A HIVE OF DEAD MEN

Geoffrey Jenkins graduated from a highly successful Fleet Street career in journalism to that of
a bestselling author of fourteen titles published
worldwide. *A Hive of Dead Men* is his fifteenth
adventure thriller. Three of his books – *A Twist of
Sand, River of Diamonds* and *In Harm's Way* –
have been made into major films.

Geoffrey Jenkins now lives in Pretoria.

GEOFFREY JENKINS

A Hive
of Dead Men

Fontana
An Imprint of HarperCollins*Publishers*

Fontana
An Imprint of HarperCollins*Publishers*
77–85 Fulham Palace Road,
Hammersmith, London W6 8JB

Published by Fontana 1992

1 3 5 7 9 8 6 4 2

First published in Great Britain by
HarperCollins*Publishers* 1991

ISBN 0 00 647256 7

Set in Linotron Plantin by
Rowland Phototypesetting Ltd,
Bury St Edmunds, Suffolk
Printed in Great Britain by
HarperCollinsManufacturing Glasgow

AUTHOR'S FOREWORD

The Cape of Good Hope silver Vice-Admiralty oar, one of South Africa's rarest historical treasures, came under the spotlight of public attention recently when it was reported by the media to have been offered for sale in London. Fortunately, this did not materialize, and the oar is now in the possession of the Cultural History Museum in Cape Town as a showpiece.

The existence of a second silver oar in my novel is fiction; equally fictitious is the lineage and ownership of the actual Cape oar, which in fact passed into the hands of the then Chief Justice after the dissolution of the Vice-Admiralty Court in 1891, when its functions were taken over by the Supreme Court. The characters of my book bear no resemblance to the persons of history or of the present day.

Neither is there any link between the famous Confederate raider *Alabama* and the Cape silver oar. The wreck of the *Alabama* was located off the French coast in 1987.

The original pioneer of Churchhaven – that beautiful spot on the shore of Langebaan lagoon on the Cape west coast – and his descendants as sketched in my book are likewise imaginary. The present friendly incumbent of the earliest dwelling, who was so helpful to me in my on-the-spot researches, has no connection with the sinister plotters in my story who occupy it.

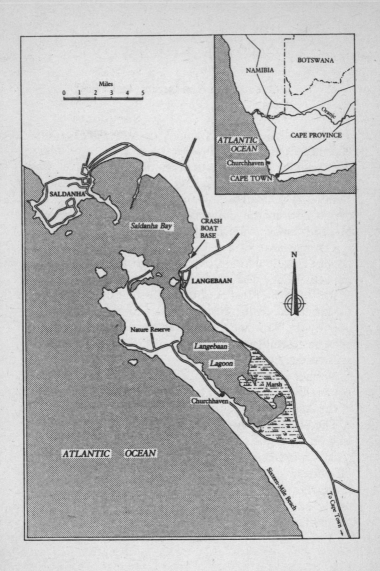

Miles
0 1 2 3 4 5

BOTSWANA

NAMIBIA

ATLANTIC
OCEAN

CAPE PROVINCE

Orange

Churchhaven

CAPE TOWN

SALDANHA

Saldanha Bay

CRASH
BOAT
BASE

N

LANGEBAAN

Nature Reserve

Langebaan

Lagoon

Marsh

Churchhaven

ATLANTIC   OCEAN

Sixteen-Mile Beach

To Cape Town

A hive of dead men buzzes, and I hear
A stir

SOPHOCLES
Lost drama

Prologue

The black, sinister, leather-clad figure made its way furtively under the low vaulting which had seen nine centuries of Britain's history come and go. That history was enshrined in lifelike effigies in the museum towards which the intruder headed. Its feet made no sound on the ancient tiles. They were clad in felt overshoes which were issued to tourists to preserve the flooring.

It was pitch-dark, nearly midnight. Had there been any stray reflection from among these cold, eleventh-century stones, it would have caught the gleam of the six-inch, saw-edged commando knife at the ready in the figure's right hand.

The steps moved confidently, if cautiously, towards the museum's shut door which was its objective. It knew the way – how many boring hours had it been a faceless tourist listening to guides' patter while all the time the logistics of the operation were being planned and the lay-out of the place studied?

The door was close at hand, now. Would it have to be forced? Would torchlight have to be risked . . . ?

A thunderous crash from overhead froze the figure in its tracks.

The sound roared down the tomb-like passageway, banging and barging past the closed door – the first of twelve measured strokes at inexorable intervals.

The intruder straightened up, moved swiftly towards the door. Here was opportunity not only knocking at the door but yelling its head off. The sound of those mighty strokes from Big Ben would conceal any slight noise she might make in forcing the door.

She. The knife-wielder was a woman.

She wore black leather like a biker's outfit and her hair was lost under a skull-fitting cap.

The door – was it locked? No need to risk the flashlight beam before she had found out. She pushed down the handle firmly. It yielded. The abyssal darkness seemed even blacker inside. She could smell the preservatives used on clothing centuries old. Predominating, however, was the odour of wax, bland and furtive, a little repulsive.

She closed the door behind her, snicked on her flashlight. The light fell on a blotched, contorted face – some old king, she remembered the guide saying, who had died of a stroke and here was his death-mask in startling effigy. With the crash of midnight still booming in her ears, it was startling, macabre.

This was the museum of Westminster Abbey in which were preserved wax effigies of personalities famous in England's history. In glass cases, some stood, some lay. The intruder made her way quickly past the figures of William III, jacked up on a low pedestal to bring him up to his consort's height, then a striking woman in full social array (was it Charles II's Duchess of Richmond?) with a withered parrot at her shoulder.

Then – the torch picked out the famous face she was looking for. The almost equally famous cocked hat was not on its head but on a small bracket above.

Bastard, she said to herself. The face was so lifelike it might have been real. Except for the fixed stare of the eyes. But the enigmatic countenance with the lock of hair over the right eyebrow was unmistakable; women had swooned over it, strong men had died for it.

The knife-woman eyed the face as dispassionately as a surgeon. She knew that the body under the ornate uniform was fashioned of wood and only the head was of wax: where was the join under the elaborate nineteenth-century cravat, heavy gilding of the thick collar, and the ribbon carrying the Order on his chest?

The showcase door lock was child's-play with the tip of her knife. She went in. Unhesitatingly, she plunged the blade into the collar, started ripping it clear of the effigy's throat with the saw-edge. The eyes were disconcertingly alive now that she was so close. Which one had been blind? She could not recall.

Here it was!

The joint between wooden body and wax head became exposed, now that the cravat and collar were more or less out of the way. How much would she have to break or chip to prise it loose?

She sawed with the commando knife. Fragments of wax, brittle with nearly two centuries of age, broke away. She drew the blade across the Adam's apple, as if cutting his throat. That is what someone should have done all those years ago, she told herself savagely, and not elevated this aggressive little male into a demi-god of English history.

A bigger chunk of wax broke away and revealed a wooden spike which linked the head to the body.

She changed the knife-blade into a lever – suddenly the whole head started loose and would have fallen, had she not grabbed it round the chin with both hands.

It was a lover's grip. For a mad moment, she had an irresistible desire to press the famous lock against her breast – after all, how many times had it been done to him in life, by a woman as famous in love as he had been in war? It was said that she had even arranged this selfsame lock of hair on the wax head . . .

She dismissed her impulse angrily. That's the way it goes with men. It had happened to her. If it hadn't, she wouldn't be here tonight after the passing of that sexual death-sentence on her. For what a man had done to her.

She put the head on the floor, pulled a plastic super-market bag from a pocket, and shoved her trophy unceremoniously into it.

She found a card which she stuck into the collar of the now headless effigy. (She had hand-printed it before-hand.) It had two words, 'Rote Zora'.

She turned to go. As she did so, the torchlight fell on the showcase card above the decapitated figure's right shoulder and empty right sleeve.

It read

HORATIO, VISCOUNT NELSON
(1758–1805)

Chapter 1

The silver blade flashed like a dagger-strike from the past between the two men.

It wasn't a dagger or a knife. It was flat and broad and blunt, the shape of a battleaxe head maybe, except for the stylized engravings chased into the precious metal. Steel would have been the choice for an offensive weapon like an axe: this was silver, and too soft. A shaft was linked by means of an ornamental knob to the head. Overall, the paddle-shaped object was some eighty-four centimetres long, the blade about a third of that length. Paddle – no paddle ever looked like this.

'*What is it?*'

The question was jerked from the older of the two men like something dreamlike out of the sleep from which he had just been torn; he was in pyjamas and a dressing-gown. The younger, fully dressed, was tense and alert. He had brought the discovery; he had hammered on the other's door until it had opened. It was after midnight.

He shifted to lean across the table towards the engraved head. The top of a belt holster snagged on the table edge. He drew the gun and laid it alongside the silver trophy. The security-beating plastic Glock 17 looked as out of place as a space shuttle in a stage-coach.

'*What is it, for Pete's sake?*'

The younger man freed the silver object from the remnants of the sacking in which he had transported it from the coast. There was also a strip of half-decayed oilcloth. It smelt of the deep sea.

The 'paddle' lay exposed: it was solid silver, having a

long cylindrical shaft and two moulded knobs, top and bottom. The bottom knob looked as if it might unscrew. It was on the flat blade at the head, however, that their eyes riveted. Even the dulling effect of sea water had failed to hide the group of engravings, chased and exquisite under the electric light.

'Where did the raider get its hands on a thing like this?' went on the older man.

'I went through all the records before we began the salvage operation,' replied the younger. 'Everything aboard was well documented – all the seventy ships' chronometers which the raider collected as loot, ten thousand dollars in gold in the strongroom, all the odds and ends which she picked up during her raiding career. But nothing remotely resembling this. Nor was there in the records of the arbitration court which sat after the raider's sinking.'

'Why didn't you signal me from the wreck site immediately instead of this cloak-and-dagger single-handed effort in bringing it here yourself? A proper security operation –'

The younger man made a half-gesture towards the Glock 17 on the table, as if that explained everything.

'Powys the diver who found it did the right thing,' he retorted incisively. 'He kept his mouth shut – tight shut. He brought it to me still wrapped in a piece of rotten tarpaulin – which I suppose dates from the time of the raider's voyage – like any other insignificant bit of stuff recovered from the hull. He realized he was on to something big. If he'd made a song and dance about it, every Frenchman and American on the site would have been alerted to the fact that we'd made a big find. A security operation such as you mention would have had the same end result. The news would have been around like wildfire, and everyone would have been staking his claim. My way, no one knows except Powys, you and me.'

In May 1988 a French marine archaeologist and a team of twenty divers located the wreck of the famous American Civil War Confederate privateer *Alabama* about seven sea-miles off the French port of Cherbourg. The *Alabama*, which had strong ties with South Africa – the ship is commemorated in song as part of the country's folk legend – was a much-feared commerce raider which plundered and sank sixty-five Union merchant ships during the course of a two-year career which covered half the world, from South Africa to Singapore and China. She was eventually sunk off the Normandy coast in June 1864 after a duel with the Union warship *Kearsage*.

The discovery of the wreck after more than a century and a quarter became a political football almost at once. The French claimed the wreck; the Americans asserted that since it lay within international waters, salvage was free for all; while the British (who built the *Alabama* in Liverpool in defiance of the Union) also staked a strong claim to the ship. Rival diving teams started work in an atmosphere of tension and suspicion, each side searching for valuable historic objects from the raider, including her guns. She was known to have carried loot from her victims and, in addition, ten thousand dollars in gold with which her commander, Captain Raphael Semmes, paid for the ship's bunker coal.

The ship's ties with South Africa dated from her visit to Cape Town in August 1863 when she received a tumultuous welcome from the local population, especially at the touch of ruthlessness Captain Semmes displayed in capturing a Yankee merchantman, the *Sea Bride*, within sight of the crowd gathered on the shoreline. The incident is commemorated in a song, 'Daar Kom die *Alabama*' ('There Comes the *Alabama*'), which has a special niche in South African folk-lore.

'Will you have a drink?' asked the older man, whose name was Don Gibson.

'I'd prefer coffee – and something to eat,' replied the other. 'I've had nothing all day. It was cold crossing the Channel in the supply tender.'

Gibson eyed Rayner Watton. His career sheet said he was thirty. He sat on the antique chair with his back as straight as the furniture. He wasn't tense, but there was an air of controlled alertness about him as if he were ready to go into action at the first sound of the bell. Gibson noted the strong hands, the left thrust seemingly negligently into the pocket of his bomber jacket; the fingers of his right lay coiled on his knee with the same air of ready relaxation. A small beard at the base of the long, straight line of his chin was not for ornament but to hide a bullet-scar.

'Wasn't it risky using the tender rather than going to the mainland and catching a quick flight to London?' asked Gibson. 'Anything could have happened.'

Rayner broke in. 'The Americans – the French in particular – are used to the tender coming and going with supplies for our team. It wouldn't – didn't – raise suspicion when I joined it for the homeward trip carrying an old bit of dirty sacking.' A quick smile wiped clean the severity of his face. 'It worked. I don't think anyone noticed me leave. Easier, too, coming ashore at this end. Customs hardly bother about our tender any more. It would have been different on a regular plane flight. The cat would have been out of the bag.'

'Some cat, some bag!' responded Gibson.

He ran a finger in admiration, coupled with disbelief, over an engraving occupying the full width of the flat blade at the top.

'Looks like the Royal arms,' he said. 'But what in hell is this under it? – an eagle riding on –'

'A missile?' grinned Rayner.

'This wasn't crafted in our time and age – it's old,' rejoined Gibson. 'There's an anchor engraving still lower down, and then –' He rubbed at the sea-dulled metal, but the image remained unclear. 'Looks like a couple of fishes with harpoons through 'em – and then there's this old-time guy's head in a kind of medallion surrounded by a wreath –'

Gibson went on incisively. 'When Surveillicor got the job of bringing ashore salvaged objects from the *Alabama*, I retained a panel of experts to brief us on what we discovered. They're mainly marine history pundits. I think this kind of silver would be outside their range.'

Surveillicor was the company, owned by Don Gibson, which had won the contract to protect and convey from the wreck-site items found by the British diving team aboard the *Alabama*. Rayner Watton headed the scrutinizing and conveyance of salvaged objects from the wreck-site off France to the company's headquarters in London. On this occasion, he had come directly to Gibson's flat.

Gibson stroked the silver shaft. 'It's solid, solid silver. I wonder what it weighs?'

'Pounds, I'd guess,' replied Rayner. 'But it has a beautiful feeling of balance, as if it were meant to be carried.'

'Which only adds to the mystery,' went on Gibson. 'Are you sure you weren't followed, or seen with it on your way here?'

Rayner gave a clipped laugh. 'If anyone had wanted to bushwhack me, the time to have done it was when I was hiring a car in Portsmouth. No, I'm sure, and I'm equally positive that no one saw me leave the *Alabama* site with it.'

'I wonder how many lives this priceless thing cost before Semmes managed to get his hands on it?' Gibson added speculatively.

'Captain Semmes was a ruthless commerce raider, but he wasn't a pirate,' answered Rayner. 'All his captures, as I said, are well documented. It's a complete mystery how this – whatever it is – came aboard the *Alabama*. Whoever we brief to identify it will have to be sworn to secrecy.'

'I'll get down to the wreck-site and warn Powys myself –' said Gibson.

'That would be a mistake, Don. Your presence will only draw attention to him – and you. Everyone watches everyone else all the time like a bunch of card-sharps at a crooked game. I trust Powys.'

'I'll get coffee and a bite,' said Gibson. 'I won't sleep again tonight. You spend the night here and we'll stand guard in shifts. I'm glad you brought a gun.'

Rayner ran a finger along the smooth silver of the shaft.

'A priceless thing like this invites guns,' he said.

Chapter 2

'*What is it?*'

Don Gibson asked the question almost rhetorically for the hundredth time that morning, eyeing the silver object lying on his office desk.

'We'll know soon enough when Christie's man arrives – what'd you say his name was?'

'Hendey – Charles Hendey. He's not only their top boy in the silver line, but the boss as well. I told 'em I wanted someone who would keep his mouth shut. Hendey informed me, from something of a height, "Secrecy is the name of our game."'

Rayner and Gibson were at Gibson's office in the City of London next morning. It was shortly after nine. Gibson had deliberately arrived early so that none of his staff would see the prize which Rayner had brought from the *Alabama*. Conveying the oar by car had smacked of a cloak-and-dagger operation. Gibson had wrapped it in old newspaper, and Rayner had sat at the back, armed with the Glock, with the parcel next to him.

In daylight, the superbly chased engravings on the flat blade were more striking than under artificial light: the topmost one was plainly the British Royal coat-of-arms; the next was an anchor surrounded by a wreath which supported what looked like a large bird riding on some unidentifiable object; followed still further down, where the blade joined the shaft, by the strange double fish emblem; and, finally, a medallion head surrounded by an ornate wreath.

'What continues to puzzle me more than anything is, where did the *Alabama* capture such a splendid piece of loot?' said Rayner. 'I told you last night, everything has been most meticulously documented.'

'I know, I know,' Gibson replied tautly. 'That's what worries me. By grabbing this thing, we may be lighting a fuse which could end in one hell of an explosion from the French and Americans.'

'Is that likely to worry you overmuch?' asked Rayner ironically.

Gibson shrugged. 'We're in the *Alabama* salvage game for money, and, by heavens, this is money. The silver alone must be worth a fortune, not to mention the historical value. I'll have our legal guys working overtime, as soon as I know what sort of fish we've landed.'

'Powys the diver said he'd found it near the strongroom entrance.'

'Strongroom!' echoed Gibson. 'How'd he manage to keep the French and American divers away from the strongroom? They know as well as we do that Captain Semmes stashed away ten thousand dollars in gold in there.'

Rayner laughed. 'That's what makes Powys the top salvage diver he is. That's why he isn't likely to blab about this to the other diving teams, or even our own.'

There was a knock at the door. Gibson hastily threw the newspaper over the silver object.

'Mr Hendey from Christie's, Mr Gibson,' the secretary said.

Hendey was as burnished in his regulation suit, striped shirt and well-nourished complexion as the engraved blade might look after expert valeting. Living in the presence of beautiful things had made him a little precious also. His eyebrows lifted when Gibson locked the door after him.

'Charles Hendey – Rayner Watton.' Gibson introduced them perfunctorily, and whipped away the newspaper with a conjuror's air of the dramatic.

Hendey's intake of breath was noisy, involuntary, from shock.

He walked across to the desk with measured steps, which gave him time to pull out his glasses and recover his dignity. He ran a finger along the bevelled edge of the blade, but it was by reflex. It was his eyes which were locked on the engravings.

'Where did you get this?' he asked in a curiously strained voice as if his vocal cords had not yet recovered from the sudden breath blitz.

Gibson glanced at Rayner, and Rayner at Gibson. Hendey could not miss the exchange.

He said stiffly, 'I must warn you right at the outset, Christie's will have nothing to do with *objets d'art* which are not legally vouched for. There are rogues in the art world, as well as in any other.'

Gibson replied, 'What I shall disclose is in the strictest confidence.'

Hendey regained his professional air. 'I told you on the phone, secrecy is the name of the game. *Legal* secrecy, that is. We are not interested in anything underhand.'

'My firm, Surveillicor, is busy salvaging the wreck of the Confederate raider *Alabama* off the coast of France,' Gibson answered. 'Rayner here is our man on the spot and is responsible for bringing back salvaged material to London.'

'So? The *Alabama*?'

But Hendey's attention was only half on what Gibson was saying. He was concentrating on the third of the five engravings, that depicting an anchor in a wreath.

'One of our divers found this the day before yesterday, and Rayner brought it with all speed to London.'

'I have never seen anything like this,' said Hendey. 'Solid silver.' He picked it up and weighed it in his hands and then put it down again with the reverence of a knight laying his sword before the altar on going to the crusades.

He took out a white silk handkerchief from his breast pocket and rubbed the medallion head engraving. Then he breathed on it and wiped off the condensation.

'It's very furred,' he remarked accusingly. 'No treasure like this should be allowed to get into this condition.'

'It has been under the sea for a century and a quarter,' Rayner replied dryly.

'*What is it?*'

The demand was fired from Gibson.

Hendey's reply was maddeningly slow in coming. First, he tried rubbing the anchor image with the silk, and then he took a small folding magnifying glass from his pocket and studied it.

'I'd say, hazarding a guess, of course, because it needs authenticating . . .'

'Go on, even if it's only a guess,' snapped Gibson.

'A guess, you understand, with no commitment attached to it . . .'

'Go on!'

'That head looks like George the Third, but it is the anchor which is the clue. The foul anchor in a wreath of oak leaves – sometimes the wreath is omitted – is the symbol of the Admiralty.'

'Meaning?'

'If this is what I think it is, it is quite priceless and unique.'

Hendey should have been a showman; he knew the value of the dramatic pause.

'And what do you think it is?'

'I don't rightly know. But I think it could be what is known as a silver oar of Admiralty. The foul anchor bears that out. I've only heard vaguely of silver oars. They're too rare . . .'

Rayner came into the conversation to try and pressure Hendey into a direct answer, but he'd ridden out too many pressures over anything from a Van Gogh to a gold chalice to be driven into a snap answer.

'What did the Admiralty do with a thing like this?' he asked.

'Speaking always subject to correction, the silver oar was used as a symbol of Admiralty authority when Admiralty Courts sat to consider marine cases.'

'But the *Alabama* had nothing to do with any British Admiralty Courts!' exclaimed Rayner. 'She was an American, a raider, outside the province of any British court . . .'

'She wasn't a pirate,' interjected Gibson. 'Let me make that quite clear. She was a fighting ship, a commerce raider for the South. And a very successful one, too.'

Hendey eyed Gibson narrowly. 'You have legal rights to salvage the raider?'

'Of course. Signed, sealed and delivered.'

'I would have to check if we decide to handle this – er, silver oar, we'll call it for the moment.'

'We have not got as far as deciding whether or not we'll put it up for sale,' said Gibson. 'We want to know first what it is.'

'My suggestion is that you contact the Greenwich National Maritime Museum and see what they can tell you about Admiralty oars and their background.'

'Noways!' replied Gibson. 'The fewer people who know about this, the better. Only a hint, the slightest leak, and the media will be on to it like vultures. Then all hell will be loose.' Gibson eyed Hendey. 'The media ban goes for you, too.'

'I learned my lesson years ago,' he answered a little tiredly. 'Sensationalism, that's what the media are all about. If I may coin a phrase, discretion is the better part of Christie's.' He put his silk handkerchief back in position. 'What I suggest is that, if you want me to go ahead, you give me a little time to do some homework on the silver oars . . .'

'Without consulting Greenwich,' added Gibson.

'Without consulting Greenwich.' Hendey managed a thin smile.

'Priority,' said Gibson.

Hendey made a gesture towards the oar. 'It's one of the most striking things that has ever crossed my path. Personally and professionally, I am what is described as being fired up. I'll clear the decks to see what I can find out.'

'By tomorrow?' Gibson pressed him.

'Certainly.' Hendey disarranged his silk handkerchief and flicked fussily at the seawater patina covering the engraved blade.

'A beautiful thing like this requires proper cleaning up,' he said. 'We have an expert at Christie's. I could arrange . . .'

Gibson shook his head. 'I'm not letting it out of my strongroom.'

Hendey replaced his handkerchief. 'It would look quite stunning. Well, until tomorrow.'

He left.

Next day, again in Gibson's office, Hendey pronounced judgement, but with less certainty than any Admiralty Court had ever done.

'I was right yesterday – up to a point – when I said the oar had something to do with Admiralty Courts –' he began.

'So it is an oar, then?' Gibson demanded impatiently.

'In my opinion, yes. A ceremonial oar. But I must reiterate that my knowledge is scanty in the extreme. There is an Admiralty oar, I was able to find out discreetly from my enquiries yesterday, which has been used here in London since the Middle Ages at sittings of Admiralty Courts. What for, I do not know.'

'This can't be it – aboard a Confederate commerce raider!' Rayner interrupted.

'No. I gather – without breaking my confidence about Greenwich – that it is still in ceremonial use and has never been outside London. But several likenesses – not copies of the original – were made for places elsewhere in the world where the Admiralty's authority ran, by virtue of the Royal Navy.

'One of these was the Cape of Good Hope. My belief is that what is in your strongroom at the moment is that oar or silver mace, which was in use at the Cape from sometime shortly after the Battle of Trafalgar. Where it has been in the meantime –'

'At the bottom of the sea,' interjected Rayner.

'If it is the Cape of Good Hope silver oar, it has had a great mystery attached to its whereabouts for a very long time,' added Hendey. 'I don't know. I can't find out. No, that is incorrect. I can find out – with your consent.'

'Greenwich is out –' Gibson began.

'Fortunately, within our own family, so to speak, the family of Christie's, we have someone who is recognized – even by Greenwich – as the world's top authority on silver oars of Admiralty.'

Gibson jumped to his feet. 'Then why in hell didn't you bring him along today . . . ?'

Hendey smiled. 'First, it's not him, but her. Second, she's ten thousand kilometres away. She works for Christie's Cape Town office. I want your permission to fly her to London and examine the oar.'

Gibson was grinning. 'How soon can we get her here?'

It was Rayner who was fated to ask her name.

'Fenella Gault.'

Chapter 3

'Fenella Gault?'

'You must be Rayner Watton.'

Their eyes held, that quick penetrating first assessment which far outranges the physical sight and colours a relationship for the future. Her eyes were dark, but with a luminousness discernible in Rayner's short glance at her. Eyes which, although inscrutable, were as much part of the vitality of a face which could at will shut out the world as the pull of forces which were not visible now in the laughter-lines at the corner of her mouth. Rayner had asked Hendey for a description of the woman from Cape Town he was due to meet at London airport, but Hendey was obviously better at the finer points of silver than the hallmarks of woman. Dark – he had been correct in that – but otherwise so vague that Rayner had twice accosted the wrong person before finally getting it right with Fenella herself.

He was not expecting beauty, nor hair so black, neck-length. It had a straight sweep from a left-hand parting to over her right eye, giving only a partial view of a strongly arched eyebrow beneath, not enough to reveal that it was blacker than the hair itself. She inclined her head to the right as she smiled, revealing a complementary dimple of her left cheek, a counterpoint to the almost severe cast which the firm nose with its fastidious nostrils and the concealed forehead gave to the face.

Nor had Rayner been expecting, from Hendey's description of 'medium height', anyone so slight and small; the unzipped anorak she had on revealed nothing of her breasts, only a loose mushroom-coloured shirt. Her pants were an indeterminate matching colour, creased from the long flight from Cape Town.

It was over a week since the silver oar consultation at Gibson's.

She said apologetically, 'I'm sorry you had to wait so long for me to come through, but it was outside my control. They've been searching everyone's baggage in there for the past hour and a half.'

The long straight line of his chin made her think of one of those dangerous rock-climbs up the face of Table Mountain, the tight set of his mouth added to the effect of toughness and inaccessibility. Or was it anger at being kept waiting?

A quick smile wiped the slate clean; there were really two faces here, and she liked both.

He gestured widely. 'The whole airport is crawling with Scotland Yard men. As a security man myself, I can understand.'

'What's going on?'

'You heard about the Westminster Abbey affair?'

'Nelson's head? Yes, the news broke just as I was leaving. The media went to town on the story. Someone broke in and cut off Nelson's head – or rather, the head of his effigy in the Abbey museum. That's all I know – I've been out of touch, flying.'

He leaned down and hefted her luggage, effortlessly, and headed for an exit. 'It doesn't feel as if you have the missing head in this lot,' he grinned.

26

'What exactly happened?'

'The night before last, someone – Scotland Yard says it was a woman – broke into Westminster Abbey in the middle of the night, hacked off the head, and made off with it. The next day the media received an anonymous telephone call to say the way-out action had been carried out by a feminist terror group called Rote Zora. Until then nobody, in Britain at any rate, had ever heard of Rote Zora.'

'The way you put it, Rote Zora is known elsewhere.'

'We've had columns in the papers and hours on the air about its background ever since yesterday – this thing has stirred up and shocked the British public very greatly. Rote Zora is a small women's terror group which is a branch of Rote Zellen, or Red Cells, in Germany.

'It is a kind of loose association of women who apparently live legally blameless lives but in their spare time engage in terrorist activities to underline their social or political grievances. Acts like bombing or setting fire to offices or cars of doctors who refuse to perform abortions, attacks on sex and porn shops, and on organizations which procure wives from the Far East for German men, which they say is slavery.'

'Rote Zora – it's an odd sort of name.'

'Apparently the group adopted the name of a girl in a German children's story who steals from the rich in order to give to the poor. Something like Robin Hood.'

'I don't see how Nelson could possibly qualify as a target.'

'You must have heard the official announcement a few days ago that the Simonstown naval agreement between Britain and South Africa is to be reinstated and that the British Prime Minister is to fly out to South Africa in the near future?'

'Of course. The ceremony is to take place at the Simonstown naval base itself. The signing has been hailed as a great breakthrough in relations between the two countries as the old naval pact lapsed under the British Socialist government way back in the sixties.'

Rayner's easy strides took them towards a group of plain-clothes detectives who were checking at the exit.

'Well, the anonymous phone caller said that cutting off Nelson's head was a protest against the reinstatement of the Simonstown agreement and the Prime Minister's visit to South Africa, as well as against hero-worship of male aggressiveness in the person of Nelson.'

He liked the way she laughed and glanced at him, without responding. Then she said:

'We've had our share of excitement, too.'

'The *Medusa* figurehead?'

'Yes. People felt shocked at the crudity of defacing Nelson's flagship's figurehead like that.'

As the news had broken in London of the Nelson theft, the newspapers had been tipped off by the anonymous caller to inspect the figurehead of Nelson's one-time flagship, HMS *Medusa*, which was mounted in a Cape garden overlooking a river at Port Elizabeth. Reporters who had sped to the scene found that the figurehead had been given a patch over one eye with spray-paint to match the famous admiral's, and hung round its neck was an artificial penis, the sort of thing sold in sleazy porn shops.

Rayner and Fenella reached the exit and one of the detectives said, 'Ah, Mr Watton, sir, so this is the lady from Cape Town you came to meet?' He grinned at Fenella. 'You picked the right person to carry your bags, miss – he's about the only person except one of ourselves we'd allow in and out on his own recognizance, so to speak.'

'I've been hearing about Nelson's head,' replied Fenella.

'A bad business, miss – the public doesn't like that sort of thing. I think maybe everyone's a bit shocked.

So everyone said in a spot-check TV interview on the streets.'

Rayner asked, 'You haven't got any inside clues about the woman yet?'

The man shook his head. 'Nothing beyond what's been published. Pity that copper who spoke to her in the street near the Abbey immediately afterwards wasn't more wideawake. Carrying something in a supermarket bag at midnight! He never guessed what she had in it!'

'It's not the sort of thing anyone might expect, Nelson's head being carried away in a plastic bag in the middle of the night,' answered Rayner.

'Well, there are some other straws in the wind which may help us,' said the detective. 'Black leather outfit, close-fitting cap, and she spoke educated-like. Best of all, though, he got a glimpse of her hair. Coppery-coloured . . .'

Coppery-coloured. On the other side of London, a woman stood before a mirror in a second-class hotel bedroom and checked her hair. She was about thirty years old, but both physical and mental pain had pinched her face so that at times – not now – she would have passed for ten years older.

Her name was Zara Hennessy. She was the leader of the Cape cell of Rote Zora.

It was she who had cut off Nelson's head.

The bed was strewn with newspapers, both that day's and the previous, headlining the theft from the Abbey and stridently voicing Britain's anger at the defilement of their public hero.

Coppery-coloured.

Zara had listened to every radio news bulletin she could but had avoided the TV in the lounge downstairs; she did not want to draw attention to herself in an empty lounge listening to successive news bulletins. Her bedside radio was on. The Scotland Yard hair clue was again given prominence.

Zara examined her hair. It was a poor clue, she decided. Her hair wasn't coppery but dark, tinged auburn; it was only when the electric light caught it at a certain angle, as now, that there was that gleam of copper.

Zara didn't feel anxious; she felt good. She had felt good ever since that moment she had ripped into Nelson's cravat with her commando knife and sawed away at the effigy's neck. (There were plenty of news photographs showing the forlorn spike which had held the wax head and wooden body together.) Perhaps it had been because she had felt so good that she had been able to carry off her chance midnight meeting with the policeman near the Abbey while she carried the loot so nonchalantly in her hand. He'd obviously thought her a tart; she had played up to that and laughed off his good-natured tolerance. If he could have guessed! She felt almost sorry for the man. He'd be collecting all the flak from his superiors now.

Zara smiled at her image in the mirror. It pulled to momentary softness the lips which two years of anguish had drawn to harshness, but it couldn't help the gaunt settings of her dark eyes which could burn and flare when the terrible inner rages avalanched over her.

It wasn't anger, now. Zara was on a high. What the Abbey theft itself and the subsequent bombshell of publicity had given her she needed, needed as a counterweight to the crushing medical judgement which had been pronounced on her. Up to the last, these past weeks, she had hoped against hope, but the specialist in Germany was emphatic, final.

She'd never be more than a sexual vegetable.

That was final, final.

For a moment Zara allowed herself to slip back into a

gear of self-pity, hatred and regret. The man who had seduced her in Cape Town and made her pregnant had thrown her on the rubbish-heap after refusing to carry out an abortion himself (he was a leading geneticist and surgeon). He had suggested to her a high-risk French abortion pill, which had had disastrous consequences. Alone and desperately ill, she had made her way to Germany and thrown herself on the mercy of the parent organization Rote Zora. Rote Zora had stood by her nobly and had secured (under pressure) the services of a German specialist who had been obliged to carry out drastic surgery in order to save her life.

He had told her to come back in a year's time for a check and see what her chances were. Even at that stage, she realized that she would never be a woman again, not half a woman.

Now Zara was on her way back to the Cape from Germany via London after the final, catastrophic diagnosis, after the year had elapsed. It was the end of her as child-bearer, woman, sex.

Her hatred for the man who had done it to her knew no bounds.

She had had time to kill in London before her plane connection to the Cape; she had been bitterly miserable and unhappy. She had visited the famous tourist spots simply in order to do something, anything to keep her mind off herself.

Then, at Westminster Abbey's famous museum of effigies of British celebrities, she had been sickened by the eulogies to Nelson, whom she regarded as a symbol of male aggression and superiority. It had fuelled her already burning hatred for men, which had been a part of the Rote Zora credo anyway.

As she had stood there with other tourists gawping, the idea had hit her. Maybe the connection had taken place subconsciously with the announcement, the day after her arrival in London, that the Simonstown agreement, moribund since the 1960s, was to be revalidated, and the British Prime Minister was to fly out for the occasion.

Cut off his head!

She did just that.

She had intended the action as a demonstration against male chauvinism, a protest against the Prime Minister's kow-towing to male superiority, and to show that Rote Zora, which had not operated in Britain before, was a force to be reckoned with.

What she had not foreseen was the violent reaction of the British public, nor, for her own part, the therapeutic, cathartic effect the action had had upon her mental state. She felt good, good.

Zara left the mirror, decided she must speak to Renate, first lieutenant of the Rote Zora cell in Cape Town (there were four other girls in the gang besides herself). Renate had carried out the *Medusa* desecration to coincide with the Abbey theft, after Zara had telephoned through her masterplan. She had left the detail and logistics of the operation to the big girl with the strong hands (Renate was a horticulturist at a Cape Town garden centre).

How successfully Renate had set the cat among the pigeons could be judged by the matching uproar the *Medusa* defacement had evoked to the London theft amongst the media and the public. The rubber penis had been a derisive touch of genius.

Zara started for the phone, but decided to check Nelson's head first, now lodged in her suitcase under the bed. She pulled out the case – the security checks at London and Frankfurt had not been sophisticated enough to detect the layer of Semtex plastic explosive which enclosed the frame of her suitcase, in the best Lockerbie tradition. The girls at Rote Zora in Germany had brought the original sinister suitcase concept with the odourless, inert but lethal high-density Czech explosive to a state of the art. She had passed through the checks unsuspected; as unsuspected as the Glock 17 nine-millimetre security-busting plastic pistol, specially designed to beat airport security checks, had been.

She opened the case. The head was there.

She dialled Renate's garden centre number in Cape Town. She had to have someone to unburden to.

'Renate?'

'Zara! What is wrong? Why are you phoning? We agreed we wouldn't contact one another for safety's sake . . .'

'Nothing's wrong.' Zara's voice had a lilt in it.

'Then you must be crazy –'

'Crazy – maybe. A little drunk the way things have gone. It's wonderful, wonderful!'

'You're sure you're all right, Zara?'

'We really tickled 'em up, you down at the Cape and me here in London. Everyone from Scotland Yard downwards is running about like bluebottle flies.'

Renate remained tense, anxious. 'The papers say Scotland Yard has a description.'

Zara's amusement and contempt tinkled over ten thousand kilometres of undersea telephone cable.

'I've just been laughing it off in front of the mirror. If that's the best they can do, I feel sorry for them.'

'Well, go on feeling sorry, Zara. Don't take any stupid risks. You got away with it once, you mayn't be so lucky again.'

Zara went on, still amused. 'You can't imagine how stirred up the British are over an old wax head. One of the papers makes a personal appeal to the thief not to destroy what it calls "a priceless piece of Britain's heritage" and begs me not to mess up the lock of hair over the right eye, which was arranged by Lady Hamilton herself. Can you believe it!'

The distance made Renate's voice sound huskier than normal. 'You've got rid of it, I hope?'

'What is it?'

'I don't want to say the word, in case we're being overheard.'

'You mean, the head? It's here, under my bed, in my suitcase.'

'You're crazy to keep such a thing! Throw it away, dump it, drop it in the Thames – anything!'

'Don't get your knickers in a twist – it's quite safe here with me. It makes me feel good just to look at it.'

'You're playing with fire, Zara! Do as I ask. What about when you come back – what happens then?'

'I'll see.'

'I'll have sleepless nights until you get back,' said Renate. 'When is it?'

'I can't get a firm date out of the airways yet – the next four or five days, I reckon. I'll let you know.'

'Zara – listen to me!' Renate went on urgently. 'Don't do anything in that time to draw attention to yourself. You've had a wonderful run of success with this head business, now leave the rest of it alone. For your sake, as well as ours in the gang here at the Cape.'

Zara was playful. 'I'll try, but I won't promise. Depends whether I need to feel good again, the way I feel now.'

'I haven't heard you like this in years.'

Zara said, with laughter in her voice, 'It was so simple – easier than drinking a bottle dry or giving oneself a shot.'

Renate is right, Zara. Cool it. You're only one small step away from the bomb and the gun.

Chapter 4

'It can't be real, yet it *is* real!'

The silver object Rayner had brought from the *Alabama* lay on the long table in Christie's boardroom, resting on a special soft green cloth to prevent scratching. It had been polished by an expert; it was a stunning sight. The corrosive seawater marks had vanished, and the five engravings on the blade stood out bright and clear.

Charles Hendey, Don Gibson, Rayner and Fenella bent over it. Fenella was still in her anorak: she and Rayner had come directly to Christie's from the airport without calling at her hotel in order to save further delay. They had hurried to the boardroom for Fenella to pass expert judgement.

'How real is real?' demanded Gibson at Fenella's excited exclamation as she leaned over the silver surface, her fingers first exploring the engraved blade, and then the long smooth length of the shaft down to the terminal button at the bottom, where there were some punch-marks struck in the metal.

'It's priceless – it's a silver oar of Admiralty.'

Hendey wasn't going to be upstaged. 'That was my thought, too.'

'But only a thought, that's why we flew you here from the Cape,' added Gibson. 'What exactly is a silver oar of Admiralty?'

Fenella pointed to the anchor engraved on the blade. 'The oar was a symbol of Admiralty authority, both in the special Vice-Admiralty Courts, and in arresting offenders for all sorts of crimes connected with ships and the sea. This is a foul anchor, the Admiralty's own special emblem. The silver oar also had an important role in court proceedings, where it was on display in front of the presiding judge.

'But the oar's functions did not end there. Traditionally, the silver oar was carried in procession by the Admiralty Marshal when a hanging was due to take place – just ahead of the executioner. The silver oar is specifically mentioned at the hanging of the famous pirate, Captain Kidd, at Execution Dock in 1701.'

Gibson glanced triumphantly at Hendey and Rayner, and asked Fenella, 'You said priceless a minute ago, Fenella – how priceless?'

'Only seven such oars were ever made for Admiralty Courts throughout the world, centuries and oceans apart. The oldest reaches right back into British history – to the reign of Elizabeth the First.'

'You're using the term priceless historically . . .'

Fenella smiled at Hendey. 'Not only historically. Mr Hendey here can give you an idea what this oar is worth for its weight of silver alone.'

Hendey said, 'I'd stick to the word priceless.'

Gibson went on, 'You say seven oars only were ever made – which one is this?'

Fenella indicated the medallion head at the place where the blade met the shaft. 'That is George the Third and here –' she showed the men the marks near the large silver button at the foot '– is the date. 1806.'

She eased herself out of the anorak, now too warm for the hot air-conditioned room, and gave it, as with some unexpressed privilege, to Rayner. The action provided a dramatic pause before her next words.

'This is the Cape of Good Hope Vice-Admiralty oar. It was crafted by one of the great silversmiths of his time, William Frisbee of London. Here is his hallmark next to the date. The oar remained in use for over eighty years at the Cape until the functions of the Vice-Admiralty Court were taken over by the Cape Supreme Court in

1891.' She flicked a self-deprecating smile at Rayner. 'I sound like a book.'

Gibson said, 'It's the sort of book I like to hear.'

Fenella inclined her head and said, 'Now it's my turn to ask questions – and I've got a lot.'

'Shoot,' replied Gibson.

'First, how did this oar come to be aboard the *Alabama*?'

Gibson passed the question to Rayner. He replied carefully, 'I went through all the available records connected with the *Alabama* before we began the salvage operation. After all, Surveillicor isn't in the salvage business for its health. Captain Semmes kept meticulous records of all the loot he captured from Yankee ships, and there's certainly no mention anywhere of a silver oar. There were also the proceedings of the international arbitration court which sat after the *Alabama* had been sunk – again, nothing.'

'It grows curiouser and curiouser,' said Fenella. 'We know that the *Alabama* was in Cape Town harbour in 1863, about a year before she was sunk off France by the Yankee *Kearsage*. How could she possibly have got hold of part of the trappings of a British Vice-Admiralty Court? In any event, the court went on functioning for nearly thirty years after the raider's visit and the silver oar was in regular use.'

Gibson flicked a warning glance at Hendey. 'There could be a lot of legal wrangling over this oar later. I'm already beginning to see tough legal implications – and then there's Surveillicor's rights of salvage as well.'

Fenella went on, 'Before I ask what I consider the sixty-four dollar question, I also want to know where the Marshal's baton is that goes with this silver oar – it was part of the ceremonial.'

'My oath!' exclaimed Gibson. 'Is there more treasure down there in the wreck? Marshal's baton – what's that?'

Hendey regarded the group with a satisfied, almost smug, smile. His protégée from the Cape was coming up trumps.

The light reflecting off the polished silver blade formed an unintended spotlight on the classic planes of Fenella's face and brought an air of drama to what she had to say.

'There was a rigid form of procedure and protocol connected with the silver oar, both in the courts and for executions,' she explained. 'The central figure in it all was the Marshal, wearing his ceremonial uniform and bearing over his right shoulder the silver oar. In his left hand he held a six-inch-long circular staff or baton of ivory. It was surmounted by a royal crown in silver and encircled by a silver band on which was engraved the Admiralty's emblem, the foul anchor, which you also see here on the blade of the oar.

'The head of this baton could be unscrewed, revealing a space inside in which was conveyed the warrant issued by the Admiralty Court.

'When the Marshal carried out an arrest aboard ship, for example, he always carried the baton as a symbol of his authority.'

'The way you describe it makes it sound like a stage show,' commented Gibson.

'Anything but.' Fenella smiled. 'It was a very serious business, I assure you.'

'We'll have to be doubly careful with our claims regarding all this Admiralty property,' observed Gibson.

'You've pre-empted my next point,' said Fenella. 'I think you should understand clearly that neither the silver oar nor the baton was the property of the Admiralty. They were the private possessions of the Marshal.'

'What!' exclaimed Gibson. 'I think we'd better all sit down while I absorb that.'

Hendey added, 'I think some tea is indicated.'

Rayner found a place next to Fenella and hung her anorak over the back of her chair.

She continued. 'The biggest point of all comes next. You say – and I accept it – that this silver oar came from the wreck of the *Alabama*. But what about the silver oar that remained in ceremonial use at the Cape for many years after the *Alabama* sailed away and was sunk?'

Gibson looked stunned, and gestured at the splendid object on the table in front of them. 'But this . . .'

'The other oar is at present in Cape Town,' went on Fenella. 'It is the property of the original Marshal's descendant – a very prominent public figure and geneticist. His name is Professor Vivian Pittock-Williams.'

Gibson was given time to get his breath back by the arrival of the tea. Hendey did not allow the secretary to see into the room but collected the tray himself.

Gibson gulped at the hot liquid and asked incredulously, 'You mean to say there are *two* Cape of Good Hope silver oars?'

'It looks like it.'

'Looks like? Haven't you examined this professor's silver oar – ?'

'No,' replied Fenella. 'I believe he has it locked away somewhere. He's not – ah, a very approachable person.'

Rayner said, 'Maybe he has the ivory baton also.'

Fenella turned to him, and he was aware of the deeps of her dark eyes. She might have been addressing him alone.

'Maybe. He has every right to it. It's his property as the Marshal's descendant.'

Her eyes held his for a split second longer, and then moved back to Gibson.

'Strictly speaking, therefore, Professor Pittock-Williams must also be the owner of this oar in front of us. And this, moreover, is the original.' She referred to

39

Hendey. 'Look, here are Frisbee's hallmarks struck at the base of the loom.'

'Loom?' demanded Gibson.

'Shaft,' explained Fenella. 'The shaft is also known as the loom.'

Gibson made a gesture. 'We've suddenly dropped into water deeper than the *Alabama*'s grave.'

Rayner added, 'Pittock-Williams is only one side of the story – imagine what will happen if the French and American diving teams get to hear about our discovery?'

Gibson shook his head doggedly. 'We are front-runners in the ownership stakes, by right of salvage.'

'That would be disputable in a court of law, especially when there's this sort of money involved,' answered Rayner. 'The French have claimed right from the start that the wreck lies inside their territorial waters. The Americans dispute this and argue that it is international water, and that they own the ship. There's also another question-mark – does the present American government actually have that ownership? The *Alabama* belonged to the Confederacy and not the Union – the two hadn't come under one flag at that stage.'

Gibson shook his head in slow dismay. 'What a feast for the lawyers! And now comes Williams with his particular stake in the shape of another silver oar!'

'Pittock-Williams,' Fenella corrected him. 'He's very particular about his double-barrel name.'

'Fenella,' said Hendey quietly, 'you say you haven't examined Pittock-Williams's silver oar?'

'No, I haven't even seen it. I only know from my researches that it is in his possession.'

'Nobody can get past these hallmarks of Frisbee's,' Hendey stated emphatically. 'This is, and remains, the original. The other oar may be spurious.'

'Yet the inescapable fact remains that it seems to have

continued in use for many years and nobody ever queried its authenticity,' said Rayner.

'Where was this oar in front of us during that time?' demanded Gibson.

'Anytime after 1864 when the *Alabama* was sunk off France, it must have been at the bottom of the sea,' replied Fenella.

A silence fell over the gathering. Gibson swallowed a second cup of tea noisily and then said:

'I need time to think about the implications of our discovery. I can't see how I cannot bring in our legal advisers, but once that door is open, there is no knowing where things will end, eh Rayner?'

'It'll also open up the road to publicity, and that's just as bad,' he answered.

Gibson nodded and addressed Hendey. 'Your life wouldn't be worth a packet of crackers once the news-hounds got loose on the story.'

'I've handled them before, but over nothing as tricky as this silver oar,' he replied.

'What I suggest is that we all meet here again tomorrow after we've had time to sleep on it,' said Gibson. 'Would it be OK to keep the oar in your strongroom for tonight?'

'No problem. Even my staff don't know about its existence.' He collected from a cupboard a long grey plastic cover, which he unzipped.

'Specially made, to hide it from curious eyes,' he explained. 'Even so –' he addressed Rayner '– I'll ask you to accompany me there, as a security man. I believe you were in the SAS once . . .'

'. . . Special Air Service, yes. I was in the force for a couple of years.' Rayner smiled across the restaurant table at Fenella. 'It's got a lot of glamour in the public eye, but it can be boring at times.'

It was evening. The meeting at Christie's belonged to

the morning. Rayner had pre-empted Hendey's rather avuncular invitation to dinner when he had returned with the silver expert from the strongroom by asking Fenella out; Gibson had only woken up too late as he brooded over the complicated cross-fire of claims and counter-claims arising out of the silver oar discovery.

It was a small, select restaurant where Rayner was known, and which he visited occasionally.

The arrival of the wine interrupted Rayner.

'It's the Cape Chardonnay you asked for, Mr Watton,' said Theodore, the owner. 'I hope it's up to standard.'

Rayner said to Fenella, 'Theodore's is one of the few places in London where you can be sure of a good Cape wine. I thought it might be fun, seeing you're from the Cape.'

'From the Cape?' Theodore deftly poured a taste for Rayner.

'Cape Town itself,' said Fenella. 'I only arrived this morning.'

'If I may say so, miss, you don't look much travel-worn.'

Rayner had thought at the airport that even in her sloppy clothes she had looked lovely; now she was ravishing. She wore a severely cut black-and-white dress with a single row of pearls at the neck. Her black hair – carelessly-carefully groomed – was highlighted by gold earrings in the form of two leaping dolphins. The only other ornament was a scimitar-shaped platinum brooch across her right shoulder, with a minute ruby at each end. The dress showed off her slender figure; the plain V of the neck revealed the fine curve of her breasts.

'I've got a cousin out there,' went on Theodore conversationally. 'In one of the suburbs, I think – you live in the city itself?'

'I've got a place on the slope of the mountain – it has a beautiful view.'

Theodore poured Rayner's wine and indicated his glass to Fenella.

'Always drinks with his left hand. I don't know the reason – you ask him why. Perhaps he'll tell you.'

Rayner merely laughed, but said when Theodore had gone, 'It's part of the SAS story, really.'

Fenella was acute. She had noticed his hesitation and said quickly, 'You don't have to tell, if you don't want to.'

He shrugged, as if putting aside something unpleasant from the past.

'I was sitting with an SAS chum at a pavement café in Gibraltar. I had my wine – in my right hand – at my lips. From nowhere, it seemed, an IRA terrorist appeared and shot him, as he sat there next to me. If I'd had my right hand free, I could have got him with my pistol. But I didn't. Ever since, it's been my left.'

The slight forward thrust of her face with her chin up, to which the artifice of her hair contributed as if by its weight, made for an identification with the painful incident which made him feel good.

'Is that why you left the SAS?'

'No, it was nothing like that. I'm simply not the type who takes to regimentation. I like to be on my own.'

'But you're part of Surveillicor.'

'You've got it wrong, Fenella. I'm a freelance, doing a freelance job for Don Gibson. Part of his set-up – no.'

Fenella eyed the controlled relaxation and built-in vigilance of the man opposite her, his right hand lying seemingly negligently on the tablecloth.

She asked, 'Why do you call yourself an Intelligencer?'

She was to learn later that when a sudden question was fired at him, Rayner would absorb it with a quick blink and sideways shift of the eyes and small involuntary quirk of the eyebrows.

She added quickly, 'I've never heard the word.'

He smiled, at ease now. 'It's an archaic old term, long out of use, which I came across early on in my freelance career when I was given the job of setting up security for some medieval books and manuscripts in an old manor-cum-abbey down in Devonshire. It appealed, and I stuck it on my nameplate at my London office. It seemed to work and draw customers – maybe they thought it meant something special. Even the SAS itself threw me some crumbs from their table when they wanted to make quite sure that something they were putting under surveillance could not be traced back to them. You see, I was in their Intelligence and Security Group, which handles only covert surveillance work.'

'That doesn't seem to cover the *Alabama*.'

'My work as an Intelligencer covers a multitude of sins.'

'How did you come to join the SAS in the first place if you felt it wasn't realizing your potential?'

He dropped his eyes and said, 'I was talked into it by a good friend of mine, Hugh Perrot. He's now a top boy in Scotland Yard's Anti-Terrorist Squad. What I had been doing up to then didn't seem – to either of us – to have much future.'

'And that was?'

'I was a professional salmon fisherman in Greenland.' His offhand shrug killed her further questions. 'Silver oars are much more interesting. What I'd like to know is, how you came to be involved in such a way-out interest? Hendey said you were the world's leading expert.'

'I love silver,' she said simply, 'the feel of it.'

He remembered how lovingly her fingers had caressed the blade and loom (as she called it) of the oar.

'That in itself is an acquired taste.'

'I suppose so. My parents' home was full of antiques, paintings and beautiful things and one night at a dinner party there a guest I was sitting next to exclaimed over the silver spoons and showed me what hallmarks were. Perhaps you know that there is a whole branch of silver relating to the Cape called Cape Silver. Those hallmarks seemed to have some special mystique for me, and the cryptics connected with hallmarking were like suddenly becoming aware of what ancient Egyptian writing was all about. Whatever it was, it sparked my interest.'

'You haven't explained the *feel* of silver you spoke about earlier.'

'It was born that night, too. I became aware of the peculiar quality connected with the metal, quite unlike the feel of gold or platinum or any other precious metal. It's part of silver's mystique for me also.'

'Is that how you got involved with Christie's, then?'

She laughed softly. 'Christie's are top experts. They wouldn't take on anyone simply because silver appealed to them. No, I happened to be working at a museum called the Cultural History Museum in Cape Town – my first job after university – and it has probably one of the finest collections of Cape Silver there is. It's odd how the wheel seems to come full circle – would you believe it, the building which houses the museum was once the venue of the Vice-Admiralty Court at the Cape, home of the silver oar?'

Their eyes held each other's for a long moment, and then she said:

'It was there that I first became fired up about silver oars.'

'And then graduated to Christie's?'

Suddenly her face seemed to close and the depths of her eyes – Rayner thought he had never seen so dark a lavender-violet in anyone – became clouded and inscrutable with some inner recall.

'It was a very unhappy period of my life,' she replied. 'I also lost both my parents – killed in an air crash. Yes,

I graduated to Christie's because I suddenly found myself broke, and in desperate need of money.'

'But the house full of antiques and choice silver –'

'Rayner,' she broke in. 'Let's talk about something else. What I'm saying can't be of any possible interest to you. After tomorrow's meeting we'll never see one another again.'

Chapter 5

'Did any of you hear the news this morning?'

Rayner eyed Gibson with surprise. The Surveillicor chief wasn't given to conversational gambits. He must be desperately tense and unsure of himself to kick off with a trite remark for what was likely to be a make-or-break meeting to decide the future of the *Alabama* oar which again lay, in Excalibur-like splendor, on the big board-room table at Christie's.

It was next day. The four of them – Charles Hendey, Don Gibson, Fenella and Rayner – were meeting as had been arranged after Gibson had had time to decide on the legal and financial implications of the discovery.

To both Rayner and Fenella, the meeting had an air of finality. Rayner had taken upon himself the prerogative of fetching Fenella from her hotel, but their anticipation of what was likely to transpire made both of them silent, in contrast to their easy exchanges the previous night.

'About the Prime Minister, I mean?' jerked out Gibson.

Hendey seemed the only relaxed person of the four. His dark suit was in sharp contrast to Rayner's grey bomber jacket and grey cotton shirt, ribbed black-and-grey V-necked jersey and grey moccasin shoes. Fenella's severely tailored white suit was the perfect foil to her hair.

Rayner and Fenella shook their heads, but Hendey replied, 'Yes, I did. There was nothing new. The Prime Minister simply repeated that the visit to South Africa in about five or six weeks was still on, despite the desecration of Nelson's head and the threat from that women's terror group, Rote something or other.'

'Rote Zora,' supplied Gibson.

'Don,' asked Rayner impatiently, 'what has this to do with what we've come to discuss?' He indicated the silver oar.

Fenella's eyes had the closed, clouded look which had come over them the previous evening; Rayner felt shut out. She was indulging as she sat in an unconscious little idiosyncrasy he'd noticed the previous day when she was examining the silver oar – in her left hand, which she propped at chin-height on the elbow, she revolved a thin silver pencil between the fingers, slowly round and round, until she needed to emphasize a statement, when she would direct the pencil like a blackboard pointer.

'Everything,' retorted Gibson.

'Perhaps I'm dim this morning, Don, but I don't see it,' said Rayner.

Gibson banged both his hands, palms down, on the table.

'Listen! I've spent a hell of a lot of time trying to work out how we could handle this thing, and every avenue landed me up at the same place – a court battle, millions in legal costs, buckets of unwanted publicity, the lot. Something kept nagging at the back of my mind, but I couldn't bring it out. That news bulletin about the Prime Minister did it.'

He leaned back, grinning. Fenella's pencil orbited more slowly.

'There's been no announcement yet about what sort of

ceremony will be held for the signing of the new agreement, but you can bet that for an occasion like that there's going to be loads of ceremonial, and that the emphasis will be naval.

'What if we give them one small shove and suggest that as a piece of historic symbolism there should be a ceremonial exchange of silver oars between the two heads of government to mark the signing?'

Involuntarily, Fenella's eyes sought Rayner's in astonishment. 'It's breath-taking!' she exclaimed.

Hendey added, 'I don't know what to say!'

'You'll never get away with it, Don!' Rayner said. 'I've never heard such a daring proposition in my life!'

'All the more reason to go for it,' answered Gibson excitedly. 'There are the two oars, ours here and Pittock-Williams's there. Just think of the financial and publicity benefits Surveillicor could win from such a ceremony! You can't put a price on them!'

'It means making public our discovery –' began Rayner.

'Of course it does – in due time,' replied Gibson. 'But it also draws the teeth of the powerful objections which we all know are bound to come from the French and Americans. In my plan, the oar would no longer be the property of a private firm but that of the British government itself. It puts the find on a different basis altogether, especially as we know it was the British who built the *Alabama* for the Confederacy out of affection for their cause and closed a blind eye to a lot of things during her raiding voyage . . . the mere fact that the *Alabama* oar is to be given away and not sold for the millions it is worth takes a lot of the steam out of foreign arguments.'

'You're not going to *give* it away, are you, Mr Gibson?' Hendey was appalled.

Gibson grinned at him. 'I'll come to that in a moment.'

'You seem to have done a lot of hard thinking in a short time, Don,' observed Rayner.

'There's still a lot more to be done – there are loose ends everywhere which have to be tidied up.'

'One of them is, how do you convey the idea to the Prime Minister?' asked Fenella.

'Or to the South African President,' added Rayner.

'Let us keep London and Cape Town separate for the moment.' Gibson was talking fast, animatedly. 'Downing Street first. The whole scheme would abort if we are naive enough to simply announce the discovery and publicize the exchange idea. We need to sell the idea behind the scenes, put it over in high places, and make the exchange a *fait accompli* by the time it gets to the media.'

'Easily said,' remarked Rayner.

'And for my part, easily done. You see, I have a high-up contact in the Prime Minister's office, a top official I did a particular service for about eighteen months ago. He's my jumping-off point to the ear of the Prime Minister.'

He addressed Fenella. 'Of course, they wouldn't take my unsupported word for it that we have the original oar. You'd have to vouch for it personally, as an expert.'

Hendey nodded. 'I'll go along with that.'

Fenella said, 'Of course.'

'You've side-stepped the point of the money involved,' said Rayner.

'I haven't,' answered Gibson. 'Can't you visualize the glamour of the occasion? Two heads of government, a famous old naval base oozing history, ambassadors, naval uniforms, warships –'

Rayner laughed. 'You don't have to sell *me* the idea, Don! Keep it for your high-up!'

'I am quite sure, with the correct approach, the British government will see it in the correct light and be willing

49

to – ah, reimburse Surveillicor in line with –' he turned to Hendey '– an expert valuation from Christie's.'

'Nothing would give me greater pleasure.'

Fenella twirled the silver pencil in her fingers. 'To me, the biggest obstacle of all remains – Professor Pittock-Williams. In strict law, he owns *both* the *Alabama* mace and the one he has in his own possession, which we don't know anything about. But it is a silver oar. As the Marshal's direct descendant, he also has another essential item of the ceremonial, the Marshal's ivory baton. I also know that he can be very difficult.'

'Difficult – in what way?' asked Gibson.

'I've never met him, but I am told he is egotistical, overbearing and arrogant. It was on the strength of this that I never attempted to follow up my researches person-ally with him. I was sure, from what I had heard, that I would get the brush-off.'

'Every man has his price,' said Gibson sententiously. 'Where is the Achilles' heel of this professor?'

'He's always in the public eye over something,' answered Fenella. 'He's chairman of a number of public bodies, among them an influential one on the en-vironment.'

'We'll give him more publicity over the silver oars than he ever got from all the rest combined,' said Gibson. 'He'd be right in the forefront as the Marshal's heir –' He let his words trail away into a silence which took in Rayner and Fenella.

Then he said incisively, 'Rayner. Fenella. I propose that you two act as my emissaries and get out to the Cape as soon as you can and approach Pittock-Williams for his consent.'

It was axiomatic that, after their epitaphic dinner the previous night, their eyes instantly sought one another's, and Rayner watched the colour flood into Fenella's face and the vanished luminousness take over eyes which had, up to now, been hooded and were now wide with joy and elation.

Fenella reached out and put her hand on Rayner's arm.

'Wonderful! Of course! I've got a whole big empty house where I live by myself and Rayner can come and stay!'

Rayner was grinning. 'Difficult, high-handed – I don't give a damn! We'll handle Pittock-Williams, Don! We'll make this crazy idea of yours work!'

'I'm beginning to think it is more brilliant than crazy,' interrupted Hendey. 'There's a tremendous amount of staff-work to be done, though.'

'Undercover is the word,' grinned Gibson. 'We must play our cards right, and time is of the essence. How soon can you leave for the Cape?'

'Tomorrow, if you want,' answered Fenella excitedly. She suddenly remembered Christie's. 'That's if it suits you, Mr Hendey.'

He nodded amusedly. 'I'm being swept along with the tide.'

Gibson went on, 'Rayner will need your full expert support in convincing Pittock-Williams, Fenella. I'll be very curious to hear your opinion of the oar he has.'

'We may never get as far as that, but we'll try,' replied Fenella.

'We need a lever strong enough to persuade Pittock-Williams,' began Rayner.

'If I can get enough encouragement at official level from Downing Street that the Prime Minister favours the idea, that would be a start and a powerful weapon against Pittock-Williams,' said Gibson. 'You won't be able to leave before I can obtain some kind of hopeful hint or even half-promise. The announcement will obviously have to come later, officially, from both Britain and South Africa. I intend to start the ball rolling now, this morning. It may take a day or two –'

It did, in fact, take three – three days of hard, skilful undercover diplomatic work by Don Gibson, culminating in the arrival by car at the Prime Minister's Westminster offices of Gibson, Rayner and Fenella. The silver oar, zipped up in Hendey's grey plastic cover, was on the car's back seat. So was Rayner, with the Glock 17 thrust out of sight under the flap of his jacket. Part of the ploy was that Gibson's contact was to remain faceless; he would be addressed as 'Mr Smith'.

Gibson slowed the car and was stopped by two policemen at the entrance. Rayner thought he had managed to slip the Glock rather neatly and unobtrusively from his belt into its holster as one of the policemen held up a hand.

He started to back out of the rear door. He didn't get further than that when one of the men moved in on him, snatched the pistol from Rayner's holster, and moved back out of range of any counterstrike with a speed and professionalism which left Rayner gasping.

'No guns in here! Noways!'

Gibson rushed to the rescue. 'It's not for here, officer. You know who we are and that we've got something special there in the back. The gun was to guard it in the streets. You can check with Mister – ah, Smith, about our credentials.'

'I know all that, sir. But there was no mention in our briefing of this – some gun, too, if I may say so.'

Rayner saw the chances of their meeting the anonymous Mr Smith slipping away. Fenella realized the implications, too.

Gibson pulled out a typewritten sheet of letter-headed notepaper from his pocket and passed it to the man. The other policeman had the pistol and was slipping out the magazine.

'Full magazine also. It'll have to be checked and sealed.'

Gibson said, 'We're not up to anything, officer. But what we've got there in the back is something which could have big implications for the Prime Minister's forthcoming visit to South Africa. This lady here has been flown from Cape Town specially to identify this – ah, precious object.'

'The gun –'

'Keep it, if you want to, and seal the magazine,' answered Rayner. 'It's all in order. I acquired it when I was in the SAS.'

The man gave Rayner a long searching glance. 'That makes things kind of different. SAS, eh? Before you go in, though, I'll want some facts from you so that I can double-check.'

It took ten minutes before Rayner, Gibson and Fenella finally confronted 'Mr Smith' in his office. He was polite but cagey – until Gibson unzipped the 'golf-bag' cover and slid out the silver oar.

He stopped being expressionless. His face took on the lineaments of an astonished and excited human being.

'My oath!' he exclaimed softly. 'I've never seen anything like this! Nor has the Prime Minister – you won't want any showmanship if there's to be an exchange! And there are two of them like this, you say?'

'Not quite identical, but very nearly,' explained Fenella.

'I told you, it's at present at the Cape,' went on Gibson. 'We need the consent of its owner before we can clinch things from that side. But with some encouragement from this office –'

Rayner thought, Don Gibson's jumping all the hurdles in-between and giving a scintillating PRO performance. Fenella thought, if it fails to come off, there won't be any joint mission to the Cape –

'Of course, at this stage I cannot give any commitment from the Prime Minister's side but, having seen the oar myself, I can say that I am greatly impressed and will do my best.'

Gibson knew the right vibes when he felt them. He also knew when to get out while the going was good.

He gathered up the oar. 'If the Prime Minister should wish to see it . . .'

'Mr Smith' smiled. 'Maybe. But I hope my word alone will be accepted.'

Gibson cleared his throat and said diffidently, 'One of the guards at the gate confiscated a pistol Mr Watton was using to protect the oar on the way here. I wonder if you could phone the gate and clear us?'

'Of course. You shall have the pistol back.'

'A most unusual weapon, sir,' said the policeman when he handed it back as they were leaving. 'I'll bet there's not another one like it in London.'

But there was. In Zara's Semtex-framed suitcase, waiting in preparation for the heat to cool off the effigy head search before she flew back to the Cape in a few days' time.

Chapter 6

'I don't care if you sent the whole of Christie's staff along. I'm not interested. Is that clear? I'm simply not interested.'

The voice at the other end of the line to Rayner was abrasive, offhand. It was that of Professor Vivian Pittock-Williams.

Rayner was phoning from Fenella's home in Cape Town, with her by his side. They had arrived the previous evening from London, too late to set in motion the wheels of their assignment. Time, as Gibson had said, was of the essence, and they had left London together the day after their Downing Street meeting.

The phone was in the hall and from it Rayner looked out past the big mahogany front door with its heavy brass fittings to the lawn and terraced garden of the Villa Montana. It was a lovely old double-storeyed place on the slopes of Table Mountain close to the cable station, with a superb backdrop of massive peaks and crags behind, and a splendid view of Signal Hill and the ocean in front. Gay awnings over wrought-iron balconies upstairs and a group of twenty-metre stone pines by the swimming pool, basking now in the bright autumn sunshine, gave the place a Mediterranean air. This was the place Fenella had told Rayner in London she had inherited on the death of her parents in an air crash.

They had first tried making contact with Pittock-Williams at his home in Constantia, a fashionable suburb in a beautiful setting to the south of the city itself. The mechanical answering service told them to try the professor at Groote Schuur hospital. Here the human barrier was more obstructive than the mechanical one at his home. They rode out brusqueness and near-rudeness from at least four secretaries, until they cornered Pittock-Williams himself.

Fenella whispered to Rayner as this was going on, 'If Charles Hendey hadn't phoned in advance from London, we wouldn't stand a chance of talking to him.'

It didn't look like much of a chance, even now.

'Christie's in London phoned me to say that two of its representatives would be approaching me for an appointment,' barked Pittock-Williams. 'I suppose you're after the Admiralty oar? I repeat, I am not interested. Period.'

'It does concern the Admiralty oar in your possession —'

'Then don't waste my time further.'

Rayner managed to slip in his words hurriedly as he

55

sensed that the phone was about to be slammed down the other end. 'But it also concerns the British Prime Minister.'

Rayner felt the phone come back into circulation again, and gave Fenella the thumbs-up sign with his free hand.

'Who are you?' snapped Pittock-Williams (Rayner had given his name at the outset). 'What's your status, to make a remark like that?'

Rayner replied carefully, 'It's something which simply can't be discussed over the telephone, Professor Pittock-Williams. I – and Miss Gault from Christie's – have to see you face-to-face. And – confidentially.'

'You're not playing the ass with me and saying something to get in so that you can then make me an offer I can't refuse, are you? Because it won't wash, I tell you.'

'It's up to you,' replied Rayner. 'But I assure you, there's no money involved.'

'But my silver oar is.'

'Yes. So is the British Prime Minister.'

'Listen,' snapped Pittock-Williams. 'I still think you're trying to con me with a very clever sales approach. I don't believe a word. Nevertheless, I'll see you – this evening. I have a big environmental meeting scheduled for eight o'clock. I'll give you half an hour before that. If you're late, you don't get in, see?'

'You may feel you will need more time, once you've heard –'

'Seven-fifteen!'

Rayner found himself holding a dead instrument.

'It looks as if we're in for a rough ride,' remarked Fenella.

'We'll need all the heavy metal we can find to bombard that fortress of prejudice.'

Pittock-Williams's home was a fortress, in more ways than one. If Rayner had been critical of the Villa Montana's security system – antiquated and inadequate, when he had seen it for the first time guarding the paintings, carpets, porcelain and *objets d'art* – he had no grounds to cavil at Pittock-Williams's: a patrolling private security guard, a couple of savage Alsatian dogs, an announcement system, infra-red scanners and a closed-circuit TV monitor at the massive wrought-iron gates.

They were finally shown in to a small side-lounge. Even if it had been designed for second-class guests, the paintings on the walls proclaimed it first-class.

They waited. Rayner checked his watch.

Pittock-Williams used an extra five minutes over time to make his entrance – a tallish, bull-necked, slightly balding man whose footsteps kicked impatiently at the thick carpet. He was jacketless; once trim surgeon's shoulder muscles had run to fleshiness, as had his hands. At first glance, neither Rayner nor Fenella liked him any more than they had done over the phone, and yet he had about him an odd air of compelling magnetism coupled with his aggressiveness.

There was no preliminary handshake, no offer to sit down.

Instead, he jerked out, 'What's your name? What's your business? What's all this about the British Prime Minister? What in hell has it to do with my Admiralty oar? I'd have you know that the oar was the private property of the Marshal, and it did not belong to either the Admiralty or the government. Mine belonged to my great-grandfather and has been inherited by the family –'

'That is perfectly correct,' said Fenella quietly. 'If the oar you inherited was the original Cape of Good Hope Admiralty oar. But it isn't.'

Pittock-Williams's eyes swivelled from Fenella to Rayner, a small breathing-space while Fenella's words sank in. That they had sunk in, was shown by his immediate attempt at aggressive bluster.

'Bah!' he sneered. 'If this is what you came to tell me and try to make a bargain basement offer on the basis of unsubstantiated nonsense, I think we should terminate this interview right away and you get out of here.'

Rayner admired the way Fenella kept her cool.

She said, 'It isn't unsubstantiated nonsense, professor.' She opened her handbag. 'You see, we have the original oar –' she spread the photographic blow-ups of the *Alabama* oar out fanwise in front of Pittock-Williams. 'If you look at this particular one, you'll see the maker's name with his hallmarks and date. "William Frisbee, London. 1806."'

Rayner noted the thin film of sweat on Pittock-Williams's upper lip as he swung his head from side to side like an angry bull.

'Where'd you get this?' His voice was hoarse.

Rayner glanced at his watch. He said with exaggerated considerateness:

'We know that you have an important meeting at eight – the time you gave us is running out. Would you like to postpone this discussion to another time? We can be at your disposal whenever is convenient to you – however, I haven't said what I really came to say.'

Pittock-Williams flicked the photographs with a contemptuous fingernail. 'Where the devil did this oar in the pictures come from?'

'From the wreck of the Confederate raider *Alabama*, seven nautical miles off the coast of France,' answered Rayner.

The effect of Rayner's reply was as dramatic as it was unexpected.

'So that is where the bastard went!' he burst out. 'The dates would be right! So he ran off and hid in a goddam Yankee warship out of reach –'

Fenella smiled and interrupted the vehement explosion. 'The *Alabama* wasn't a Yankee – just the opposite. She belonged to the Confederacy, the Yankees' enemies. The Civil War. She was their most successful merchant raider –'

'Damn it, it was a slip of the tongue!' rapped out Pittock-Williams. 'What is the connection between the oar and the *Alabama*?'

'We were hoping you would be able to tell us,' rejoined Fenella.

'It also depends which oar,' interjected Rayner.

'You're trying to twist my words and my arm,' asserted Pittock-Williams, swinging his head again like a trapped bull looking for an opening. 'It's all part of the game of driving a tough bargain! It won't work, do you see? Those photographs – they could be anything! Probably fakes!'

'We arrived from London only last evening, where I examined the *Alabama* oar myself,' replied Fenella. 'It *is* the original, I assure you.'

'So you take it upon yourself, as a prejudiced party representing Christie's, to state that?' he sneered.

'She is recognized as the world's top authority on Admiralty silver oars,' said Rayner shortly. Pittock-Williams's hectoring was starting to needle him.

'What is the purpose of this discussion? Let's get to the point!' Pittock-Williams went on.

Rayner said, 'What I want to ask you has nothing to do with the authenticity of either the *Alabama* oar now in London or the one you have in your possession. I'm here in a kind of pseudo-diplomatic role –'

'Pseudo, all right!' retorted Pittock-Williams.

Rayner ignored the jibe. 'I'm here with the unofficial blessing of Downing Street –'

'Now I've heard everything!' snapped Pittock-Williams.

'You haven't,' rejoined Rayner. 'There will be an approach at official level once I have your views on our

59

proposition. What is suggested is that there should be a ceremonial exchange of silver oars – the original from the *Alabama* and the one in your possession – to mark the signing of the Simonstown agreement when the British Prime Minister flies out to South Africa shortly.'

Pittock-Williams looked incredulously from Rayner to Fenella for a long moment. Then he rapped out, 'Sit down!'

Some of his blatant aggressiveness seemed to lessen. He's on the hook, thought Rayner.

'Go on!'

Fenella assumed control of the conversation. 'As you rightly said at the start of the discussion, the Admiralty oar –'

'Or oars.'

'Oars – are private property. One is in your hands, the other is in ours –'

'Who is us?' demanded Pittock-Williams. 'You're Christie's. You don't own the London one.'

'The company I work for does,' interjected Rayner. 'Surveillicor. Ownership by right of salvage. Our divers brought it up from the wreck of the *Alabama*. But what we don't know is, who owned it *before* it got aboard such an unlikely place as an American Civil War raider? Or *how* it came to be aboard. Did she capture it? If so, from which of her sixty-five victims? Least of all, how would a treasure like that, the official symbol of the Admiralty at the Cape, have found its way aboard an American ship, let alone a Confederate raider?'

'I'll tell you,' replied Pittock-Williams. 'It belonged – belongs – to the Cape Vice-Admiralty Court Marshal –'

'How then did it vanish and turn up again, after a hundred and thirty years, amongst the buried loot of a Confederate warship which was known to have docked at the Cape? And where did the substitute oar come from, the one which descended through your family to you? What *happened*, Professor Pittock-Williams?'

'In strict legal terms, the oar Surveillicor claims to have salvaged belongs to me – my great-grandfather was the Admiralty Marshal.'

'Does it?' demanded Rayner. 'What about our salvage rights? They override your ownership claims.'

The discussion was interrupted by the arrival, after a tentative knock at the door, of a middle-aged woman who looked as if she had been steamrollered by the years. She had, living with Pittock-Williams.

'What is it?' Pittock-Williams demanded testily.

'Dear, your meeting has just telephoned for you. It's late.'

'It's my privilege to be late,' snapped Pittock-Williams. 'Tell them I have been delayed by an emergency. I'll be along shortly.'

'Yes, dear.' She went, for the millionth time the ham in Pittock-Williams's sandwich.

Rayner resumed. 'The question of legal ownership is dicey, to say the least. You might well own one, perhaps both oars. However, what I am entrusted to approach you about is whether you will agree to the ceremonial exchange of these two silver oars – the one by the British Prime Minister and the other by the South African President – at the signing ceremony of the new Simonstown treaty in about a month's time. I am authorized to tell you that Downing Street looks with favour on the idea.'

'You must be joking,' exclaimed Pittock-Williams.

'I've never been so serious about anything,' replied Rayner.

Fenella read her man well. 'You would not be forgotten in the ceremony, professor. As the lineal descendant of the Cape Marshal, the spotlight will fall upon you.'

'You mean – ?'

'You will have a key role in the ceremony, since your

grand—, er, great-grandfather, was the last Marshal to hold the office at the Cape.'

There was another tentative knock at the door and Mrs Pittock-Williams sidled in with long-practised adroitness.

'Dear, your meeting has phoned again –'

Pittock-Williams got up. 'Come back tomorrow, and we'll have an in-depth discussion about your proposal. There is a lot I need to know.'

Rayner and Fenella knew they had hooked their fish. 'Naturally.'

Pittock-Williams instructed his face muscles to smile.

'Some coffee? A liqueur? Mildred, get my appointment book and fix – er, I've forgotten your names.'

'Fenella Gault. Rayner Watton.'

Mildred came back at the double-shuffle. 'The diary is pretty full tomorrow, dear –'

'Fix 'em up!' snapped Pittock-Williams.

Chapter 7

They were fixed up: they met Pittock-Williams the next morning, still in the second-class visitors' lounge, after another close security check.

From the moment Pittock-Williams came in, both Rayner and Fenella realized that he was in an oddly different frame of mind – not so aggressive but, to start with, a kind of controlled elation which neither of them could fathom.

His first question was shot at their heads straight from his ego.

'What precisely will be my role in the Simonstown ceremony – always providing I agree about the oars? They both belong to me, never forget.'

This was the question Rayner and Fenella had discussed by phone the previous evening with Don Gibson, who had been elated to hear that the initial meeting had gone so well and that further discussions were on track.

Rayner wrapped up his reply in a way to keep Pittock-Williams's ego well under the spotlight.

'If you agree, Fenella and I will pass it on immediately to our principals in London, and then, so Don Gibson informed me last night, the British ambassador and the South African Department of Foreign Affairs will both be in touch with you to give official sanction to the idea. The logistics of the signing ceremony are still under discussion – as you can imagine, such a programme takes considerable working out, not to mention the timing.

'However, it has already been agreed that the signing ceremony will take place in Simonstown itself because of the naval base's long association with, and significance to, both countries' navies. Admiralty House there has been chosen because of its deep historical links –'

'I know it well,' Pittock-Williams interrupted. 'I was there recently as a VIP to mark its restoration – the South African Navy today reserves the place for top VIPs and naval staff.'

'As to procedure –' Rayner handed the explanation to Fenella.

She said, 'The old Vice-Admiralty Court at the Cape followed very much the same procedure as still takes place in London on the first day of the Michaelmas Law Sittings – the procession of judges is headed by the Marshal carrying the silver oar. Inside the courtroom itself, when the President of the Admiralty Division is hearing Admiralty cases, the silver oar is laid in front of him by the Marshal on a pair of brackets fitted immediately below the bench. In the case of the Simonstown ceremony, it has already been tentatively agreed that there will be a procession of dignitaries instead of judges, headed by the two heads of government –'

Pittock-Williams bridled. 'You've forgotten the Marshal's leading role. His place must be in front.'

Fenella remained patient. 'If you agree, professor, then you will be the Marshal who will act as mace-bearer with the oar and lead the procession. The ritual goes back centuries in history.'

Pittock-Williams dodged the question of consent and remained cagey.

'You've pronounced the oar from the *Alabama* wreck as being the original, and the one I have as a substitute –'

'I didn't call it a substitute,' replied Fenella. 'All I said was, you have another silver oar in your possession. Where it came from, and who made it, I don't know.'

'I have to have a concrete undertaking that the oar in my possession will not be underrated, or in any way relegated to an inferior position or status,' asserted Pittock-Williams.

'None whatsoever,' Rayner reassured him. 'It will, in fact, be the oar which will be donated to the British Prime Minister, just as the *Alabama* oar in turn will be donated to South Africa.'

'I don't like your continual reference to what you term the *Alabama* oar. It didn't belong to the *Alabama*.'

'An easy way of identification, that's all,' answered Rayner. 'We still don't know how it came to be aboard the raider.'

Fenella felt that Pittock-Williams again resorted to aggressiveness to hide something to which he knew the answer.

'Am I expected to donate two priceless silver relics without any monetary compensation?'

'I simply don't know, at this stage,' replied Rayner.

'But both governments will be made fully aware of the value of the two oars.'

'What if I don't agree to this exchange ceremony?' Pittock-Williams demanded.

'Then we will be obliged to break the news of our find, and the dramatic way it was salvaged. In that event, your oar won't be more than a second-stringer when the story comes out. We will also back up the authenticity of our oar as the original. We also know that the news will evoke an uproar. The French and Americans have been watching our team like hawks.'

'And you them,' added Pittock-Williams.

Rayner shrugged. 'It's the name of the game. We've landed the ace in the pack.'

'How did you get it past them?' asked Pittock-Williams.

Both Rayner and Fenella realized that Pittock-Williams was marking time before coming up with a new point.

Then he said abruptly, 'I'll agree – on one condition.'

'It depends whether the condition outweighs your consent,' replied Rayner.

The studied way in which Pittock-Williams put his proposition made it clear that he had worked things out the previous night and that his agreement was a foregone conclusion to the second day's meeting.

'The public at large today has no idea what the functions were of the Vice-Admiralty Court at the Cape in the past –'

'Why should they?' interrupted Rayner rhetorically.

'– except a few historians and antiquarians.' He inclined his head towards Fenella. 'Nor of the ceremonial involved.'

'I myself don't, beyond what I've picked up from Fenella,' said Rayner, wondering what Pittock-Williams was leading up to.

'Nor the status of the Marshal.' Pittock-Williams's ego broke through the wrapping of words. He added pontifically, 'I am convinced, therefore, that the public needs to be enlightened – *before* the ceremonial exchange of oars takes place at the signing ceremony proper.'

'Before?' echoed Rayner. 'I am sure the media –'

'It's not the media, but the public, the man in the street, that I am concerned about.'

'What are you driving at, professor?' asked Rayner.

Pittock-Williams addressed Fenella. 'You know the Old Supreme Court building in Adderley Street, just below the Houses of Parliament –'

Fenella glanced at Rayner and smiled. 'I worked there, in the Cultural History Museum, before I joined Christie's.'

'The centenary of the hand-over of this building when the Vice-Admiralty Court ceased to function there is at hand, which would also be an appropriate occasion for what I am about to say. My proposition is – purely for the edification of the public, you understand – that there should be a kind of mock trial staged in this old building, and that a procession should take place from it towards parliament next door – in period costume, of course.'

It was only Rayner who was able to detect the inflexion in Fenella's voice. 'Led by the Marshal with his silver oar.'

'Naturally.'

A neat bit of double exposure, Rayner told himself inwardly. First, to the fore in the mock trial procession and then, for real, at the Simonstown ceremony itself.

Aloud, he said, 'I can't see there can be any objections. Except the time factor. I wonder if the authorities can manage to arrange such a function in time?'

'You don't have to bother about the authorities and arrangements,' answered Pittock-Williams over-eagerly. 'I will organize it myself. As a matter of fact, I have already taken some preliminary steps in that direction. Last night I spoke to the director of a leading theatre group and sounded him out. Actors and actresses will be available, he assures me. I myself still have the Marshal's original uniform in my possession. I can wear it, or have it copied –' He went on self-deprecatingly when Rayner and Fenella remained silent. 'It's all a bit of historical nonsense, really, but it will serve to inform, ahead of the main ceremony.'

'We can leave it to you, then?' Rayner asked blandly.

'Absolutely.'

'Are you willing to risk a public showing of your silver oar?' asked Fenella quietly.

Pittock-Williams nodded, and then said with studied nonchalance, 'Would you like to see it – now?'

It was something Fenella had been hoping for, without much prospect. Rayner asked in surprise, 'You keep it here – in the house?'

Pittock-Williams laughed. 'Try and get past my security, and see what happens!'

He led them through to his study, but before entering he paused at the door to immobilize the alarm system. He said confidentially, 'Everything in the security line that opens and shuts – video scanners, infra-red beams, the lot.'

Rayner was impressed. More so, when Pittock-Williams opened a combination lock safe and took from it a long object wrapped in a purple velvet cloth.

He laid it on his desk and whipped the cloth aside, like a magician's act.

'What do you think of that?' he asked Fenella.

With the *Alabama* oar fresh in mind, Rayner himself was able to see the difference in the oar in front of them. It looked about the same length, but the blade itself seemed flatter, wider. The top was engraved with the Royal arms like the *Alabama*'s, but the engraving below it, that of the eagle mounted on a thunderbolt, was missing altogether, while the Admiralty's foul anchor emblem seemed to lack the flourish of Frisbee's original. There had been an attempt to copy (clearly from memory) the medallion head of George the Third at the base of the blade, but it lacked the grace of Frisbee's master-craftsmanship.

'Good!' exclaimed Fenella, bending over the base of the loom or shaft to study the hallmarks. 'Made by Heinrich Schmidt, grandson of the famous Cape silversmith Daniel Schmidt. Schmidt the younger did some very fine work.'

But Pittock-Williams seemed to be waiting for some further comment from her. She said, 'Of course, the blade is differently engraved from the original –'

'There was no pictorial record of the original,' replied Pittock-Williams defensively. 'The record says this one was done largely from recollection. What else?'

'Here's the big difference.' Fenella pointed to the object which projected from the base of the long shaft, which made it look longer still than the original. It was white, like ivory, in contrast to the silver of the shaft, and was topped by a Royal crown fashioned in silver, and encircled by a silver band engraved with the customary Admiralty anchor. It was about six inches long.

'Marshal's baton,' she said. 'But the way it screws into the base of the shaft is an improvisation. It wasn't that way in the original. The oar and the baton remained completely separate.'

Pittock-Williams unscrewed the baton from the shaft. 'I said, Schmidt never had the benefit of viewing the original – how could he have had?' He went on to unscrew in turn the Royal crown which constituted the head of the baton and indicated an empty space inside.

'That space was for carrying the warrant issued by the Vice-Admiralty Court –' Pittock-Williams stopped short in mid-sentence. 'By heavens, this gives me an idea! Why not let the treaty document the two heads of government are to sign be housed in this space and then ceremonially removed before the signing proper! It would be in complete harmony with the tradition of Admiralty courts!'

And give the twentieth-century Marshal yet another opportunity to steal centre stage, Rayner thought.

Aloud, he said, 'I'll put forward the idea to London.'

Pittock-Williams looked to Fenella for further backing. 'You agree?'

She answered levelly, 'As you say, fully in keeping with the oar traditions.'

'Agreed, then? There's a great deal of work to be done. Mock trial, the actual signing ceremony. You can count on my full co-operation, at all levels. I presume you'll be reporting to London on the outcome of our meeting? You can use my phone if you wish.'

Rayner smiled to himself. Some of his comments were for Gibson's ear alone. 'It won't be necessary, thanks. I must muster my facts first. I'll speak from Fenella's place when I have.'

Fenella said, 'Your oar might be different, professor, but it is a masterpiece in its own right.'

Pittock-Williams started to wrap up the oar in its velvet covering and said to Fenella:

'Is it correct that the blade derives its shape from that of a thirteenth-century iron battleaxe, which was a formidable weapon?' He finished wrapping the head. 'No trace any longer here of an offensive weapon.'

Don't be so sure, Professor Pittock-Williams. Modern man has a devilish ingenuity when it comes to killing his fellow-beings.

Chapter 8

'His ego must be the size of Table Mountain,' commented Don Gibson.

'Plus some of the other big mountains hereabouts thrown in,' laughed Rayner.

Rayner and Fenella were telephoning Gibson in London from the Villa Montana after their second interview with Pittock-Williams. They had driven back from Constantia slowly, basking in the perfect morning, in the autumn colours of the oaks along the tree-lined roadway, in the magnificent views and (although they did not define it) in themselves.

It wasn't a morning for work, smiled Fenella when they reached the villa, but they had to communicate Pittock-Williams's proposal of a mock trial to Gibson and in turn know what the London reaction was.

'– and your man all togged up in his greatgrandfather's old Marshal's uniform!' chuckled Gibson. 'Well, I don't see it can do much harm, especially as we're not called upon to do anything about organizing the affair. Agreed?'

'That's what Fenella and I both thought when he came up with the proposition,' replied Rayner. 'He's already set the wheels in motion with a theatrical company, and I'll bet his list of invited guests will read like a snob garden party.'

'We – that is, myself and my Downing Street man – were working on the assumption that Pittock-Williams would accept, but it will take a few days before the official announcement can be made, jointly in London and South Africa. There's a mass of protocol attached to a thing like this. Now that you've both seen the man and his mace,

I'm more curious than ever to know how its twin came to be aboard the *Alabama*.'

'He knows something, but he's not saying – why, I don't know,' answered Rayner. 'But it's a misnomer to call the oars twins. Here's Fenella – she can explain the differences better than I.'

'Pittock-Williams's oar was made from memory, not from Frisbee's actual designs,' she told Gibson. 'Also, the size is slightly different, and the engravings on the blade aren't the same. In fact, one is missing altogether.'

'But it's near enough not to spoil the look-alike exchange idea?'

'It's very close – in fact, it's very well done, in its own right. The big difference comes in regard to the Marshal's baton.'

'How?'

'Frankly, I think the arrangement in Pittock-Williams's oar is better than in yours,' replied Fenella. 'It has a special screw-in arrangement at the base of the shaft, and forms part of the oar itself when it's in position. It can be unscrewed for the Marshal to carry it as his symbol of office, if he wishes.'

'These are all minor technicalities,' said Gibson.

'They have a bearing on a further point which Pittock-Williams wants Downing Street to consider,' went on Fenella. 'The Marshal's ivory baton has a hollow body, in which the old-time Admiralty warrant of arrest was carried. What the professor suggests is that the document for the new Simonstown agreement which the two heads of government will sign should be conveyed in this, and duly removed by the Marshal at the appropriate moment.'

Gibson said, 'More spotlight on the Marshal!'

Fenella laughed softly. 'That's the way he thinks.'

'Well, whatever the motives, I think it is an excellent idea – a neat little touch out of the past,' answered

Gibson. 'I am sure that neither of the two governments will object to it. I think you can inform your professor that we favour the idea, pending, of course, formal agreement.'

'We'll do that, Don.'

'I'd like to speak again to Rayner. Rayner, this is now your field. We've already had in-depth discussions here about the security precautions which will have to be put into force once the discovery of the *Alabama* oar has been announced officially. Already there have been media murmurings and probing hints from the French that the British have come up with something big.'

'Who leaked the news?' demanded Rayner. 'Not Powys, I'll lay an even dollar.'

'They haven't got anything concrete, it's just speculation,' added Gibson. 'But it's there, and will erupt once the actual news is broken.'

'Where is the oar now?' asked Rayner.

'In Christie's strongroom. There's no problem there, but it's getting it to South Africa for the signing ceremony that will require the security. Big security. The thing is worth millions.' His voice assumed a note of satisfaction. 'You'll probably be interested to know that I have negotiated the security contract for Surveillicor.'

'Interested, but not surprised,' said Rayner dryly.

'We'll know how to handle it,' added Gibson.

'Meaning?'

'You're the man who slipped the oar into London all unknown in the first place, and you are the man to slip it out again. I've decided that you will be responsible for conveying it safely to South Africa and handing it over to the South African authorities in Cape Town.'

'You've decided – just like that!' exclaimed Rayner ironically. 'Take one priceless silver oar, stash it in your hand luggage, quick-talk your way through the customs, and present it to some faceless guy in Cape Town!'

Gibson seemed more amused than resentful at Rayner's reaction. 'You are Surveillicor's Number One smart guy, Rayner. In any event, you'll carry a gun.'

'Under those circumstances, I'd feel stark naked without it!'

'Now listen,' continued Gibson. 'We're going to be very crafty about this operation. I – and others – have given it a lot of thought. Coinciding with the official announcement about the exchange of oars will be a statement that the *Alabama* mace, because of its value, will be conveyed to South Africa by a special hand-picked security team –'

'I prefer to work on my own – you know that, Don.'

'You won't be one of the team, Rayner. All the publicity about the team will be a blind, a decoy, a smoke-screen. True, the team will protect a parcel – but it won't contain the silver oar. It will be the time-honoured story of the double-take. It's the way they conveyed the world's biggest diamond, the Cullinan, all those years ago. You throw a big public spotlight on a team of armed police, special safe, etcetera, etcetera. You build it up so that all eyes are focused on the team. My guys won't have anything in their parcel except a Shape and a Weight. You will have the real silver oar. You'll travel alone. You sneered just now at hand luggage. That's exactly what it will be. It'll be in a cover, just like a golf club. It's about the same length as a club. No one will know what you are carrying, and no one will know who you are. Just to follow up the ploy, the tough-guy team will be met in Cape Town by another tough-guy team from that end. The "oar" will be wafted away from the airport in a police vehicle amid the wail of sirens and a motor-cycle escort.'

'And me – when I arrive?'

'Fenella can meet you. Private car. You can then take

it direct to whoever the South Africans designate. I'd guess, their Security chief.'

'There's only one small snag to your scheme,' said Rayner, unable to keep the note of sarcasm out of his voice. 'No customs officer has yet been born dumb enough to mistake a solid silver oar for a golf club.'

'Of course, you'll be cleared in advance. Everyone concerned will be briefed ahead of the operation,' answered Gibson testily. 'And, see here, Rayner. You will be the target of a lot of unsuspected surveillance yourself. Even when you leave your seat in the plane to go to the toilet, there will be someone watching, watching. But, for the purposes of the exercise, you will pass through customs checks just like any other passenger.'

'It all seems a bit cut-and-dried, too ready-made,' replied Rayner thoughtfully. 'No provision for contingencies.'

'That's the plan, unless you can think up a better,' answered Gibson shortly. 'You can stand by for trouble, especially from the French, once the news breaks. They're adamant in their claims that the *Alabama* lies in French territorial waters, and therefore belongs to them. And everything in it. It's just because nothing of the calibre of the silver oar has cropped up that they've rather unwillingly accepted the situation as it is.'

'That's not my problem,' said Rayner.

'It could be. OK. I'll phone you in advance exactly when the joint announcement will be made. You'll get yourself back here to London –'

'Before or after Pittock-Williams's mock trial?'

'After, I think. You'll want to see the fun, won't you?'

'Fine. We'll have to work out the precise date with the professor, though. He mentioned tentatively that it would be about ten days hence. It mustn't be too close to the signing ceremony itself. We can't have him upstaging the VIPs.'

'Ten days shouldn't be cutting it too fine,' replied Gibson. He added, as an afterthought, 'By the way, as the man who has acted as go-between, as special envoy if you like, between the various parties, you will be mentioned in the official announcement. Fenella too, as the world's top expert, to back up the authenticity of the oar.'

'I'd prefer to remain anonymous,' said Rayner. 'It's the way the best security works, out of the public eye.'

'It's too big for that,' responded Gibson. 'There'll also be need of someone authoritative to speak to the media, go on camera – all that jazz, you know.'

'You're quite capable of that yourself. Better keep the eyes of the cameras on you than on me –' Rayner started to say.

'We'll sort that out later,' he replied airily. 'Bye!'

Rayner put down the phone and turned to Fenella. 'Once something like this breaks loose, there is no knowing where it is going to finish up,' he said.

Chapter 9

'Open it – it's a surprise,' said Zara.

'It looks like a hatbox,' responded Renate dubiously.

'It *is* a hatbox,' replied Zara, smiling. It softened the tight, strained lines of her face which had been so prominent in London; perhaps the late afternoon light coming in a wash off the great lagoon in front of them had an added cosmetic effect.

Renate, Zara's right-hand woman in the six-strong Rote Zora gang in Cape Town, had met Zara's plane on her return from London and had driven her the hundred kilometres northward, up the west coast or Atlantic seaboard, to this remote cottage high on a cliff overlooking the magnificent lagoon.

It was autumn. It was two days after Fenella and Rayner's second meeting with Professor Pittock-Williams.

Renate eyed Zara acutely. 'You've been on a high ever since you arrived this afternoon,' she observed. 'What happened there in London?'

'Open the box,' Zara replied.

'The way you say it makes me wonder whether it isn't part of the high,' said Renate. She was bigger, taller and slightly younger than Zara, with strong hands which had enjoyed defacing the *Medusa* figurehead.

'Could be,' answered Zara, still smiling.

Renate unloosed the plastic catch a little uncertainly, and opened the lid. The hat which came into view was frilly and lacy and far too feminine for Renate's big frame.

'Look, Zara,' she said a little desperately, 'it's very sweet of you, but I don't wear hats, and certainly not one like this anyway. They're not my scene.'

'Take it out and make sure,' insisted Zara.

Renate, more dubiously than before, withdrew the confection from the box. Below, the container was stuffed with scented tissue paper and flimsy wrappings.

Zara still had the air of a magician producing a rabbit from the hat. 'Go on – there's more.'

'There can't be another one – it's all packing.'

'Fortunately, that's what the customs thought too,' replied Zara.

Renate gave the leader another puzzled glance and pulled out a handful of wrapping.

She stood, transfixed. 'Oh, sweet Jesus!'

Zara's hat had not disturbed the lock of hair over the right eye; the eyes gazed sightlessly out of the famous waxen face.

76

'You must be mad, mad, mad!' she burst out. 'This is the craziest, riskiest thing –'

Zara lifted the effigy out of the box. 'May I introduce Horatio, Lord Nelson, victor of Trafalgar and symbol of male dominance, newly arrived from Westminster Abbey!'

'*You brought the damn thing with you!*' Renate gasped unbelievingly. 'The whole of Scotland Yard and half the police forces of the world are on the alert for this head!'

'So, the safer it will be at Churchhaven,' replied Zara.

It would have been difficult to find anywhere a more remote and little-known spot than the narrow, 25-kilometre strip of dune-land which separates the sea from the splendid lagoon called Langebaan stretching south-ward from the great naval base and harbour of Saldanha. Churchhaven peninsula owes its centuries-old isolation (it still has no telephones) to its unique geographical situation, being cut off from the north by water, and from the south by a formidable barrier known as Sixteen-Mile Beach. This barred access before the advent of the four-wheel drive vehicle, reinforced by a wilderness of salt-ings, mudflats and reedy marshes crowning the head of the lagoon.

The lagoon, some fifteen kilometres long and four wide, is populated by immense hordes of birds – cormor-ants, herons, sandpipers, flamingos, pelicans, plovers, gannets and Northern Hemisphere migrants from Siberia and even Greenland. Zara's cottage lay below cliff-top level, facing out across the great lagoon (or eastwards). The last part of the road – more properly an upgraded track – by which they had come traversed the spine of the peninsula, which was so narrow (only about one and a half kilometres to the sea at this particular point) that the thud-thud of the Atlantic breakers formed a continual counterpoint to the immense silence of the place.

The autumn day was on its way out to a lavender

evening: the muted half-tones of blue, violet and mauve had taken over the dun bracken colours of the cliffside and the water's edge; away to the right, the purplish light emphasized without obliterating the veins of open water between the bright green lakeside lawns which were mudflats and marshes. Between the marshes and the water proper was a wide pink streak which might have been a stray wodge of sunset; it was, in fact, the colour from thousands of flamingos standing motionless in the shallows.

The magic was lost on Renate.

'What are you trying to prove, Zara, by bringing this blasted head here to South Africa? Wasn't it enough that you got away with the theft in the first place?'

'I proved what I set out to prove,' answered Zara coolly.

'That was?'

'Rote Zora's protest against the reinstatement of the Simonstown agreement, and the fact of the Prime Minister making a special trip to perpetuate male dominance.' She gestured towards the effigy. 'There's the male who symbolized the legend of male superiority, worshipped, practically deified. So I cut off his head.'

'You communicated those reasons to the media?'

'Yes. Anonymous telephone call.'

'Fair enough. You had fun, and created a hell of a stink –'

'So did the *Medusa* figurehead back here at home. The media overseas ran out of words about the rubber penis hung round the figurehead's neck – degrading, filthy, disgusting!'

Renate laughed, despite her anger with and disapproval of her leader. 'It was a lark and a laugh, and it came off. So did your effort. Enough's enough. That's what I'm trying to say. This head can only lead to trouble. Why didn't you just dump it in a shopping-bag somewhere and make your getaway clean and sweet?'

'No one is going to find the head here at Churchhaven. Even the customs didn't suspect a thing.'

'I don't like it, Zara,' repeated Renate.

'Get us both a drink before the light goes,' retorted Zara. 'I want to drink in the scene along with the gin. Hell, if you only knew how I longed for my lagoon in those concrete jungles in London and Germany!'

She stared broodingly out across the water while Renate went inside to fix the drinks. The light became more tender; half behind her, to the left of where she stood on the terrace, a shaft sneaked over the tip of the road and illuminated, like a lighthouse of faith in a pagan world, a twin pillar of whitewashed bell-tower and its bell. Behind it, a little higher up the cliff slope, was the church – a low, somewhat crudely built place – from which Churchhaven took its name. On the farther side the sun wandered among gravestones – lavender stone like the evening colours, some crumbling and pathetic, some new and brash – in what Zara considered the most beautiful graveyard in the world. Its silent inhabitants would face out for all eternity across that breathtaking view of the lagoon.

Renate came with the drinks. 'Zara –' she began.

'In a moment,' Zara replied sharply. 'Let me enjoy it while I can, will you?'

'While you can?' echoed Renate.

The serene mood, which had coloured Zara's outlook ever since, earlier, their car had rounded the track at the marsh end of the lagoon and left the grey scrub of the rest of the countryside behind for the first glimpse of the lawn-like fringes of the head of the lagoon, seemed to evaporate.

'For a hundred and thirty years, all my family has wanted is to be left alone – left alone at Churchhaven,' she said in a low, pulsing voice. 'That's why the first guy came here – to be alone. He built this house and he built the church, just as you see them now. In time, when others came over the years, there were only eleven houses altogether, strung out at a good arm's length from each other, along this narrow strip of land. Four of them are still occupied by original Churchhaven settlers' families.'

'Isn't that OK, then?' asked Renate.

Zara picked up her glass and took a deep pull at its contents. She slammed it down.

'Pittock-Williams, Vivian bloody Pittock-Williams,' she got out savagely. 'As if he hasn't done enough already to ruin my life!'

'I thought you were only personally involved –'

'Jeez!' Zara burst out in reply. 'Is that your description for it – copulation, seduction, pregnancy, abortion, operations, cutting out my guts and my womanhood so that I'm useless to any man – is that what you call personally involved?'

'Take it easy, Zara,' said Renate. 'All of us know you've had a rough ride – and you haven't yet told me the result of your medical checks in Germany. But what has all this to do with your saying Pittock-Williams wants to take Churchhaven away from you? He can't just step in and dispossess you of a place which has been in your family for over a century.'

'Get me another drink,' Zara answered harshly. 'No, I won't get it myself. If I do, I'll take it straight out of the bottle.'

Renate brought back the drink. 'Here.'

The light beyond the terrace and the conspiracy of colours ceased to have meaning for Zara.

Zara said, 'Naturally Pittock-Williams wouldn't stick his neck out and try straightforwardly to dispossess me. He's far too cunning for that.'

'And you've got too much on him also,' observed Renate cynically.

'I haven't, that's the trouble,' replied Zara. 'You may think that an affair, making me pregnant and then refusing to do an abortion on me – he could have done it, but he chose to keep his nose clean –'

'He surely didn't just wash his hands of you?'

'That's not his way, and it's not his way now, trying to rob me of Churchhaven. He always opts for the sneaky, roundabout way of keeping his yardarm clear. No, when I confronted him with my pregnancy he was responsible for, he gave me some bum advice about using a new-fangled French abortion pill. Very smooth and professional, he was. The French pill provided the medical alternative to surgical abortion, he said. What he didn't tell me – I found this out only later when I fled to Germany for skilled help – was that after swallowing the French pill you had to go back to hospital some thirty-six to forty-eight hours later and be treated with a second drug, which had to be used to reduce the risk of incomplete abortion. This has to be administered systematically until the process is complete.'

'You never told me – us, the other girls – all this before,' said Renate, eyeing Zara.

'I'm telling you now,' retorted Zara.

She stood and looked out across the lagoon, drink in hand.

'My abortion was incomplete. Pittock-Williams wouldn't handle the complications – why should he? A neat case of professional ethics. He wouldn't admit an unknown woman into his hospital with a series of complications through some stupid act of her own. I went to him, begged him for help. I was haemorrhaging, crazy with pain and worry. The bastard! He simply sat there, detached and professional, on his bloody high professional horse. What was I to him? He'd got me to sign a document before he gave me the French pill stating that I was aware of the danger and risks of foetal malformation. The ball was in my court. I found for myself an underground doctor, struck off the medical register for drug-taking, who did the job. But it wasn't a job, he messed me up still further. I flew to Germany for the first time and threw myself on the mercy of Rote Zora. They were sympathetic, understanding, loyal to a fellow Rote Zora in trouble. They had the black spot on a surgeon, a good man, and they sent me to him. He operated under duress, under threat that Rote Zora would expose or bomb him if he didn't. He did the job – and left me less than a woman. That was about eighteen months ago.'

'Then why did you go back to Germany now?'

The vehemence of Zara's outburst stunned Renate, raking, searing, despair-plummeting words.

'Do you want me to strip and show you? All that is left of the woman which was once me is a couple of tits – the rest is gone, gone, gone! I couldn't sleep with a man, even with a pervert! Can't you understand, all my sexual equipment has been ripped out of me!' She turned her face from the placid lagoon and ran her hand, palm inward, up and down her body, from breast to crotch.

'If *you* want a man, all you have to do is go out in the street and get one – you've got it all there! I haven't – any more. You ask me why I went back again to Germany this time. I went because when the specialist originally operated, he said there might be some hope – slender enough, God knows, but still hope – that something of my womanhood might be left after the healing processes (which took longer than he expected) had taken place.'

Her voice died, only its ghost spoke. 'There wasn't. A sexual vegetable. That was his diagnosis. Final.'

It was Renate who spoke after the long silence, broken only far away by the sad, spectral cry from some bird flying home in that ephemeral moment when the last light glints off the water.

'Then why,' she asked, indicating Nelson's head, 'did you do this?'

'I'll tell you why.' Her voice picked up momentum. Savage momentum, but it was life.

'Try killing time in a great lonely city like London with the sort of judgement I had on my mind,' she answered. Renate saw the evidence of it, of the hope-against-hope torment in the engraved scorings round Zara's mouth and eyes. It could almost have been a beautiful face once, under its cap of auburn hair, tinged copper.

'I wandered about, looking at every goddamn tourist sight in the days before my plane was due to leave. The Tower, the Horse Guards, St Paul's – you name it. I don't remember any of them. But in Westminster Abbey our tour group was shown a museum containing effigies made for the lying-in-state of great personages in British history. Suddenly I saw amongst all the junk –'

She repeated the word angrily. 'Junk! Old clothes draped on bodies of wood and heads of wax –' she half-gestured at the effigy head on the table '– that. Suddenly everything came together, and I knew how I could get this thing out of my system – for a while, at least. A male, hero-worshipped by millions for his maleness, and a male had done this thing to me!'

She laughed; Renate didn't care for the sound of it.

'I went back, with a knife, broke in. It was almost midnight. Big Ben struck. It scared the wits out of me. But I went ahead, sawed off this bastard's head. I shoved it in a shopping-bag, and went back the way I had come, back into the street.'

Renate said very seriously, 'You were seen. The papers made great play of it.'

'A fuzz came down the street. So I strolled along, swinging the shopping-bag. He said, kind of matily, "Quite late for shopping, isn't it, miss?"'

'I made the smart come-back. "Depends what you're

shopping for at this time of night, officer." He thought it a big joke, but I got on my way before he could throw more chat at me.'

Renate said, 'That encounter is Scotland Yard's strongest clue.'

'I was wearing a biker's outfit – leather – and my hair was out of sight under a cap,' Zara replied. 'He didn't get much of a sight of me.'

'The media trumpeted it abroad –'

'But I got out of London safely, with the head.' Life began to steal back into her voice, as if it had been on a drip. 'I'm here, aren't I?

'I'll tell you.' Zara's voice was suddenly strong with hate. 'As I started to saw at his neck, I felt good. Good, good, good! I knew I'd hit on the right antidote to the prognosis passed on my womanhood. If I want to feel good again, I know how to set about it.'

'For Pete's sake, not again!' exclaimed Renate.

'Come!' said Zara. She led Renate to where they had put down Zara's suitcases. She took the smaller one, snapped open the lid, threw the contents untidily on the floor, and then tugged loose the cloth binding covering the suitcase's skeleton.

She made a dramatic gesture at it. 'There!'

Renate examined it carefully. 'The frame looks as if it has been given a coating of something. Not paint.'

'I'll make a bomber out of you yet!' Zara said. 'That, ducky, is the way the Lockerbie disaster was engineered. Plastic explosive. Moulded to the ribs of the suitcase. No smell, no giveaway, undetectable explosive. There are several kilograms of the stuff there. Semtex. Rote Zora in Germany gave it to me as a kind of parting gift. I didn't know what I intended to do with it, but it's a good thing to have around.'

'For what?'

'No targets defined – yet. Rote Zora also gave me

another little present, as undetectable as the Semtex.'

She pulled loose more lining, and secured to the bottom of the case was what looked to Renate like a thick piece of moulded plastic.

Renate shook her head, and Zara said, 'It's not really a fair question. It's a handgun, partially dismantled. The Glock 17, semi-automatic. There are other bits and pieces distributed through my luggage. It passed through all the airport metal detectors and scanners. That is what it was made for. Austria's gift to the cause of terrorism.'

Renate banged down her glass and asked tightly, 'OK, you've got a unique gun. You've also got kilograms of the latest security-beating explosive. What is all this hardware in aid of?'

Zara's dark eyes had a glow which may have come from her mind, or from the last light coming off the water.

'I haven't made a plan – yet.'

Chapter 10

'Let's forget it for the moment,' said Zara abruptly. 'Now I'm ready for another drink – and ready to enjoy the lagoon and Churchhaven with it.'

Renate returned to find her leader still staring out across the fading lagoon.

She gestured towards the far shore, still visible across nearly four kilometres of water.

'My great-grandfather and his young wife arrived here on a Christmas Day, on that landward shore of the lagoon,' she said. 'They were starving, broke. He fired a shot and a fugitive who had settled on this side rowed across and shared his Christmas fare with them. The couple stayed. In fact, they stayed on here for the rest of their lives. He named it Churchhaven, built the church and this house, died here.' She indicated the mauve tombstones in the cliffside graveyard. 'That's his, the big tomb, with the best view. I envy him.'

'Churchhaven's yours, so what are you complaining about?' asked Renate. 'How can Pittock-Williams take it away from you? Why should he? Hasn't he done enough to you already?'

'Some wise guy said it is in the nature of a man who has wronged someone to hate that person – Pittock-Williams hates me.'

'So what? Let him hate. He's a chapter in your life that is closed.'

'He knows I love Churchhaven,' went on Zara. 'I brought him here when our relationship first sparked into something which I thought was The Big Passion. Churchhaven was our perfect funk-hole. Far away from Cape Town, far away from all his cronies on all the public bodies he serves on. Far away from that ninny of a wife of his. We first made love here, in the bedroom overlooking the lagoon. Nothing could have been sweeter. He used to come here at weekends: he told Mildred he was away on a congress, a conference, any old excuse. We used to walk along the beach down there by the water's edge, and I told him briefly how my great-grandfather came from Cape Town long ago. He never suspected a thing. Nor did I, at that stage.'

'You mean, that you were pregnant?'

'No. That came later. About the man who founded Churchhaven. I suppose he didn't see the connection, because the names were different.'

'What are you driving at, Zara?'

'I only told P.-W. the romantic side of it – after all we, at least I was passionately in love. I told him how my great-grandparents (his name was White) lived here all their long lives.' A savage note took over her voice. 'Good

86

fairy-tale stuff. They lived happily ever after. I liked to think it would be the same with Pittock-Williams and myself.'

'Go on,' said Renate.

'It took him so long to get wise to who my great-grandfather was because the names were different.' She gave a kind of choked, semi-hysterical gurgle. 'It would have put P.-W.'s genetics to the test, if he'd guessed when he bedded me down. Was it incest, between the two of us?'

'Zara,' said Renate firmly, 'pull yourself together. This is a load of bull.'

'I wish to God it was,' she answered. 'I told you, his name was White. That's the name there on the tombstone. George White. But, in point of fact, his name was Williams.'

'Ah!'

'Williams, without the Pittock. That came later, when the Williamses became leaders of Cape society. I can't think of Pittock-Williams without the handle to his name.'

'How were the original Williams and the original White connected then?' asked Renate. 'I don't get it.'

'They were brothers,' answered Zara. 'Both were sailors, based in Cape Town in the early 1860s. George –' she indicated the graveyard '– was a merchant captain who ran his own ship from East Africa via the Cape to England. It was a prosperous little enterprise – cloves, spices, general cargoes. The other brother, John, was a Royal Navy officer who commanded one of the anti-slavery ships of the Cape Station. At that time East Africa was still one of the centres of the slave trade, and it fell under the Cape Station, which was in fact Simonstown.

'Both brothers wanted to marry a pretty Cape Town girl. John, the Navy man, lost, George won. He married the girl. John never forgave or forgot. The Williamses are great haters.

'He saw his chance of revenge against his brother when his Navy ship intercepted George's merchantman on its way back from Zanzibar to England. He had as a passenger one of the minor Zanzibar sultans, with his harem and a retinue of servants.

'John saw his opportunity. They were not servants, he maintained, they were slaves. George, he asserted, was slave-running. He arrested the ship and hauled it in to Cape Town for George to stand trial before the Vice-Admiralty Court. Slaving was a very serious offence: he stood to lose his ship and possibly be transported for life. The young wife was distraught.

'A few days before George's trial began (it was early in August, 1863, the time of the American Civil War) a great sensation had been created in Cape Town by the arrival of the Confederate raider *Alabama* under her famous captain, Commander Raphael Semmes. The ship had shown its mettle by capturing, in sight of the crowds gathered on the shore to welcome her, a Yankee merchant vessel. The Cape was strongly on the side of the South. The *Alabama* received a wildly enthusiastic reception when she docked. You know the song, of course, "There Comes the *Alabama*".

'George Williams's trial before the Admiralty Court began. George was a tough, resourceful man who knew that the odds had been cleverly stacked against him. Legally, he realized he wouldn't stand a chance.'

'Where did you get all this detail from?' interrupted Renate.

'It has been handed down by word of mouth in our family,' replied Zara. 'Part of the procedure of a Vice-Admiralty Court used to be that a silver oar, which was carried by the Marshal, was laid in front of the presiding judge as a symbol of authority. George was brought in between two Royal Navy guards but, luckily for him, he wasn't shackled. The mace – he could use it as a weapon! He leapt out of the dock, grabbed it, and, swinging it like a battleaxe, knocked one guard unconscious and injured the other. He then burst out of the courtroom and raced down the main street towards the docks, with the court officials in hot pursuit. George knew his way around the docks; he dived into a well-known sailors' brothel. The madam was a friend of George's; they'd settled many disputes amicably when George had had to go in search of members of his crew on the loose after weeks at sea.

'She hid him, and denied all knowledge of his where-abouts when the Navy patrols came searching for him. That night George, still with his Admiralty oar, made his way aboard the *Alabama*. He offered his services as a crewman to Captain Semmes, plus the silver oar. Semmes was delighted to have another skilled sailor for his crew: no fewer than three of the *Alabama*'s officers were British. He accepted the silver oar; he had no intention of surrendering George for trial.

'The Royal Navy scoured Cape Town for the missing prisoner, but of course they could not venture aboard the *Alabama*, being a foreign warship. George was safe. The *Alabama* sailed away a few days later until she was finally sunk about a year later off the coast of France by a Fed-eral warship. Captain Semmes, George Williams, and most of her crew were rescued.

'Eventually George, still a fugitive from justice and a wanted man in the eyes of the law, made his way in secret back to Cape Town. He found his wife Jane in a pitiful state. During his absence, she had been harassed continu-ally by the Royal Navy searching for her escaped hus-band, and pestered by John Williams. George found her living in poverty and distress.

'Aboard the *Alabama*, he had heard of an isolated

peninsula near where the raider had made her first land-fall in South African waters. It was on the shores of a great lagoon; here, with Jane, he could be safe. Here, as I told you, they came and lived their whole lives, cut off from all past associations. They changed their name to White. George feared all his life that the law might catch up on him –'

Zara laughed and said suddenly, 'You asked me what I was going to do with Nelson's head. Now you've given me an idea. Come!'

They started to walk through the lounge which adjoined the terrace; Zara paused at an outsize glass fish tank which stood by the sliding doors.

Not only was the tank extra large: in it was a fish about half a metre long with a repulsive, tentacled head and three big fins, one on its back and two on its sides.

'Thank you for looking after him while I was away overseas,' said Zara. 'I wouldn't like anything to happen to him.'

Renate said, 'It gives me the creeps. Look at those hideous eyes.'

'I've been talking about Churchhaven history. He, or the likes of him, are part of the Churchhaven tradition. There's always been one like this, ever since George White's day. It was his ultimate insurance against being taken alive.'

'Insurance?' echoed Renate. 'I don't get it.'

'It's a sea-barbel,' answered Zara. 'It's more dangerous than a snake. If you look, you may spot what looks like a hard sharp bone hidden away behind each of his fins.'

Renate peered at the brute, but shook her head. 'I don't.'

'Well, they're there. You can't spot them because they're hidden by a slimy skin. Each spine has a saw-edge and teeth pointing down at the tip. The spines are coated with a venomous slime: one deep stab, and you're a dead woman. They say the pain is unbelievable. Even the touch of a spine could knock you unconscious.'

'Where did you get hold of such a monster?' asked Renate.

'The occasional one finds its way into the seaward end of the lagoon. That is where George White must have got his first one,' said Zara. 'They're dreaded by fishermen.'

'It seems old George White was choosing the hard way out,' commented Renate.

'He had another insurance, less painful, if the law ever came for him,' went on Zara. 'I'll show you.'

She fetched a key. They left the house, crossed the dusty white track which separated the house from the church, and then made their way past the white bell-tower to the church door. The early evening, the long white beach below them, and the soft incandescent lagoon were breathtakingly lovely.

Zara led the way to the altar, after lighting a small oil lamp from a table inside. She went down on her knees. Renate was nonplussed. She hadn't expected such a gesture from Zara.

But Zara wasn't praying. She held the lamp high and felt down the wooden front of the altar. She seemed to find what she was looking for. She unlocked a catch, and a whole wooden front panel swung open. Inside, the light showed a short flight of steps, and a second closed door beyond.

'There are more steps down to the other side of that door,' she said. 'It's old George White's bunker, funk-hole, call it what you like. It's the perfect place to stash away Nelson's head. There are no exits. George kept it stocked with food and water all his life. But they never came. He died a serene old man.'

'What is down there now?'

'It's the Rote Zora gang arsenal,' grinned Zara. 'Limpet mines, detonators, Makarov pistols, a brace of

AK-47s, and my Semtex is going to join them. Where'd you think the stuff we use came from?'

'I never thought about it. Just accepted.'

'Want to go down?' asked Zara.

'No. You wouldn't think a beautiful spot like Church-haven had so much hate. Let's get out of here. There's too much dynamite around, both past and present.'

'Dynamite!' exclaimed Zara. 'That was too mild an explosion for the way Pittock-Williams blew up when I told him about George White and Churchhaven.'

'You actually told him?'

'I was a fool. I knew the story from our family's side, of course, but not from the Williamses'. Not only John Williams but all the subsequent descendants have spent their lives trying to trace what happened to George – and the silver oar. To show you how they felt about it, when John Williams settled at the Cape – and he feathered his nest the crafty way by buying his brother's ship for a song when it became forfeit by the court and setting himself up as a prosperous businessman – he commissioned a Cape silversmith to make a substitute silver oar for the Admiralty Court. The gesture made him very popular; he became the next Admiralty Marshal.'

They reached the church door and Zara blew out the light. The lagoon's lights were muted now; the white birds stood out like lamps among the dark marshes.

'The Williams family kept alive the vendetta against George White for over a century,' Zara said. 'When I told Pittock-Williams what had happened to him, it was like stirring up a hive of bees. Every bee became fighting mad; every old hatred from all the past years came alive and exploded. He was stunned to know who I was – the woman he'd been sleeping with was a blood-link of the detested George White! I think he hated me from that moment. The pregnancy news hit him at the same time. He couldn't handle it. He even drew me a little genetic diagram showing the dangers of consanguinity. Again, like a fool I listened to him. I was terrified, I had no one to turn to. I trusted him because I loved him and believed that a genetic expert and surgeon like himself would have no problem in ending it. That was the beginning of *my* end. Williams, White, a silver oar, a runaway prisoner, Churchhaven, a hatred spanning four generations and still ready to blow up —'

'Talk about a powder-keg!' exclaimed Renate.

Zara paused with her hand on the lock of the door.

'Powder might have been OK in Williams's day,' she said. 'Today we use Semtex.'

Chapter 11

'Bokkems!'

'Come again?' Rayner looked quizzically from his corner seat under the room's heavy sloping raftered beams to where Fenella crouched on her hunkers in front of a log fire in a wide, old-fashioned grate.

Fenella threw him a glance over her right shoulder; her dark hair half-masked her smile, but the amusement rippled through her voice.

'You tell me you're a professional salmon fisherman from Greenland, and you don't know what a bokkem is?'

'Was,' he said. 'The Greenland days are over. A lot of water has flowed under the bridge since then.'

'Carrying the salmon with it?'

She swung round, and sat looking at him. The firelight silhouetted her hair; it found its way past its thickness to reflect off one of her big gold earrings, the pair he admired with the tiny leaping dolphins. They might almost have been duplicates of the intertwined dolphins engraved on the *Alabama*'s oar blade.

'Bokkems and mulled wine,' she said firmly. 'That's the staple menu of the Rommel Room.'

'Two enigmas in one short sentence,' he grinned at her, catching her mood. 'Bokkems and rommel. I don't know what either means.'

'You're experiencing both – or are about to experience them,' she answered.

It was two days later. Rayner and Fenella were upstairs in the Villa Montana, in what Fenella termed her 'Rommel Room', waiting for the joint official announcement on TV which would make public the news of the ceremonial exchange of the two silver oars at the Simonstown ceremony in a little over three weeks' time.

Fenella and Rayner had been informed in advance of the announcement, since they had already pre-recorded (together with Professor Pittock-Williams) an interview in which Fenella would explain the significance of the two silver oars, Rayner the discovery of one of them aboard the wreck of the *Alabama*, and Pittock-Williams the historical background of the second oar in his possession. Beyond his momentary outburst in front of Rayner and Fenella at their first meeting, he had disclosed nothing of how the original silver oar had found its way aboard the *Alabama* in Cape Town.

It was a while before eight in the evening, time for the main TV newscast of the day. The north-wester filtered the cold rain between the branches of the great old stone pines which were grouped near the swimming-pool.

'Rommel means junk, lumber,' she explained.

'You're trying to sound like you did on the TV telling about the two oars, but you haven't got it quite right.'

She laughed at his sally. 'I didn't have a heckler then to put me off. What more junkish than this lot?'

She gave a broad sweep of her arm which took in the rafters which stretched right down to the floor in the corner where Rayner was ensconced on a warm, padded, yellowwood seat; a battered old chair (Fenella's favourite); books and magazines scattered about, some in shelves, some lying loose on low tables; a static keep-fit exercise bicycle; a word processor on an antique desk which looked as out of place as a T-shirt at a Victorian society wedding; a haversack pitched into a corner; a pair of binoculars in a leather case; some dried wild-flower specimens hung up in bunches with fishing line; the whole scene being presided over by a stuffed penguin.

'A good contrast to the remainder of the Villa Montana,' he observed. 'There has to be some kind of counterweight to all the valuable antiques and things in the rest of the house. It must be hard to live with objects of virtu.'

'They've always been there, part of my life,' replied Fenella. 'That's why I wouldn't part with the villa after Dad's death. Even Alpha and Omega, absurd as they are – they're part of the Fenella scene.'

Alpha and Omega were two ridiculous calf-sized ceramic camels which knelt on either side of the Rommel Room door, at the head of the main stairway. They had caught Rayner's eye when he first entered the Villa Montana; they looked like a piece of nonsense pitched in amongst the magnificent carpets, the superb antique furniture, irreplaceable ceramics and fine silver in display cabinets.

'Every time I look round, I shudder at the security system,' answered Rayner. 'You should really do something about it, Fenella. Even a dumb burglar wouldn't have problems about bypassing what you call your security.'

She ignored his seriousness. 'So, R is for rommel, and J is for junk,' she proclaimed light-heartedly. 'And B is for bokkems which I hope you as a fisherman enjoy. I have a particular old Malay woman called Marta I buy them from, and she has her own source of supply on the west coast near Saldanha. They're also known as harders. They come in huge shoals and the locals literally harvest the sea. They split them open, salt them lightly and hang 'em up to dry. They're part of my Rommel Room ritual. Bokkems and mulled wine.'

She reached for a bottle of red wine, which she poured into a crockery jug, added some herbs and spices, and then took a small poker.

'This is the fun part,' she said.

'Do you do this often, Fenella?'

'In winter, yes. I said, it's fun.'

'Fun, in a great big old empty house by yourself.'

'Here, at the Villa Montana, I've always been by myself.'

'Meaning, there was a time – elsewhere though – when you were not alone?'

She pulled the poker from the fire, and turned and sat cross-legged facing him. Her face suddenly went disconcertingly still. But her luminous dark eyes were eloquent under the strongly arched black brows, although their language was unfathomable to him.

Her words came arduously, at first.

'He never came here – never to the Rommel Room – and I'm glad now because it belongs to the inner me. He used to come quite often to dinner with my parents at the Villa Montana. That was before the cold-blooded and deliberate dissection of my heart.'

The planes of her face were lovely and well defined, her mouth supple but untwisted by bitterness, her head capped by the drift of black hair.

Rayner had straightened from his relaxed pose on the padded seat and now sat facing her, one knee caught in his hands.

She went on, 'I love the Villa Montana, Rayner. I know all its disadvantages, but it's my childhood home, that's why I stuck to it after the crash. Double crash, I should rather say. The air crash which killed my parents, and the crash of the Gault industrial empire after that.'

Her eyes were so deep that it seemed to Rayner he could dive into them and drown in whatever tragedy she was about to unveil.

'Go on.'

'I told you before, my first job after I graduated was at the Cultural History Museum –'

'So you went there to study silver.'

'Nothing of the kind. I came out of university – social sciences, psychology – a dilettante. Poor little rich girl. I was a rich man's daughter, there was no need for me to work, do anything, except become a social butterfly.' Her words bled. 'That's the way *he* wanted me, the way my father wanted me.'

'But it's not the way you wanted.'

'You're wrong, Rayner. It was. I knew no other. The only trace of stiffening in my whole existence was made of silver. I graduated from Cape Silver to the esoteric subject of silver oars of Admiralty.'

Rayner said, 'It wasn't an Admiralty oar which cold-bloodedly and deliberately dissected your heart, Fenella.'

'No,' she replied. The fire at her back deepened the shadows round her eyes, which looked inward and not at Rayner. Her face looked so young, so vital, so withdrawn as to be impenetrable.

She said quietly, 'His name was Wayne Gerber. He was an up-and-coming young business executive whom I met through my father's business interests. Dad held him in considerable esteem for his business ability. Wayne knew how to lay on the charm, when he wanted to. He was about ten years older than I was.'

'When was this?'

'About four years ago,' she answered. 'Wayne wanted to charm because – I was to find out later – the charm was a way in to a stake in the Gault industrial empire.'

'Industrial empire? You hinted earlier that all that was left for you after your parents' death was the Villa Montana.'

'When Dad was alive he presided over and controlled via a holding company called Gault Enterprises half a dozen thriving Cape Town manufacturing concerns – components, electrical goods, suchlike. Wayne admired what he had built up, and envied it, too.'

Fenella drew up her knees and rested her chin on them. It was the sort of posture someone might take up to escape a blow from behind.

'I went to live with Wayne. Dad was old-fashioned enough to disapprove of that kind of modern relationship. His bait to Wayne (of course, I didn't know it at the time) was by offering him, as his son-in-law, a big block of shares in Gault Enterprises. This would have left him pretty close to a majority shareholding if he could have got control over my own interests of about ten per cent, plus a minority holding by other shareholders.'

'Talk about wheeler-dealing!' exclaimed Rayner.

'When I got to know about it, it sounded more like the marriage deals negotiated by primitive tribesmen – so many cattle for the bride.'

'How did you find out?' asked Rayner.

'The deal had already been finalized on promises from Wayne that he would regularize our affair and marry me. In fact, some shares had already been ceded, and others were in the process of being ceded, when Dad and my mother were killed. Unfortunately for Wayne, the whole underhand plan was unmasked when investigations began into Dad's estate; I realized I was no more than a financial pawn in the game.'

Rayner said slowly, 'You must have cared for him in the first place to go and live with him.'

'I did – at first. But later, there were straws in the wind which made me unhappy and doubtful about the prospect of marriage. Wayne changed towards me as the share deal hardened in his favour. The air crash was something he couldn't possibly have foreseen. The cool cynicism of the deal killed anything which I might have felt for him. My emotional and sexual life backfired when I found out what he really was. I saw everything in the context of the exploitation of myself, my body, my heart, my whole life. That is why I described it the way I did, the cold-blooded and deliberate dissection of my heart.'

'I still don't see how you were left with very little from your father's estate.'

'Wayne tried very hard, even when his whole ploy was unveiled,' continued Fenella. 'However, by then I knew what his protestations meant. We broke up. But even when he realized he had lost out with me, he wasn't going to lose control of the Gault empire. By offering shareholders a completely inflated price for their interests, he gained majority control over the holding company, and then proceeded to put the screws on me until I was forced to sell out, so that I was left with a trifle instead of a fortune. One important thing I managed to salvage from the ruin was the Villa Montana.

'My play-play job at the Cultural History Museum all at once turned out to be very important money-wise, and when Christie's offered me a position at their silver department in Cape Town, I jumped at it.'

Later, when the death-threat was upon them, Rayner was to call back to his mind's eye the picture of a girl sitting in front of the fire with a high, heroic look about her, the bones of her cheek and chin delicate and defined by the brush of firelight, and the eloquent, hurt dark eyes.

The north-wester rattled the branches of the stone pine against the balcony outside.

Fenella looked at her watch. She said, in a completely different tone of voice, 'It's almost news-time. We'll miss out on our TV appearance and the announcement if we go on talking. And there's bokkems and mulled wine to follow, never forget.'

She reached out her hands to him to help her up, and together they sat on chairs in front of the TV set.

Chapter 12

Fenella had switched out the main light and only the small TV backlight remained. Her face was an enigma, shutting out the pull of forces which had tugged at her mouth and eyes when she had told Rayner about Wayne Gerber.

The announcer said:

There has been a surprise development in regard to the projected visit in just over three weeks' time of the British Prime Minister to South Africa. A joint announcement by the British and South African governments, released simultaneously in London and Cape Town, states that the ceremony will not only take place in a setting with a time-honoured naval tradition behind it, but will be marked by an exchange of two items of priceless historic value. The existence of one of these was unsuspected until a few weeks ago; its rediscovery is surrounded by a mystery which has yet to be cleared up.

The ceremony is to take place at Admiralty House in Simonstown, which has an association dating for over a hundred and seventy-five years with the Royal and South African navies, and for many decades was the official residence of admirals commanding the Cape Station. Admiralty House has equally historic connections with British Royalty going back to Victorian times; the present Queen visited there in 1947.

The official announcement goes on to say that the occasion will be marked by an exchange of two silver oars of Admiralty. These oars, hand-crafted from solid silver, once symbolized the authority of Admiralty Courts and were displayed in the courtroom while the court was in session. The use of the silver oar can be traced to the reign of Elizabeth the First. Two such silver oars, both associated with the Cape, will feature during the signing ceremony at Admiralty House –

'Wait for it!' interjected Rayner softly.

– the announcement says that it was well known that one such silver oar had been in use at the Cape since the early years of the nineteenth century and, after the functions of the Admiralty Courts had been taken over by the Supreme Court in 1891, the oar had passed into the possession of the then Marshal and his family.

It has always been accepted that this silver oar was the one made by the London master silversmith William Frisbee in 1806.

Now, however, the background of the oar has taken a bizarre and dramatic turn with the announcement that one of the two oars which will be exchanged has been salvaged by British divers from the wreck of the Confederate raider *Alabama* off the coast of France. How the Cape silver oar came to be aboard the famous raider is a complete mystery. The news of the momentous discovery, the official announcement goes on, had been deliberately withheld to allow authentication of the oar and accord it a role in the Simonstown ceremony –

'That news will make the French blow a gasket all right!' exclaimed Rayner.

'Wait until you come on the air after the newscast,' she replied. 'You'll be the focus of attention, after your part in its discovery!'

The announcer went on:

The oar which had been in use for so long is at present in the possession of the noted surgeon and environmentalist Professor Vivian Pittock-Williams, of Cape Town. In an attempt to clear up the mystery surrounding the two Cape oars, we have with us in the studio tonight Professor Pittock-Williams himself, as well as the man who was responsible for conveying the oar from the *Alabama* wreck to London, and Miss Fenella Gault of Cape Town, the world's top authority on Admiralty oars –

The newscast switched to Rayner, Fenella and Pittock-Williams sitting in a group.

'Professor Pittock-Williams,' said the interviewer, 'we have just heard how one silver oar has recently been salvaged from the wreck of the *Alabama*, and yet you claim still to have the original which was in use for many years.

'In view of the importance of the signing ceremony which is to take place at Admiralty House, can you offer an explanation of the mystery?'

'No. Less still, how the oar came to be aboard such a famous raider as the *Alabama*.'

'You bloody liar, Williams!'

Zara's words were not yelled or ejaculated particularly loudly; they spilled out almost in uncontrolled reflex action, like toxin from a fatal ulcer. Had she shouted at the screen backdropped against the dark water of Churchhaven's lagoon it would have pointed to an emotion less savage, less caustic, than that which the sight of Pittock-Williams's bland face on the screen evoked in the woman sitting alone in the room. A room built by the hands of the man who stood like a ghost behind the story of the two silver oars – George Williams, or White. Pittock-Williams knew the story as well as Zara did.

'You smooth, double-talking hypocrite!'

The added viciousness came out strangled and unreal in the silence. Zara wanted to kick over the coffee tray on the low table in front of her, make some physical proclamation of the pain which lanced through her mind. The TV screen seemed to take on a remove to her inflamed mind and its three actors a distance like demons dancing in front of a window in a blazing house.

The interviewer went on, addressing Fenella. 'You have examined both silver oars, Miss Gault. Would you consider the Cape Town one a fake?'

Fenella was firm. 'I have examined both oars, as you say. The hallmarks on the one recovered from the *Alabama* –' she gave a small sideways glance at Rayner '– are the authentic hallmarks and signature of William Frisbee, and the date, London, 1806 –'

'Stop playing games!' It was more a moan of pain than a reprimand from Zara. 'Stop it! You know the story – you got it from me! Tell them, tell the world, for Pete's sake!'

Her loaded words were lost in the cross-fire of professional TV questioning. Her head felt as if it had a charge of Semtex inside it. She had to do something – she couldn't take the sight of the face of the man who had ruined her life with his smooth talk, here, right here in this house, his smooth love-talk –

She got up, holding her crotch with both hands, as if that would help bring back her womanhood. She stumbled to the bedroom door and stood looking at the bed where it had happened –

Behind her, the TV went on remorselessly.

'– had the lettering, and the engravings, which I understand figure on the blade, not been defaced by the oar's long immersion in the sea? After all, the *Alabama* went down a century and a quarter ago.'

'When I first examined the oar in London,' replied Fenella, 'it had a kind of patina which I understand is characteristic of gold or silver objects which have been long under the sea. But the maker's signature and the engravings on the blade were still clear and in splendid shape.'

The interviewer switched to Rayner.

'It was your company, Surveillicor, which discovered the oar – you yourself played a prominent part in its recovery, did you not, Mr Watton?'

'One of our divers, not me, discovered it and brought it to the surface. I merely conveyed it safely to London.'

'Merely!' commented the interviewer. 'The oar must be worth a fortune! My next question is about the security which will have to be observed to bring it safely to South Africa for the signing ceremony.'

Rayner gave a half-smile. 'Security is my job.'

The interviewer threw a quick, low punch.

'I am not implying anything, Mr Watton, but is there not the possibility that the oar – which Miss Gault herself admits was in excellent condition – could have been planted aboard the wreck?'

Zara wheeled on the empty room at her back. 'Shut up, for pity's sake, shut up! Can't you leave me alone?'

Yet she knew she could not switch off the set, kill the image of the man who had done all this to her. She stared at the trio. Rayner and Fenella, she told herself, must be in cahoots with Pittock-Williams and his bloody Admiralty oar, they were shadow-boxing with the interviewer so that he wouldn't get at the truth –

Rayner was clever and tough, she admitted, watching him handle, suavely and without losing his cool, the question whether the oar had been 'salted' aboard the *Alabama* wreck. (The implication was clear, by his own outfit.) And Fenella, she was beautiful: Zara could picture those eyes dropping their guard and lighting up for a man, maybe the man in the studio with her now. *She* could go to bed with him, love him, feel the warmth and intimacy of his body, while for the rest of her life Zara would remain an exile from any loving, just as George Williams had been an exile from life.

She felt as if she were suffocating, as if there was something closing round her throat, at the savage prospect which her overheated mind threw up.

She ran through the lounge, out the side door, leaving the TV still on, across the dusty pathway and up to the bell-tower by the church door. Her breath came in short, shallow gasps; she put a hand against the tower to support herself. A dark shadow rose lazily from somewhere across the lagoon and made a smear across the starlight like an angel of death rising out of the cliff-top graveyard.

The TV was addressing the empty room.

'– yes, I have also examined the oar owned by Professor Pittock-Williams here,' Fenella was saying. 'It isn't an exact replica of the Frisbee oar, but it's very good. The style of craftsmanship is Cape silversmithing, and the maker was Heinrich Schmidt, grandson of the famous silversmith Daniel Schmidt, a noted silversmith in his own right. I'd estimate the date at about the middle 1870s.'

'Which would be about ten years after the *Alabama* visited the Cape on her raiding voyage,' interjected the interviewer.

'Correct,' replied Fenella.

'And this is the one which will form South Africa's gift to Britain at the signing ceremony, and the Frisbee oar will come to South Africa from Britain –'

The words, indistinguishable at the distance except as a jumble, filtered across to Zara at the bell-tower. She had never felt like this before, even in a hotel room alone in those dark days in London.

She yanked open the church door and edged into the darkness. London had been bad: she needed something cathartic now to purge her of the agony. Then, she hadn't had Pittock-Williams's living image in the forefront to torment her, only her memory of him. Now, seeing him as she did on the TV made it worse.

Her eyes grew accustomed to the dark interior. She could make out the brass candlesticks on the altar. She would need a more powerful psychic purgative than Nelson's head tonight.

The secret altar panel to old George White's hide-out was visible as a dim outline.

She stood, transfixed.

Inside there was Nelson's head.

The plan avalanched through her mind in the same way as the plan to steal the famous head from the Abbey had done.

Kill him!

Kill Pittock-Williams!

Kill him using Nelson's head!

Chapter 13

Zara stood rooted, her eyes on the secret panel which opened the way to the funk-hole. In the darkness, the burning of her eyes in their deep settings seemed to take up half her face and provide a kind of illumination whose name was vengeance. Down there was the wax head, down there was Rote Zora's arsenal of explosives, fuses, mines, detonators –

She would booby-trap Nelson's head and send it to Pittock-Williams!

When he opened the hatbox – her mind raced so that she had already decided on her own hatbox as the means of conveying it – the sensitive fuse would detonate the explosive!

She had to view the instrument she would use to kill him – now!

She also had to have a flashlight to see down in the hide-out, as cold and dark as death itself, in order to plan the logistics of the death-trap.

Her body gave a sudden spurt of movement and she was moving swiftly down the aisle, out of the church door and across to the house, where the bright cathode light of the TV screen hurt her as yet unadapted eyes.

'– security,' the interviewer was saying. 'Surely there are to be special precautions not only in bringing the silver oar from London but also in protecting Professor Pittock-Williams's twin here in Cape Town?'

Zara paused on her way for a torch. For once, the focus was off Pittock-Williams but the ruthless TV medium left a picture as he sat next to Rayner of a somewhat brutal face above the bull neck, and the shut, selfish eyes: how could she ever have loved him? The bitter hurt lay quiescent now, and she viewed his face as dispassionately as an axeman might the head he was about to sever on the block.

'– the security on both fronts will naturally be of the tightest.'

Rayner's words followed Zara as she found her flashlight.

'But you will be involved?' probed the interviewer.

Zara headed back past the set on her way to the hide-out.

Rayner fenced. 'You wouldn't naturally expect me to discuss in advance what our strategy will be, but it will be stringent, I assure you. However, I have seen Professor Pittock-Williams's precautions and I am satisfied.'

The water of the lagoon moved uneasily on the suggestion of a wind, the harbinger of the half-gale and rain which was plucking at the stone pines outside Fenella's room at the Villa Montana as they, too, watched themselves on TV.

As she moved towards the church, Zara had no time even to glance at the black space between the water and stars which she loved; there was elation in her heart that, in a roundabout way at least, old George White was contributing to her plan. It had taken a long, long time, but now the wheel of revenge was making its full circle.

Zara flicked open the secret altar panel and felt her way down the wooden ladder into the depths of the funk-hole. The chill struck first at her feet, and then her whole body. The place was roughly L-shaped; in the inner angle of it, the light picked out on the floor what she was looking for: several grey shapes, half-round on one side, with a lighter grey projection under a protective plate jutting out of one end.

Limpet mine! Mini-limpet mine, the deadliest terror weapon and one of the easiest to conceal, its six-inch length holding a couple of kilograms of modern Soviet explosive.

Zara was familiar with them, and now her mind raced on the expertise required to load a deadly charge into Nelson's head. The mini-limpet mine would have to be inserted in the hole through which the spike holding the wax head to the wooden body projected.

Would it fit?

It was awkward using only one hand while the other had the light. She put the flashlight down, lifted out the head carefully. The eyes shone disconcertingly alive as the light caught them.

As Zara upended the effigy, she realized that a limpet mine was too broad and too long to fit into the space. Even if the neck-hole were wider, the fuse-end of the mine would still show.

She sat back in disappointment.

Melt the wax?

Melted wax would be an immediate giveaway to anyone observant enough not merely to grab hold of the head at first sight.

Zara's hands were shaking from the cold and frustration. Nothing would marry the mine to the head.

Suddenly, there was a message in her face, and she laughed, a sound which masqueraded as a laugh, but its message was death.

Semtex!

Malleable, mouldable, any shape, any form, the most cunning and deceptive of all terrorist explosives!

She would pack the hole in the base of the head with Semtex (as much as it would take) and set a sensitive fuse which would trigger it. An IRA trick, perfected and adapted by Rote Zora. They had schooled her in Germany on the technique. So simple, so lethal!

She'd overlooked the Semtex at first because she'd left it still moulded round the frame of her suitcase, which was in her bedroom.

She hurried up the wooden steps into the church. Even in the short time she had been below, the wind had risen. This was the classic way winter came, first on a north-wester and then on the back of a south-wester, and the water was disturbed and uneasy.

She eyed Pittock-Williams on the TV (he was now occupying centre stage again) with less distaste than earlier, now that she had the solution.

He was talking about the mock trial.

'I have discussed the matter with the authorities here, who think that my suggestion of an actual living – ah, charade, if you like to call it that, of how an Admiralty Court trial was held in the past is excellent. The public will be able to come to terms with the procedures, and the role of the Marshal in carrying the silver oar as a symbol of the Admiralty's authority.

'I have been entrusted with the privilege of arranging such a mock trial, which will take place in ten days' time at the Cultural History Museum. Entrance will be by special invitation only, but outside the building the public at large will be able to view the procession on its way towards the Houses of Parliament . . .'

Rayner added a little dryly, 'Security will be the tightest. It is the first time in nearly a century that this particular oar has been paraded in public. All invited guests will be screened, as an additional precaution.'

Zara gathered up her suitcase and hurried back to the hide-out as if she meant to set about arming the head right away.

Security, that was the snag!

How could she arrange so that the loaded head went directly into Pittock-Williams's own hands?

And where?

It had all seemed so straightforward, in that splendid concept moment of burning revenge, but now the logistics of the kill were daunting.

His home at Constantia?

She discarded the idea the moment she thought of it. She herself knew, from her visits there during the affair, that unauthorized admission even to a lover was virtually impossible. Nothing – no parcel, nothing as blatantly ostentatious as a hatbox parcel – would stand a chance past the guards' scrutiny at the gates. Even the grocery deliveries were checked, that she knew.

There was no way she could insinuate the head into the Constantia home.

The mock trial, the one they had been discussing on the TV?

Zara seized on the idea. But then, like a bucket of icy water, she remembered Rayner's warnings about the tight security. To try to get a bulky parcel to Pittock-Williams in the middle of a public function at which he was the leading figure bordered on the absurd.

Zara found her teeth chattering in the chill of the hide-out. She climbed the wooden ladder dejectedly, slowly, and made her way back to the house.

The TV interview was winding up. Zara eyed Pittock-Williams. He had on his suave, committee face. Her eyes, deep-set and flaring, searched the screen. There must be a way!

Subtly, by some sleight of emphasis by the cameras perhaps, the focus had switched away from Pittock-

Williams to Rayner. It was he the interviewer seemed to be concentrating on in the last minutes of the interview. His air of authority, of concealed power perhaps, came across, and its impact forced Zara's attention away from her target.

What onward role would Rayner be playing in bringing the oar from London for the signing ceremony? In fact, that was what the interviewer was trying to extract from Rayner now.

Without realizing it, Zara's focus of interest was on Rayner. He wasn't playing for the spotlight like Pittock-Williams, but his overall function in the ceremony was not less vital. Killing Pittock-Williams with Nelson's head would have put an end to the entire ceremony, she felt. Did it, her inflamed mind raced on, need to be him? That would satisfy her personal revenge, but could the same result not be achieved in a more indirect way, by using the same weapon against one of the other principal actors in the forthcoming male-elevating charade?

Rayner, for example?

Or the girl? The silver expert – Zara couldn't recall her name.

A big bomb blast, the death of one of the principal characters involved, might well be enough warning for the authorities to call off the subsequent Simonstown ceremony with all its trappings of male domination. Instinctively, her mind selected the male who would be so deeply involved – Rayner!

She felt no personal animosity against him there on the screen, but he would have to die because he stood in the cross-fire. It would be clear to the world because Nelson's head would have been the vehicle to convey the bomb that Rote Zora was the perpetrator. The threat to the signing ceremony might also be enough to warrant the cancellation of the mock trial at which Pittock-Williams planned to parade his ego.

Zara was so lost in her own thoughts that she missed the fact that the interview was over. She switched off the set.

How to get the hatbox and the head to Rayner?

Where was he staying in Cape Town?

Zara's mind was cold, unlike the rush of hot blood when she had first thought of Pittock-Williams as her target.

She turned her plan inside out in her mind. How would the authorities know that the bomb had been concealed in Nelson's head and consequently be able to pinpoint the terrorists responsible? The thing would be blown to pieces by the explosion. Rayner – *he* would perhaps catch a first and last glance of the effigy as he opened the parcel, but dead men tell no tales.

The same problem arose if she attached a note saying Rote Zora had been responsible. The only other means was an anonymous telephone call afterwards to the media. That was the way it would have to be.

How would she find out where Rayner was staying? Zara's mind was running effortlessly as she overcame the logistical problems of the blast one by one. The girl who had been on TV with him, she had been from Christie's, and a call to someone else in the firm would soon establish Rayner's Cape Town address.

Delivery of the bomb?

It would be by one of the Rote Zora girls living in Cape Town: there were five to choose from. One who would not be remembered afterwards for any distinguishing characteristic. She started to run over the gang in her mind, and then pulled herself up. No! The theft of the head itself had been a lone effort on her part, and she had pulled it off successfully. Equally, the bomb would be another lone effort by herself.

Besides, the next get-together of the gang – Renate, Rikki, Menty, Gemma and Kerry-Ann – was scheduled only for next weekend, and she had to work fast, be unencumbered with doubts and reservations which would arise from a round table discussion. She *knew* she was right, she *knew* how she would carry it out, she *knew* what the blast would achieve. Zara thrust the question of killing an innocent man on to the back-burner. Hers was the grand concept, the stakes were high, she would play the game alone. She would deliver the bomb alone, herself.

Zara closed the big glass door against the uneasy wind which cleaved the night and excoriated the surface of the lagoon, flicking the tall reeds among the marshes like fretwork whips. She did not feel the same about this bombing – that splendid, irresistible, all-swamping urge like uncontrollable sex – as she had done over the Abbey theft. This was a clinical, calculated affair of checks and balances.

The killing of Rayner Watton was to be a cold-blooded strike.

Chapter 14

Rayner sat on the front porch of the Villa Montana in the morning sunshine, looking down the steeply terraced garden towards the main gate. It was a wrought-iron affair through which the busy roadway could be seen. Fenella had gone off to work, although she had promised to be back early, before lunch. The charwoman was not due that day.

It was the second day after his TV appearance with Fenella and Pittock-Williams. The mock trial was still eight days away, and almost immediately after the function he was due to fly to London to bring back the silver oar.

The question of conveying the silver oar in the way Gibson had proposed worried Rayner as he sat watching the last wisps of mist clear from the mountain and the sea. He had a gut feeling it was too simplistic.

With one ear Rayner heard a car pull up outside the side gate of the villa; its brakes squeaked as it came to a halt on the steep slope. This road ran parallel with the villa's side. There was another which formed the corner on which the house stood, fronting the grounds. The main entrance opened on to this latter road, while there were two entrances on the downhill side. One of these was a pedestrian gate with a solid wooden door which led directly on to the terrace; the other was simply an unbarred entrance to parking in the villa's kitchen yard. This pedestrian door was a security Achilles' heel in Rayner's opinion. He had urged Fenella that it should stay permanently locked, but she found it easy and convenient for access to the street.

It was outside this gate that Rayner vaguely registered the click of a car door and then, soon after, his mind was brought to focus on what was happening beyond the gate when he heard a vehicle begin to run engineless down the slope, only to kick-start as it neared the corner.

Rayner in his relaxed mood was mildly curious, and opened the street gate. He was just in time to spot a cream-coloured car, a Toyota, accelerate hard away from the corner stop street, where it had been held up by the traffic. It picked up speed fast through a right-hander S-bend, a dangerous thing to do on such a steep slope in the face of a constant stream of traffic from a hospital only a few hundred metres further on.

Then – Rayner saw the parcel.

The ribbon-wrapped, box-shaped package had been placed between two large flower-tubs flanking the wooden door. Rayner moved to pick up the box. He stopped. Subconsciously, by virtue of his long anti-terrorist training, the alarm bells rang in his mind as it raced over the sounds of the past few minutes – that furtive car-halt, the more furtive getaway. It would have been the normal thing for the driver to leave the engine running for the brief time needed for him to deliver the parcel.

He?

Rayner wasn't sure whether the Toyota driver had been a man or a woman. He thought he had spotted a woman's auburn head.

Rayner stood eyeing the empty roadway down which the car had vanished, and then the parcel. Was he reading something into a harmless situation, his SAS-trained mind notching an orange alert over something which had no substance at all?

Now he saw – there was a small envelope attached to the top of the parcel.

On it was printed (roughly, Rayner logged in his mind) 'Mr Rayner Watton, Villa Montana. Personal'.

Rayner did not touch it or the parcel, but kept a stand-off distance, like a suspicious sniffer-dog.

Who in Cape Town would send him a parcel? Besides Fenella and Pittock-Williams, he knew no one. Some unknown who had seen him on TV? – there are always nuts willing to hitch themselves to a celebrity or public figure.

A practical joke by some hoaxer?

The card would give a clue. He reached down decisively, flicked it loose, and slit it open with the small penknife he always carried in his trouser pocket.

A plain card read: 'In Admiration'. The same rough printing.

As he read the message, Rayner's orange alert glowed brighter. 'Admiration' – a bait to open the parcel and see what was inside!

Some built-in suspicion, animal instinct maybe,

warned him to be ultra-careful. He'd seen too many men in Ireland be maimed or killed through becoming blasé about 'loaded' parcels.

Rayner tested the box. It had a heavy, 'dead' feel.

The bomb syndrome pulsed through Rayner's mind.

Pick it up? Might it go off?

He dismissed that fear. Whoever had delivered it, had done so by hand, and that meant it had been carried the few metres from the car at the kerb. *Ipso facto*, it must be safe.

He snatched up the box, entered through the still-open side door, and put down the parcel on a terrace table.

Now.

He sliced some of the wrapping clear with his small knife.

He froze, knife poised. Red alert! Red alert!

At one corner, the lid had a small blob of something putty-brown.

To anyone less keyed to danger, less trained to know that his life hung on his smartness against hellish ingenuity, the blob would have passed as a spot of carelessly spilt adhesive.

To Rayner it was equated with a blob of plastic explosive which had been negligently allowed to stick to the parcel during the packing operation.

There was a rule-of-thumb test for finding out, quickly. If the drop had any smell, it was not plastic explosive. Semtex, the terrorists' favourite, was completely odourless.

He put his nose gingerly to the drop.

Even one small drop of Semtex could injure. It was powerful stuff, and under test one gram had been known to fling an army steel helmet fifty metres.

There was no smell. No 'marzipan-and-nuts' odour of other plastic explosive.

Rayner considered the parcel again quickly. He could

– if he wanted to make a possible fool of himself – get on the phone and summon a police bomb disposal squad.

On the other hand, that parcel with its weight and bulk contained something else besides Semtex.

Also, Semtex would have to be triggered – *what kind of fuse?*

Rayner coolly assessed the possibilities.

If a 'trembler' device – wired into a detonator which would be activated by even the smallest movement – had been used, it could not, in the first place, have been transferred from the car and, next, to the terrace.

A 'command' device – a radio signal to the parcel itself – was equally unlikely. That implied the 'command' being given from somewhere quite near and some kind of receiver antenna on the parcel, however well camouflaged. There was none.

That left a timer of some kind, hidden inside the bomb itself. It could be ticking away as he stood here weighing the options. At any moment it could blow him, and a sizeable piece of the Villa Montana, against the side of Table Mountain.

He would have to open the parcel, soon.

Wasn't that just what the 'admiration' card was designed to do? To induce him to open it?

Rayner held himself back. He had been stationed in Belfast when the SAS had made its big breakthrough into how innocent victims were being killed by mystery parcels which exploded at the moment of opening.

He had been present at a secret demonstration which had been given, using as a guinea-pig an IRA mystery-killer bomb which had neglected to explode because of a failure in its electric circuitry.

The bomb had been triggered by light falling on a photo-electric cell secreted *inside* the parcel. During arming, the SAS audience had been instructed, the cell would be covered with black paper, the sort of thing used by photographers.

Once the explosive charge had been placed securely inside the box (a box was always used, he remembered grimly, eyeing the hatbox in front of him) the black paper would be carefully eased off from the outside. If the terrorist were careless enough during this tricky operation to allow any light into the parcel, the cell would blow the charge in his face.

The use of the light-sensitive cell meant that bomb disposal experts, the moment they opened the box, triggered the bomb and blew themselves up.

The trick of this type of device was that the photoelectric cell had to be placed near the top of the box's contents so that the black paper masking it during arming could easily be withdrawn and so render it 'live'. This had to be done in the dark, and the wrappings secured before it could be risked in the light.

Rayner himself had been present at a nail-biting incident when such a suspected parcel had been defused by another SAS expert. Rayner remembered the eternity (it had seemed) while the bomb expert rustled the wrappings, fumbling in the dark under a blanket, slicing the securing tape loose; the grunt, half of fear, half of satisfaction, when his fingers lighted on the small round killer eye of the photo-electric cell, and the savage oath as his groping fingers found the wires to the nest of small batteries and plucked them loose –

Rayner examined his parcel. A dark room, a knife, a blanket – that was all he needed to draw the teeth of the lethal thing masquerading so innocently in front of him.

The Rommel Room! It had the long heavy curtains necessary for darkness.

Rayner picked up the box and strode up the stairs. It was only a moment's work to test the curtains, with the light off, and decide that this was the place for the operation.

Now, a blanket.

He found one on his own bed and then carefully made some quick preliminary cuts along the seams without disturbing the paper sufficiently to admit the entry of any light. Soon the wrapping was loose enough all over for him to be able to feel his way around.

He decided that he would grip the points of paper on either side, under the blanket of course, and rip them upwards and sideways, clear of the box. From then on, it would be by guess and by God.

Rayner made one quick final check.

Now!

He switched off the light, walked cautiously back to the low table in the dark, squatted down on his hunkers before it with his hands holding the blanket draped, like some esoteric eastern religious ritual.

He had to make certain that the blanket masked the whole box. One disastrous chink of light would be enough. Rayner crushed the fear from his mind. Decisively, he grasped the parcel and tore the outer wrapping upwards and outwards.

There was no going back now.

His ultra-sensitive fingers detected a second layer of wrapping.

He got his hands in under it in an attitude something like a man about to whip the shirt over his head.

He lifted.

The paper snagged. He felt the blanket start to pull clear of the table as the box rose – light!

He eased it back hastily. He dared not – not now – risk the flashlight to try and locate the obstacle.

His fingers felt, searched, probed, like a blind man desperately looking for a lost Braille figure on which his life depended.

So did Rayner's life. He could not go backward now; he could only go forward.

The realization made him sweat. He wanted to throw aside the choking warmth of the blanket, throw open the wide glass doors on the lovely garden below, bathed in the sun –

Fenella! Oh God!

The recollection avalanched through his mind. Fenella said she would come home from work early, about mid-morning, and they would have the rest of the day to themselves.

Rayner's arms were soaked up to the elbows in sweat.

He pushed aside the thought of her, concentrated on trying to find the snag.

It was somewhere under his left hand, so he worked his fingers slowly downwards, using a thumbnail in a seam as his guide.

He felt the offending strip of adhesive tape, not more than a couple of centimetres long, between his thumb and index finger. He carefully removed it and prised at the wrapping.

It came away smoothly. He pulled it clear, like finally getting the shirt free of one's head.

He shoved it to one side, felt again.

The box top simply came away in his hands.

He had expected it to be taped down, but it wasn't.

He fingered the smooth cardboard.

His next move would reveal, either a joke – or death.

Once that top was off, the killer-eye would be hungry for its ration of light.

No point in waiting. He had made up his mind, right at the start, to go for it.

He lifted off the top of the box, pulled it clear.

He reached into the box.

He snatched his right hand away, jerked backwards on

his haunches. He wanted to be sick. He had enough sense left not to pull the blanket off.

His hand had touched human hair.

Someone had sent him a human head in a parcel.

He pulled as far away as he could from its loathsome contents. The moment the stench of decomposing flesh hit him, he knew he would be able to take it no longer. The blanket must be masking it, for the moment.

Rayner sat there, swaying backwards and forwards.

Why wasn't the smell coming through? Was it a booby-trapped bit of corpse, or a macabre, mind-boggling practical joke?

Whose head was it he had felt?

He steadied his revolted senses and tried to make his mind work rationally.

Had it been human hair that he had touched? His fingertips were still vibrating. It was hair, all right. Human? Only a sight of it would provide that answer. He still did not give way to the overwhelming desire to pluck away the blanket and put on the light.

Had hair been all that his fingertips had touched?

Rayner paused. There *had* been something else! His fingers, seared from shock, *had* touched something cold – metal?

He had to force his hands back in there and find out.

Rayner steeled himself and, linking his thumbs so that his hands had a full eight-finger spread, put them back.

A little metal cylinder was the first thing he came in contact with. Next, hair.

Rayner's mind was running swiftly, coolly. He realized the parallels with the IRA booby-trap demonstration. That is the way the photo-electric cell had been planted. *On top* of the box's contents.

His fingertips explored the object. Cylindrical. He knew what it was when he went further and encountered the glass eye at the extremity, the malignant, death-dealing eye.

It was a photo-electric cell, all right!

He knew what he was after, the other end of the electrical circuit, in the vicinity of the severed neck.

There it was! Wires running from the cell past the nape of the neck into the body of the box to the batteries for the cell, no doubt.

At that moment, he heard Fenella on the stairway landing.

If she opened the door, they were dead.

His voice came out, crucified. 'Fenella! Stay away from that door! Don't open it, for God's sake! *Don't open it!*'

Her voice came back, breaking the spell of the short yet stunned silence which followed his strangled yell.

'What's going on, Rayner? Not open . . . !'

He tried to get his voice under control. 'Light – there mustn't be light – it will kill us –'

'I'm coming in. This is nonsense.'

'Fenella!' What was in his anguished reply stopped her.

'There's a bomb in here – it's sensitive to light – I'm trying to defuse it – in the dark, under a blanket –'

'A bomb? In the Villa Montana? Rayner –!'

'Just accept what I say,' he called. 'I've found the solution – detonating wires – give me a minute. Once they're cut, I'll let you in. But if you come before I say – Fenella! I'm not joking!'

He thought he could almost see the quiet seriousness wash over her fine features and flood her eyes from the way she replied:

'I'll wait right here, Rayner.'

'Go away – anywhere – downstairs – in case it explodes prematurely –'

'I'll stay here. Those are my terms for not opening the door.'

He responded briefly. 'I'm going ahead now.'

'Keep you, Rayner.'

Rayner found that his forearms and hands were wet with sweat. He had hung on to the fateful wires while he had addressed Fenella; now he must cut the umbilical cord and abort the certain death.

He followed one wire with his pocket-knife until he found its connection with the cell. He gripped it with one finger and thumb, cut. He did the same for the second wire. Unnecessarily, his trained mind told him. But he wanted to make assurance doubly sure.

The final act!

He jerked the blanket free, pitched it aside. He directed the flashlight into the box.

Nothing happened.

Safe.

'Come!'

Fenella found him like that when she threw open the door and let in the light which a minute before would have killed them both.

Chapter 15

Fenella came swiftly across the room, stood behind the kneeling figure, and put both her hands on his shoulders, one on either side of his neck. The way the pressure of her fingers moved from side to side and round under the curve of his neck, relayed the emotions avalanching through her. She stood so that his head rested against her stomach. She slid her hands under his chin and pushed his head firmly back so that he felt every contour of her body, the soft sweep of her from navel to crotch.

They remained locked like that for a long minute; then she leaned over him, trying to see into the box.

'It's a head, all right.' They were the first words he had spoken, and his voice came out as if rusty with years of disuse.

He went on, 'Don't look. This is a job for a pathologist.'

But she did, craning further. 'How do you know it is a bomb, Rayner? There's nothing here.'

He squirmed sideways, seeing her face now for the first time. The shock which had blanched it highlighted the make-up round the fine bones of her cheeks, widened her dark, enigmatic eyes, and pencilled in more strongly the arched black brows which were darker than her hair. Their eyes held, mutually recognizing the message and language of her fingers.

He held up the now detached photo-electric cell. 'This is a cell which reacts to light. When light – any light – falls on it, it triggers an impulse –' he got to his feet and indicated the box '– an electrical impulse which activates the detonator, and the explosive. Kaput.'

'How did you know – guess –'

'I could have made a fool of myself. I had a hunch. I'll tell you about it when I've taken a thorough look.'

'Rayner,' said Fenella slowly, 'that looks more like a wig to me than human hair.'

'It's the first chance I've had of *seeing*, instead of *feeling*, it,' he answered.

Fenella asked, a little unsteadily, 'Is it a man or a woman, Rayner?'

They were looking down on the back of the head; its features faced away from them.

'What worries me still, Fenella, is that there may be a second booby-trap, just as an insurance against the first not working. A trembler fuse is a favourite second-string of terrorists. I'll check. Please leave me, and go downstairs. You know enough of the story for the authorities if anything should go wrong. Five minutes should be enough for me. I'll come and call you when I'm through.'

Her eyes flared for a moment with the inner affirmation they were making. 'We're in this together, Rayner. Go ahead. I'm staying.'

'I'll remember that a long time, Fenella.'

'I'll help you get it out.'

Four hands slid their fingers under the neck.

'Rayner!' she exclaimed. 'There are bits and pieces of electrics here –' Then she burst out. 'Rayner! This isn't a human head! It's a dummy! Feel! It's wax!'

They pulled it clear of the box, trailing wires and batteries, and they saw for themselves the face Lady Hamilton had vouched was a living likeness of her famous hero-lover. The lock she had arranged over the effigy's right eye was still in place.

'Nelson's head, by all that's holy!' he exclaimed.

'Here in Cape Town!' Fenella exclaimed incredulously.

'With a bomb attached,' added Rayner. He was down on his knees again by the low table, checking the base of the neck where the wires entered. He tugged gently, and a little bright metal tube, slightly thicker than a fountain-pen but about the same length, came away.

He indicated a putty-like blob which remained stuck to the metal.

'Detonator,' he said tersely. 'Semtex. The head is stuffed full of it.'

'Semtex?'

'Plastic explosive,' he explained. 'Whoever armed this thing knew what they were doing. This is a professional job.'

Fenella sat down on the low table alongside the head. 'It doesn't seem to have been damaged much.'

'Some of the wax has been broken here at the base of the neck,' he said. 'By and large, though, it's a smart piece of work.'

'But *here*!' repeated Fenella. 'What is Nelson's head doing here in Cape Town? And why was it sent booby-trapped to you? What have you to do with it? And why –' she stumbled over the words '– try and kill you?'

He said quietly, 'It was a women's terrorist organization called Rote Zora which no one in Britain had heard of before which claimed responsibility for the theft of this head from the Abbey. At the same time, the figurehead of Nelson's one-time flagship was defaced, here at the Cape. It seems a straightforward deduction that the same group is operating in both countries. Here's the proof.'

'The box has a London address on it,' observed Fenella. 'Where did you find it before you brought it indoors?'

'There was a car –' Rayner explained how he had been attracted to the car's odd behaviour, and its high-speed exit.

'The fact that the driver might have been a woman ties in with Rote Zora,' she remarked. 'I still can't figure why you should have been their target.'

'Until I appeared on TV, the only people who knew I was in South Africa were yourself and Pittock-Williams.'

'Pittock-Williams is the real celebrity, if anyone wanted a public figure to bomb,' answered Fenella.

'The working of a terrorist mind has always been a riddle,' replied Rayner. 'The theft of the head in itself would seem to have achieved their aim. Now it reappears with the bomb as the cherry on the top, so to speak.'

'Perhaps something to do with the silver oars?' she suggested.

'You may have something there,' Rayner answered thoughtfully. 'Not the oars themselves, maybe, but what they stand for. That means the Simonstown ceremony. It becomes clearer. First, the mere theft in London which was billed as a feminist protest against the new

Simonstown agreement, and now a much tougher protest in the form of a bomb.'

'That reasoning doesn't include you,' argued Fenella. 'If it had been directed against Pittock-Williams, I would go along with you. It looks to me like a blind swipe around the wicket, at anyone connected with the affair in any way. And you *are* connected with the original discovery of the *Alabama* oar. That makes me frightened for you.'

He added, gently, 'And you, if anyone is looking for blind targets.' He went on incisively, 'What this means is that you and I will have to go on red alert from now on.'

'What does red alert imply? Against what? Against whom?'

'Against anything which in any way seems a little out of the ordinary.'

'That seems so broad a spectrum that one could reduce oneself to seeing shadows in regard to almost anything.'

'We'll talk it through later,' said Rayner. 'For the immediate present, Don Gibson's got to know about the head. And Scotland Yard. South African Security.'

'Speak to Don Gibson first,' said Fenella. 'That will clear the ground for the next steps.'

When Rayner dialled Gibson, the Surveillicor chief's reaction set the line vibrating.

'My oath!' Gibson exclaimed. '*You*, Rayner! You!'

'That's what Fenella says,' observed Rayner dryly.

'It's your connection with the *Alabama* oar,' asserted Gibson dogmatically. 'There can be no other reason.'

'How can it possibly be?' demanded Rayner. 'Don, nobody but you, Fenella and Pittock-Williams know at this stage about the plan for me to bring the oar to South Africa.'

'I'm anxious for you, Rayner.'

'So is Fenella. But what possible connection can there be?'

'I think you should ask for police protection.'

'Noways. If I am capable of spotting a bomb like the effigy head and disarming it myself, I don't need anyone to nursemaid me – thanks.'

'I'd feel happier.'

'I wouldn't, Don. That's flat. Imagine my being hamstrung by a bodyguard in my investigations.'

'What investigations?'

'Into who sent me the bomb, of course. You don't think I intend to let the matter rest, do you?'

'Have you contacted your local Security people yet?'

'No. You're my first call, they're next. But I want you to get on to Scotland Yard right away and inform them. Head, Anti-Terrorist Squad – got that?'

'There'll have to be consultation between the two security outfits, here and in Cape Town,' replied Gibson. 'How the news is to be publicly broken, for example. There's more than just a bomb and the effigy involved, Rayner. There's the security surrounding the Prime Minister: it's hellishly involved. Toes are bound to be trodden on.'

They were, when Rayner finally managed to get through to Brigadier Neels Keyter, head of South African Security, past a network of obstructive underlings. Before he did so, however, Fenella, as the implications of the bomb threat homed in on her, urged Rayner to call off his courier mission to London. He would be a marked man from now on, she said apprehensively; Gibson could employ someone else.

He smiled at her, but the steel was clear in his reply. 'I'm not the sort to call off a mission simply because of an undefined threat.'

When Keyter spoke, Rayner had a mental picture of disbelief spilling from a tough, close mouth set in a square, close-shaven jaw. His image of the man was accurate, when he came to see him later.

'Nelson's head? Bomb?' exclaimed Keyter. 'Is this a hoax?'

'Come and see for yourself,' answered Rayner, not caring for the abrasive response. 'It's here at the Villa Montana, quite close to the cable station.'

'What's your authority?' barked Keyter.

'If you don't believe me, perhaps you'll tell Scotland Yard when they phone you any moment now.'

'You've informed Scotland Yard – in advance of your local Security?'

'It's their head.'

'It's my territory.'

'I've worked with them. I know the set-up. I've also informed my chief at Surveillicor in London.'

'Anyone else? You haven't forgotten the media, by any chance? It sounds like your golden opportunity for a bit of personal publicity.'

'The media are your prerogative. I'm sure you will know how to handle this hot potato.'

'My oath, I do! Bomb – you say there is a bomb. How do you know that?'

'Come and look. The inside of the head is stuffed full of Semtex.'

'And you defused it – by yourself – without expert help?'

'I like to think I know about these things.'

'We'll soon see. I'll be right round with my men.'

Rayner put down the phone and said to Fenella, who had stood next to him during the two calls, 'Before the brigadier and his merry men arrive, I think we should let Pittock-Williams know and put him on his guard against any suspicious parcels. After all, he's more deeply involved with silver oars than I am.'

Fenella put her hand on Rayner's arm. 'Before you do, won't you reconsider your *Alabama* oar mission?'

He covered her hand with his own. 'I couldn't live with myself as a security man if I chickened out.'

Her eyes were very deep and luminous. 'It hurts, but I'll try to understand.'

Pittock-Williams seized on only one thing in Rayner's conversation, the thought that the Simonstown ceremony might be called off because of the bomb discovery, and that the mock trial might fall on its face as a result.

'The publicity about Nelson's head could kill them both!' he exclaimed. 'Everything's been set in train from my side! The mock trial is only eight days away! My tailor is busy refurbishing the old Marshal's uniform to fit me –'

'I can't do anything about the media,' Rayner responded. 'In fact, I prefer to stay well clear of them.'

'They have their uses,' interjected Pittock-Williams. 'They can make a positive contribution sometimes.'

'I hope you'll bear in mind my warning about parcels,' Rayner started to say.

'Yes, yes, of course. My personal security is sound, as you know. Now see here, you say this brigadier fellow is on his way –'

'Right now.'

'Then listen. I have it. The gods alone know what he'll tell the media, but I aim to forestall him. I'm going to jump the gun on the official announcement of the mock trial and so make sure that it still takes place, whatever. Agreed?'

'It's your trial, professor, and your pigeon,' replied Rayner ironically.

Pittock-Williams rushed on. 'Once the announcement has been made and the news becomes public property, it will be very hard to recall it.'

The sound of a police car's siren in the roadway outside

the villa cut into Pittock-Williams's ego-trip. Rayner wasn't sorry.

'Here's the Security force,' Rayner told him as the sound of more sirens reached him, and the thump of running footsteps from heavy booted feet. 'Goodbye.'

Brigadier Keyter saved Rayner the trouble of having to answer the door. He was inside before Rayner could reach it, plus four men, all in camouflage uniform with pistols at their belts. Through the open door Rayner and Fenella could make out more uniformed men surrounding the Villa Montana at the double.

'Where is this thing?' Keyter's lips moved only wide enough for him to articulate: the words seemed to originate somewhere deep in the broad, square shoulders.

'Upstairs.'

'Why is it upstairs when you say you found it outside in the street?'

'Because I needed a dark place in which to defuse it.'

'That's a new one on me.'

'Perhaps the type of booby-trap is, too. Come.'

Rayner led them to the Rommel Room, where the effigy head stood on the low table, along with batteries, wires, detonator, and the photo-electric cell.

Keyter eyed the head. 'Looks like what was shown on TV.'

'It's full of Semtex. Look –'

'Leave it!' snapped the brigadier. 'It could go off.'

Rayner gave a derisive laugh, ignored the order and up-ended the head. He indicated. 'Semtex. I reckon there could be about three kilos or so.'

'You seem to know a great deal about Semtex, Watton.'

'Enough to recognize it when I see it. Here –' he picked up the photo-electric cell '– is the joker in the pack.'

Keyter turned to his men. 'Know this?'

'Never seen one like it, sir.'

'Nor me. I've heard about them, read the info, of course. How did you come to recognize what it was? In the dark, as you allege?' he demanded from Rayner.

'I don't allege anything. I've seen this sort of booby-trap in Northern Ireland. When the bomb is being armed, the terrorist puts a strip of black photographic paper over the cell to keep it from exploding, then withdraws the paper as he is about to seal the parcel. After that, if light falls on it, it sets it off.'

Keyter suddenly rounded on Fenella. 'And where were you while all this was going on?'

'I came back to the house from work to find Rayner busy defusing the head. I waited outside the door until he had finished. Then I helped him get the head out of the box.'

'Close co-operation, eh?'

The flush rose to Fenella's cheeks, but she kept her cool.

'It was a matter of life or death.'

'Both of you seem to have been extraordinarily confident about what you were doing.'

'It was agonizing,' answered Fenella simply.

'Fingerprints all over this thing,' said one of the men, busy with dusting powder and a brush.

'I'll want your fingerprints, both of you,' snapped Keyter. 'Saliva tests, too.'

'What on earth for?' demanded Rayner.

'I want to check the flap of the envelope with the card.'

'I didn't lick it, if that's what you're driving at. Nor did Fenella.'

Keyter eyed them with his cold eyes. 'So you say.'

'Are you hinting that we stage-managed this whole business?'

'I didn't say so. I have my investigations to carry out. Now – you allege that you heard the sound of a car in the street, went outside and found the parcel near the side door?'

'I don't allege. That is what happened.'

'Thousands might believe you. Frankly, it sounds pretty thin to me. Have you anyone to substantiate what you say?'

'Of course not. I was alone. Fenella was still at work.'

'Can you prove that, Miss Gault?'

'The office staff saw me.'

Keyter seemed almost regretful at her alibi. 'Then – according to you – you saw a car accelerate away after a kick-start with a woman driver who had copper-coloured hair?'

'It was only a glimpse. I'm uncertain about the hair. It was my impression.'

A man, in camouflage uniform, came in holding Rayner's Glock 17 pistol. 'Found this during our search of the house, sir. Hidden in a drawer. Plus this –' He handed over a box of shells.

Keyter drew in his breath sharply, eyeing the plastic butt. 'Something else I've only read about,' he said sharply. 'Glock 17. Terrorist weapon.'

'It is. It's mine. I brought it from London with me.'

'Did you declare it?'

Rayner gave a short laugh. 'I wanted to see if what the makers claim about its being security-proof against airport checks was true. I proved my point.'

'You smuggled in a lethal weapon?'

'I'm a security man myself.'

'That's no answer, Watton. I'm confiscating this gun for ballistic and other tests.'

'If you're trying to put the bite on me, brigadier –'

Keyter ignored Rayner and said to his men, 'Get this stuff together. Finished?'

'We can do the rest of the tests at headquarters, sir.'

Keyter said coldly, 'I could arrest you, you realize that, don't you?'

'Why don't you?' asked Rayner sarcastically.

'You will report any of your movements outside this house, until I have completed my investigations.'

'You can keep Scotland Yard informed.'

'That is my business. There is a strict protocol between countries in delicate matters like this. None of your security-beating pistols and heads in a hatbox.'

'I don't think I care for that remark, brigadier.'

Keyter shrugged. 'You'll hear from me.'

He went, taking the velvet glove in which he had unsuccessfully concealed his iron fist, with him.

Rayner and Fenella listened to the lunch-time news. The very paucity of the announcement about the effigy head was revealing.

It said briefly:

Security headquarters in Cape Town has announced that the missing effigy head of Lord Nelson, which was stolen from Westminster Abbey recently, has been located in Cape Town. Two detectives from Scotland Yard's crack Anti-Terrorist Squad will be flying to this country at the earliest opportunity to liaise with Brigadier Neels Keyter, South African Security chief, who led the task force which took possession of the effigy head.

No further details have been released, and Brigadier Keyter stated that he has no comment to make.

It has also been made known in Cape Town by the well-known public personality, Professor Vivian Pittock-Williams, that a mock trial at which the old Vice-Admiralty Court practice will be followed is to be held in eight days' time in the Cultural History Museum adjoining the Houses of Parliament. Professor Pittock-Williams, whose great-grandfather was the last Admiralty Marshal at the Cape, will figure in the mock trial and lead a procession in period dress, carrying the silver oar which is to be exchanged with one presented by the British Prime Minister at the Simonstown ceremony. Part of the ceremonial involves the display of the ivory-and-silver Marshal's baton, the symbol of the Admiralty's authority in bygone days. As Marshal, Professor Pittock-Williams will also carry this in procession.

The purpose behind the mock trial is to enlighten and inform the modern-day public of the ceremonial involved in an Admiralty Court sitting, and the significance of the Marshal and the silver oar –

Chapter 16

The news announcement blew Zara's euphoric mood into Churchhaven lagoon. Had it been the bomb itself, the impact on Zara could not have been more stunning.

Even as she had accelerated down the hill away from the Villa Montana after dropping off the hatbox at the side entrance, Zara had felt the cathartic mood wash over her; it grew as she hightailed it out of Cape Town by the quickest route back to Churchhaven. By the time she had reached the lagoon, she began to experience the same sort of therapeutic benefit from her action as she had done on the night of her theft from Westminster Abbey.

She had spent the time between her arrival and the midday news enjoying the great peace of the lagoon and rejoicing in the fact that she had taken a couple of weeks' leave over and above her overseas break from her job (she was a computer programmer) just to be at the place she loved.

She had kept the radio going in case of a snap announcement about the bomb; by the time the actual bulletin arrived she could not sit still.

A four-punch combination ending in an uppercut could not have flattened her more when it did come. She could not believe her ears. All that was revealed was that Nelson's head had been found: no mention of the bomb! What had gone wrong? Why hadn't the booby-trap worked? The baldness of the announcement left her with a thousand unanswered questions. Who had discovered the head? Where? Had Rayner himself been far smarter than she thought and become wise to its contents? Had he rendered it harmless? She never credited that anyone outside a handful of top terrorists in Europe would have been able to handle such a sophisticated trap. Yet he must have!

With the avalanche of questions, came a panic-slide of fear. Fingerprints! She had deliberately not gone to much trouble to clean up the head or the box in the certainty that the force of the explosion would destroy all evidence.

In Cape Town, it was Renate's habit to have a snack lunch in a shade-house of the plant centre for which she worked and listen to the radio. All her relaxation vanished in a flash as she sat idly listening to the bulletin. She was flabbergasted, filled with fear at the vagueness of the announcement. Cape Town – did that mean the city proper, or its environs at large (the way the term was often used)? If the latter, did the finger point straight at Churchhaven, and the secret underground bunker? How had Zara's perfect cover been blown?

She rushed to a phone. The rest of the gang had to know. They had to decide, quickly, what they would do in case Rote Zora's set-up had been discovered. The news had come like a lightning-flash out of a clear sky. None of the girls had been in Zara's confidence about using the head as a booby-trapped bomb.

Renate dialled the gang in quick succession: Rikki, the hotel receptionist, was first because she was quickest to contact; Gemma, who worked in a laboratory manufacturing serum; Menty, a lay-out expert in a publishing house; and Kerry-Ann, PRO for a catering concern.

None of the girls had heard the news before Renate phoned. They shared Renate's fears and assigned her to get up to Churchhaven that same afternoon and establish from Zara (if she was not under arrest) what the situation was. Since there were no telephones at Churchhaven, it was impossible to reach Zara otherwise than personally.

Renate took the afternoon off, and left immediately.

She was not to know the black despair which had overtaken Zara, who knew she had boobed, and that the consequences could be disastrous, not only for herself but for the rest of the gang. The very isolation of the lagoon which had filled her earlier with such quiet joy was now like an unseen hand throttling her. Yet, she dared not leave, dared not risk going to spy out the Villa Montana.

She should, she told herself, have gone for Pittock-Williams, made a more concerted effort (somehow) to insinuate the booby-trapped head into his home or office. Now it was too late. Either she had had a wicked piece of ill-luck, or Rayner Watton was far cleverer than she gave him credit for.

Pittock-Williams! She had hardly paid attention to the announcement about the mock trial which had followed that of the head's discovery. Now it started to come back to her. There was to be a mock trial and Pittock-Williams (of course) would be back in the public spotlight leading the procession –

Leading the procession! Out in front! A clear target!

The idea hit her, clear, complete, uncluttered by technicalities.

She would gun down Pittock-Williams with her own hands as he led the mock trial procession!

She moved quickly through to her bedroom, stood for a brief moment looking at the bed where he had seduced her, and then opened a drawer and pulled out her Glock 17. This was it! Good that she had a silencer for it, if she was to fire from the crowd. It was down there in the bunker with the rest of the hardware. She had refused the silencer at first, but her hosts in Germany had insisted that she should take it, since there might be a use for it.

Now there was that use!

One straight shot!

It was late afternoon when Renate arrived at Churchhaven.

She parked her car about a kilometre and a half short of Zara's house behind a small peninsula which blocked the approach road from sight. She climbed down through the cliffside's rough vegetation to the water's edge, in order to stake out the house from the beach. The long low light would help.

When the roof of Zara's house appeared, Renate dropped down on all fours (she still wore her faded working jeans) and inched her way towards her objective. Nothing stirred. Had the security men taken Zara away and left their guards behind?

There was only one way to find out. Renate forced her way again through the cliffside undergrowth to the road at the top and warily reached a point where she could command the back of the house.

There were no police vehicles, no sign of anyone.

Renate edged closer, and then sprinted to the shelter of the graveyard, which was masked from the house by the church.

Nothing.

She could see Zara's own car in the garage with the doors open, as she always left it.

Then – Zara appeared from the house, walked swiftly across to the church, and went in.

Renate first made a searching check, and then followed her.

Zara knelt at the altar, using a torch and key to open the secret panel leading to the bunker.

Renate watched her disappear, took a seat in one of the deep old pews, and waited for her to return.

When she did, Renate saw what was in her hand. It was a silencer for a pistol.

'Zara!'

Zara spun round, every nerve on edge.

'Renate! What are you up to here?'

'I could ask the same of you! What the devil are you up to, Zara?'

'What do you mean?'

'You know perfectly well what I mean. You heard the news?'

'Yes,' Zara admitted reluctantly.

'How did the security people get hold of the head? I – we – all believed it was safe down here in the bunker. Did they raid the place? Why aren't you under arrest? Why –'

'So the rest of the girls know?'

'They sent me here. We're all in a blind panic. Is our cover broken? Is –'

'You'd better come to the house. I'll explain.'

'You'd better. None of us think this is very funny. You're sure there's no danger?'

Renate couldn't understand the leader's calm and apparent lack of concern.

'There's no danger. The security guys haven't been here, if that's what you're wetting yourself about.'

'Hell's teeth! Don't you realize what's happening?'

'I realize.'

What Renate couldn't realize was what the afternoon had brought Zara. Now that she was formulating the logistics of her plan to shoot Pittock-Williams, it had a soothing effect on her whole personality. She fiddled unconsciously with the silencer. Yes, she would have to employ it if she was to fire from the crowd –

'Come!' she repeated, and led the way.

'Now!' demanded Renate, when they reached the house. She was truculent, tight with tension.

'What do you want to know?' Zara fenced. She realized from Renate's attitude that her status as leader had been dented.

'For God's sake!' burst out Renate. 'The news about the head which the police and the public in two countries have been looking for breaks and you're at the heart of it and all you can say is, what do you want to know?'

Zara remained unruffled. She seemed to Renate to be operating on another wavelength. She was. She saw from Renate's mood, which probably reflected the rest of the gang's, that it was useless trying to involve Rote Zora in her latest plan against Pittock-Williams; they simply wouldn't play ball.

Zara said, 'It is correct that the head was found in Cape Town. I took it there.'

'You took it there!' echoed Renate. 'When it was safely stashed away in the safest, most isolated spot –'

'It's a long story,' said Zara.

'And I'm not going to listen to it, at this stage,' retorted Renate. 'I was sent here by the rest of the girls to find out two things, first, whether Rote Zora's cover has been blown and, more important for the moment, how safe are we? Unless you are willing to meet them all for an emergency meeting tomorrow afternoon and explain yourself, you'll find that the gang has fallen apart at the seams.'

'OK. Go back and tell them all that no one saw me with the effigy head, that no fuzz came to Churchhaven, and that there's not a thing to point to Rote Zora as being involved.'

'It sounds as if you are papering the whole thing over,' replied Renate angrily. 'If we're going to hold an emergency session, it had better be here. I'm not so sure about Cape Town.'

'Have it your own way, Renate.'

She studied Zara's calm, unworried face and distant eyes.

'Don't be so bloody smug!' she snapped. 'You'd think nothing had happened!'

Zara came back to the present and lent a double meaning to her reply. 'It hasn't – yet.'

'I'm getting back to Cape Town right away,' snapped Renate. 'You can account to us all tomorrow for your actions. You're sure we won't find ourselves walking into a trap?'

'It's safe – I told you.'

Renate shrugged impatiently and stalked out.

Zara stood by the big glass door, looking out across the lavender water and far hills of the lagoon. She realized that she had been a fool in not taking the rest of the gang into her confidence over the effigy head; it was only when she faced their ostracism that she realized how lonely she was. The girls, for all their waywardness, were important to her, and she had to re-establish herself in their eyes. They had admired her dash and finesse over the Abbey theft; if she gunned down Pittock-Williams in full public view and got away with it, they would come running back to her and restore her to the pedestal which she now was in danger of losing.

A flight of flamingos painted the complementary hues

of the lagoon: her Churchhaven sanctuary was under threat also from the man she detested. She would kill him, save Churchhaven, reinstate herself. It all came back to Pittock-Williams.

'. . . Professor Pittock-Williams –' the TV set behind her threw the name into the silent and darkening room '– has come along to the studio this evening to explain details of the mock trial procession which was announced earlier today and which will take place in eight days' time at the Cultural History Museum, once the venue of the Cape's Vice-Admiralty Court.'

Mock trial! Zara doubled back into the room, dodged the big fish tank with its repulsive occupant, to get into position to view the screen. Mock trial! The situation was playing into her hands! The glow of hot, revenge-laden exhilaration which swept through her was altogether different from the calculated coldness of the effigy head affair. She was half-glad now that the bomb plan had gone astray. This was for real!

The camera began with a splendid exterior shot of the magnificent, old, white, double-storeyed court building with its green shutters and double entrance door to the street, and, above it, an ornate fanlight above a stuccoed pediment.

The view then switched to the courtyard inside, where an old slave well, overhung with trees, and historic tombstones of the founders of the Cape (including the first Dutch commander, Jan van Riebeeck and his wife) let into the walls, added time-honoured nobility to the architecture.

Then – the camera zoomed in on a big door near the slave well: it swung open with an invisible theatrical movement to show Pittock-Williams standing at the top of a small flight of steps.

Pittock-Williams's gesture was as stagey as the door's opening.

'This is the spot where the procession will debouch into the courtyard, led by myself in the uniform of an Admiralty Marshal, and carrying the silver oar and ivory baton as symbols of the Admiralty's authority at the Cape,' he said. 'In the procession also will be a lay figure of a pirate in chains being led to execution. Such an event was always headed by the Marshal and his oar, which was, apart from its ceremonial uses, also the symbol of retribution –'

'Retribution!' The word slipped past Zara's lips before she could check the upsurge of feeling inside her. Here the detailed lay-out of the stage for retribution was being presented to her on a plate!

She hardly heard Pittock-Williams going on to outline the procession's route through the courtyard and then out via the big main front door into the street beyond, thence towards the Houses of Parliament situated in the famous gardens next door.

'Retribution!'

She missed Pittock-Williams's disappearance from the screen, but came alive to the announcer saying, 'Because of the value of the silver oar, both historically and monetarily, the strictest security will be in force both inside and outside the old court building during the mock trial. Admittance to the interior will be by invitation only; even those invited will first have to be cleared security-wise.'

Zara killed the image, and stood staring at the dead screen.

By invitation only! To be cleared security-wise! She would never be able to smuggle in the Glock! Once again, Pittock-Williams had slipped her killer-punch.

At the Villa Montana, Rayner and Fenella watched Pittock-Williams's ego-trip. They were in the Rommel Room, where Fenella had arranged one of her 'bokkems-and-mulled-wine' suppers. But it had an air of constraint, although both of them had tried to gloss over Fenella's fears about Rayner's trip to London to fetch the *Alabama* oar. He had gently but firmly refused her renewed request to ask Gibson to substitute another courier for him. If the Rote Zora gang were well informed enough to know where Rayner had been staying in Cape Town, they could equally follow him to London – and back, she had maintained.

Fenella sat on a cushion on the floor. She wore her favourite faded tartan pants and a soft beige shirt. She had changed her hair-style slightly so that instead of the sweep of black masking the right-hand side of her forehead, it was now lightly blown and arranged with a careless natural grace on top, and also clear of her ears.

She said, not looking at Rayner, 'The fact is, Rayner, you are a marked man. The bomb attempt proves that. The gang may try again, and the next time you mayn't be so lucky.'

There was a heavy knock at the front door, heavy enough to carry all the way up the stairs to where they were.

Fenella gave Rayner a startled glance. He knew what she was thinking.

He got to his feet. 'I'll answer it.'

She was up, too. 'Rayner, please! Be careful! Check before you open!'

He smiled gravely at her. 'I'll be as careful as I promise to be when I go to London.'

She heard Rayner's query at the door, and the sound of a man's voice in reply. Two sets of footsteps came up the stairs.

Rayner said, 'Fenella, it's Brigadier Keyter.'

Keyter wore civilian clothes, a loose jacket over a sweater. He gave a searching glance round the Rommel Room, and forced his lips into what might have been a smile.

'Very cosy, if I may say so, Miss Gault.'

'Would you care to join us in some wine? I was about to do my thing with a red-hot poker.'

'Thank you, no. This is not really an official visit. I came to return this.'

He pulled the Glock from his jacket pocket, and from another the confiscated box of ammunition.

'It could have waited, brigadier. I'm in no hurry to have it back. There was no need for you yourself to bring it.'

'No problem.'

An awkward silence fell. Keyter broke it. 'It still seems to me a strange weapon for a civilian to carry.'

What was Keyter after? Rayner asked himself. He could have detailed some underling to bring back the Glock. Tomorrow, any day. There was also a rasp at the back of Keyter's voice that he didn't care for.

'You can check my track record with the SAS and Surveillicor, if you want to.'

'I already have, Mr Watton.'

Checkmate.

Fenella said, 'Are you sure you won't sit down?'

'I'll be on my way in a moment.' Then he said suddenly, 'Did you know the Semtex in the head had been newly manufactured, which means that it must have been brought to South Africa very recently?'

'Meaning?'

'You came recently from London.'

Here it was. Rayner had known all along that Keyter hadn't come merely for the ride. There was a suspicion that Rayner had had something to do with the effigy head, apart from being the target he claimed.

'Are you implying – ?'

Keyter added, 'After the Lockerbie air disaster, the Czech manufacturers of Semtex agreed to representations from several governments in Europe, including Britain,

146

to deliberately add an impurity to Semtex to make it detectable. The older Semtex could beat any security check. The stuff in the head couldn't. It was new. How'd it get through?'

'Should I know, brigadier?'

'I just thought I would ask.'

Rayner made up his mind in a moment. 'Listen, brigadier, if both the British and South African Foreign Offices felt unhappy about me, in the way you apparently do, they would not have asked me to undertake the silver oar mission.'

Keyter's thinly veiled cordiality evaporated. 'What are you talking about?'

Rayner had presupposed that Keyter knew about Gibson's decoy plan. He couldn't go back now.

'You know that I am to bring back the *Alabama* oar – on my own – to South Africa for the Simonstown ceremony.'

'I know nothing of the sort. This is news to me.' He considered Rayner. 'I don't like my sources of news to come to me from persons outside my profession. Whose authority have you for this?'

'Ask Scotland Yard. They're arranging the decoy force. They must be acting in collaboration with you.'

The last vestige of Keyter's social approach vanished. 'Listen, Watton, there is a strict protocol in this sort of thing, and I don't care for the manner in which you go your own way as if you stood above the security forces here. And in London also, it seems. Does anyone else know about this so-called courier business?'

'Professor Pittock-Williams.'

'So you broached a highly confidential plan, of which I know nothing, I repeat, to another civilian?'

'The *Alabama* oar, strictly speaking, belongs to Professor Pittock-Williams. It was only common courtesy to let him know.'

'And common courtesy that I should know.' Keyter's eyes went round the Rommel Room, as if seeking further indictment amongst its pleasant jumble of Fenella's things. Then he snapped, 'See here. I can't stop you going to London, but there are straws in the wind I don't care for. Don't start ferreting around thinking you can make your own private investigations and run rough-shod over my organization. I advise you to watch your step from now on very, very carefully indeed.'

Chapter 17

'That brute gives me the shits.'

Renate stood by the big fish tank in Zara's lounge with three of the other Rote Zora girls. It was late the next afternoon. They had travelled together from Cape Town in Renate's minibus for the confrontation with Zara. The fifth member of the gang, Menty, could not link up with the others and was due shortly in her own car.

As if in response, the lethal sea-barbel did a backward loop-the-loop, giving the girls a full view of its repulsive, tentacled head.

The antics of the fish gave them something to make small talk about; Zara herself, like an awaiting-trial prisoner, had made herself scarce in her bedroom until the gang's number was complete. All of them were uneasy, none of them really wanted to haul Zara over the coals. The crisis and their reluctance to keel-haul their leader highlighted just how much Rote Zora meant in their lives, unexpressed, but vital.

It also revealed unconsciously that they all had a very real loyalty, even affection, for Zara. 'Taking her apart will be like undressing your sister' was the summing-up delivered on the journey to Churchhaven by Rikki, the hotel receptionist with the tousle of rather untidy blonde hair and professional smile. Rikki was smoking now, the only one of the gang who did.

Terror gang. Outwardly, the group looked like a gathering of everyday, under-twenty-five young women – what had gone wrong in their life that they should each find themselves drawn to the life of a terrorist? A women's terror gang proclaiming anti-male shibboleths and tossing about (so far) pinprick bombs?

Renate, tall, big-boned, dark. It was she who had defaced the *Medusa* figurehead with her strong gardening hands. Her short-fuse temper was apparent now as she chafed at having to wait for Menty's arrival. Renate admired the panache of Zara's theft from the Abbey and, because she deplored what she reasoned must be bungling by Zara in its subsequent discovery, she was willing, as her first lieutenant, to lead the attack for an explanation.

Rikki stubbed out her cigarette and lit another. It was her only giveaway; in her life, there was none. Somewhere behind Rikki's outwardly balanced friendly air and wide grey eyes something had gone astray – a man? a teenage sexual assault? a genetic inhibition? No one would ever know.

Gemma, the gang's fuse expert, cruised about pretending to concentrate on the magnificent view. She worked in a serum laboratory in Cape Town; it bored her stiff, but it did provide the tools to indulge her character quirk of making fuses. Fuses gave her a sense of power, counterweight to the pale, man-shy personality which hid behind a rather toothy uncertain smile under a too-large nose and big eyes, capped by a head of thick, coarse hair which neither she nor any hairdresser could keep within bounds. She had met Zara through computer programming of her lab's success rate; she had been drawn into Rote Zora like iron filings to a magnet.

Kerry-Ann was as well groomed now as if she were out on a cocktail party for the catering concern for which she was PRO. Her blonde hair was piled up to give her a deliberate 'ungroomed-yet-groomed' look. With her soft but studied clear enunciation she could have been a preschool nursery teacher, but her smile did not extend beyond her broad lips and the double dimple of her left cheek. Where did she go wrong? Even Rikki, with whom she had the nearest to friendship among the gang, had no idea what made her tick. She had been drawn into the gang by Rikki; catering and hotels are not far apart. In her job, circulating in public places, she had been a stalwart in planting bombs. Renate mistrusted her; she did not know why.

'Where the hell is Menty?' exclaimed Renate impatiently.

'She should be here any moment. Her driving's not all that hot,' began Rikki, when Zara came in. She was relaxed and composed.

'Ready?'

'Menty's not here yet.'

'So the kangaroo court's not complete?' she mocked, glancing round the group, who avoided her eyes.

'You're not on trial. It's an explanation we want,' began Renate uncomfortably.

Kerry-Ann came to the rescue. She handed Zara a newspaper.

'The papers came on the streets just as I left,' she said. 'There's something here about the head.' She indicated.

Zara read the piece in silence. 'Nothing new in this.' She half-smiled round the group. 'What you're looking for is the inside story, no doubt.'

Kerry-Ann tried to damp the tension which was building up behind the exchange of words.

She said rapidly, nervously, 'There's a bit here also about a mock trial which is going to be held before the

Simonstown affair. It's all concerned with – ah, Professor Pittock-Williams. I thought you might –'

'I don't want to hear about it,' snapped Zara.

'There's a colour picture of the invitation cards,' blundered on Kerry-Ann.

Gemma broke in. 'Here's Menty. I hear her car.'

A tight silence fell over the group and they heard the sound of a car being parked at the back of the house.

From the expectation, one might have thought Menty was worth waiting for. She wasn't. She was a mousy young woman with indeterminate-coloured hair caught up behind with a ribbon more in the style of a schoolgirl than a woman. Her style of dress – straps over bare shoulders and big buttons – was an under-twenty mode which would have been derided by her contemporaries. She rode into the room on a tentative, too-ready, hesitant smile. There was no giveaway in the smoky haze of her eyes. One hand was already on its way to her teeth to gnaw at her nails, dirty as always with printer's ink. She worked as a lay-out artist for a publishing house. She lacked no accomplishment when it came to her work, which had mutated through some deep-down deviation into forgery. As yet, the gang had had little need of her expert services.

Renate said, 'Right, here we go. Zara, what I and the girls feel, if our necks are to be at stake through some unilateral action of yours, the least you could have done was to inform us in advance. What in hell's name made you remove the effigy head from what was a perfect hiding-place in the bunker and take it to Cape Town? Why? Who found it there? What is the story?'

Zara looked round the gathering. There was little sympathy in their somewhat scared eyes.

When Zara did not reply immediately, Renate went on impatiently, 'What *happened*? We have to know!'

Zara decided to come clean. It was her only option. Her leadership hung in the balance.

'I took the head to Cape Town myself,' she answered. 'It was meant to kill a man. I armed it with a booby-trapped charge of Semtex.'

Renate's dumbfoundment rippled through the group. 'What a bloody crazy thing to do!' Her mind jumped to the same conclusion as the other girls at the mention of a man. 'How did you ever expect to get it through Pittock-Williams's security system?'

'It wasn't Pittock-Williams,' Zara told her astonished audience. 'It was the other guy who appeared with him on TV. Rayner Watton. The security expert who brought back the silver oar from the wreck of the *Alabama*.'

'Now I've heard everything!' Renate spoke for the whole gang, who nodded agreement. 'You tried to kill someone who means nothing to you – why? How'd you ever expect to get a bomb past a security man whose job is bombs and guns! *What happened?*'

Zara dropped another couple of notches in the leadership stakes. She realized instinctively that it was hopeless to try and rationalize what was essentially irrational.

'Listen, all of you,' she said in a low, slightly theatrical voice. 'I wanted it to be Pittock-Williams. When I saw the bastard who had seduced and chucked me aside there on the TV, something snapped inside me. It brought back everything he had done to me. Through him, I'm less a woman than a spayed cat –'

Renate broke in. 'OK, OK, Zara. We know it all. We know how you feel, and we sympathize.'

'Sympathize! Jeez, is that all you can say!'

'We understand your motivations, but why did you risk a bomb?'

'I'll tell you! The sight of Pittock-Williams grabbing the limelight with his role as Marshal at the Simonstown ceremony made me puke! I couldn't handle it, can you understand? I had to hit out. I knew, as you've already said, Renate, that it would be impossible to get past his security screen. I still had to hit at the heart of the ceremony itself, even if I didn't go for my man. What if I killed off one of the persons involved – Rayner Watton? I meant him to die so that the whole ceremony would be called off and so rob Pittock-Williams of his moment of triumph. There are more ways of killing a cat – I don't know where the plan went astray.'

When Gemma, the fuse expert, spoke, Zara knew that the gang had been impressed by her explanation, and that her own come-back was just around the corner.

'What sort of detonator did you use, Zara? Where did you slip up?'

'I primed the head with about three kilograms of the Semtex I brought back from Germany,' she answered. She saw that she had the gang's undivided attention. All perhaps bar Menty. 'I used a photo-electric cell as a trigger – you know, Gemma, the sophisticated IRA trick with the black photographic paper.'

'I wish you'd brought me in on it, Zara. I would love to have tried my hand at it.'

'Everything seemed in perfect order.' A faint smile came to her face. 'With that gadget, you can't open the parcel and double-check, or else it's –'

'Kaput,' replied Gemma.

'Where did you plant it? In what?' demanded Renate, who wasn't as carried away by the fuse expertise as Gemma.

'At the Villa Montana, in the Gardens. That's where Rayner Watton was – is – staying with the girl, the silver expert from Christie's you saw on the TV feature with the two men. The bomb was in the same hatbox as I showed you, Renate.'

'What about fingerprints?' Renate demanded further.

'I presume you cleaned up everything before you let the head out of your possession?'

'I expected the whole thing to be blown to hell, strewn all over the neighbourhood, along with Watton.'

'You're saying you didn't?'

Zara nodded. Kerry-Ann's clear enunciation grated on her. 'I've always planted the gang's bombs. I should have been in on this act.'

Zara explained briefly how she had offloaded the hat-box at the villa's side entrance and had shot off down the hill.

'Inviting attention,' said Kerry-Ann carpingly. 'You did all the wrong things, Zara.'

Renate added, 'The authorities now have your finger-prints and I'll bet you licked the flap of the charming little card you left for Watton, so that they also have a record of your spit, when they catch up on you!'

After an embarrassing silence, Renate resumed control of the gathering, although none of the gang had called Zara's leadership directly into question.

'So it seems that at this stage our headquarters here at Churchhaven is not under threat of discovery? It seems that we've been let off the hook for the moment, but the danger is very real still, especially with all those clues on the effigy head.'

'I don't like the way the announcement made no mention of the bomb or the booby-trap,' argued Gemma. 'It seems to me as if they have some important clue they're holding out on.'

Zara came back, more strongly now, and more confidently.

'You're all seeing shadows. Nothing has really happened, and Churchhaven is safe. Everything will be OK if we all watch our step and keep our mouths shut.'

Renate said, 'Zara, the sooner you get back to work

154

and stop sitting around here on your own brooding, the better for you and for all of us.'

'I like being here,' retorted Zara.

'Think about it, Zara.' She checked her watch. 'It's time we all got back to Cape Town.'

Menty addressed Zara. 'Do you think I could sleep over here tonight? It's a long drive back to Cape Town in the dark on my own.'

Zara didn't want to be burdened with this ninny. All she wanted was to be alone in order to work out her plan against Pittock-Williams.

'If you like.'

'I'll be off first thing in the morning –'

'I said, it's OK,' rejoined Zara sharply.

Menty crawled back into her shell; the others crawled off down the appalling road to Cape Town.

'Have a drink?' asked Zara.

Menty's puritan progenitors would have struck her down dead if she had.

'I don't drink. Something soft, please.'

Zara shrugged inwardly. She needed the brandy she splashed into a glass for herself. She was in for a heavy evening.

In spring, thaws come from unexpected quarters. The thaw in the lounge came equally unexpectedly, from Menty.

She sipped her orange juice. Her eyes swivelled on every object in the room except Zara.

She said in a tiny voice, 'I – I think I sympathize with you, about the effigy, that is, I mean to say. I'd also hit out blindly if – any man had done to me what he did to you.'

Zara held back from pulling the trigger on the sarcastic bullet which loaded into her throat. Was the mouse trying to make a genuine overture of understanding?

Menty mistook her silence, and blurted on, 'But it

couldn't be, with me, I mean. I don't think any man will ever want me. You see, I'm a virgin, and I'm ashamed of it.'

'We were all virgins once.' Hell, she sounded like Whistler's great-grandmother.

She couldn't return Menty's half-look, and her eyes strayed to the newspaper Kerry-Ann had brought. The colour picture automatically drew her attention. It was of one of the VIP invitation cards for the mock trial.

Menty rushed on, seeing she had an audience and not a brush-off. 'I think the other girls were rather hard on you – I want you to know that. But it was no good my saying anything, they wouldn't have listened. But I can say it now we're alone –' Her voice trailed, and then she added with a tremendous effort, 'Zara, if there's anything I can do –'

Pittock-Williams and his helpers must have done some first-class staff work to have got out an invitation card with such an imaginative and elaborate design so quickly. It was based on some of the engravings on the blade of the silver oar, the Admiralty's foul anchor symbol, and the two dolphins intertwined on crossed tridents. The Royal arms were missing; even Pittock-Williams hesitated to hijack them to add lustre to the occasion.

Zara's glance went swiftly from the invitation card to Menty, who was busy twisting her mental knickers out of embarrassment and diffidence.

She had it!

A prototype invitation card, and a master-forger sitting begging her to let her help!

She leaned forward and said in a completely different, confidential tone of voice which immediately had Menty's full attention:

'There *is* something, Menty. I think you're wonderful to offer.'

Menty couldn't find words, and Zara went on quickly, indicating the picture of the invitation card.

'Do you think you could draw' (she avoided the word forge) 'an invitation like that so that I could get inside the building for the mock trial?'

Menty vibrated to the roots of her ribbon-tied hair.

Zara decided to put her cards on the table. 'You see, Menty, I have a plan –' Before she was halfway through, Menty was down on her knees at the picture. She held it up to the light, studying it acutely as Zara spoke.

'Go on!' said Menty. 'I want to consider this while I listen to what you have to say.'

When Zara had finished, there were tears in Menty's eyes; Zara was afraid she was going to kiss her. Her voice was alive, vibrating like her hair roots.

'I understand, I understand!' Schoolgirls in dormitory confessions use the same tone. 'What name shall I put – you see, the space is open here in the picture?'

'You'll do it, then?' asked Zara.

'I want to, I'd love to do it! I've got just the right sort of paper at the office, and I'll use script for the name! I'll make a dummy tomorrow as soon as I get back!'

'Listen, Menty,' said Zara, a new enthusiasm underscoring her words. 'What about the two of us staking out the place during your lunch-hour tomorrow? I'll come specially to Cape Town, and we can go over the set-up together and pick the best spot for the shot.'

'Wonderful! I'll be there, you can be sure!' enthused Menty.

A thought struck Zara. 'Menty, there's another thing I'll ask your help with. I'll have to have a getaway car after the shooting. Will you drive mine? We'll find the best place tomorrow to park.'

'No, I'd rather use my own car. I'm familiar with it and won't make any silly mistakes as I might with a strange vehicle.'

'Agreed then?'

'Agreed!' Zara thought this time she would really kiss her. The mouse wouldn't sleep much tonight.

Menty asked suddenly, 'The name on the invitation – you won't use your own, will you?'

'No. Too risky.'

'What shall I put?'

Zara's voice lifted and she gestured at the still lagoon with the sleeping church on the cliffside.

'Old George White would love this,' she said. 'Put the name, Ms Z. White.'

Chapter 18

Zara would not have been elated about her name next day had she been at the Villa Montana when the original name George Williams cropped up. Less so, to have known it was on Scotland Yard's lips.

Rayner was alone at the villa; Fenella was at work. Rayner was busy trying to do something about the villa's security system, but his mind was only half on it. How could he get going on his single-handed investigation into who had sent him the bomb? He had decided to ignore altogether Brigadier Keyter's warning to leave it to the professionals, which also meant a blanket denial of fingerprints or other clues Keyter's men might have. Keyter had made it clear that he thought Rayner was too big for his boots and was undermining his own security set-up. There was also his attitude of veiled suspicion, as if Rayner had stage-managed the head affair, which made him keep Rayner at arm's-length.

The villa's phone rang.

'Hugh Perrot!' exclaimed Rayner delightedly at the

sound of a well-known voice. 'Hugh! Where on earth are you?'

'Right on your doorstep. Not more than a couple of kilometres, in fact. Can I come round?'

'What are you doing in Cape Town?'

'Never talk on the phone,' admonished the voice banteringly. 'OK to see you?'

'Of course. Are you alone?'

'I've got Peter Imbrie with me. One of the Anti-Terrorist Squad.'

'Come right away.'

Hugh Perrot was the man who years before had talked Rayner into joining the SAS with him. Now he was one of Scotland Yard's crack anti-terrorist men.

Within ten minutes, Rayner was shaking the hand of the tall, sandy-haired gangling figure who shambled up the pathway from the main gate. Peter Imbrie was a short, dark man who sported a small black beard and phlegmatic air to hide a razor-sharp brain.

'Quite a place you've got here,' commented Hugh with a smile.

'The security system is up to maggots,' grinned back Rayner. 'I was having a go at it when you phoned. Can you believe it, it doesn't even extend upstairs? And downstairs it is in the veteran category.'

Imbrie asked, 'They wanted to blow this up with the bomb?'

Rayner laughed grimly. 'I was the target, not the villa. It wouldn't have made much difference in the long run which was meant to be which. Three kilos of Semtex.' He indicated the side door. 'It was dumped outside there.'

Hugh said, 'I want to hear details in a moment. That's what Peter and I are in South Africa for, about Nelson's head. But first I have something here from Don Gibson which he's sure will be of interest to you – and Fenella Gault.'

He handed Rayner what looked like a photocopy of an old-time handwritten document, grey with age.

Rayner read the date aloud. 'The tenth of August, 1863. What's this, Hugh?'

'Don Gibson asked me to tell you that your diver Powys recovered the crew muster book of the *Alabama* recently from the wreck. That entry is in Captain Semmes' own handwriting aboard the ship in Cape Town.'

Rayner read:

> Today signed on George Williams (master's certificate), escaped prisoner from British Admiralty Court in Cape Town. Williams explained to me how he had been unjustly arraigned before this court by his brother; story credible. *Alabama* needs seamen of his calibre; Williams owned his own ship before the trial. Williams brought on board with him a silver oar, part of the court's accoutrements, with which he fought his way out of the court. In view of the value of the oar, and the fact that it could be Admiralty property, the oar has been locked in the *Alabama*'s strongroom along with the gold used for the purchase of bunker coal and other stores. It is not being held with the chronometers and other prize items captured by the *Alabama* from Northern ships. The oar will, on completion of the *Alabama*'s cruise and return to home port, be submitted to relevant impartial arbitration to determine whether it should be returned to the British Admiralty.

'This is a piece of a jigsaw puzzle which has intrigued both myself and Fenella,' said Rayner. 'It involves the present owner of the silver oars, Professor Pittock-Williams. Exactly how, I don't know. Fenella will have to sort that one out. I'm very glad to have it, though.'

'Don Gibson thought you could have fun with it. There's some sort of mystery about the two oars, he said,' Hugh Perrot added.

'It's more historical than anything. It doesn't affect the actual exchange ceremony at the Simonstown signing.'

'That's on our schedule also,' said Hugh. 'For the moment, however, we're concerned with the effigy head. What's the story?'

Rayner and Hugh talked the same language. Rayner explained that his instinct had made him suspicious, how he had defused the bomb in the darkness of the Rommel Room after discovering the photo-electric trigger device.

'What do you think, Peter?' asked Hugh. 'The photo-electric cell is pure IRA, but the Semtex to my mind has all the hallmarks of the Abu Nidal group – the renegade Palestine Liberation Organization officer who developed the method of moulding Semtex round suitcase frames and fitting the bomb with a barometric-pressure trigger to explode at a predetermined altitude. You remember, that was the method used in the Lockerbie air disaster crash over Scotland.

'However, the marrying of the two techniques is something new in my experience, and of course the photo-electric cell in place of the barometric-pressure trigger is a devilish variation on a theme.'

He eyed Rayner. 'Fellah, you were either very lucky or very smart to have got away with it.'

'It gives us a strong lead in tracking down the bomber,' interjected Imbrie. 'You know, Rayner, the Yard has its own system of identifying suspects. Not by name, but by technique. What you've already told us narrows the field considerably.'

'Let me fetch something which I hope will narrow it still further,' said Rayner. He went to his room and returned with a printed paper for Hugh.

Hugh whistled. 'Where'd you get this, Rayner?' He passed it to Imbrie.

'In the box with the head,' answered Rayner. 'In view of Keyter's suspicious attitude, I thought I'd hang on to it and not pass it on.'

'You know what this is?' asked Imbrie.

'I can guess, but you tell me.'

'It's a set of assembly instructions for do-it-yourself bombs. It's drafted in Syria and circulated to extremists, especially Arabs.'

Hugh added, 'Our investigations have shown that this is how radio-cassette bombs – stocks of them are known to exist at terrorist points in Europe and Britain – are assembled. They are prefabricated in Syria, and then the terrorists assemble them on the basis of these instructions.' He slapped the paper. 'Now we're really making headway about the identity of the Nelson's head bomber! We already know it is a woman from her call to the media about the Abbey theft and the card mentioning Rote Zora. The gang is based in Germany. It's logical to assume she picked up the Semtex she used for your bomb there.

'The stuff she used was from a new batch from Czechoslovakia.'

'Where'd you discover that, Hugh?' asked Rayner.

'Your Security boss's report to us on the incident.'

'I'm glad to hear he parted with some information.'

'Listen, Rayner,' went on Hugh. 'Shortly before we left London, our counterparts in Germany made available to the Yard the confession of a Palestinian accused of offences in that country – he'd been trapped with a half-completed bomb in his flat. He thought if he blew the gaff, it would help his marble.

'He revealed that there was a specialist bomb school in West Germany, where operatives were known only by their Christian names. There was only one woman. Her name was Zara.'

'Zara!' echoed Rayner. 'Nothing more?'

'Unfortunately not. But it's a good start. This instruction pamphlet proves that whoever loaded Nelson's head had been a member of the specialist school in Germany. You won't begrudge her her technique, either!'

'Are you intending to tell all this to the South African Security chief, Hugh?' Rayner asked.

'I'm a bit shy of him, to tell you the truth, Rayner. He was pretty tight-lipped about the discovery of the head, and his image hasn't improved by what you have told me. No, we'll sit on this info, for the meantime.'

'It could be tricky later on,' observed Imbrie.

'Why?' asked Rayner.

'This is top-secret, of course,' said Hugh. 'True, we're here to follow up on Nelson's head, but in addition both of us are to form part of the Prime Minister's bodyguard during the Simonstown ceremony. We'll have to establish some kind of working arrangement with Keyter.'

'He's very prickly and touchy,' said Rayner. 'Rather you than me.'

Hugh glanced at his watch. 'We'd better be in good time for our appointment then, Peter.' He grinned at Rayner. 'The date was made a couple of days ago, from London. That gives him plenty of time to have put up his keep-off-the-grass notices.'

However, it was Rayner who felt he was treading on thin ice when Fenella returned before lunch. He greeted her enthusiastically with the news of Hugh Perrot's arrival together with Peter Imbrie, and how Hugh had been able to supply him with the name Zara as a powerful clue as to the identity of the Nelson's head bomber.

As he outlined the terror chain and expertise connected with the use of Semtex and barometric fuses, Fenella's eyes became remote and she interrupted him.

'Please, Rayner, don't go on! There was talk at the time of the plane crash which killed my parents that it was also a Lockerbie-type bomb which had been used. That's bad enough, but the crash was the thing which threw the door wide open on Wayne and his double-dealing, and put an end to a chapter in my life which I'd rather forget. Now you're trying to trace and revive a lot of things which are better left dead.'

'But Fenella, these are clues to a killer!'

'I'm not interested in killers, only in my happiness – and yours. All you've told me only goes to satisfy Scotland Yard's professional pride and your own. The same thing applies to your courier mission – Rayner, again I beg you to tell Gibson your part in it is off!'

'No, Fenella. I don't think and operate that way.'

'You've already done more than enough, defusing the effigy head bomb. Even Brigadier Keyter admits it was beyond him. Now the whole thing is snowballing with the arrival of these London detectives. It's becoming a trial of strength, Scotland Yard, you and Keyter on one side, and terrorists on the other. I don't want it, Rayner, I want it the way we started off, you and I.'

Rayner did not respond, but for a reply handed her the photocopy of the *Alabama*'s muster book and explained how Hugh had brought it from Don Gibson.

He was taken aback at her reaction.

'It only adds to what I am saying, Rayner! It's all starting to take on a strange pattern! Why revive something from a sinister past and make it part of the present, *our* present, Rayner, which is becoming more ominous at every turn! It's clear now from this that Pittock-Williams has suppressed his knowledge of how the oar came to be aboard the *Alabama*. It could have all kinds of repercussions for the Simonstown ceremony. This –' she banged the muster book page '– is something which was better left at the bottom of the sea.'

Chapter 19

Menty walked tall. Ran, rather, with a breathless patter of feet to the entrance to the Cultural History Museum where Zara stood waiting. It was their lunch-time date to reconnoitre the historic old building on the basis of the TV feature, and select a suitable firing-spot for Zara. It was an effusive non-stop talking greeting – from Menty's side at least – in contrast to the silent, unhappy meal Rayner and Fenella were having at the Villa Montana.

Zara backed away from a potential kiss from Menty, whose words poured out. 'I'm sorry I'm late, but it's the parking –'

'You're not really late, only two minutes overdue. That won't harm anyone.'

Menty put her hand on Zara's arm, companion, confidante in crime. 'You're so understanding.'

There was a trickle of people coming in and out of the big green double doors on to the main street. Zara turned to go in.

'Can we wait just a moment?' asked Menty with a shadow of her old cringing psyche. 'Something I want to show you first. Here.'

She pulled something from a big front pocket and handed it to Zara.

It was the fake invitation card to the mock trial ceremony. A perfect reproduction of the photograph in the newspaper, it was a superb piece of forgery. Even Zara's name, 'Ms Z. White', was so realistically inscribed that unless the entrance screen was lynx-eyed, it must pass.

'It's – perfect!' Zara exclaimed.

'It's just a rough and I had to knock it out in a hurry

this morning. I wanted it to be ready to show you. I'm not sure whether the texture of the paper is right.'

'Menty, you're a genius!'

She was. With a little more initiative, she could have knocked out banknotes for an easy living.

Menty blushed with pleasure. 'Something which worries me, though, is the serial number I'm sure will be on the cards themselves.'

'We'll worry about that later.' Zara was smiling. She felt good. When she had selected her pitch for the shot, she would feel better still.

They went in. Zara rejected the entrance foyer with its fine old stairway as unsuitable for her purpose. She had already half-decided, from the TV feature, that the famous old courtyard with its cobbled surface and entrance close to the old slave well offered the best opportunity.

They found their way to it, and joined a handful of sightseers examining the historic tombstones and plaques, and the reproduction of a five-centuries-old Portuguese navigation cross.

The history was lost on Zara. She stood under a big tree by the slave well and checked: the courtyard was overlooked by green-shuttered windows on all four sides. The well, which Pittock-Williams must pass, was a focal target point, but it was partially masked by foliage. The trees would obstruct her sighting: she wanted a clear, one-time killing shot.

Zara inclined her head and said in a low voice, 'That's the spot, Menty.'

The double door which debouched on to the courtyard from the inside via a short inner stairway (she knew this from the TV) was the exit by which the procession, led by Pittock-Williams in the uniform of a bygone Admiralty Marshal, would emerge first to public view. It would then file across the courtyard. Zara had no intention of letting him get as far as that.

Menty said, 'How close?'

'Keep your voice down!' warned Zara. 'We don't want any backlash later from anyone who may have seen us here.'

They moved back as nonchalantly as they could to stand by the big door, now shut.

Zara eyed the windows, both upper- and lower-storey.

'That's the one!' she said to Menty. 'That upper one, there in the corner.'

'There's nothing in the way!' added Menty.

'Let's get up there and see what it looks like on the spot,' interrupted Zara, who had begun to fear Menty's enthusiasm.

They hurried upstairs, paying no attention to the wealth of exhibits in the museum cases. Their guide-window was taking them to the Silver Gallery, which contained one of the finest collections of Cape Silver known.

As they hurried towards it past a full-size replica of a shop window, Menty gave a little gasp.

'Look, Zara! They could be alive, they're so lifelike!'

The dummy customers in the old-time apothecary's shop might have stepped living out of the past in their period costume. The full-scale shop itself, with genuine old fitments, coloured glass bottles and advertisements, was as lifelike as the dummies.

Zara paused a moment to look, and commented, 'There'll be enough period dress around in Pittock-Williams's procession without having to bother about any more here.'

They entered the gallery. They were as indifferent to its superb silver as the groups of tongue-tied onlookers were reverent.

Close to the entrance, on the apothecary-shop side,

was the window Zara had chosen from the courtyard.

Menty rushed to it.

'Take it easy,' cautioned Zara. 'We're supposed to be looking at silver.'

The old sash-type window was opened at the bottom and Menty leaned out. 'Zara! It's perfect! Look!'

Zara glanced round circumspectly and said, 'It gives a very narrow firing-angle, though. I'll have to be mighty quick, once I've got the pistol out of my handbag. Look, I'll take the door above the handle as my bull's-eye. If he stands there only for a moment, he's a goner. It won't be a full frontal shot, but side-on to the head.'

'And then?' asked Menty.

Zara indicated the entrance to the gallery. 'I beat it out there. There's bound to be a lot of confusion and milling around after the shot. I'll push my way through the crowd under cover of it.'

'But you'll still be inside the building,' Menty pointed out.

'Let's have another look-see.'

They went down the main stairway. Near the bottom, Menty spotted a small passageway leading off it, lit by several makeshift overhead electric lights. A notice read: 'Private. Staff toilets'.

'Where does it lead to? Or does it run dead?' asked Zara in a low voice. She was not to know that this was once the judges' private entrance from a small narrow side-street which divided the museum from the Houses of Parliament.

'If someone comes, just say we lost our way looking for a toilet,' said Zara.

Menty nodded. 'I could do with one, I'm so excited.'

They walked quickly past a quartet of toilets and a small storage place which was once a judge's robing-room. A small door, with a key in its lock, blocked their onward way.

'Quick – where does it lead?'

They turned the key, found themselves facing the quiet lane beyond.

Menty started forward, but Zara restrained her. 'The key – plasticine – we could need a duplicate on the day.'

Zara had brought along a wad of the stuff for just such a contingency. She took a hasty impression of the key, and restored it to the lock.

'We'll find a place for the car somewhere at the back,' she whispered. 'You'll be able to wait for me there. It's a backwater. There won't be parking problems.'

No judge ever slipped out of the private door with more of a fugitive's stealth than the two Rote Zora women.

Chapter 20

Rayner and Fenella stood together at the far end of the Silver Gallery. It was the exit furthest away from the apothecary's shop.

It was five days later.

They were waiting, along with hundreds of other invited guests, for the mock trial to begin. All windows and vantage points, both upstairs and downstairs, were packed as the crowd buzzed in anticipation of the court-yard door opening and the procession, headed by Pittock-Williams, emerging.

Pittock-Williams had chosen the day with the eye of a master self-publicist. It was a Friday before a long weekend holiday; it was to be a colourful preliminary to a relaxed break.

Between Rayner and Fenella, however, there was an undercurrent of tension, which would increase as the time drew nearer for Rayner's departure the following

Monday night for London to bring back the *Alabama* oar. Both knew it was a stumbling-block to their deeper relationship; it was too late now for either to do anything about it without a pride-sacrificing climbdown.

Rayner had seen little of the two Scotland Yard men, Hugh Perrot and Peter Imbrie. They had been in touch with London, but nothing fresh had emerged as to the identity of the mystery woman named Zara. The two detectives had been very occupied setting up security arrangements at Admiralty House for the Simonstown signing ceremony. Rayner had begun to have second thoughts that the person called Zara had indeed had anything to do with the Nelson's head bomb.

Pittock-Williams had been in frequent touch with Fenella about Admiralty Court procedure for the great day; neither she nor Rayner had passed on to him the muster book secret because of Fenella's deep and growing apprehension of ill-omen connected with the oars.

Zara also waited for the procession to begin. She had taken up her firing position at the end of the Silver Gallery, the opposite end to Rayner and Fenella's, at the window which she and Menty had selected overlooking the courtyard doorway.

Zara had had bad moments. The first had been when she had presented her fake invitation at the entrance. She and Menty had finally decided to omit a serial number from the card in case of duplication with a genuine guest. The door was not manned by police, as she thought it might be, but by civilians – women. She had held her card so that her fingers covered the spot where the number might have been expected to be stamped, and hoped against hope that VIPs had not been allocated designated window positions. A big map (seating?) had been spread out at an adjoining table. The crowd thronged the queue behind her, impatient to get in.

The woman gatekeeper glanced briefly at the name,

'Ms Z. White', and said, under pressure from the guests behind, 'You're far down the alphabet – the "Ws" have been put in the Silver Gallery. An usher will show you –'

Zara had managed a forced smile. 'No need, thanks. I know the museum well. I can find my own way.'

The checker looked grateful. Zara hurried at her best speed up the stairs. Past the apothecary's shop. Would her vantage window be occupied already? She had come extra early to avoid such a disaster.

The Silver Gallery crowd was streaming in. Her window was empty!

The next forty minutes were like forty years to Zara. No one addressed her; she seemed the only person on her own. Her handbag with the Glock and its silencer seemed to get heavier as the time dragged on.

Zara became more uptight as the crowd filled all the window spaces adjoining hers. Soon, someone must come to hers. Who would it be? For the moment would come – nearer and nearer now – when she would have to tug open her bag and draw the gun –

Mrs Stenner-Cartwright arrived with a camp stool, a middle-aged daughter in attendance and a social status which gave her immediate access to the best view from Zara's window. She had shouldered aside more formidable social opponents than an unknown woman standing at a window.

Zara saw an immediate advantage in the situation, and surrendered her place graciously. She had been afraid all along that she would be hemmed in at the rear and unable to escape. Now she could fire over Mrs Stenner-Cartwright's head and make an unimpeded break. It was unlikely that anyone would want the poor view that they would get from the back of the trio, plus the camp stool also obstructing access to the window.

There was a stir, a buzz, a hush from the crowd. The

courtyard door opened. A costumed trumpeter emerged, sounded a flourish. An announcer with a microphone followed (there were loudspeaker relays everywhere) and gave a brief sketch of the significance of silver oars in Admiralty Court proceedings. He also stated (what everybody knew) that there would be an exchange of silver oars at the Simonstown ceremony in just under a fortnight's time.

The trumpeter gave another resounding flourish. It was through the generosity of Professor Pittock-Williams that such an exchange had been possible, he proclaimed, since, legally, he was the owner of both oars; he would donate them to the two signatory countries, Britain and South Africa.

Zara bit her lip. The ego-massage made her sick. Let him come – quickly!

There was a further trumpet flourish. The big double door swung wide open. Zara tautened. Her moment of truth was at hand. The old lady craned forward on her stool, opera-glasses to her eyes, peering. Zara cautiously undid the clip of her handbag. Her hand closed on the cold butt of the Glock.

The gun was half out of her handbag when the first figure emerged.

It was not Pittock-Williams.

It was a man dressed up as a condemned pirate, complete with chains, on his way to execution. By time-honoured custom the condemned preceded the Marshal. It was as colourful a piece of stage-managing as anyone could hope for.

Then – with measured step, bearing the silver oar on his left shoulder (the side nearest Zara), Professor Pittock-Williams in period dress stepped into the lime-light and the cameras.

And into the firing angle.

The silencer's long barrel snagged on the lining of

Zara's handbag. It was only for a second. Zara tugged, got it free.

That brief moment when Pittock-Williams had paused like an actor waiting for the applause had been to Zara's advantage: it gave her time to sight the gun.

Pittock-Williams started forward into the courtyard. He began transferring the silver oar from his left to his right shoulder.

Zara held his head in her sights, fired.

Pittock-Williams spun round as the bullet took him. The oar went flying.

The sound of the muted shot did not carry far. Spectators at some of the windows across the courtyard from Zara scarcely heard it, even in the expectant silence which followed Pittock-Williams's emergence from the doorway.

Mrs Stenner-Cartwright levered herself round on her stool, in disbelief, shock and age-related non-reaction. Her daughter wrenched her eyes away from the figure writhing on the courtyard cobbles in deafened, stunned surprise. The shot had gone off close to her left ear.

How much she comprehended it was Zara who had fired it was anyone's guess. Like lightning, Zara had jammed the pistol into her handbag, snatched a handkerchief from it, clapped it against her mouth and lower face as if about to be violently sick, and reeled away in the direction of her getaway point.

The act was part of her escape strategy; the handkerchief served to conceal her face. The crowd parted from the gagging figure, obviously about to throw up.

The crowd remained paralysed for a brief moment, then all hell broke loose. No one recognized the faint plop as a shot, but the consequences were clear on the floor of the courtyard.

But the plop was recognized – and specifically identified – by one man.

Rayner, at the other end of the gallery, knew what a silenced Glock sounded like. Yet he had been told that his was the only Glock in the country.

Rayner gave Fenella an electrified glance, gestured down the gallery in the direction from which the sound had come. His view of Zara's window itself was obstructed by showcases full of silver, apart from the crowd, now terrified and fighting their way towards the exits.

Rayner went into them, shouldering, sidling, bullocking, like a Rugby maul.

He reached the apothecary's shop. There was no one around who looked like a would-be assassin. Beyond the old-time shop, he progressed faster down a long, wide passageway which ran the entire length of the building.

About halfway down this passage, there was a branch with a small set of stairs which made a double upward kink towards a locked door which had a notice: 'No entrance. Staff only'.

Rayner checked in his headlong rush to see if there was anyone suspicious trying to get out in a hurry.

A woman, alone, sank down on the small stairway landing as Rayner approached. Was she his suspect? Rayner covered the stairs two at a time.

Then – the woman was violently sick. She groped in her handbag for tissues, her lower face covered by a handkerchief.

Rayner tried the handle of the staff door. It was firmly locked on the inside. No chance that a suspect got away there.

He dodged past the kneeling woman, still gagging, back into the mainstream of the crowd, now funnelling through the big passageway towards the already thronged main entrance.

It was hopeless to try and get through. The flood had been stemmed by the closing of the main street doors.

He turned, shouldered his way back against the human

174

tide. There was no sign of the retching woman on the short stairway landing. He was about to pass on (he had asked Fenella to wait for him in the Silver Gallery) when his eye spotted a piece of paper at the place where the woman had been. He recalled her groping in her handbag. He edged himself clear of the crowd, made for the place.

The piece of paper was, in fact, an invitation card which had probably fallen out of her bag with the tissues. He rammed it into his pocket, and threw himself once again into the human maelstrom.

The TV cameras and media were having a field day. All lenses had been focused on Pittock-Williams's dramatic entrance. Now they were working overtime on the bloodied figure squirming on the cobbles in his comic-opera uniform. There was enough blood to satisfy the most rabid picture-editor. One thing was certain: Pittock-Williams was not dead – yet.

Zara was on a high. She slipped away from her pitch on the small stairway landing into the crowd – nobody paid any attention to her – and found herself carried away down the big main stairway in the direction of the entrance. Near its foot, she managed to insinuate herself off the main stairs into the small passageway which headed towards the judges' old private entrance. She and Menty had staked out the route; since there were no windows on this side, and moreover it was at the rear of the courtyard, there had been no onlookers.

She was now able to progress. She followed the arrow which read 'Private. Staff toilets' and found herself at the former robing-room and – beyond – the small door on the narrow lane between the building and Parliament.

There was no need of the duplicate key she and Menty had provided; the original hung in the lock.

She opened it cautiously, checked, slipped out into the lane. The baying of police and ambulance sirens from the main street entrance drowned the sound of her hurrying footsteps.

As she reached the far end of the lane, she saw a man in camouflage uniform moving away from Menty's car. Some half a dozen of his mates started off at a trot as he joined them, up the other side of the building towards the main entrance, which buzzed like a disturbed hornets' nest.

For a brief moment Zara hesitated. She heard Menty start the engine. She sprinted to the car, whipped open the door.

Menty was white-faced. 'No parking – he told me to move on – now!'

'Do as he says.'

'Did you get him?'

The question was redundant. Menty had never seen Zara look like this.

She laughed. 'Move! Churchhaven!'

Chapter 21

The nearest Rayner got to the Silver Gallery, the easier his progress became. By the time he reached the apothecary's shop, there were only knots of people instead of the solid phalanx further down the main passageway and stairs. The palpable air of panic amongst these groups seemed to have been supplanted by intense curiosity at the scene being enacted in the courtyard below.

Pittock-Williams lay in the centre of a police and first-aid cordon which had been thrown round the immediate area of the old slave well.

Loudspeakers were blaring. Appeals to the crowd to remain calm were interspersed with urgent requests for any doctor in the crowd to make his way to the scene of the shooting and assist. The crowd was warned that all exits to the building had been sealed off, and that in order to leave, all inside would have to produce their invitations or otherwise satisfactorily identify themselves before being allowed out.

There was also a police appeal for anyone who had seen the shot fired to report immediately to them.

Rayner stopped at the entrance to the apothecary's shop. Such a place could be an ideal lurking-place for the assassin. He checked, but the door was locked. There was nothing to be seen inside through the shop windows.

All Rayner's senses were keyed to concert pitch: he wondered about a light folding stool he saw standing by a window. He went to it, by a window overlooking the courtyard scene. As he reached it, ambulance men carrying a stretcher came trotting over the cobbles, and behind them paramedics carrying mobile drips and emergency resuscitation equipment.

Rayner did not wait to see Pittock-Williams being removed. As he stepped back from the window, his foot crunched on something. He picked it up.

It was a spent cartridge case.

Rayner smelt it. It had been newly fired. The stench of fresh cordite was unmistakable.

Unmistakable, too, to his trained eye, was the type of shell.

It was a Glock 17.

Rayner pocketed it, hurried to Fenella, whom he could see standing at their original position at the other end of the gallery.

'Fenella —' he pulled the shell from his pocket, explained hastily. 'Over there — where that camp stool is standing by the window. We must get downstairs and give this to the police. They're busy checking everyone.'

The time they spent getting through the crowd dove-

tailed their arrival almost to the second with that of Brigadier Keyter from the street outside.

Keyter was venting his anger on cowed subordinates.

'My oath!' he ground out. 'An elaborate security net
penetrated and a top VIP shot under your noses! Where
in hell were you all?' He swung on one unfortunate. 'Will
Pittock-Williams live?'

'They say so, sir. I haven't seen for myself –'

Rayner and Fenella reached Keyter's elbow un-
observed.

Rayner broke in on the silence surrounding the Security chief's outburst. 'He was moving when they brought
in the stretcher – that's a good sign.'

Keyter rounded on Rayner. 'You! What in hell are you
doing here?'

For a reply, Rayner held out his hand with the spent
shell in his palm.

A galvanic thrill passed through the group of security
men.

It was difficult for Keyter's tough face to make way
for much more ugliness and rage.

'Did you fire it?' he snarled. 'You're always at the
rock-face of trouble, aren't you, Watton? First the bomb,
now the killing!'

'He isn't dead.'

'You're always around when terrorists strike, it seems
to me.'

'I'll show you where I found it.' Rayner had trouble
in keeping his voice level. 'Smell it, it's just been fired.'

'Do you think I'm dumb?' he demanded. Nevertheless, he smelt it, and then snapped, 'Glock 17. You've
got the only Glock in the country that I know of. Where
is it? I want to check it.'

'At the Villa Montana.'

'It had better be, Watton!' he retorted unpleasantly.
'Take me to where you found this.'

Security men opened a way through the now silent crowd waiting on the stairway. Rayner felt like Pittock-Williams's pirate being led off to execution. Fenella walked silent at his side.

When they reached the Silver Gallery and Rayner had indicated the place by the stool, Keyter rapped out, 'Where'd this stool come from? Is it yours?'

'It isn't. Nor Fenella's.'

'Where were you at the time of the shooting?' Keyter went on.

'At the other end of the gallery. With Fenella.'

'Can you prove that?'

'Fenella will vouch for it.'

'I don't accept her word – she's a prejudiced witness. She'd say anything.'

'You can check at the door against our invitation.' Rayner suddenly remembered the other invitation he had picked up, also in his pocket. In the light of Keyter's attitude, he had no intention of revealing it, now.

Keyter told his men, 'I want everything, but everything, checked in here. Is that clear? Report anything right away to me. I'll be at the Villa Montana.' He addressed Rayner and Fenella: 'You're coming with me, right away. In a police car, not your own.'

They returned downstairs. As they approached the entrance door, there was a whirr of television cameras and men with shaggy hair and girls with short hair thrust microphones into the Security chief's face.

The questions could have been fired from a machine-pistol.

'Whom do you suspect?'

'Has anyone been arrested yet?'

'Have you got any strong leads?'

One of the girls eyed Rayner and Fenella. 'Why are these two with you, brigadier? They appeared on TV with Professor Pittock-Williams –'

'Mind your own business,' retorted Keyter. 'Don't try and sabotage delicate investigations.'

'Then you admit that investigations are at a critical stage?'

'I admit nothing,' snapped Keyter. 'Haven't you got enough dramatic footage without pushing your luck further today?'

'Brigadier,' said a girl in over-sweet tones. 'This broadcast is live.'

Keyter wheeled on Rayner and Fenella. 'Come.' He said to the cameramen, 'And don't try and follow me.'

To a media man, that is the biggest open invitation in the book.

Several transposed themselves somehow with their bulky equipment to the entrance as the main door was opened. The coverage of Rayner and Fenella being ushered into a police car with flashing roof-lights and a gawping crowd in the background was complete. The car's siren provided appropriate background music as it accelerated away.

At the Villa Montana, Rayner led Keyter and four other security men who had followed in a second car to his room, unlocked a drawer, and handed his Glock to Keyter.

Keyter still tried to brazen it out. 'Where is the ammunition? – this is not enough for me.'

Rayner produced a couple of boxes of shells, still with police seals on them.

Keyter glanced round the room, as if that would help him. He told Rayner, 'I want you to hold yourself available for further questioning at any time.'

'And my gun?'

Keyter sniffed at the barrel for the second time, as if his olfactory senses had missed some lingering trace of powder from his first inhalation.

'It will have to undergo exhaustive ballistic tests.'

Rayner was glad that Hugh Perrot's information-seeking call came a few minutes after Keyter and his squad had disappeared. There was no knowing what construction Keyter might have put upon it.

'Rayner! Peter and I saw you from the street being whipped off by Brigadier Keyter like a wanted felon! What gives, man?'

'It's a story of a Glock – two Glocks –' Rayner explained the situation.

'Why doesn't he stop wasting his time and do something constructive?' was all Hugh's response. 'Look, can Peter and I come round and have a drink with you and Fenella this evening? We can discuss it all better on an eyeball-to-eyeball basis.'

'I've got something to show you, too.'

Rayner could almost hear Hugh's mental machine go into overdrive.

'You have, eh? Good!'

'I'd like your opinion about it.'

'I can't wait. By the way, how is your victim?'

'My shooting's deteriorated, Hugh. I think I missed. It's bound to be on the lunch-time news.'

It was. Pittock-Williams himself could not have wished for better visual coverage.

The announcer said:

According to a hospital spokesman, Professor Pittock-Williams was not seriously wounded in the cowardly attack by an unknown gunman. The bullet grazed his left shoulder, causing a superficial flesh wound.

He is at present in hospital suffering from shock, and his wife Mildred is at his bedside. However, he is expected to be discharged from hospital in a day or two.

Meanwhile, an official spokesman has stated that

the police have a strong clue about the would-be assassin, and are following up several promising leads –

Chapter 22

At Churchhaven, the news they had been waiting for ever since their return to the lagoon stunned Zara and Menty when it came, and filled them with fear. What strong lead on the assassin were the police following up? The usual benign face of the lagoon looked troubled as it crumpled under the first thrust of a cold-weather bringing wind.

The bulletin also brought unease to Renate, having her usual shade-house sandwich lunch at her garden centre. Had Zara been somehow involved? she wondered. Some instinct told Renate, since Pittock-Williams had been the victim, that she had been. It was, however, impossible to confirm by phone since there were no phones at Churchhaven.

Instead, she spoke to Gemma, Rote Zora's fuse girl, to Rikki, the listening-post girl, and Kerry-Ann, the bomb-planter. They agreed that the finger pointed at Zara; they arranged to travel that afternoon after work to the lagoon, instead of waiting until next day, the original plan for the long weekend. Renate also warned the others about the police's 'strong lead' and that, if any of them should be approached, they were to keep their mouths shut.

Menty was last on Renate's phone list. Renate's anxiety was fuelled when her workplace said she was away for the day. Yet, Menty! Surely Zara wouldn't call on Menty!

But, against all the odds, Renate knew she had when

she saw Menty standing by Zara's door in the half-dark as her minibus containing the other girls pulled up that evening at Churchhaven.

Menty didn't greet the gang: she looked cowed and defiant.

It was Zara who immediately assumed centre stage as she called out with a kind of spurious bonhomie, 'Hallo, girls! What brings you all here? I thought you were only coming tomorrow for the long weekend.'

Renate jumped down from the driver's high seat and cut her short.

'You know that Pittock-Williams has been shot?'

'Yes.'

The circle of girls, their faces tense and strained, closed on Zara. Zara had merely been under the gang's whip previously over the effigy head; now her leadership itself was in the melting-pot. Menty made herself scarce on the outskirts with her usual adroitness.

Renate snapped, 'Did you have anything to do with it?'

Zara eyed the others. It was inevitable that her part would come out.

'I pulled the trigger.'

Renate grabbed Zara by the shoulder with a powerful hand and propelled her backwards into the lounge.

She said savagely, 'For the second time, you've acted on your own and put the black spot on all of us! What right had you to do it? You've got a hell of a lot of explaining to do, Zara, before we'll be satisfied about your leading the Rote Zora group and putting a noose round our necks for no damn reason at all!'

'I thought he was dead,' said Zara defensively.

'As if that explains everything! If you thought he was dead, it makes the danger all the worse for us! Now you've endangered all our lives and safety for the sake of a bum shot which only winged Pittock-Williams! In full sight of hundreds of people! Do you want to throw away our lives – and your own? What in hell are you playing at, Zara? We want to know!'

'I meant to kill him.'

'Instead, you shot him in the shoulder – merely grazed him – bah! I – we – ask ourselves, why?'

The question enabled Zara to try and divert the heat by a counterburst of anger on her part: 'You – all of you – ask me why? Because of what Pittock-Williams did to me as a woman!'

'We've heard all that crap before,' retorted Renate. 'What we want to know is whether your crazy attempt at revenge has put a rope round all our necks! That's what we're here for. Is the heat on the Rote Zora gang? You must have been spotted, in a crowd that size. The news said the shot was fired from an upper window. Is that so? Our necks are on the line! Why didn't you send him that effigy head in the first place instead of wasting your efforts on that security guy from London? He never did anything to you! Or, better still, you could have kept it among your souvenirs of a misspent youth.'

The crack touched Zara on the raw. 'Watch your mouth, Renate! It's only a few hours back that I had a man in my gun-sights. I don't want the next to be a woman.'

'Which means you brought the gun back here?'

Zara replied, 'The Glock.'

'Get rid of it, hide it, throw it in the sea, anything!' snapped Renate. 'It's key evidence against you, against us all. Now – did anyone see you fire the shot? How in hell did you get inside the building in the first place? How'd you get clear afterwards?'

Menty was still hanging round on the outskirts of the conversation. Renate demanded, 'You, Menty, what do you know about all this?'

Zara broke in. 'Menty faked an invitation for me, so

good that it beat all the checks. She drove me back here afterwards.'

'Which means that the two of you had worked out a plan, a very detailed plan, beforehand,' Renate went on accusingly. 'Days beforehand, I'd guess. But you didn't see fit to tell any other one of us. Talk about a dirty piece of double-dealing! Now the rest of us will have to take the rap.'

'There's no rap – yet,' replied Zara. 'Pittock-Williams is still alive. No one is wise to Menty and me.'

'Ever heard of a charge of attempted murder?' sneered Renate.

'I'll get you the invitation, just to show you how good it is,' said Zara.

Menty was grateful for the small crumb of consolation thrown her way.

Zara's bag lay on the table. She snapped it open. The Glock was there, with the silencer still in place.

'My oath, how careless can you be!' accused Renate. 'Lying there for everyone to see!'

'There's been no one all afternoon, except Menty and me.' She put the pistol on the table, rifled through her bag. A note of alarm came into her voice. 'Menty, did you take it? It was here.'

Renate went on sarcastically, 'Nothing like scattering clues everywhere for the benefit of the fuzz! And with your name on it, no doubt, just to make it easier for them!'

'Menty made it out to Ms Z. White, not Hennessy. It must be around here somewhere.' She tipped out the bag's contents. The others waited. Zara said unhappily, 'I know I put it back.'

'It's news-time,' said Gemma, taking the heat off Zara for the moment. 'Let's see what the latest is about Pittock-Williams.'

The latest was Pittock-Williams sitting up in a hospital

bed with his left shoulder heavily bandaged. The sight threw Zara.

'There's your dead victim,' jeered Renate. 'A graze wound in the shoulder. Out of hospital in a day or two. You'd better brush up on your assassination techniques for the future, Zara.'

The picture cut to a view of a police spokesman demonstrating the oar which Pittock-Williams had been carrying. He pointed to a score across the blade, and explained how the would-be killer's bullet had been deflected at the critical moment as Pittock-Williams had transferred it to his right shoulder, the correct side, according to protocol.

The picture cut back to the hospital, and the interviewer asked Pittock-Williams whether his role as mace-bearer at the Simonstown ceremony would now be out.

Pittock-Williams with a brave smile assured him that he certainly would not be deterred from fulfilling his honoured and traditional part as Marshal, in spite of his wound.

The police spokesman added that security precautions at the ceremony would be of the tightest, and repeated that the police were actively following up strong leads in regard to the mock trial shooting.

Zara sat silent, staring at the TV screen, as if mesmerized by the sight of Pittock-Williams alive.

Renate's anger and bitterness reflected the gang's fear and anxiety as well as her own.

'Thinking of when you'll get another crack at your lover-boy?' she taunted Zara. 'If you couldn't shoot straight when you had the chance, you'd better forget it, quickly. You heard about the security. You won't get a second chance.'

Zara continued to stare riveted at the TV screen, although it had passed on to the next news item. Then she said, half to herself, 'I'll make a second chance.'

Chapter 23

'Forget it –!' began Renate.

But Zara jumped to her feet, snapped off the TV, and stood facing the accusing circle. Her eyes, which seemed to have fallen back in their sockets and become totally inscrutable during her transfixed stare at the screen, were now prominent and blazing. Here was the fire and charisma which had knitted together the miscellaneous group of women in the first place and led them to follow her own feminist terror ideal. Those qualities had now been given a terrible new dimension by her craving for revenge.

She asked, rhetorically, 'When, you ask, will I get another chance for a crack at Pittock-Williams?'

'First get rid of that bloody murder weapon.' Renate started to gesture at the Glock lying on the table.

But Zara cut her short.

'Where,' she demanded slowly, eyeing each one of the women in turn, 'is that silver oar being kept until the signing ceremony?'

'You'd know, better than any of us,' retorted Renate, who continued her previous tone of confrontation, although she was puzzled by Zara, who seemed to have slipped the noose of being the accused and instead had become the improviser and innovator.

'I expect Pittock-Williams's home has all kinds of fancy gadgets to protect the family heirlooms –'

'Zara was too busy with the other family heirlooms when she was sleeping there to bother much about the security system,' sneered Rikki.

Zara did not, surprisingly, rise to the jibe, but said

rather reminiscently, 'I had the key to immobilize the system – once.'

'What happened to it?'

'I threw it in his face.'

'It must have been a cosy set-up, you switching off the system and wifey –' Rikki went on.

'Shut up!' said Zara, but it lacked heat. 'That's in the past. I'm living in the present, and the future.' She eyed the others acutely. 'A bomb's the thing. The signing ceremony's the thing. It would make our name, Rote Zora's name, ring round the world. We – all of us here – would be remembered, for ever.'

Zara's words were so compulsive that Renate had half-fallen under their spell. Only half.

'What are you talking about? One moment you're wanting to shoot Pittock-Williams, and the next you're bullshitting about a silver oar.'

'Listen, listen all of you!' retorted Zara, talking rapidly, articulately. 'We can kill two birds with one stone, this way, my way, this new way. My bird, Pittock-Williams. We'll also register the protest of all the world's women against this glorification and entrench-ment of male aggression with the reinstatement of the Simonstown agreement. Navy, Nelson – bah! That's why I took his head in the first place! This will show the world that Rote Zora's not bluffing!'

'Say what you are trying to say in simple, one-syllable words so that we all can understand,' said Renate.

'In under two weeks from now,' Zara went on, 'the British Prime Minister and the South African President will sign the new Simonstown agreement. We've been told that to mark the occasion, two silver oars are to be exchanged, not so?'

'It's been all over the news,' interrupted Renate.

'What if,' continued Zara, 'what if one of the silver oars exploded in their faces as it was handed over?'

'Go on, Zara.'

The gang was listening now, half-captivated, but under Zara's spell. All but Menty, who was sitting (the others all stood) biting her nails and looking like a kicked mongrel.

'Semtex,' Zara replied. 'That is what it is all about. What if the shaft of one of the oars was filled with moulded plastic explosive and detonated as the handing-over took place? Bye-bye Pittock-Williams, bye-bye Prime Minister, bye-bye President.'

'This is crazy – we'd never get away with it!' exclaimed Renate.

'You can imagine what kind of security screen is going to be thrown around the VIPs for a ceremony like that,' interrupted Rikki. 'You won't be able to get near!'

'We don't need to be near – remote control trigger,' replied Zara.

Gemma, the gang's fuse expert, came in on the discussion.

'Aw, shit! Remote control! Talk about old hat! Those security boys are so clued up that you couldn't get anywhere close enough to be effective with a radio transmitter, even if you managed the bomb, although God knows how you'd manage that – silver oar, you say?'

'Yeah. That's the principle.'

'The principle is fantasy and the logistics – impossible,' retorted Gemma.

'The principle is sound,' replied Zara. 'We – you – can lick the logistics.'

Gemma laughed. 'It's like stuffing, the principle's easy, but the practice is consummately difficult.'

Her remark about sex rattled Zara. She tried to keep her voice steady and muster her argument.

'Pittock-Williams is to act as Marshal at the signing ceremony and carry the oar we've just seen on TV,' continued Zara. 'Also, there's the Marshal's ivory baton, it's part of the silver oar. They fit together somehow –

'*I've got it!* When he takes them apart, our bomb goes off, detonated by a self-activating fuse!'

Zara's idea was so way-out that the gang latched on to it as an amusement and relief to the tense accusing air which had prevailed.

Rikki broke in, 'I love bed-time stories and, by heavens, this is one! Little Rote Zora, our patron, would adore it! The fuse is self-activating at the wave of a wand, the hollow shaft of the silver oar is stuffed with Semtex – if the shaft isn't hollow, you make it so, for the sake of your story! Sheer imagination! And you expect us all to risk our necks, for the sake of it!'

Gemma said, 'A trembler fuse would be easy enough, it's an old IRA trick. It could be activated by the oar and the baton being taken apart, as Zara says. A trembler is as sensitive as hell. You only have to blow on it and up it goes.'

'There you are,' said Zara. 'If you really put your mind to a thing, you can always come up with an answer.'

'You don't know whether the oar's shaft is hollow or solid,' pointed out Renate. 'We don't know anything about it, in fact.'

Zara thought she detected a slight softening of Renate's attitude, and she continued.

'Another big loose end is how to prime it, even if you assume the rest is really a practical proposition. 'The oar is going to be so closely guarded –'

'What about the other oar, the one from London?' interrupted Kerry-Ann. 'The papers said, a special security team has been detailed to bring it to South Africa next week.'

'Security, beating the odds, that is what our game is all about,' said Renate. Her tone was changing. She had come to Churchhaven to accuse; she might stay to detonate.

'Look at the mock trial affair,' she continued. Zara stiffened. Menty did not look up. 'Look at the security odds there, but you licked 'em and got inside.'

'Thanks to Menty,' added Zara. Menty, however, seemed immune to praise; some deep-seated inferiority complex was tearing her apart inside. Outside, it was chewing her nails to shreds.

The gang left Menty to her complexes.

'Like Zara says, this could be the big one, the big one for us girls, the big one for Rote Zora. Even Rote Zora in Germany never pulled off one like this,' said Renate.

'Are you selling Zara's idea for her?' asked Kerry-Ann in her nursery-teacher voice. 'What about the rest of us? If it's going to be a deal, it includes all of us.'

Renate said, unexpectedly, 'You all know I rated the Nelson's head job as tops. I've also told you what I think of this bungled shot at Pittock-Williams. It may yet sink us all. But what if it doesn't? Are we just going to sit around and hope we get away with it? Or are we going to do something else, while we've got the opportunity? I enjoy a touch of flair. I need something more in my life than plants and seeds.'

'Stimulus,' chipped in Rikki. 'A man.'

'You stand all day behind a hotel reception desk and smile – and smile – at the passing crowd,' went on Renate. 'It's your defence mechanism, Rikki. I'd like to know against what.'

Rikki coloured and retorted, 'Bugger you, Renate.'

'That's what I say to myself,' Renate responded with an ironic grin. 'What I'm trying to say is that Zara's idea switches me on. I haven't an idea whether it's feasible or workable or not. But let's all go along with it, just for the hell of it to start with, anyway. If it doesn't work, or can't work, too bad. We will have had some fun meanwhile kicking the ball around.'

Zara followed up the breakthrough. 'Rikki?'

Rikki smiled her easy professional smile. 'What the hell!'

'Gemma?'

'Fuses are my fun. I like 'em. Maybe I can work out something, even if it's only on paper.'

'Kerry-Ann?'

'It'll pass a long wet weekend.'

'Menty?'

She replied in a hurt schoolgirl voice, 'It doesn't sound as if there's any place for me.' She went back to her nails.

Zara said briskly, 'First, we've got to know what the drill is for the signing ceremony, how exactly Pittock-Williams fits into his key role. He must be close enough to the heads of government for the bomb to kill them all.'

'Jeez, what a stink it will cause!' exclaimed Renate.

'Second, we need to know where the silver oar or oars will be kept beforehand so that we can prime 'em,' went on Zara.

'Both?' asked Gemma in surprise.

'We don't know at this stage,' replied Zara.

'The bedtime-story stage for our patroness Rote Zora,' mocked Kerry-Ann. 'The fantasy stage, no less.'

Zara ignored her. 'Third, we need accurate, first-hand information about the design and construction of the silver oar.'

'Without that, this whole exercise could become a damn dangerous kid's story, which could cost one of us a security bullet in the guts,' said Renate.

'Spare my ovaries – don't shoot below the waterline,' jeered Rikki. Her tone showed how seriously she took the plan.

'Accurate, first-hand information about the oar,' brooded Zara. 'Where to find that?'

She had the answer for the gang at breakfast next morning.

'Kidnap the girl we saw on TV – the silver expert from Christie's.'

Chapter 24

'I like a good laugh with my breakfast. It helps the digestion,' said Rikki with her non-giveaway professional smile. Her wide grey eyes equally revealed nothing.

Kerry-Ann's overloud crunch on her toast was a good substitute for a raspberry.

But Gemma – had she been dreaming of becoming a kind of feminine Gilbert McNamee, the convicted IRA master-bomber? – put down her cutlery with a clatter and jutted out her too-big nose.

'With what specifically in mind, Zara?'

Zara eyed the group. Her proposition was aimed to shock acquiescence from the gang: would it, or would they simply shrug it off? Each one of them had a character quirk, an unaccountable weakness somewhere, and there was no knowing which way the cat would jump. That is what bonded them into Rote Zora.

'I said last night, we need accurate, first hand information about the construction of the silver oar.'

'A feasibility study, in other words?' asked Gemma.

'That's it, Gemma. Some of you –' she singled out Kerry-Ann with her glance '– said last night the whole idea was a dream. All I'm suggesting is that we test whether it is just that, or worth following up.'

Zara did not know whether the idea had sparked Renate's love of panache, the sudden strike and quick get-out, when she asked:

'A kidnap seems a hell of a risk. You can't go back on

it if it doesn't work and say to your victim, thanks, lassie, but we don't need you any more. It's a serious crime, you know that?'

'I'm not suggesting we kidnap the girl immediately: what I propose is nothing beyond a recce of the place where she lives, the Villa Montana, to see whether a snatch is feasible. It'll provide a little excitement, even if it doesn't come to anything.'

Renate gestured beyond the big glass door. It was a cold, overcast day with intermittent showers which from time to time blanked out the lagoon and turned it into a grey, uninviting blanket.

'I could do with something to zap me out of the prospect of sitting here all the holiday weekend playing cards. This place is a dead loss when you can't swim and sunbathe.'

She might have included Menty in her definition of dead loss. She was silent and hangdog, as if Zara's shooting failure could be laid at her door. The others ignored her.

'Why stake out this villa place? There are other ways of getting our hands on her,' said Kerry-Ann.

Zara smiled to herself. The girls were taking the bait. It could become a serious proposition, not merely a diversionary lark.

'Such as?'

'A fake phone call to her at Christie's saying that guy Rayner Watton wanted to see her at a particular place –'

'I mean to leave Watton out of it,' interrupted Zara. 'I told you how he came storming past me on the stairs after the shooting. He could remember my face, although half of it was hidden in my handkerchief. I think he's smart.'

'Before I could think of priming an unknown object like a silver oar, there's a great deal of technical detail I'd have to know first,' said Gemma.

'That's exactly why I am proposing we get hold of the fountainhead itself,' replied Zara.

A spatter of rain lashed against the big glass door.

'When?' asked Rikki, who with Kerry-Ann remained lukewarm.

'No time like the present. Tonight.'

'The whole crowd of us can't go along. We'd be falling over each other,' objected Kerry-Ann.

Renate eyed her big hands, as if recalling what they had done to the *Medusa* figurehead.

'I'll go with Zara – just the two of us.'

They went, that evening.

It was the perfect night for a stakeout: a strengthening north-wester which made the stone pines round the Villa Montana creak and groan, and a cold, thin, driving rain which would keep most honest citizens indoors. Zara wore the same black leather biker's suit which she had done for the Abbey break-in ('It brought me good luck then, it will bring me luck again'); Renate had on jeans and a waterproof anorak. Both women wore ankle-hugging sneakers.

Zara avoided the downhill side entrance to the Villa Montana where she had left the hatbox bomb; instead, she parked her car round the corner by the villa's main entrance where the road was not so steep. From there they could keep watch on the house.

The villa was clearly occupied; the lights were on, and there were two cars in the back-door parking area.

The rain dripped down.

Their vigil and the blackness were broken momentarily when an ambulance, with rooftop lights flashing, went past their car and headed down the hill for the hospital only a block and a half away.

'See the "Metro" sign on the side?' asked Renate.

'What makes it different from other ambulances?'

asked Zara. It provided a minor topic of conversation in what promised to be a long, long watch.

'It's specially equipped for rescuing mountain-climbing casualties,' explained Renate, a climber herself. 'I saw one of them operating once on the mountain – special lightweight stretchers to which they strap casualties to carry 'em down the slopes, ropes, drips, paramedics – everything that opens and shuts.'

'Let's just recheck our own gear for tonight,' said Zara.

Renate produced a small jemmy, a pair of insulated, wire-cutting pliers, and a multiple-bladed screwdriver. Zara had the same commando knife she had used to cut off Nelson's head in the Abbey. Both also had flashlights.

At Churchhaven, Zara had wondered whether she should bring the Glock, but the vote was against it; the gang regarded the night's outing more as an escapade than a serious undertaking.

'Look!' exclaimed Renate under her breath.

The villa's front lights went off; a shaft of light showed a door opening; one of the cars, headlights on, pulled out of the parking area and went down the hill.

Zara was grinning. 'Couldn't be better! They could have gone off together for dinner. Let's go!'

The curtain of rain was perfect cover. They slipped into the villa's grounds from the swimming-pool side (the opposite side from where Zara had dumped the hatbox) where the place was all flower-beds and trees. Close by the house, Renate indicated a notice nailed to a tree. It read: 'Protected by Roving Eye alarm systems'.

Renate gave a grin and made a thumbs-down sign. She nevertheless remained cautious, taking the lead from Zara, and where the patio side of the villa opened on to the pool area, she pointed out the alarm wires to Zara. Her derisive grin said, easy!

They went on: a little further, towards the front of the house, Renate pointed out in dumb show a natural fea-

ture of the house which fitted the job she had in mind –
a small wrought-iron balcony, roofed over by a sloping
continuation of the main roof (clearly an afterthought)
and, fixed to the side wall next to it, a complex of
water- and drainpipes serving several bathrooms on the
villa's top floor. The different pipes had been joined
together to one big central down-pipe, for easy servicing.

Almost overhanging the balcony (it dipped now in the
strong wind) was a big branch from the twenty-metre
stone pine overlooking the pool.

Renate indicated the pipe complex – up! It hardly
needed a mountaineer's skill to shin up such a burglar's
delight.

Renate led, Zara followed, up and over the balcony
rail. Facing them was a big glass sliding door, heavily
curtained on the inside.

Renate was as derisive about the villa's security system
as Rayner was. A quick check showed no electric sensors
here; she thought they must be confined to downstairs.
Forcing the lock with a fine screwdriver was a moment's
work for Renate.

Behind the floor-length drawn curtains was a bedroom,
a woman's bedroom: toiletries on the dressing-table, the
clothes, and the pretty pillows on the bed.

The door leading from the room to the stairhead landing was open; light coming in from it saved the intruders
having to resort to their torches.

The young clothes in the wardrobe told Renate and
Zara that this was Fenella's bedroom suite; a door gave
on to the bathroom. Near to the balcony sliding door was
a big three-quarter bed with candy-pink pillow slips and
sheets. Sitting up against its wooden bedhead, Fenella
could look out on the impressive bulk of Lion's Head
immediately on her left and, beyond, Signal Hill.

Zara gave the thumbs-up signal; they went on to
explore the rest of the house.

Two more bedrooms led off the stairhead landing, facing the front of the house. They were not in use. There was also another bathroom whose pipes linked with Fenella's to provide the ladder used by the Rote Zora women.

Where was Rayner housed? Zara asked in dumb show. Clearly not in this area.

They tried the remaining doorway on the floor. It was flanked by two absurd half-size kneeling ceramic camels, in sharp contrast to the valuable *objets d'art* in cabinets, and magnificent Persian carpets hanging on the walls flanking the stairway to the bottom.

It was Fenella's Rommel Room, clearly in use, but not as a bedroom for Rayner. If there was to be an attempted break-in, both women recognized Rayner as the main danger.

They sneaked downstairs. Renate warned Zara to walk carefully and keep to the side of the stair treads in case there was an alarm pressure plate hidden under the carpet. Nothing happened.

They found more rooms on the ground floor, including a beautifully furnished lounge, and a small bedroom clearly occupied. A quick search revealed men's clothing. That the room was Rayner's was borne out by his name on a suitcase tag.

Zara signalled Renate. They had found out all they had come to discover; they would not push their luck any more with the obsolescent alarm by attempting to penetrate further.

They returned via Fenella's room. Zara lingered before they went down, studying the balcony railing and the branch overhanging it.

Then – down the wall pipes, through the garden, and back to their car.

It was after midnight when they got back to Church-haven. The gang (all except Menty) were waiting agog for news, and had hot coffee and sandwiches ready against the cold and the rain.

Zara was triumphant.

'This is how we'll do it –'

Chapter 25

The barometer fell both outside and inside the Villa Montana all weekend.

The initial drop paralleled the weather's on Friday evening when the two Scotland Yard men, Hugh Perrot and Peter Imbrie, arrived for drinks, full of curiosity about the Pittock-Williams shooting.

Rayner explained about a Glock pistol having been used in the assassination attempt and how, after he had taken the spent shell to Brigadier Keyter, the Security chief had become suspicious of him, and had returned to the Villa Montana to confiscate his own Glock 'for ballistic tests', despite the fact that it was clear it had not been fired.

'Here's something more to show you,' went on Rayner. He produced the faked invitation card. 'After Keyter's attitude, I felt it wiser to keep mum about it.'

'Where'd you get this?' demanded Imbrie, turning it over (he himself was an expert on handwriting and counterfeiting).

'There was a woman throwing up on the stairs –' Rayner explained.

'Have you got a magnifying glass?'

Fenella, who had remained silent, nodded and fetched one.

Imbrie examined it closely. 'This is a fake, a very clever bit of faking,' he said slowly. 'Also, it hasn't a serial number. Surely all the invitations were numbered?'

'Ours was, but whether they all were, I don't know. I haven't had any opportunity to follow it up.'

'It's the "Z" of the initial which takes me to town,' interrupted Hugh. 'It could be a pointer to the bomb trainee we know of in Germany. If it's the same, we're getting into very deep waters. What did this woman you saw vomiting look like, the one who must have dropped the card?'

'Difficult to say,' replied Rayner. 'She had a handkerchief over her face. But it seemed that her hair was kind of coppery.'

'Kind of coppery,' repeated Hugh. 'That's what the guy on the beat said about the woman's hair he saw near the Abbey that night.'

'It thickens,' said Imbrie with a grin. Both men were excited.

'Listen,' said Hugh. 'I'll be sorry to cut this little get-together short, but I'm going to get on to the Anti-Terrorist Squad right away by phone. It's now become urgent, urgent. I'll have them double-check all the "Zs" on their files. I'm beginning to have a feeling that her identity may point to an international terrorist lurking in the wings in readiness for the Simonstown ceremony.'

'Go for it, Hugh!' exclaimed Rayner enthusiastically. 'Can I also ask something else – I haven't any status to make such a request – but what about the Yard asking the organizers of the mock trial to check their invitation list? It might give us a further clue to who "Z" is.'

'What about Brigadier Keyter?' asked Imbrie.

'I think we'll bypass him for the moment, until we have some really solid fact to go on,' replied Hugh.

Fenella had remained very silent during the exchange between the Yard men and Rayner, but now she broke in strongly, but with an air of restraint.

'Why should an international terrorist, if this is what you think it is, want in the first place to kill Rayner with

200

a bomb? And, second, why Pittock-Williams? Rayner has no part in the Simonstown ceremony, although the professor has, a key role. But why, in any event, single him out? He will only be the Marshal, he's not one of the principal VIPs. If he had been killed today, what difference would it have made to the Simonstown ceremony?'

'It could be terror tactics, to force the ceremony to be called off by accounting for one of the pawns and leaving the king and queen alone at this stage,' answered Hugh. 'Pittock-Williams was a soft target at the mock trial.'

'But why Rayner?' repeated Fenella. She said, fear in every word, '*Unless* they know – somehow – that he is bringing the *Alabama* oar back next week. The security smokescreen, the decoy story, could have been penetrated.'

'I don't see how,' said Hugh. 'There's a great deal of sorting out to be done before we have the answers. Meanwhile, I foresee great difficulties in trying to get a check on the mock trial invitation list in the next couple of days. It's a long holiday weekend, remember. But in London, the Anti-Terrorist Squad never sleeps. Rayner, when I speak to them right away, I am going to request permission for you to visit the Yard next Tuesday when you arrive in London. By that time, I feel sure more light will have been shed on the identity of the mysterious "Z". Even if we only set the wheels in motion tonight.'

Fenella said, 'You're welcome to use the villa's phone.'

Hugh smiled and shook his head. 'Thanks all the same, but who knows who might be tapping it? Maybe Keyter's men, maybe even "Z" herself.'

They went.

Then Fenella said, 'Rayner, that warning of Hugh's about the phone – it all adds to my sense of being watched and followed. It makes my foreboding worse.'

'You're reading things into the situation, Fenella. Nothing is going to happen to me.'

'Rayner!' she went on, a note of desperation in her voice. 'I feel, as I did over my break-up over Wayne, that I am being compelled – inexorably – by unknown forces into a no-win situation, in which there's more trauma and heartbreak waiting for me. Then it was heartbreak and death. Now it is something which will snatch away someone who is special to me.'

She turned away so that he could not see her eyes. She realized she had almost given away the fact that she was in love with him.

She resumed, keeping her voice as level as she could. 'Your previous security role has ballooned into something quite different and more sinister. You're now involved in international terrorism. They've already shown their hand and tried to kill you. Next time you won't be so lucky. This single-handed courier business –' she made a throwaway gesture with one hand '– you're a sitting duck. I'm sure they're watching every move you make.'

'This is a superheated view of things –' he began, but she went on passionately.

'These unknown forces are closing a stranglehold round my throat. I could run away from it all! I am being squeezed by forces beyond my control. Escape seems the only way out.'

On Monday, Rayner was to remember her words.

Now, he said placatingly, 'Once I've safely brought the *Alabama* oar to Cape Town, my job will be done.'

'It won't be!' exclaimed Fenella. 'You'll be drawn into tracking down more facts about this mystery woman "Z" along with Scotland Yard! It's in your blood. I now bitterly regret having gone to London and set the wheels in motion which will only bring me – and you – grief and unhappiness. The situation is rapidly getting out of control. I was involved at the start, now you all are, and I am left standing on the sidelines.'

Not the sidelines, Fenella. You are slap in the target area.

Their last Rommel Room party on Sunday night was not a success; the magic seemed to have gone out of it. By tacit consent, they broke it up, and went early to bed.

Outside, in the streaming night, Rote Zora stood poised, waiting, watching.

Chapter 26

It was about nine o'clock.

The plan to kidnap Fenella was in train.

The whole Rote Zora gang (except Menty) was taking part. She had been left behind at Churchhaven; the gang could not make out what was bugging her. Ever since Zara had expounded her plan regarding the silver oars at the Simonstown ceremony, Menty had lapsed into near-autistic impenetrability and had retreated completely into her shell – some shell!

Zara and Renate occupied one car, and the other three – Gemma, Rikki and Kerry-Ann – another. The two vehicles were parked apart, Zara and Renate in the street fronting the villa, and the others in the roadway flanking it, the 'hatbox' side.

At a pre-determined signal, the three would start off on their part of the mission. When they returned, Zara and Renate would go for the kidnap proper.

The Rote Zora vigil began.

Surprisingly early, about nine o'clock, Zara and Renate spotted the villa's main lights going out. However, this was followed by the upstairs light above the swimming pool going on (they recognized this as

Fenella's) as well as Rayner's downstairs light, which they could also identify.

It took nearly an hour before Fenella's light went out; Rayner's in turn disappeared about half an hour afterwards.

The kidnap was on!

Renate slipped out to the second car. She said tightly to the trio in it, 'OK! You're on your way!'

This car, driven by Gemma, headed down the S-bend hill towards the hospital. Would they find the Metro ambulance in the parking bay where Zara said it would be? Would there be anyone around? Would the whole kidnap plan abort right at the start?

The Metro ambulance was the kingpin.

Rikki, the hotel receptionist, had the task of forcing the ambulance's door and starting it, without keys, if necessary. At Churchhaven, there had been wisecracks about Rikki's lock-picking talent, that she had picked so many hotel room locks that it was second nature to her. She could start a car in less than two minutes flat.

The girls' car pulled into the hospital forecourt. Because of the weather, there was no one around, although lights were blazing behind closed doors.

The Metro ambulance was parked in its special place on the far side of the building.

Gemma made for it. As the car pulled up, Rikki jumped out, went for the ambulance door. Gemma swapped places with Kerry-Ann, who would follow the ambulance (they hoped) back to Zara and Renate.

Gemma quickly joined Rikki. The locked door swung open. To their surprise, the vehicle's ignition keys were in place, ready for an emergency call.

Gemma fired the engine, edged forward as quietly as she could. It was only a short distance to pick up the downhill slope again. As soon as they reached it, she cut the engine. The ambulance slid like a ghost through the night. Kerry-Ann followed.

There seemed to be no pursuit from the hospital. When she judged that they were well clear, Gemma restarted the engine.

There was an agonizing moment when she fumbled with the unfamiliar controls and set the flashing lights on the ambulance roof in action.

'Jeez,' exclaimed Rikki, 'all we're short of now is the siren!'

Gemma managed to kill the offending lights, and circled several blocks back to where Zara and Renate were gnawing their nails in anxiety. The ambulance suddenly appeared ghost-like and pulled over to Zara's side of the road.

The gang wasted no time in words. A key on the ambulance ring opened the rear doors; they piled in, just as Kerry-Ann drew up in the getaway car.

Zara knew what she was looking for, a lightweight aluminium stretcher, with straps to hold down a casualty. It took only a moment to slide it off its runners. One girl could easily manage it, it was so light and compact.

Zara also grabbed a roll of broad adhesive bandage from a shelf.

'Got the ropes?' she fired at Renate. 'OK! Then we're on our way!'

Zara carried the stretcher, Renate the ropes. They made their way to the foot of the balcony. There was no sign of movement beyond Fenella's glass door. From now on, it would be all hand signals, no words.

Renate slung the nylon rope coiled round her shoulders like a mountaineer; Zara started upwards, leading. The weight of the stretcher was not a factor, but she had barely begun when one of the aluminium runners clinked against a down-pipe.

They froze.

An unaccustomed sound like that, soft though it was, could disturb a sleeper – how fast asleep was Fenella above?

At the thought, Zara shifted the Glock deeper into her waistband. She did not want another metallic noise.

Zara and Renate remained clinging to the pipes, hard against the wall. It was a highly vulnerable position: someone passing in the street, or the fleeting illumination of a car's headlights, might expose their black figures against the white wall.

Zara waited until she thought the coast was clear, then pushed upwards, careful to keep the aluminium runners well clear of the pipes.

She was equally careful as she swung a leg over the wrought-iron balcony rail, then froze for the second time.

Fenella's door was open – about half a metre!

Renate could not see what had stopped Zara in her tracks. She waited, seemingly for another eternity. When finally her face got level with the bottom of the balcony rail, Zara indicated in dumb show: the door was open!

Renate came over the rail with her rope on a wash of creaks and groans from the stone pine branch in the wind.

Zara laid down the stretcher on the balcony floor, slipped out the Glock, and signalled Renate to be ready with the adhesive bandage which she had passed to her, and then the rope.

She gave a further hand signal, eased herself through the open door (obviously left open for ventilation) and threw herself at the figure in the bed.

She went for the head, the mouth, and the ear. She knew at the first tingling touch it was Fenella. Her left hand clamped across the mouth, the right rammed the Glock against Fenella's left ear; Renate was on top of the sleeping girl from the other side and pinioned her to the bed by sprawling across her.

Fenella tried by reflex to shake her head free of Zara's palm around her mouth, and thrash herself loose with her legs and lower body from Renate's weight. She emitted a strangled, terrified gurgle; her eyes, even in the almost non-existent light, were wide, staring, terror-struck.

It flashed through Zara's mind – she smells warm and sleepy and all woman! The thought, like a goad, tightened her finger muscles like a tourniquet round the mouth trying to bite at her hand. She rammed the dark head back into the pillow.

Fenella tried to kick free, but Renate altered her sprawl so that her weight rested across Fenella's lower body like a clumsy lover.

Zara gripped in her teeth one end of the adhesive roll which Renate had presented to her as Renate herself slackened her grip on Fenella's shoulders with one hand to help reel it out for a gag.

Fenella squirmed aside at the loosening pressure, but the two Rote Zora women were too quick. In a split second, a strip of tape had been clamped across her mouth, silencing her. Zara whipped out her commando knife, cut the gag free of the main roll.

Fenella's free legs were still a hazard. While she could use them a lucky kick might change the situation.

'The rope!' Zara had spoken. For the first time the thought crashed home to Fenella that she was being attacked not by men but by women.

Renate was back in an instant.

'Legs!' snapped Zara. Her grip was starting to slip from the perspiration of Fenella's body.

She snatched back the blankets. Fenella's pyjama pants had been pulled down to her knees by her struggles. Zara saw the smooth white length of her belly and the dark patch in her crotch. Smooth, white, desirable. Her own belly was a criss-cross of cobbled purplish skin from surgical cuts and craters.

Fenella tried to haul herself up into a sitting position to hide her nakedness; Zara held her down; Renate pulled up her pants, secured one flailing leg, and followed it up with the second.

Together they turned Fenella face-down with her arms behind her back and secured her wrists with more rope.

Fenella was making a choking noise as she fought for breath. Renate went quickly to the inner door and closed it carefully. Rayner could be awake downstairs.

'Next!' ordered Zara.

Renate followed a well-rehearsed pattern, opened the balcony door a little further, and brought in the Metro stretcher. They laid it transversely across the bed – Fenella was too trussed to offer any real resistance – and put Fenella on it, face-down. She could not be carried with her arms behind her back. Once they had untied the stretcher straps, they would take care of them.

To keep Fenella passive, Zara held up the Glock threateningly for her to see, and shone the flashlight for a moment on it.

The light caught Fenella's eyes. Zara cursed herself. Remember the first adage of terrorist torture, never look into their eyes!

She held up a hand to Renate – wait!

She went to Fenella's dressing-table, snapped open a couple of drawers, and then found what she was looking for. A scarf, to serve as a blindfold. Fenella was plunged into darkness as the silk went round her eyes.

Zara said, 'Clothes!'

Fenella heard the wardrobe door being opened, there was a pause, then the ropes round her ankles were eased while a pair of what she recognized as her own warm trousers were slipped on. A warm shirt came next, then a jersey. They were warm; what was cold was the muzzle of the Glock thrust against her head by one of the attackers. The other did the dressing.

She was forced into a lying position again on something – she could not identify it as a stretcher – and strapped to it.

There was another pause. She could not know that Zara and Renate were searching for warm socks, shoes, and something to keep out the rain. But enlightenment came when the socks were dragged on, and a pair of sneakers. A waterproof anorak, reversed, was put over her upper body.

The stretcher was picked up, and she felt the cold rain in her face as they carried her out on to the balcony.

Renate had coached Zara how to sway a limp body down a cliff-face and, by the same token, the nylon rope was threaded through the stretcher's runners with a guide-rope at Fenella's feet. Zara and Renate fed the stretcher, feet first, over the balcony rail, like a sea burial over a ship's rail.

Using the rail as a kind of block-and-tackle, Zara eased their burden earthwards while Renate clambered over and steered it clear of the down-pipes.

Finally, Zara too threw a leg over the balcony and joined Renate on the ground.

'Keep to the pathways – no footprints!' snapped Zara.

Carrying the stretcher, they went at a brisk trot through the garden.

As they reached the smaller gate to the street, two figures in long waterproof cloaks and hats awaited them. Renate spotted them first. It was too late to do anything about them now.

The two came forward, not menacingly but help-fully. They were, in fact, Gemma and Rikki, wearing buff-coloured Metro waterproofing taken from the ambulance.

The ambulance itself was waiting, back door ajar.

'OK?'

'A piece of cake.'

Zara and Renate moved towards the ambulance's doors. Half a block away a car, lights cutting through the rain, pulled up at the downhill stop street. The driver could not help but see the white bulk of the Metro vehicle and the cluster of figures.

Renate hesitated. Zara rapped out, 'Keep going! Act normal!'

The halted car seemed to be waiting overlong, seeing the street ahead was empty. The other girls tried to walk alongside the stretcher as if in attendance on a casualty.

'Should have brought a drip bottle, just to add realism,' whispered Rikki.

The car pulled away now, following the S-bend down towards the hospital.

Fenella was loaded in. Zara took station with the Glock on a low seat alongside the stretcher.

'The rendezvous! Quick as you can! Don't hang around here!'

Fenella was in her own black world: the touch of the metal runners, the alien hostile medical smell of the vehicle's interior, brought an avalanche of fears. If only she could see or speak!

There was the noise and vibration of an engine starting, and a second similar sound from outside. The vehicle's ride was soft and comfortable. Rayner – where was Rayner? Had they killed him first, before capturing her?

The rendezvous between the two gang cars and the ambulance was a secluded pull-out among trees near the cable station. When the ambulance stopped and the doors were flung open, the straps holding Fenella were freed; she felt again the cold snout of the pistol and an equally sinister companion, a knife-point, against her neck. She was marched a few paces, forced into the back seat of a car.

Zara said, 'Don't try anything – you're safe while you don't!'

Zara ordered Rikki and Gemma, the original hijackers of the Metro vehicle, 'Get this thing back to as near the hospital as you can without arousing attention and dump it. I'm on my way to headquarters. Follow with Kerry-Ann as hard as you can.'

Renate and Zara waited until the clumsy vehicle, plus the second getaway car, had started towards the hospital before their own car headed in the opposite direction for the highway – and Churchhaven.

It was a little before midnight.

Chapter 27

'Zara –' The name stabbed at Fenella like a full-scale thrust of the commando knife which was pricking her neck into leaving the car.

She was hardly aware of the rest of Renate's question to the gang leader: '– into the house or down below?'

Zara's car had just pulled to a halt at the foot of the muddy driveway (usually dusty) which led from an equally muddy, corrugated road which traversed the spine of the Churchhaven peninsula leading down a steep slope to Zara's cliffside house overlooking the lagoon. Far across the water on the opposite shore, a searchlight cut through the murk from a naval Search and Rescue crash-boat heading out to sea to a ship in distress in the gale. Hard on the heels of Zara's car came the second car with the rest of the gang.

Zara! The name had stunning implications for Fenella, knowing as she did its background and involvement in the Abbey theft, the bomb attempt on Rayner, and the mock trial shooting.

Now – herself!

Fenella shrank away from the leather-clad figure next to her on the car seat.

'The house – to start with,' answered Zara.

Strong hands (Renate's) led her by the shoulders down the rough path to the house. There was a smell of the sea in the air; there was a muted thud-thud which could have been breakers.

They entered the house. Without an order being given, the blindfold was whipped off Fenella's eyes.

The sudden inrush of bright electric light and the impact of an alien room – big windows and door overlooking the lagoon, a television set, a grotesque fish squirming in its lighted tank, and the sight of her captors upset her balance and she swayed on her feet.

The leather-clad woman with the gun (was it indeed Zara?) said, 'Renate, get her into a chair. Also, get that gag off her. No need for it now.'

Fenella was pushed into a chair. The other women eyed her curiously.

Renate addressed her in a nurse-to-patient voice.

'Pull your lips in hard, or else it'll drag them with it, and it'll hurt like hell. Better to do it quickly. Right?'

Fenella looked at her and nodded. Renate thought, God, for those eyes!

Involuntary tears started from them when Renate, helped by Gemma, flicked off the tape. Fenella sucked in deep gulps of air.

Zara moved close to her, the Glock in her right hand.

She said roughly, 'Skip the obvious questions such as, what is the meaning of this outrage? Where am I? Who are you? We all need some coffee, and then we'll talk.'

Fenella moved her stiff lips round the words. 'There's nothing to talk about from my side.'

'That's what you think,' retorted Zara. 'Coffee – where in hell is Menty? Why wasn't she ready waiting with it?'

Rikki came through from another part of the house and grinned. 'Menty says she's sleeping – leave her alone. Gemma and I can fix it,' she added.

'Something to eat also,' said Renate. 'Kidnapping is an appetite-making business.'

'Save the cracks,' replied Zara shortly. 'They don't go with one-thirty in the morning.'

Fenella said, the adhesive still making her lips feel thick, 'This isn't Cape Town.'

'No, it isn't Cape Town.' The tone in which Zara said it killed further talk. There was no sound but for the wash of the rain, and the curious thud-thud which could be waves.

Before the coffee arrived, Zara jerked out, 'You can make it very easy for yourself – or very hard.'

Fenella took a shot in the dark. 'It was you who tried to kill Rayner Watton.'

The first animation Fenella had seen flared red in Zara's eyes, part fear, part bravado.

'If you know that, we already have plenty to talk about when I interrogate you – later.'

'I don't like the word interrogate.'

Zara shrugged. 'Call it anything you like.'

Fenella went on, 'You used Nelson's head for that bomb. In London, Rote Zora claimed responsibility for the theft. That means you are Rote Zora.'

Zara waved a hand mockingly at the other girls. 'Rote Zora.'

'What do you want from me?' demanded Fenella. 'I've nothing to do with bombs and terrorism –'

'All this will wait till morning,' retorted Zara. 'You will sleep in this room tonight. What happens to you after that is up to you. One of us will be on guard all night, so don't try and be heroic.' She gestured at the pistol. 'It won't work. Now – shut up! Coffee!'

*   *   *

'I want information – expert information,' said Zara briefly.

It was after breakfast next day. Fenella sat on a chair in the lounge, facing the big windows and glass door and a half-moon of all the Rote Zora gang: Zara, on a low stool in the centre, and the others – Renate, Gemma, Kerry-Ann, Rikki, even Menty, who had insinuated herself into the group at the last moment.

The gang had their backs to the light, Fenella faced it. This was the light which had risen over the far pale grey rim of the lagoon into her face and had awoken her out of a troubled sleep. Through a latticework of foliage by the window, she had had a sight of rose sky in the east melting into the greys and purples of the lagoon, flanked by emerald marshes.

First, a kidnap; now, a kangaroo court.

Zara went on, when Fenella did not respond. 'Expert information, about the two silver oars which are to be exchanged at the Simonstown ceremony.'

'The media has been full of them,' answered Fenella. 'You didn't have to go breaking into my home, dragging me out of bed at pistol-point and bringing me to some unknown spot to find out about them. Where *is* this place?'

'Far enough from Cape Town to be safe.'

'Unsafe – for me.'

'Don't quibble over words,' retorted Zara impatiently. 'I want information, and you're the one who possesses it. Supply it, and I – we – guarantee nothing further will happen to you. We'll take you back to Cape Town and you can go home as if nothing had ever happened. Subject, of course, to various undertakings.'

Fenella laughed derisively. 'Undertakings! What sort of undertakings have you in mind? For me to keep secret that you are the Zara who stole Nelson's effigy?'

'Shut up! I know who I am and what I have done, so

214

do the other girls. But you're putting the cart before the horse. First, I want to know the following facts about the two oars: the two are not identical, so the papers say. How are they different – ?' She consulted a sheet of notepaper.

Fenella responded. 'If the papers say they are not identical, then they're not identical.'

'Don't let her get away with that kind of answer, Zara,' broke in Renate. 'It means damn-all.'

Zara handed the gun to Renate to check her notes. Fenella noticed that her hand was trembling.

'Are the handles –'

'Loom is the word,' said Fenella. 'If you mean the shaft.'

'For crying out loud! Of course I mean shaft, or loom, or whatever,' snapped Zara. 'The thing which holds the top –'

'The blade,' said Fenella.

'Don't try and be smart,' went on Zara in the same overbearing tone. 'It won't do you any good in the long run.

'Is the shaft hollow? What is its diameter inside?'

Fenella remained silent.

'There are ways of making you talk, but I'm trying to make it easy for you,' Zara went on. 'Next question. At the mock trial Professor Pittock-Williams –' she kept her voice neutral, but Fenella saw Gemma flick a glance at Rikki, and Menty now seemed to be showing an interest in the proceedings '– carried the baton separate from the oar. Previously, though, when the TV showed him talking about the oar, it seemed to be all one piece. Now, does the baton screw into the shaft? Is it part of it, or not part of it?'

'The oar belongs to Professor Pittock-Williams – why don't you phone him and ask?'

A spurt of strangled laughter erupted from Kerry-Ann.

Zara snatched the pistol from Renate and held it on Fenella. The blood which suffused her face seemed to be pumping into her eyes.

'Mind what you say!' she burst out. 'Mind what you say! I said, don't play the ass with me, or else you'll be sorry!'

Fenella went on calmly, 'You didn't drag me here the way you have done merely to obtain some harmless information. You intend using it –'

'Put her in the cooler for a day or two and she'll change her mind,' interjected Renate.

'I'll probably be missed already,' replied Fenella. 'Rayner Watton is a security man, and he won't overlook the clues you left scattered about in my bedroom, and down to the street.'

'That's our problem,' retorted Zara. 'Now, are you going to answer?'

Fenella shrugged.

'OK, here it is. Either you answer, or else Rayner Watton –'

Fenella's reaction was too quick, too anxious.

Zara smiled grimly. 'Ah!'

'He knows nothing about the silver oars –'

'I know, and I don't intend to ask him.' She changed the Glock's aim. 'He showed himself pretty smart about the effigy bomb. That trick wouldn't work twice with him. But this –' she gestured with the gun '– is a different proposition.' She raised it and squinted along the barrel. 'Line of sight, they call it. You know for sure, your man's at the other end, and that it's him.'

Fenella sat very still, taut, unbelieving. Even during the kidnap, Zara had done her no physical harm; the snatch had constituted an outrage, but not, until this moment, a real threat. Now the death threat was against Rayner. Zara had missed killing him once; his second chance lay with her, Fenella. However, what Zara and the others did not know was something she did: Rayner was leaving for London tonight. Once he was clear of Cape Town, he would be beyond Zara. If she could buy time until then –

Her reply came slowly, softly. 'What you're saying is, if I don't tell you all about the make-up of the oars, you'll kill Rayner Watton?'

'That's it, in a nutshell.'

Buy time, buy time!

'What else do you want to know? You've only mentioned one oar, that belonging to Professor Pittock-Williams.'

'Is the handle – the shaft – of the other one from the *Alabama* wreck hollow?' persisted Zara.

Fenella kept quiet. Should she lie, or pretend she didn't know? What was behind the questioning? What was the gang, particularly Zara, up to? What did they intend to do with the information she knew she could supply in a moment?

Zara sensed she had made progress in regard to her threat to Rayner. She leaned forward expectantly. 'Where are the oars being kept when the one arrives from London later this week? The media's been full of the security arrangements. A whole team of specialists is accompanying it on the flight.'

So Zara didn't know about the decoy plan, hadn't even guessed that Rayner was involved! While she kept silent, he was safe!

'How are the oars being guarded before the Simonstown ceremony? Where?' Fenella found the gang's unremitting stare unnerving. 'Where? *Where?*' demanded Zara.

Fenella said, 'I ask you, why? Why do you want –'

'You're in no position to ask anything,' retorted Zara. 'Will you, or won't you, answer?'

'I want time to consider.'

Renate intervened impatiently. 'She's stringing you along, Zara. Show you mean business about Watton. You saw the way she reacted, there's something between them.'

Zara ignored her first lieutenant. 'How much time?'

What time did Rayner's plane leave? She knew it was after dinner tonight. If she held Zara at bay until dark, that would give the opportunity for him to get clear away. Then, they could do their worst to her.

'Put her in the cooler, it'll show you're not bluffing,' insisted Renate. 'Sitting here with all of us waiting on her hand and foot doesn't give her any notion that we mean what we say.'

'I'm giving the orders round here,' Zara told Renate sharply. She addressed Fenella. 'How long?'

'Until this evening.'

As she said it, Fenella realized that the answer was too pat, too premeditated.

Zara eyed her suspiciously for a long time, until some of the other girls seemed to become embarrassed. Menty sat with her eyes downcast, like a penitent nun. Except that somewhere this little nun had jumped over the wall.

Now Fenella recalled Rayner's exact plane time – 8.30. She'd have to stave them off, take account of how long it had taken the gang to reach here from Cape Town. Say, an hour and a half at least. Until darkness, she would make her condition; that would be safe. Rayner would be away from the Villa Montana long before that.

'If you're conning me –' Zara began threateningly.

'That's my answer.'

Zara thought a moment or two and then said abruptly, 'We'll all take turns on guard in this room with the gun. Two at a time, for safety.' She snapped at Fenella, 'Your time limit expires at seven o'clock. That's the time it gets dark here. I warn you, after that it had better be good.'

Chapter 28

Fenella was still within Rayner Watton's eyelids as his mind rose out of sleep that morning at the Villa Montana. It was about six o'clock, and still dark.

As he lay for a moment islanded between sleep and wakefulness, it was her eyes which were his focus, dark, counterweighted by an extraordinary clarity and depth, set above the classic line of her cheekbones –

Rayner lost the image as conscious thought barraged him. He was leaving her tonight for London; above all, he was leaving with unfinished, troubled business between them which could only deteriorate progressively in the coming days of his absence and the public run-up to the Simonstown ceremony in ten days' time.

The thought had lain all night at the forefront of his mind so that intermittently he had awoken to hear the rain and wind and the arthritic complaining of the old stone pine's branches above Fenella's bedroom balcony. Now, the bad weather seemed to have passed.

Rayner checked his watch. This was the time of a little ritual Fenella had developed since he had been at the villa: she would come with a tray of Earl Grey tea and share it with him, sitting on the foot of his bed. The thought continued to bug him – had they mutually lost something this weekend, culminating in her withdrawn silence and early bed-time last night?

Suddenly, forcefully, the issue hit him – she was in love with him, and he with her!

Rayner made up his mind. He would go and tell her so – now.

And, pre-empt her delightful early morning ritual by himself making the tea, and taking it up to her room.

He pulled on a dressing-gown and hurried to the kitchen, which was empty. He was surprised that during the ten minutes or so that it took him to prepare tea, Fenella did not put in an appearance.

Finally, Rayner got the tray ready, and took it upstairs. Fenella's door was closed. Unusual for her. She had told him, when he had criticized the antiquated alarm system, that she always slept with the door open.

Rayner paused uncertainly. Was it more than simply a closed door – a keep-out warning to him? He decided that he was being over-sensitive. There had been nothing, nothing definable, at any rate, in Fenella's attitude the previous night to indicate that.

Rayner knocked.

As he did so, the door opened a crack: it had not been fully latched.

'Fenella –' Rayner stood still, tray in hand. The door was not open wide enough for him to see in.

He shifted the tray to one hand, rattled a tea-spoon. 'Tea, Fenella!'

The non-response from inside the room had a strange quality of deadness.

He gave the door a push with a slippered toe, still standing at the doorway.

The bed was empty.

Was she in the bathroom? Yet its door from the bedroom also stood open.

'Fenella!'

Something cold, something wholly irrational, targeted his heart. He dumped the tray down and went to the bed. He eyed the rucked-up pillow and bedclothes. Now that he was close, they looked more churned-up than rumpled. His eyes went to the vacant aperture of the sliding door to the balcony. What if –

He took a grip on his arcing thoughts. There was a simple everyday explanation. Fenella had had a disturbed night, and had slipped out quietly for an early morning jog round the block. Any moment she would be back. Except, it was half an hour later than her usual time.

Rayner moved swiftly across to the curtains to draw them back, then stopped.

He felt the gravelly grit through his fine-leather slippers.

What if –

All his professional senses went to action stations. Leave it! Footprints! Fingerprints!

What was he treading on? If Fenella had gone for a jog, she could have brought the ground in on her sneakers, but that presupposed that she had already been out, had returned, and gone out a second time. Why? Because of him?

Or – the thought crashed home like a homing Tomahawk missile: had she gone, escaped, run away from him just as she said she had escaped from her live-in lover when the emotional heat of the kitchen had become too great?

There was no sign of her pyjamas. But her dressing-gown was thrown loosely over a chair. The wardrobe door was closed, but not locked. He opened it, using a handkerchief to handle the catch. Dresses, pants, blouses, shoes – nothing seemed to be missing, as far as he could tell.

He had deliberately shelved checking the carpet and the door to the balcony in the hope-against-hope that he would find some reassuring clue which all his professional senses told him was not there. She had gone, she had gone, walked out on him!

Rayner crossed rapidly to the partly ajar glass door to the balcony. The carpet there was a passageway of muddiness, but it was round Fenella's bed that the real mess lay. On both sides. To have achieved that, she must have had a couple of pairs of shoes and wiped them clean on the carpet. There was also a strange, ruler-straight smear across the blankets.

Rayner was tempted to pull back the blankets and check, but left it. One side of his mind kept telling him, this is a police matter, while the other side said, play it cool, she'll be back. Don't make a fool of yourself and her by panicking.

Rayner checked the balcony. If anyone had entered that way, the rain had been his ally and washed away the tracks.

Perhaps, he told himself desperately, she had taken her car and gone out without his hearing. It was a holiday, and she might have been short of provisions – hardly, at six in the morning, he corrected himself. Nevertheless, he checked the kitchen yard. Both cars, hers and his, were there.

Rayner decided to wait an hour before setting the official wheels in motion. By that time, Fenella might have returned. If not – He crushed down the prospect of a fresh encounter with Brigadier Keyter. This would have to be a security matter, not an ordinary police investigation.

An hour.

Some hours are a lifetime. It doesn't take a lifetime to bath and shave and dress and drink fresh tea in the kitchen.

Almost as the time was up, the thought came to him. He could still keep this security matter in the club, so to speak, by getting hold of Hugh Perrot and obtaining his verdict on her bedroom before Keyter and his men came into the act.

Rayner dialled the Scotland Yard man's hotel. 'Hugh?' Rayner's voice was taut and dry. 'I thought I might have missed you.'

'What's wrong?' Hugh wasn't the sort to indulge in polite chat when he heard a voice like that.

'Fenella –' Rayner told him tightly. When he had done, he asked, 'Will you come now?'

'Rayner, you say you went upstairs just after six. Why wait all this time?'

'I didn't like to seem to be panicking. I hoped she'd come back with an explanation.'

'I'll be right round. No need to tell you not to touch anything.'

'It's all as it was, still.'

'As it was,' echoed Hugh a while later standing in Fenella's room, his face grave. 'And that was, hours ago. I'd guess, well before midnight from the state of the mud.'

'That seems to make it worse, somehow.'

'You heard nothing, Rayner, you say?'

'That old tree there creaks and groans like a ship in a seaway. Apart from that, nothing.'

'Look at this mud, it's quite dry.'

Hugh went down on his hands and knees by the door, and then followed the blurred imprints to both sides of the bed.

'The bed wasn't warm when you came in with the tea?'

'Quite cold – on the surface at any rate. I didn't try further, so as not to disturb anything.'

'She was upset, you say, when you went to bed?' He eyed Rayner acutely. 'Did you have a bust-up?'

'No, nothing like that. She was silent and withdrawn. She had bad vibes, she said, about my going to London to fetch the *Alabama* oar.'

'Maybe that hunch should have been directed at herself,' said Hugh. His eyes were everywhere. 'You're sure she didn't go outside after you'd gone to bed?'

'Certain. I'd have heard if she'd used either the front or back doors. My room's strategically situated.'

'But she could have used the balcony.'

'In the rain? Without a ladder?'

Hugh drew back the curtains with his handkerchief masking his fingers. He indicated the complex of bathroom pipes. 'Easy substitute for a ladder for a determined man – or woman.'

'You're saying Fenella climbed down there in rain and pitch darkness, for unknown reasons –'

'Hey! Look at this!' Hugh indicated. The paint on the balcony rail had been scuffed off for a strip a couple of inches wide.

'New,' said Hugh briefly. 'And carrying a weight. Whoever came up this way, went back again. Two of them.'

'Two of them, Hugh?'

'Take another look at the footprints on either side of the bed. One set belongs to a bigger person than the other. It's clear to read. What about the garden?'

'I haven't checked. There was too much to see up here.'

'Let's go.'

The day's lovely mood, shining through the trees and flower-beds, revoked the night's dark anger and happenings. However, the traces were there, to Hugh's keen eye. He pointed out to Rayner a footprint at the foot of the balcony, away from the slated section of path, and several others in the direction of the smaller garden gate on to the street.

When he had cast round like a sniffer dog and found no more, he summed up. 'My reading of the signs is, Fenella was abducted from her bedroom and brought down here.'

'That's crazy, it's absurd!' Rayner's pent-up feelings burst loose. 'Fenella! Why Fenella?'

'Why did they try and kill you?' Hugh countered. 'You're both up to the neck in this silver oar ceremony. Fenella even more than you, with her expert knowledge. Pittock-Williams was also a target.'

'By heavens!' exclaimed Rayner, clutching at a straw. 'I wonder if he has had any word of Fenella? I'm going to phone him!'

'You're wasting your time, and you know it,' retorted Hugh. 'The longer you stave off Brigadier Keyter, the more suspicious he's going to become of you and your motives. After all, you were the only person in the house, weren't you?'

That realization, defined, struck Rayner for the first time like a chunk of Table Mountain falling off the heights above on to the Villa Montana.

Hugh went on, 'This is a serious matter, Rayner, a criminal one. You've got to bring in the authorities. I have no standing. My brief concerns the Prime Minister's safety. Keyter is your man.'

'Come with me,' said Rayner. 'I want you to witness what I say. First, Pittock-Williams, then Keyter.'

The faithful Mildred stalled until Rayner insisted on speaking to Pittock-Williams.

'Listen, Watton,' he said. 'My time is precious, even on holidays. Unless you have something of significance to tell me.'

'Have you seen or heard from Fenella Gault?'

'I am not Fenella Gault's keeper.'

'She's disappeared. Without a trace. And I am scheduled to fly to London tonight, as you know.'

'Does her disappearance affect the signing ceremony in any way?'

'Do you know anything of her whereabouts?'

'Of course I don't, damn it! Have you called in Brigadier Keyter?'

'He's my next call,' Rayner answered briefly. 'I'll be here at the Villa Montana if you want me.'

Brigadier Keyter was a more difficult proposition. The Security number Rayner had was an office one. His subordinates were as close-mouthed as their chief normally was when Rayner first requested and then demanded Keyter's home number. Finally, he obtained it.

His call was less of a success than even that to Pittock-Williams.

'Who gave you permission to phone me at home, and on a public holiday?' Keyter demanded abrasively. 'You're always up to something, Watton. What is it this time?'

Hugh, standing next to Rayner at the phone, made an expressive 'I-told-you-so' grimace.

'Fenella Gault has disappeared. We think she may have been abducted.'

'You're always making trouble,' Keyter rasped. 'Who is we, may I ask?'

'Inspector Hugh Perrot of Scotland Yard, and myself.'

'And where is this alleged abduction supposed to have taken place?'

'At the Villa Montana.'

'It had to be the Villa Montana, didn't it, Watton?' he retorted bitingly.

Rayner kept his cool. 'I'm phoning from the house now. It happened some time before midnight, we reckon.'

'If you've got it all worked out, why bother to ruin my public holiday?' he went on.

Rayner kept his voice level. 'Because of her involvement with the silver oars, Fenella Gault is a top security rating and as such is your concern.'

'I seem to remember that you refused a full-time security guard I offered you.'

Rayner did not reply. The ice formed on the phone connection.

Then Keyter snapped, 'I'll come round, and raise some of my men.' He banged down the phone.

Rayner said to Hugh, 'I have a third call to make. I'm cancelling my flight tonight to London. I am going to find Fenella.'

Chapter 29

'You can't just drop your secret silver oar mission – not just like that,' Hugh was aghast. 'You'll rock the boat of a whole intricate, carefully planned operation. Besides, it's not for you to say, at this late stage. You're under orders.'

'Whose orders?' Rayner demanded.

'Scotland Yard's – our Anti-Terrorist Squad chief's –'

'I'm not under anyone's orders. I'm a private individual, working for a private company. The decoy was Don Gibson's bright idea. Essentially, Scotland Yard merely fell in with Don's sales talk.'

'If you back down now, you'll do your relations with Scotland Yard everlasting damage,' answered Hugh quietly. 'Not to mention Downing Street. They're in the act, too, don't forget.'

'Fenella means more to me than all that crap.'

Hugh held his hand over the telephone to prevent Rayner dialling. 'Before you hang yourself, let me just say that the fact you are prepared to sacrifice your career, sacrifice relations as a security man with Scotland Yard for the future, and cock a snook at a Prime Minister and a President, shows just how much Fenella means to you. It's heroic, but it won't bring Fenella back. You need official security and police assistance for something like this. You've got to have official muscle behind your investigations. You by yourself can't undertake it. Call it off, Rayner!'

'Thanks, Hugh, but I know what I am doing. I'll phone the airways first, and then Don.'

But Hugh wouldn't let go. 'Phone Don first, if you won't listen to me,' he said. 'Talk it over with him before you jump overboard and commit hara-kiri.'

For a reply, Rayner took up the phone directory, found the number and said, 'Rayner Watton here. I'm booked on a flight leaving Cape Town for London at 8.30 tonight. I want to cancel it. No, no alternative dates at this stage. Just make sure it's cancelled. OK, phone me back and confirm.'

Hugh watched and shook his head.

Don Gibson in London had his Monday banish-the-blues voice on – until he heard what Rayner had to say.

'Not coming?' he echoed incredulously. 'Am I hearing you right, Rayner? You've cancelled your flight to London tonight and you're not acting as sole courier for the *Alabama* oar –!'

'You heard right, Don. That's what I am saying.'

'This is crazy! You must be mad, out of your mind! You can't do this to me, Rayner! Not after what we've built up between us over the years –'

'Sorry, Don, but that's the way it is. Here's the reason. Fenella has been abducted, shanghaied out of her bedroom in the middle of the night. There's not a trace of her. I'm going to look for her. She could be dead.'

'I – I – don't believe it! Why should anyone abduct her?'

'That's what I keep asking myself. It's what Hugh Perrot of Scotland Yard, who's next to me now at the phone, keeps asking himself. It's what Brigadier Keyter, the South African Security chief, will demand to know when he arrives in a few minutes' time. That's the reason I can't come, Don. I can't walk out on a crisis situation when she needs me and leave it to strangers.'

'You're in love with this girl?'

'Could be.'

Like a delayed-action bomb, the full implication of

Rayner's refusal detonated on Gibson at the other end.

'Listen, Rayner, I don't accept what you're saying, you've got to listen –'

'I've cancelled the flight already.'

'No, no! Get on to the airways right away – I will – abort the cancellation –'

'It's done.'

'What will Downing Street say – oh, sweet heavens above! Listen, Rayner, put the Scotland Yard man on to the line to me – now! He's got to hammer some sense into your mind!'

'He's tried already. He's said a lot of what you've said. It makes no difference, Don. I'm going after Fenella, whatever.'

The Surveillicor chief's tone hardened. 'This is all a load of horseshit you're saying, Rayner. Hear me! I'm going to hang up now and phone you back in half an hour. It'll give you time to let other considerations except the shock take effect. I'm revoking the flight cancellation myself, from this end, whether you like it or not.'

'I won't be on that plane, Don.'

Gibson went on remorselessly. 'I'm not accepting this. That's flat. You can make up your mind to that. Don't argue –'

Rayner heard a car draw up outside the Villa Montana, and Hugh indicated who its occupant was.

'Here's Brigadier Keyter now,' he added. 'OK, I'm hanging up, as you said.'

'Tell Brigadier Keyter from me –'

But Rayner had already put down the phone to face the Security chief: close-mouthed and square-set in the shoulders, squarer under his casual open-necked shirt than they appeared in uniform, which was the only way Rayner had encountered him. But the cold eyes were the same and so was the strong, close-shaven jaw.

'Who was that you were phoning?' he demanded.

'I don't have to tell you, but I will,' Rayner replied. 'London.'

'We'll deal with that in a moment,' he rasped. 'Where's the room you say was the scene of the abduction?'

Rayner led him upstairs. The Security man's penetrating glance swivelled with reptilian thoroughness round the disarranged bed, the muddy carpet, the now half-open sliding door on to the terrace.

'Are there any bloodstains?' Keyter asked detachedly.

'Not on the bedclothes on the outside.' Rayner faced the reality of the fact for the first time, and it made him cringe. 'I haven't turned them back. I wanted everything to be as it was when you people arrived.'

Keyter talked through Rayner to Hugh. 'Can you confirm that?'

'It was like this when I saw the bed.'

Keyter moved to pull the bedclothes back, but Rayner said:

'Before you do that, there's an odd sort of mark here across the foot, as if something had rested on it. The line could have been made by wetness.'

'My men will make their own evaluation.'

Nevertheless, Keyter was careful not to pull the covers back over the spot Rayner had indicated.

Rayner was glad now he hadn't seen the cruelly rucked-up bottom sheet and ploughed-up state inside of Fenella's bed previously. There was no blood.

'Whoever it was, she fought them off,' commented Keyter.

'I'd also say "they",' remarked Hugh. 'Look at those footprints.'

'My men don't miss things like that.'

'There are a couple more in the garden, off the edge of the slate paths.'

'They know their job. They'll go over the whole place with a toothcomb.'

Keyter turned abruptly to Rayner. 'Have you got a gun?'

'You took mine away, remember?'

'You could have another.'

'I haven't.'

'We'll check that. Where did you sleep?'

'Downstairs. I'll show you.'

'I haven't finished here yet.'

Before he could, Rayner and Hugh were brushed aside by an irruption of holiday-clad but business-equipped men whom Brigadier Keyter had wrenched from a day's relaxation at home: fingerprint and footprint experts, forensic experts. Like their chief, they were taking time to warm to the thought of a hunt; their disgruntlement kept them terse, monosyllabic.

Rayner's resentment grew. Every puff of black fingerprint powder, every hair removed from Fenella's bedclothes, every sweep of the fingerprint brush, was to him an intrusive breach of Fenella's own personal life.

He was glad when Keyter said, 'What about the other rooms?'

'I didn't think to check them.'

'You didn't think to check them.'

The man was turning his words back on him by inflexion and insinuation. 'She could be in any of them.'

Rayner's overwrought mind threw up an image of Fenella slowly bleeding to death while he had wasted his time on prevarication, on minor things while he stalled for time, refusing to face the fact that she had gone.

The Rommel Room was obviously unentered, undisturbed. Keyter gave it only a cursory glance. 'Next.'

He indicated the doors of the two bedrooms which faced the front of the villa.

'Spare bedrooms,' said Rayner.

'Why locked?' asked Keyter as Rayner tried the first one.

'The security system in this house is so antiquated that I insisted she should take whatever precautions remained,' said Rayner. 'The alarm works only downstairs.'

'You knew all this?'

'Of course I knew it. I was worried about all this valuable stuff.' He gestured at the cabinets, pictures on the walls and Persian carpets with his hand still on the door handle.

'Why?'

'As a security man myself.'

There was a moment of dread inside him when he opened the door. But there was nothing there, nor in the adjoining room.

Keyter asked, with the practised casualness of an interrogator hoping to catch his victim off-guard with a question he had held on to until he sensed a relaxation of vigilance, 'Who were you phoning in London?'

'My boss at Surveillicor, Don Gibson.'

'Why? What had Fenella Gault's disappearance got to do with him?' Keep off the grass – the warning was written in words of acid, and Keyter would not hesitate to throw it.

'I told him I had cancelled my flight tonight to London. I'm backing out of the *Alabama* oar mission.'

Normally the only thing which would have stopped Keyter dead in his tracks would have been a nine-millimetre parabellum slug. Rayner's words did.

When he spoke, his normally harsh accent sandpapered his outburst.

'You couldn't give a rat's arse about any interests but your own, could you, Watton? I said all along it was a mistake to bring in an amateur, and I only gave way because of your SAS track record. I was right, by God, I was right!'

'If you find Fenella alive today, I'll still go.'

'I don't want any favours from you,' he retorted. 'There's something I can't get to the bottom of about you, Watton – starting with that effigy bomb business. Something shady, something underhand. My first inclination when I arrived here today was to put you under arrest. You're the prime suspect. I still may.'

'I said, I intend finding Fenella.'

'You won't get any help – one smallest bit of help – from me or what my men find in there,' he responded. 'You want to be on your own, OK, you're on your own, absolutely and completely. I'll give orders to that effect.'

He went on: 'You realize what your action means as far as Scotland Yard's relations with ourselves are concerned? We'll have to try and unscramble all the elaborate decoy plans we made and find substitutes for them, all in a matter of hours. Lay ourselves wide open into the bargain, if anyone is contemplating a hijack of the *Alabama* oar. You realize that?'

'It can still be brought out by the British squad. They're all professionals, and armed.'

'You always have the slick answer, Watton,' he rasped on. 'Never at a loss for words!'

'Are you finished, or shall I wait?' Rayner asked.

The ringing of the phone downstairs cut across his reply.

Keyter shouted, 'Answer that phone, someone!'

One of the men from Fenella's room raced down.

Rayner said, 'That happens to be a private phone, not yours.'

Keyter gave a grunt a hippo surfacing might have envied. 'You said, your man Gibson would phone back. If it's him, I'll speak.'

'Am I under arrest, or not?' Rayner asked.

'You could be, at any moment. You'll make a full statement – a full written statement – to one of my men, now. You'll also report for the next few days to the police by nine in the morning, for checking with Security head-quarters. Do you understand?'

The man came from the telephone. 'It's a Mr Gibson from London, sir.'

'I want to speak to Mr Gibson!' snapped Keyter. 'If there's anything left to say after I've done, I'll send for you, Watton.'

Rayner never knew what Don Gibson said to Keyter; he was taken away to the Rommel Room where, with the door closed, a long and detailed handwritten statement was taken from him. The man either knew his job or had been briefed by Keyter. It seemed to Rayner that every irrelevancy the official mind could run to was insisted upon.

When they finally emerged, the villa was strangely quiet. The Security team had gone.

Later in the afternoon, there was another phone call. It was Hugh Perrot.

'Rayner,' he said. 'I've been ordered to take your place to bring back the *Alabama* oar, with the same stage props as you would have used. I thought you'd like to know.'

'Thanks, Hugh.'

'It's the best they could devise in London. I agree it's not ideal, but it was too much to unscramble the original plan in time.'

'How did Don Gibson sound?'

'I think you may find yourself without a job when you get back.'

'Fenella's more important.'

'All the odds are against you, you realize that?'

'Yes, Hugh.'

'Another thing – I'm not supposed to divulge any information about what Keyter's men found, but I will to you for old times' sake.'

'I appreciate that, Hugh.'

'You mayn't, when you hear what I have to say. It's

pretty clear that Fenella was snatched from her bed by two intruders. Apart from the footprints and finger-prints, the forensic guys found samples of two lots of hair, other than Fenella's, from the bed. Women's hair. Those straight marks on the bed remain a mystery. She was then removed –'

'What is it, Hugh?'

'Remember those scratches on the balcony rail? A dead weight was lowered by rope over it. A dead weight, Rayner. I hope you find her alive.'

Chapter 30

'Your ultimatum expires in just over an hour.'

Zara's drawn lips confided nothing; her face had a slightly ominous composure now that the deadline Fenella had set that morning was at hand.

She sat on a low stool in front of Fenella's chair as she had done for a good part of the day with the Glock resting in her lap, sharing the guard shift with several of the other girls.

It was now a little before six, too late for dusk, too early for evening, which always came tardily over the lagoon in autumn. Sunset was a thief crucified in his own blood against the Atlantic sky at their backs: the garish colours redoubled their vividness in the lagoon's reflec-tion and finally foundered on the low purple hills on the lagoon's eastern shore in maroon and saffron, like the colours of a Buddhist monk's robes.

Fenella was still unaware of where the lagoon was situ-ated. But, as the light began to ebb in the afternoon, she knew that every hour was contributing to Rayner's safety. As the hours passed, she also realized that Zara meant what she had said: behind the brooding eyes, so startling and disquieting in their distillate of pure hate, there was a menace which left Fenella very afraid.

It had been a day of activity – activity Fenella did not understand – by the Rote Zora gang. It seemed concentrated on the church, which Fenella could see on her left on its mound fronted by the bell-tower. The girls came out of the church carrying cardboard cartons, then made their way round the back of the church in the direction of the graveyard. Fenella was not to know that the cartons contained Soviet-made mini-limpet mines, SZ6 demolition mines, a nest of PMN anti-personnel mines, RG42 hand grenades, looking more like vegetable cans than weapons, and the deeply embossed evil-looking F1 grenades, scores of detonators of various kinds, and several Makarov pistols and magazines.

At one stage, Renate came in and ear-whispered to Zara, and they swapped guard stints. Zara went to supervise the packing of her favourite Semtex plastic explosive, which she wanted to be separate from the others.

The gang was, in fact, transferring their arsenal from old George Williams/White's original bunker hide-out under the floor of the church. Zara had made up her mind that, whatever Fenella's answers, she would not go free. She would be held in the dark funk-hole 'pending' – pending what, Zara had yet to clarify.

To this end, part of the gang's activity had been readying the bunker for Fenella with a stretcher, chair and washbasin. Where, the gang had debated out of Fenella's earshot, to hide the arms cache?

They had toyed with the idea of loading it into Zara's small yacht which lay at a buoy offshore in shallow water, its dinghy drawn up on a natural rock slipway at the foot of the cliff on which the church stood, but had discarded it as too risky.

Then Zara had come up with the answer. 'The tomb, of course! Old George White's family tomb!'

It was there, on the graveyard mound overlooking the stunning view, an old-fashioned brick structure with a small locked wooden entrance door leading to a kind of mausoleum chamber in which the coffins of old White and his Churchhaven descendants were stacked.

Zara had unlocked it, and the Soviet hardware took its place amongst less volatile company.

Anticipation and tension had brought the whole gang into the lounge where Fenella was long before the lunch-time radio news bulletin. Zara never took her eyes from Fenella as the first item came on. There was nothing about the kidnapping, nor in the rest of the news.

Towards the end, however, there was a minor item which had everyone interested: a Metro ambulance had been removed – presumably by vandals or pranksters – from its hospital parking bay the previous night and had been recovered, undamaged and with nothing missing, a few blocks away the same morning. A police appeal was made to anyone who had any information to report to the nearest police station.

The buzz of excitement from the Rote Zora girls told Fenella everything: she recalled the hospital smell, the stretcher, the short ride in a soft-sprung vehicle – the gang had boldly hijacked a Metro ambulance, after lowering her from the balcony on one of its stretchers!

'You guessed right,' Zara had told her. 'Don't expect to be as comfortable from now on, unless you answer my questions.'

Now, the early evening television newscast was coming on. Again, the whole gang packed into the lounge. Fenella's own interest in it was limited; she wanted that deadline of 7.00 p.m. past, then she knew Rayner would be safe.

The lead picture of the Villa Montana jerked her attention away from the time-squeeze.

The announcer said:

Security police were today called in to this lovely home in the Gardens to investigate what may turn out to be a sinister crime. According to a spokesman, Miss Fenella Gault was abducted during the night from her upstairs bedroom in the Villa Montana, to which several assailants gained entry by scaling drainpipes to a balcony adjoining it.

Fingerprint and forensic tests indicate that there were at least two women involved –

'I don't care for that,' interrupted Renate. 'How the hell did they know we were women?'

'Keep quiet!' said Zara. 'Keep your comments for afterwards.'

– there were signs of a violent struggle –

The camera showed Fenella's bed, hideously rumpled. She cringed from the sight: one's own bed being eyed by millions of viewers!

– but the security experts found no bloodstains, and it is hoped that Miss Gault has not been seriously hurt in the assault.

'How do you feel about that?' broke in Gemma, addressing Fenella.

'For Pete's sake, shut up and hear what is being said!' snapped Zara.

– a top team of security experts, headed by Brigadier Keyter, Security chief, were soon on the scene of the crime early today. In the house at the time was Mr Rayner Watton, from London. Both Mr Watton and Miss Gault have been in the public eye recently in connection with the two silver oars which are to figure in the forthcoming Simonstown ceremony, together with Professor Vivian Pittock-Williams. Viewers will recall that while demonstrating the ceremonial connected with these oars last week at the venue of the old Admiralty Court, Professor Pittock-Williams was gunned down by a mysterious sharpshooter. He has now recovered from the wound he sustained and will still lead the Simonstown ceremonial procession as Admiralty Marshal.

The announcer added:

Several strong leads are being followed up in connection with Miss Gault's disappearance.

In the meantime, in order to assist the Security authorities, Mr Watton, who was due to have flown to London tonight, has cancelled his visit and will remain –

The strain of the long day had drawn the architecture of Fenella's face to finer lines; now, at the mention of Rayner, it blanched, leaving her lips unnaturally prominent.

Zara was on her feet before the announcement had finished, brandishing the pistol at Fenella and yelling. The gang drew back from the obscenity of Zara's face, and out of her possible line of fire.

'You double-dealing, smooth-talking bitch!' she mouthed at Fenella. 'You've sat there all day, stringing me along when all the time you knew – or thought you knew – that your lover-boy would be on his way to London tonight and out of my reach –' She gestured wildly with the gun, and Fenella recoiled from the livid blueness of Zara's lips as the words spewed out. 'So you kept your mouth shut, eh, knowing that my lever against you would be gone! You weren't going to give me the information I wanted, were you?'

Zara lurched close to Fenella, so that she thought she was about to pistol-whip her face with the Glock.

Fenella said nothing; what was there to say? That had been her plan about Rayner, and she had been prepared to take the whole rap, once he was out of Zara's reach.

'I should kill you,' Zara ranted thickly. 'I would kill you, except that you still have something for me.'

'What –'

'You can make up your mind, quick!' Zara cut across Fenella's rhetorical question. 'You can answer my questions about the silver oar, or I'll go and get Rayner Watton – tonight. Tonight, d'ye hear? I know where to find him, at the Villa Montana! I know the lay-out! I'll get him! You can make up your mind – now!'

Fenella said quietly, still shrinking from the ugly blatant rage tearing at the Rote Zora chief's face, 'It depends what you want to know.'

The rest of the gang stood back in awe. The only sound was a curious little whimper from Menty. What it meant, no one knew, or cared.

It's a pity for their sakes they didn't, Menty. For your sake too.

'Here, Renate!' ordered Zara. 'Hold this gun on her while I get my list of questions. You know what to do if she tries any tricks.'

She left. Renate had none of Zara's terrible subjective anger which still reverberated about the room.

The sick sense of being pinned into an impossible situation rose like sourness in Fenella's throat. What were Zara and her feminist gang up to? Could she get away with telling her only so much? But how much was so much, when she didn't know the objective? Rayner?

Zara was back. 'Well?'

'I'll try and answer.'

'You'll try damn hard!' retorted Zara. 'If you don't, you know what will happen to Watton!'

She edged Renate, still aiming the gun, aside, and faced Fenella. The rest of the gang formed a kind of silent chorus in the background.

'First, the handle of the silver oar –'

'You mean the loom or shaft, I presume.'

There was a flare of anger in Zara's face, but it was far away, compared to the earlier outburst, like receding lightning on a far horizon.

'Don't nitpick about words!' she retorted. 'You know what I mean. Is it made of solid silver?'

'I don't know which oar you are talking about.'

'To get back to what I asked you previously, how are the two oars different?'

'Professor Pittock-Williams's is a replica, made from memory about sixty or seventy years after the *Alabama* oar. The Cape silversmith who crafted it obviously didn't work from the original design, which dated from 1806.'

'So what?'

'There are five engravings on the blade of the original, but they aren't the same on the replica –'

'I don't want to hear these piddling details,' snapped Zara. 'I want to know about the shafts. Physical detail about them. How long is it?'

'Do you mean the shaft itself, or the shaft plus blade?'

'The shaft itself, damn it!' burst out Zara. 'I'm not interested in the blade, unless it is hollow inside.'

'Hardly. The blade is a core of iron encased in sheet silver. The edges of the back fold over in front in such a way that it is held immovable without soldering –'

Zara stopped her with an angry gesture. 'You're trying to talk me down with a mass of irrelevant shit. Now, answer my questions, plain and simple, or else it'll be the worse for you – and Watton.'

Fenella replied in a flat voice, 'The *Alabama* oar measures eighty-four centimetres overall –'

'What's that in imperial terms, for crying out loud?' demanded Zara. 'Inches!'

'Thirty-three inches. The blade is twelve inches, and the shaft or loom twenty-one and a half inches.'

'Is it hollow?'

The eagerness with which Zara fired the query left no doubt with Fenella that this was the sixty-four-dollar question.

She hedged. 'Not quite.'

'What in hell do you mean, not quite? Either something is hollow or solid. Which is it? Answer!'

'Let me explain. The shaft is built from several units. There are three all told. Each is really a tube, which has been hand-crafted from thick silver plate to a diameter of about one and a half inches, with an invisible seam which runs the length of the shaft. There are, in addition, two ring-like knobs which join them into a single entity, and there is a round boss which links the shaft to the blade.'

'OK, OK. So, briefly, we have a hollow silver tube about an inch and a half in diameter?'

'Let me go on. At the base of the shaft there is a large silver terminal button, about three inches or seventy-five millimetres across. It has a cover, which is screwed in, which is engraved in the case of the *Alabama* oar but not the replica.'

Zara's eagerness was like a hound picking up a vital scent.

'It screws out, you say? What for?'

'Inside there is a flat-faced iron rod which has a deep slot cut across its face, so that it can be turned with a screwdriver. This iron rod extends the length of the shaft and where it meets the blade it is screwed into the iron core of the blade itself. So when I said the shaft was not quite hollow, that is what I meant. It has this long iron rod inside.'

'Why?'

'To give the whole structure vertical strength and support. Silver is not all that hard.'

An interruption came from Gemma, whose concentration among the other members of the gang matched only Zara's.

'She's bullshitting you, Zara. That oar has been under the sea for over a century. There won't be any iron left by now. It would have all rusted away.'

'What do you say to that?' demanded Zara.

'Several sections of the iron rod were, it is true, reduced to paper-thinness. But all the iron had been encased with silver – and Frisbee was a master-craftsman – so that the inside was virtually waterproof. However, the oar has been fully restored in London since it was recovered, and new iron cores made. Even the blade's silver rim was superbly crafted and strengthened with receded moulding, so that seawater damage was limited.'

'So if the big terminal button was removed, and the iron rod inside also screwed out, you'd have a hollow tube – of silver?'

'Yes.'

'And the same applies to the replica which is here in Cape Town?'

Fenella logged the fact that Zara seemed to steer clear of Pittock-Williams's name for some reason.

'By no means. The replica belonging to Professor Pittock-Williams looks superficially very much the same as the *Alabama* oar, but in fact it's very different.'

'How?' barked Zara.

'I told you the Cape silversmith who made it must have worked from memorized verbal descriptions, and he knew nothing of the strengthening iron structure inside the original. So he used his own ideas.'

'Such as?'

'First, the silver he used to encase the replica oar was much thinner than the original, not strong enough to form a shaft by itself without some kind of internal support. He got the length of the shaft more or less right – a couple of inches shorter – but it is not uniform in width and is tapered towards the blade, which isn't the case with the *Alabama* oar. Also, it hasn't got a big terminal silver button at its base.'

'What has it got?' The question came from Gemma.

'I'll have to refer to the old Admiralty Court procedure to give you a satisfactory answer.'

Renate said, 'Hell, fancy trying to sort all this out on one's own!'

'You couldn't – no one could,' retorted Zara. 'That's why she's here. Go on!'

Fenella found her descriptive effort a relief after the long hours of unspeaking captivity. The kind of expertise she was supplying couldn't be of use to anyone but a silversmith or an antiquarian.

With this in mind, she went on, 'The Admiralty Marshal carried, as a symbol of his authority, a small circular staff of ivory, not more than a hundred and fifty millimetres long –'

Zara gestured impatiently. 'Inches!'

'Six inches,' Fenella supplied. 'The head of this staff – which incidentally was the personal property of the Marshal and did not belong to the Admiralty – was a Royal crown fashioned in silver, which was encircled by a silver band engraved with the Admiralty's symbol, a foul anchor. This head unscrewed, and revealed a space inside which was used for carrying the Admiralty's warrant.

'Now when the *Alabama* oar was in use at the Cape, the ivory staff and the silver oar were carried separately in procession by the Marshal, the oar over his right shoulder and the staff in his left hand.

'However, with the replica, the oar and staff were made into a single unit.'

'Explain!'

Fenella went on. 'To join the two, a silver ferrule was fitted to one end of the ivory staff and a matching screw-thread attached to the base of the oar. The one was screwed into the other, making it much easier to carry.'

'The baton must have screwed into something, apart from a small ferrule,' Zara said.

'There wasn't any problem. The Cape silversmith used as his strengthening foundation a hollow iron tube encased in thin silver sheeting –'

Zara threw the words at Gemma. 'You hear that, Gemma! An *iron* tube, under the silver! By God, shrapnel – iron shrapnel fragments!'

Gemma was grinning, too. 'That's all we need! An updated version of the early IRA trick – an iron pipe stuffed with gelignite!'

Zara had started to throw her a warning look, but she was too late. Despite the threat of the pistol, Fenella jumped to her feet and burst out:

'What are you up to, all of you? You're not women, you're a bunch of cold-blooded, cowardly killers! You're going to use an innocent thing to kill innocent people –'

Zara's short-fuse temper detonated. She projected Fenella backwards again into her chair with a crash, using her left hand to crack against her face, and her right with the Glock to thrust bruisingly between her breasts.

'You've already heard too much,' she rasped. 'I wouldn't have let you go anyway, but now – You'll have to pay the price. Nothing, but nothing, is going to stop me – d'ye hear?' She swung on Renate and thrust the pistol into her hands. 'Take her away – lock her up!'

Chapter 31

It was dark outside. Renate marched Fenella, with the gun at her back, across the path which separated the church from the house.

Any moment, Fenella kept telling herself, she would wake up and find that the lovely nameless lake, the white bell-tower at the top of the steps, and the tiny, peaceful, century-old whitewashed church had evaporated with the rest of the nightmare.

Before they had even entered the church, Zara came up in support, over-keen lest anything should happen to allow Fenella to escape with the knowledge of her plan that she had.

'In!' she ordered at the church door.

When they reached the altar, Zara said, 'Turn round and face the way you came.'

Fenella could not see how Zara opened the secret panel. But the entrance gaped when she was told to about-face once again – a dark hole which Zara's torch illuminated, with a flight of steps leading down.

They descended. In the flashlight's limited illumination underground, the bunker appeared to be L-shaped, branching rightwards, which would have positioned it under the church floor in the direction of the graveyard. The place was low and cold. Zara lit an oil lantern. There was a chair, a bed, a portable radio, several heavy blankets. Fenella was glad she still had her pyjamas with her. She had shed them during the day in the house; they had been too hot under warm pants and a jersey.

Fenella's eyes were wide from darkness and disquiet. 'How long do you intend to keep me in this ice-box?'

'As long as required,' answered Zara. 'If I want more

information about silver oars, I'll give you a breather upstairs.'

Fenella said, with a note of desperation in her voice, 'You realize what you are doing –'

Zara brushed her aside. 'Toilet round the corner – portable chemical model from the boat you saw at anchor. See here, right at the start, you are wasting your time if you think you can get out. There's no way. Someone will bring you some food shortly, when we eat at the house. OK, Renate, let's go.'

They went back to the interrupted round-table discussion on arming the silver oar with explosive.

'Semtex, of course,' said Zara. 'We can tamp the interior of one of the oar shafts with Semtex. It's tailor-made for the job. It'll mould easily into the space.'

'I guess you're teaching the Lockerbie bomber a thing or two about his trade,' said Kerry-Ann in her clear nursery-school enunciation. Sitting next to Rikki, the nearest to her one friend in the gang, she wore her habitual 'groomed-yet-ungroomed' look; the smile which began on her broad lips aborted against the double dimple of her left cheek. It must have taken turbo-thrust to have got that far.

'Don't talk crap,' replied Zara. 'He was a master. The Lockerbie suitcase trick was a stroke of genius.'

'It's the type of fuse which worries me with this bomb of yours, Zara –' began Gemma.

But Rikki cut in. 'We're all making one hell of an assumption.' Her wide grey eyes and balanced tone were as cool as if she had been booking in a hotel client. 'Putting the cart before the horse, in fact. You're taking it for granted you can get your hands on one or both of the oars. Impossible!'

'I'm splitting this discussion into two sections,' responded Zara. 'The first is, how we can prime and fuse an apparently innocent thing like a silver oar with a charge of Semtex; and the second, how we can get our hands on an oar and carry it out.'

'The two problems are interlinked,' argued Rikki. 'The one depends on the other. Already we've branded ourselves as criminals by the kidnap.'

Zara shrugged. 'We will go into the logistics of the bomb first, and then see how we can dovetail it into acquiring an oar.'

'OK, OK,' replied Rikki. 'But I still say –'

Zara cut her short. 'Gemma, carry on – this is your field.'

Gemma gave a rather toothy, uncertain grin and shook her brush of untidy coarse hair. Zara had elevated her sense of personal power and pushed into the background her pale, man-shy personality. Menty in turn had thrust herself into the penumbra of the group. Zara did not realize what she was doing to the contorted psyche inside that mousy body by ignoring her.

'How much Semtex do you intend to use?'

'I've got a stock of about six kilograms I brought from Germany,' replied Zara. 'We don't need anything like that amount, and, besides, a hollow pipe twenty-one inches long won't take that quantity.'

'I like the idea of the iron pipe,' said Gemma. 'The iron will fragment much better than soft silver. Like a hand grenade.'

'That automatically points to the replica oar,' added Zara.

'Where is it being kept at present, since the mock trial?' asked Rikki.

'You're jumping the gun again,' answered Zara. 'I told you, we are dealing with the accessibility of the oars and the bomb logistics as two separate issues. Gemma?'

'Using a high-density, powerful explosive like Semtex, it should have an effective blast radius of at least five metres from the centre of the explosion.'

'Splendid!' exclaimed Zara.

'This is all theory – it may be correct enough, but we still don't know anything about the ceremonial set-up, who is going to be where, and who will be near the blast centre,' said Renate.

Zara said obliquely, but with a menace which stopped the conversation in its tracks:

'Professor Pittock-Williams is the Admiralty Marshal. The Marshal carries the silver oar.'

There was a silence. The big fish coiled and flicked its fins, plunging against the lighted side of the tank, as if offering its poison spines for use to Rote Zora. It peered and jerked at the women.

'Let's get on.' Zara ended the melt-down of the conversation which had followed the implication of her remark. 'Gemma – the detonator?'

'If the bomb is to go off as we plan during the Simonstown signing ceremony, then we need something remote-controlled, delayed-action. I don't see any of us getting close enough to detonate the device.'

'Forget it,' said Zara. 'There will be a security screen around the VIPs so tight that even a cockroach won't be able to smuggle itself in between the layers of a sandwich.

'What about a high-frequency transmitter?' she went on.

'The British learned their lesson about high-frequency waves in Northern Ireland,' objected Gemma. 'They'll be jamming all the airwaves at Simonstown during the ceremony, you can bet. Besides, that would require very sophisticated electronics built into the shaft of the silver oar. I don't think you've got anything as miniaturized and sophisticated as that amongst your collection, Zara. There wouldn't be space in the shaft, either.'

'You're also forgetting the time factor, how long it would take to prime the oar with sophisticated gadgetry like that,' added Renate. 'We don't know how long – or how short – a time we're going to have even if we get our hands on one of them –'

'That question belongs to the second half of the discussion,' Zara interrupted again. 'Remember?'

'It's hard to separate the two,' replied Rikki.

'Go on, Gemma. What do you suggest?'

'We've only got a space one and a half inches to work in,' Gemma answered. 'To my mind, our options narrow down to two choices – either a delayed-action fuse, or an impact detonator. Will the security people put the oars through an explosives check beforehand?'

Zara shrugged. 'Who knows? They certainly won't detect the Semtex, but a complicated bit of electronics is a major risk –'

'I've got it!' burst out Gemma excitedly. 'I've got it! Listen! That girl Fenella told us, the Marshal's baton will screw in and out of the silver oar shaft – if we fit a trembler device which will detonate the moment the baton is removed, but will not react so long as it remains part of the oar itself, we'll have it! A trembler – that is what is needed! The classic booby-trap! It's perfect, I tell you – a trembler's perfect for the job!'

'Let's go over this before we throw our hats in the air,' said Zara.

'If our plan is feasible enough to get off the ground, which it isn't at the moment,' added Rikki, who was filling the role of devil's advocate with remarkable ability. 'Fair enough, we needed accurate, first-hand information about the silver oars, and we got it – at a price which we haven't yet paid. Now comes the chain reaction, and the next thing is we need accurate, first-hand information about the drill for the signing ceremony, and about where the two silver maces are being kept until the ceremony. Without it, this is a Rote Zora story for the kids. And a damn dangerous one which could cost any one of us a bullet in the guts.'

'Spare my ovaries, please,' mocked Kerry-Ann. 'Don't shoot below the waterline, please.'

'Oh Jeez!' exclaimed Zara. 'Can't you stay away from sex?'

Renate took up the running. 'Let's consider as first priority the silver oar which is right here on our doorstep in Cape Town at the moment, Pittock-Williams's replica. It's also the one Gemma fancies for the bomb. We could go for it if we knew where it was being held in safe-keeping.'

She turned to Zara (it was only Renate who could get away with her remark to the gang leader). 'When you were shacking up with Pittock-Williams, didn't he ever mention the silver oar? It's a famous heirloom, after all.'

'Zara was too occupied at the time with other family heirlooms,' jeered Rikki.

A ripple of laughter went round the group.

'I said, stay away from it!' Zara burst out. 'If anyone makes another sexy crack, I'll – I'll –'

Her fury stilled the girls' laughter. There was an uncomfortable silence, then Renate said:

'I expect his home has good security?'

'The best – the bloody best,' replied Zara. 'Burglar alarms, sensors, infra-red scanners, TV monitors, the lot.' She added, a little reminiscently, 'I had a key to immobilize the alarm system, once. But that's all in the past. I'm living only for the present. That includes the silver oar bomb, however tough a proposition it looks right now.'

Chapter 32

Rayner woke with a hangover. Not a hangover from alcohol, but a hangover of guilt, doubt and suspicion – and fear. Most of all, fear. Fear for Fenella which earlier had jerked him out of sleep and had sent him up the great staircase of the Villa Montana to Fenella's bedroom. Empty, of course. And beyond, that balcony rail over which a dead weight had been lowered – a *dead* weight –

Guilt and doubt. Had he indeed betrayed Gibson and Scotland Yard's faith in him as one of the few they had trusted outside their own ranks, and he'd thrown that trust in their faces? Hugh had let him down lightly, Gibson less so. Had he acted impetuously, quixotically, swept off his feet by a woman's love for the first time in his life?

Fenella! It hurt. It was all hurt. The only way to reinstate himself was to find her, and bring her back, alive, along with her two women captors.

Where to begin? He had no status to conduct inquiries; he had no security infrastructure to fall back upon or refer to. Brigadier Keyter's outfit certainly had its door firmly closed in his face, and they had the forensic and other clues they had gathered in Fenella's bedroom. Even if it were to be a question of simply mulling over such facts to keep himself occupied, hoping that somewhere a lead would show up.

He could find only one small consolation (if it could be called that) in his darkness in the fact that Fenella had been forcibly removed from the Villa Montana, and had not walked out on him, as he at first dreaded.

With nothing to do, and the day stretching blankly

ahead, Rayner killed time by going over everything in Fenella's room and making an equally futile search of the garden. He passed the phone on the way out and yearned to get in touch with Don Gibson in order to try and heal the breach. But it was too deep for that.

Finally, he almost welcomed the fact that he had to report to the police, on Brigadier Keyter's orders.

'Passport!' snapped the lieutenant he was ushered in to see. The man was morose, perhaps modelling himself on his chief. 'One of the brigadier's specials, eh?'

Rayner felt he was in a twilight state between suspicion and arrest. 'I don't know what that means.'

'You don't have to. Just report every day at this time and we won't pull you in.'

Rayner went. The man's bearing gave a clear pointer as to how much he could expect from Keyter's set-up.

The phone tempted him again when he re-entered the villa. He longed for it to ring. But it remained sullen and autistic all day, until the evening.

'Rayner?' Rayner's heart leapt at the well-known voice.

'Hugh! Where are you? I didn't expect –'

'London. Listen, Rayner, I've got to keep this short. Right off the record, understand? No one, but no one, must ever know. Even telling you could earn me the chop.'

'I'll say my full thanks at a more appropriate time.'

'I'll take it as read,' replied Hugh. 'I was with the boss at Scotland Yard this afternoon. He got a name from the Germans via an Arab they picked up with an explosives cache. Pal of Nezar Hind-wani – you remember, the bomber who failed against a Palestine airliner at Heathrow. He wanted to make his marble good and escape the consequences by squealing to the Germans. He confessed, when his arm was twisted a little, to knowing the girl who attended the bomb school. The one with the coppery hair, remember?'

253

'Zara?'

'Her name's Zara Hennessy.'

'Zara Hennessy!' breathed Rayner.

Hugh went on, speaking fast. 'We're looking for Zara Hennessy in London, of course, but my guess is that she's on your doorstep. The boss thinks so, too. I'm under orders to give this name Zara Hennessy to Brigadier Keyter when I get back. I'll see him on Thursday. I fly again tomorrow morning, you know why. Be back Wednesday night. Gives you a headstart to find Fenella. Any word of her?'

'Keyter and I are incommunicado.'

'That's it, then. Good luck, Rayner.'

'Hugh, how can I ever thank –'

'It'll keep. Find Zara Hennessy and you'll find Fenella.'

'Admiralty House, Simonstown.'

Zara was already through the lounge door at Churchhaven, on her way to the kitchen, when the TV announcement stopped her. As the subtitle appeared over a view of the historic forty-room building, Zara moved swiftly and switched on the video recorder. Some intuition told her that what she was about to see was important to her stalled masterplan regarding the silver oars.

A thousand schemes, some practical, some absurd, had chased their way through her mind in the wake of the gang's half-decision to arm a silver oar with Semtex and a trembler fuse. But so many obstacles had intercrossed, and she had given weighty consideration to every one of them during the long day, so that now (it was after eight and the main news bulletin) she had been left with a headache. The practicalities remained insuperable.

The announcer said:

Tonight we are privileged to bring viewers visual material of the venue at which the reinstated Simonstown agreement will be signed next week by the British Prime Minister on the one hand and the South African President on the other. The ceremony takes place at the historic old Admiralty House in Simonstown, which has an association of no fewer than a hundred and seventy-five years with the Royal and South African navies.

The cameras showed the house's frontage on the busy main street which ran parallel to the Naval Dockyard, and two big wooden gates guarded by naval sentries. The camera zoomed in on one of the sentries, and the announcer went on:

Since the announcement several weeks ago of the ceremony, security has been tightened up at Admiralty House in anticipation of the function itself, when the tightest checks will be in force to protect the VIPs who will witness the historic occasion.

Zara logged the fact. How could a Semtex-primed oar get through that security screen, even assuming that an oar could be armed?

Showing another front view of the house, the commentator went on:

Admiralty House dates from the late eighteenth century and was bought near the end of the Napoleonic wars in 1814 by the Royal Navy. It was occupied by the South African Navy from 1957 to 1977, when Naval Headquarters was moved to Pretoria.

Admiralty House has a long association also with British Royalty, including the present Queen Elizabeth, who visited it with her parents in 1947.

The cameras switched to a new view, this time of the frontage facing the sea and the dockyard. A close-up followed of a small beach and pier. The announcer went on:

Not many people are aware that Admiralty House had its own private pier, which was built in 1828, but in recent years it became silted up. It has now been dredged, and this historic approach, once used by Royal Navy admirals, will be revived during next week's historic ceremony, when the two heads of government and other dignitaries will step ashore from the Admiral's barge and make their way in procession to the house itself for the signing ceremony.

The cameras tracked through the garden, pausing briefly at two old Portuguese cannon flanking the pathway, while the announcer said:

This pathway will be closely watched by an unbroken line of naval guards next week; a guard of honour will meet the VIP party at the old pierhead and accompany them to the house, where the signing ceremony will take place in a room filled with historical associations. This is the diningroom, famous for its magnificent central chandelier and blue-and-white decor and carpets, as well as massive central stinkwood table and chairs.

However, viewers will not be seeing the diningroom as it was until a few weeks ago, because a new and imaginative touch has been given to the historic room by converting it into a replica of the Vice-Admiralty Court as it used to be at the Cape – the court, in fact, never sat at Admiralty House.

Zara craned forward in her chair as the camera focused on the end wall of the room. Occupying half its height was a wooden screen topped by an arcade of five carved arches, each containing a fleur-de-lis, and broad wooden pillars on either end. Between these pillars, red curtains were draped from each fleur-de-lis arch. A judge's bench with raised central writing section stretched across the entire front of this magnificent piece of improvisation; on the wall above was a framed, painted reproduction of the Admiralty's symbol, the foul anchor.

It was the next camera shot, however, which electrified Zara.

As if from nowhere, Professor Pittock-Williams appeared.

Over his right shoulder, holding a pair of gloves in his left, Pittock-Williams carried the replica silver oar.

Zara was so stunned that for the moment she did not notice that the oar terminated in a Royal crown in silver, the head of the Marshal's traditional ivory staff of authority.

It was part of the oar itself – it had been fixed in!

Pittock-Williams advanced with studied nonchalance to below the judge's bench (there were two big Regency chairs side by side on it) and indicated what looked like four brackets fixed a few inches below the level surface of the bench.

The announcer went on:

We have here with us one of the key figures in next week's ceremony, Professor Vivian Pittock-Williams, whose great-grandfather was Admiralty Marshal at the Cape. Professor Pittock-Williams inherited the magnificent silver oar you can now see and through his generosity this priceless heirloom, as well as the silver oar salvaged from the Confederate raider *Alabama* recently, have both been donated to mark the auspicious occasion. In the tradition of Marshal, Professor Pittock-

Williams will lead the ceremonial procession from the Admiral's barge to this room –

Pittock-Williams wasn't going to be upstaged, when it came to the talking. He interrupted, with a gesture towards the two big chairs, and his most winning TV smile:

Before the heads of government take their seats, my function as Admiralty Marshal will be to lay the two silver oars, which I shall carry one on each shoulder, here in front of the judge's bench.

He advanced towards the brackets and laid the oar in position. Somewhere in the background, Zara noticed movement: the announcer explained it, the camera revealed it.

There were four armed plain-clothes security men.

Zara's eyes were now riveted on the ivory staff projecting from the base of the oar.

Pittock-Williams went on:

Here you can see the Marshal's staff, which screws into the shaft of the oar –

Zara felt slightly sick with excitement and intense concentration.

– the Marshal's baton has a hollow interior, in which will be kept the parchment which will be signed by the Prime Minister and the President to formally revalidate the Simonstown agreement.

As soon as the two VIPs are seated, I unscrew the baton's head like this –

It was coming right! It was coming right! Jubilation crashed through Zara's mind. God, for a trembler fuse and a charge of Semtex in place right now!

– take out the treaty parchment, turn and hand it to the presidential aide who will be standing next to him. The signing proper will then take place –

Zara jumped to her feet, unable to check her emotions. The baton itself was not to be unscrewed, only the head! There *could* be no bomb! The kidnap, all her elaborate expertising, had been a waste of time! Savage hatred surged through her at the sight of Pittock-Williams preening himself. He had slipped out of her trap!

He went on:

After the signing ceremony, we will come to the high point of the ceremony, when the two silver oars will be exchanged. This one here, the replica of the original, will first be presented by the State President to the Prime Minister, after which the second, the *Alabama* oar, as it has come to be called, will be presented by the Prime Minister –

Get on, for Chrissake, get on! Zara almost cried out aloud.

Pittock-Williams obliged:

I take up the replica oar, thus –

He lifted the beautiful object from its brackets.

– and make my way to the two VIPs, who a moment before were sitting but will now be standing, and take up my position next to the Prime Minister. Viewers should realize that the Marshal's baton was not part of the ceremonial oar and was the private property of the Marshal. Therefore, at this point I unscrew my baton from the oar and carry it in my left hand –

Pittock-Williams deftly unscrewed the crown-topped ivory baton.

Zara struck her clenched fist into her hand, over and over.

She exclaimed aloud: 'You will unscrew that baton, Pittock-Williams, but you will never carry it away in your left hand – or any other bloody hand!'

Chapter 33

'Shit-heel!'

As if in delayed reaction, Zara jumped to her feet; the crudity was whipped from her by the explosion of the hatred which had festered inside her for so long against Pittock-Williams.

There was no one within miles to hear Zara's yell at the TV screen except the great lewd fish in its tank. Almost as if it heard and understood her, it whorled and scratched itself against the glass like a cat preening itself. Only a cat hasn't got poison spines.

She had to see that programme again – now! She had to go over every minute point and check that her plan was watertight, no point at which Pittock-Williams might slip the noose through a technicality she had overlooked.

Zara moved to re-run the recording, then stopped. She knew what she would do, she would bring Fenella up from the bunker and make sure the expertise was 100 per cent, especially the critical moment at which the Marshal would unscrew his ivory staff.

Zara laughed, but it came out raspy because of her excitement. As she adjusted the video machine, her sense of recall became hyper-bright so that she felt she could remember even the minutest details of the ceremony.

'Bastard!' she said, less venomously than before, and went and collected the Glock.

Fenella was startled at the sound of the altar door being opened. Although she had lost her sense of sequential time down in the bunker with its darkness and cold, her watch told her this was no routine visit. She had been sitting at a spot away from the door where the radio reception seemed less bad than elsewhere, wrapped in a blanket. For one wild moment, she thought Zara had come to dispose of her.

Zara's flashlight did not pick her up immediately. 'Fenella! Where are you?'

'Here – what do you want?'

Zara heard the note of anxiety in Fenella's voice. She wanted something from her: perhaps it would be better to lead with a low card rather than take a tough approach.

'You're coming upstairs with me for a while. I want your opinion on something.'

'You got my opinion before, at pistol point. I've nothing to add.'

'You don't know whether we're talking about the same subject, although we are, in fact. Now! March!'

'Rayner – is he –?'

Zara smiled grimly. The conflicting light of the torch and the tired oil lamp sketched strange lines at the corners of her mouth.

'He's not,' she answered off-handedly. 'He's probably still chasing his tail – and yours – at the Villa Montana.'

Fenella had heard the radio news bulletins: Keyter was quoted as saying there was still no word of her, although several 'promising leads' were being followed. There had been no further word of the *Alabama* oar.

Zara said impatiently, 'You've got a job to do for me, and I've got my job to do. It depends on how well you do yours what happens to you.'

There was a resplendent moon above the line of low purple hills on the far shore. Its muted light made Fenella's eyes, wide from the darkness underground, the colour of the deepest lavender. The sigh of the lagoon's wide waters, the heaving fleece of scrub-covered dunes at her back towards the sea, had a feeling of unreality, like the mind's stirabout immediately on regaining consciousness. The serene waters had the touchmark of the prolonged autumn upon them, and the countless birds were still. Nevertheless, the night was warm to Fenella after the penetrating chill of the bunker.

They paused for a moment by the bell-tower. Steps went down from it towards the water; a few hundred metres to their right was a little rocky cove in which a dinghy was drawn up on a natural rock ramp, to serve Zara's yacht which lay at a buoy offshore.

Fenella indicated a skyward glow, far away to the left. There was enough illumination to come from a town.

'What is this place?' she demanded.

'The less you know, the better,' rejoined Zara.

They went into the house. Fenella scrunched up her eyes against the electric light. Zara noted, without concession, the unbrushed hair and rumpled clothes.

'Sit down. Keep your distance from me.' Zara gestured with the pistol. 'I am going to show you a video recording of a news feature tonight on details of the Simonstown ceremony next week. I am going to stop it where the handing-over of the two silver oars takes place. If there is anything amiss on the technical side, you will say so, is that clear?'

'Do you expect me to be a party to your hellish plan?' Fenella demanded.

'Leave the conscience to me,' retorted Zara. 'I want to know – must know – in particular, whether the way the Marshal's baton is unscrewed from the oar is correct.'

'I told you before –'

'Keep quiet! Watch!'

Zara seated herself on a stool half behind Fenella's chair, gun in lap, and started the re-run.

When Pittock-Williams made his sudden god-in-the-box appearance with the silver oar on his shoulder, Zara froze the picture. She indicated.

'Is that right? Is that how the baton is carried ceremoniously?'

Now that the motion had been stopped, the silver crown which topped the Marshal's staff could be seen projecting at the base of the oar.

'I explained that before: it's only in the replica, the one you see here, that the Marshal's baton forms part of the shaft. It's not like that in the original, the *Alabama* oar.'

'Look at it closely! Is that how it will be on the day of the ceremony?'

'That's what they're saying here, isn't it?'

'Don't come the heavy with me!' Zara snapped. 'Just reply to my question. The Marshal wouldn't have occasion to screw it out of the oar for any reason before the final proceedings?'

'I see no reason for him to do so.'

'We'll get on.'

Zara restarted the machine and they watched Pittock-Williams lay the oar on the brackets in front of the judge's bench. Zara commented, 'You see, he unscrews only the head of the Marshal's baton in order to extract the treaty parchment.'

'That answers your question then,' Fenella broke in with an air of triumph in her voice. 'The baton is not unscrewed from the shaft.'

'Don't anticipate!' Zara rapped out. 'Watch it out!'

They viewed Pittock-Williams lifting the replica from its brackets and moving round to the point where he said the Prime Minister would be standing. 'Therefore, at this point I unscrew my baton from the oar.' Zara froze the picture.

'Now – keep your eyes on it – step by step!'

Fenella saw him dexterously grasp the baton below the silver crown.

'He couldn't unscrew the baton by holding the crown, because it would itself unscrew,' she told Zara.

'I'd already noticed,' she remarked. She ran a frame or two further. Pittock-Williams had now separated baton from oar.

Her question to Fenella was rhetorical. 'That baton screws in and out of an iron foundation pipe, not so?'

Fenella did not reply directly, but said, 'Shrapnel, that is what you mentioned before, wasn't it? And shrapnel means explosives. I've had plenty of time down there in the dark by myself to think about it. You're out to kill the Prime Minister, the President, and the other VIPs, aren't you? That's what this silver oar business is all about!'

Zara answered levelly, menacingly, 'That is what it is all about. It's what you are all about. Without you, we wouldn't have known how to arm the silver oar, or what kind of detonator would be appropriate. You've served your purpose. You also know and guess far too much.' She toyed absent-mindedly with the Glock. 'The only problem now is, what to do with you.' She eyed her. 'Perhaps tonight you will hear the ghost footsteps down in the bunker. They mean death.'

At the Villa Montana, Rayner saw the Admiralty House feature, too. It brought the realization with it like a knife-thrust: unless he found Fenella within the next week, her place at the ceremony would be empty. His own was already. Brigadier Keyter had informed him, he had been struck off the invitation list.

Chapter 34

'I like it! I like it! It's a cinch!'

Gemma laughed, and it brushed out the habitual uncertainty of her smile.

'I had my doubts at Churchhaven on Monday – the whole plan seemed too airy-fairy, not enough solid fact to build on. Now we have it!'

It was next day, about one o'clock. Zara had let herself into Gemma's Cape Town flat: it was part of the gang's structure that they all had keys to one another's apartments, a funk-hole precaution in case of need.

Zara had motored from Churchhaven, bringing the video recording with her. Her idea was to have an impromptu gathering of the gang to view it later in the afternoon after they had finished work. Her viewing now with Gemma, the fuse expert, was in advance, a dry run, so to speak, in order to iron out any preliminary loopholes Gemma's technical eye might spot. Zara's presence had surprised Gemma (Churchhaven had no phones) but as the video progressed, she had become more and more enthusiastic.

Zara asked, 'There won't be any doubt about rubbing off everyone in the vicinity when the Semtex goes off?'

Gemma threw the coarse hair clear of her eyes. 'What you mean is, one person in particular?'

'The Marshal will be at the heart of the blast centre,' Zara replied harshly. 'He can start saying his prayers when the ceremony begins.'

They went through the finer points of the recording showing the ceremony's climax, concentrating on the baton being unscrewed.

Finally, Gemma exclaimed, 'It's perfect, absolutely perfect! It's a piece of cake, Zara!'

The other members of the Rote Zora gang thought so too, that evening. Except Menty. They had been summoned to Gemma's flat – Renate, Rikki, Kerry-Ann and Menty – by phone by Zara to view the video and offer their comments on it. Zara presented the scene of Pittock-Williams unscrewing the baton with the air of a conjuror.

Menty said, skilfully avoiding the other five pairs of eyes and rubbing her grubby fingers against the sleeve of her overall-type dress, as if that would get rid of the ingrained printer's ink under her nails, 'Are we all just going to sit back and watch this happen like the video shows?'

'What do you mean, just sit and watch all this happen? What else do you want?' Zara found it easy to bulldoze such puny opposition into the ground.

'I mean, are you not going to be there at Admiralty House for the ceremony?'

'I must remember to ask the organizers for my invitation.'

The others sniggered, but Menty said hastily, 'There's no need for that. I could fix an invitation for you.' She chanced a glance out of her smoky, concealing eyes. 'Just like I fixed you an invitation to the mock trial.'

Zara turned away impatiently. 'This is another ball game altogether. Besides, why should any of us be present? We don't want to get ourselves killed with our own bomb. We can watch it all happen on TV from a safe distance.'

Menty tried to re-establish her claim. 'I did a good job before – no one suspected. It was a good job, wasn't it? I mean –'

'I don't know what the hell you mean,' retorted Zara

impatiently. 'Get this clear, you and your forging skill have no place in my plan.'

'I see, I see,' she retracted. 'I just thought –'

'Forget it.'

Menty crawled away into her mousehole. It was a good way of hiding the hate in her eyes.

There was a silence, and then Zara asked, 'Any questions?'

Renate said abruptly, 'In our game, I buy only the success story. OK, we've had lots of fun over this. We've armed a unique type of bomb and detonated it in a very clever way. We've killed a prime minister, a president, and an ex-lover, plus who knows how many other VIPs. It's all there – on tape. That's as far as it will ever get. Why? Because we haven't got, and won't get, our hands on what is the key to it, the silver oar. Not a hope in hell of doing so. It's a fact which so far we've carefully swept under the carpet.'

Kerry-Ann's schoolmarmy enunciation added an edge to the malice of her words. 'Trust Renate to stamp on the plan with her big feet.'

Renate's short-fuse temper was as sensitive as a trembler.

'Yes, I am shooting it down – and down, and down!' she retorted. 'I know when a thing's crazy, and it's simply crazy to build a whole plan on something which doesn't exist. How in hell do you expect any of us to get near a silver oar between now and next week? Also, it takes time to arm it the way Gemma has plotted it with Semtex and a trembler device. The oar has to be in our possession, we have to prime it, put it back in place – wherever that might be – and then into the bargain hope that no damn fool unscrews the baton ahead of schedule and blows himself up prematurely, before it ever gets near the signing ceremony. This whole scenario is a dream, and it needs someone to rescue it!'

It was the news bulletin which rescued it. There was a strained, tense silence following Renate's outburst. To break it, Gemma switched on the TV. The camera showed an airliner coming to a halt at Cape Town's airport and four men, one carrying a long parcel, came down the steps.

The announcer said:

The historic *Alabama* oar, focal point of the Simonstown ceremony next week, is here shown arriving in Cape Town under an armed guard of a special four-man team of British detectives.

The team was met on arrival by a hand-picked South African security task force, headed by Brigadier Neels Keyter, who will be responsible for the arrangements to guard VIPs at Simonstown –

Keyter strode forward in his square-set, bull-necked way and gave the leader of the Scotland Yard contingent a perfunctory handshake; the almost brutal bones of his face were not modified by his attempt at a smile. The formidable bunch of men strode off towards the airport buildings.

The announcer went on:

Immediately on arrival, the *Alabama* oar was taken under armed security escort to an unknown destination. We asked Brigadier Keyter to give the public some idea of the security arrangements which will surround the exchange of these two priceless relics next week.

The close-up of Keyter's sun-scored face made the cold eyes appear still less confiding and trusting than they were in reality.

He said tightly, 'We are mounting the biggest security operation in South Africa's history and every available man will be on duty to ensure the safety of our distinguished visitors.'

His lips clamped shut. When Brigadier Keyter's lips clamped, a charge of Semtex wouldn't blow them open.

'Are you taking special precautions against possible terrorist attacks – ?'

'No comment.' He turned and walked away.

The announcer retrieved the interview blandly. He continued:

> Shortly before the plane's arrival, a special announcement was issued by the office of the State President regarding the two silver oars. This is to the effect that, in view of the immense public interest which has been generated in them, they will be placed on public view until the day before the Simonstown ceremony.

Zara jerked forward in her seat and threw a startled, questioning glance at Gemma.

> The venue will be the Silver Gallery of the Cultural History Museum, whose building has had intimate links with the silver oars, since it was here that the Vice-Admiralty Court sat for over three-quarters of a century before its functions were taken over by the Supreme Court –

Zara was on her feet. Her lips curled over her words like a breaking wave and showed a white line. The slack lines of her face were pulled taut by the rush of blood which mantled her cheekbones.

'The Cultural History Museum, by all that's holy! And we've been scaring ourselves pissless about how to get at the oars! Gemma!'

> – the public will be able to compare, at close quarters, these two famous and historic oars, which will be put on display in the Silver Gallery as from

tomorrow. Viewing hours will be from ten in the morning until four in the afternoon –

Zara repeated the announcer's words, flinging them around the group. 'The Silver Gallery! The Silver Gallery! From ten in the morning to four in the afternoon!'

– in view of the priceless value of the two oars, a special round-the-clock guard will be mounted by a team of hand-picked men from South African Security, who next week will fill a similar role in protecting the two oars at Admiralty House. Other security squads have been assigned to guard both the Prime Minister and the President as well as the scores of VIPs and diplomats who will attend the ceremony.

Renate said ironically, 'Ten in the morning till four in the afternoon! What time do you nominate for the heist, Zara?'

Zara didn't even hear the jibe. 'Right there, under our noses! Just for the taking!'

'You've got a plan all worked out?' asked Renate in the same sarcastic tone of voice.

'Any more information required from me?' Rikki's eyes and ears at her hotel reception desk had ensured the success of many previous, lesser, Rote Zora strikes.

'I haven't, but I will,' answered Zara. 'Just as soon as I get in and see the set-up in the Silver Gallery. Gemma, OK for tomorrow when the place opens?'

Gemma said, with surprising insight, 'I'm OK, I can get an hour off from work. But the time isn't. We don't want to rush in there with the first-comers, it might draw attention to ourselves. Over-keen. Those guys are smart, you know. Make it eleven, rather.'

'I see your point,' answered Zara. 'But an hour lost, is an hour lost.'

'What do you want the rest of us to do?' asked Renate.

'Nothing – yet. Until our recce tomorrow.'

'It's not a kamikaze act, I hope.'

'It's not me who's going to get killed.'

Menty's contribution was unsure, stuttering. 'Won't you need a ticket or something to get in there? I mean, I could, if you want –'

'Some people get hooked on booze, some people get hooked on dope, but this girl is hooked on counter-feiting,' sneered Zara. 'No, ducky, we won't be wanting either you or your undoubted talents this time. Just stay away like the rest, see?'

Menty squirmed and nodded silently.

Zara added, 'I want you all here again tomorrow at this time. We will use what Gemma and I find out as the basis for our plan.'

Renate added, 'Just don't underrate the boys with the shoulder-holsters, see?'

Zara ignored the crack. 'Till tomorrow, then. I'm get-ting back to Churchhaven.'

Beware, Zara. Menty is the most dangerous woman in your gang.

Chapter 35

Silver on black velvet.

The unstudied impact of the contrast between the two silver oars and the black velvet cushions on which they lay in their display cabinet outdid any which a jeweller might have contrived by means of special lighting and other artifices.

It was, in brief, stunning.

It hushed the crowd as they came close to the glass-topped cabinet, and left those filing past with little more

271

than monosyllables or inarticulate grunts, smiles or gestures, at the masterpieces beneath the glass.

The *Alabama* oar held pride of place in front; Pittock-Williams's replica was behind. Now that they were together, it was possible to distinguish the differences, not only of length and craftsmanship but principally, in the replica, of the addition of the Marshal's original ivory staff. This gave it a particular dimension of grace and rounded off the shaft with the three-dimensional Royal crown in silver, encircled by an engraved silver band.

It was on the staff that Zara and Gemma's eyes were riveted.

It was next day, Thursday, about eleven o'clock.

The following Tuesday the British Prime Minister would arrive in Cape Town.

The day after that, Wednesday, the Simonstown ceremony would take place.

The two Rote Zora women were part of the crowd which had been drawn in hundreds to the Cultural History Museum by the TV announcement the previous evening that the two oars would be on public exhibition.

The announcement had not exaggerated the security set-up in the Silver Gallery, either. Four uniformed guards stood, one at each corner of the glass-topped cabinet, like sentries at a VIP catafalque. Unlike mourners, their arms were not reversed. Their pistols were loose in their belts; their eyes were not downcast as they would have been at a coffin being ceremoniously guarded but flicked continually in every direction with a kind of erratic jump-ball effect over the faces and persons of the men and women who thronged the gallery.

One guard had a darker complexion than the others, and he had a peculiar trick of picking up eye-contact with a passer-by and holding it, expressionless, as his target tried to scrutinize the contents of the display case.

Zara found it disconcerting; Gemma to the extent that

she said in a whisper to Zara, 'Is that his way of looking for sex?'

'Don't whisper,' replied Zara. 'Be ordinary. Just ooh and ah, like the rest.'

The two women had met at the street entrance as they had arranged, an hour after the gallery had been opened. Zara knew the way inside the building, but even if she hadn't, the pair couldn't have gone any but one way with the press of sightseers.

Upstairs, the crowd bottlenecked at the Silver Gallery entrance door (also guarded by an armed sentry) and Zara and Gemma came to a halt next to the full-scale life-sized exhibit in the form of a reproduction of an old-time pharmacy. It was situated just outside the gallery proper.

Gemma indicated the rows of old-fashioned coloured glass bottles, fancy bins and brass containers of long-forgotten panaceas from corns to cancer. 'Reminds me of my lab. – 1900 model.'

Zara tried to loosen up enough to give a grin. 'Look at that guy behind the till: like something out of "Underneath the Arches".'

A life-size dummy in old-time apron and stiff fly-away collar above a Victorian waistcoat, buttoned up high, was handing over some medicine to a woman customer. The woman seemed to be smiling her thanks; both figures were extraordinarily lifelike. The illusion persisted in regard to the other customers in the shop, another woman and a man.

Gemma grinned again and gestured at the stylized advertisement for aspirin above the counter where one of the dummies stood, back half-turned, as if in contemplation of it.

'Aspirin was a popular number even in those days.'

A woman queuing behind the Rote Zora pair overheard Gemma's comment and said, 'Shows women haven't changed much over the years.'

Gemma grinned again and nodded back; Zara killed any further possible giveaway conversation with a warning tread on Gemma's foot.

They had moved on, and finally they had been borne along to the oar display cabinet.

Zara realized now that she and Gemma would encounter an obstacle they had not bargained for, the time factor. It would be impossible to make a prolonged study of the oars as they would have wished as the crowd jostled by. Although not being supervised or hurried by the guards, it was clear that they would not be able to linger.

They neared the display; Zara was tight with tension. She also wanted to examine the lock on the display cabinet: it would have to be forced to get at the oars. Would there be an alarm system to supplement the guards? Would there be any technical snags that were not apparent on the TV demonstration about removing the Marshal's staff itself? Or about tamping the shaft with Semtex? Finally, about screwing the baton back into position – its final death-dealing position – armed with the ultra-sensitive trembler fuse without blowing themselves up as they did so?

They were up to the display cabinet, now.

The cabinet lock was at waist-level. Zara surreptitiously ran a finger over it, like a blind man reading Braille. But her interest in the lock faded at the proximity of the weapon which would level her score against Pittock-Williams, as well as have world-wide repercussions with the death of the two heads of government. It brought such a rush of blood to her head that for a split second her vision was blurred by a momentary wave of giddiness.

As it cleared, she found that her sight was not focused on the replica but on the blade of the *Alabama* oar with its five exquisite engravings, from the Royal arms at the top to the medallion head of George the Third, encircled by an oak-leaf wreath, at the bottom.

But it was the replica which was her target. She noted, so sharp was her attention, that the Cape silversmith who had crafted it for Pittock-Williams's ancestor had omitted the dynamic engravings of the eagle and thunderbolt of Zeus which graced the original.

As she stood foursquare in front of the exhibit, Zara was aware of steady, subtle pressure from the queue behind. She threw a quick glance at Gemma. The fuse-girl's tight concentration must have set up vibes. As her eyes came away from Gemma's face, she found herself locked into the fixed stare of the dark-complexioned guard, as mesmeric and unyielding as that of a New Zealand strong-eyed dog on a sheep.

Zara wrenched her glance away, braced herself against the oncoming crowd pressure in order to win Gemma more time.

Her eyeballs seemed to be pulsing: here, within a short hand's-reach, was the instrument she needed above anything else – and she could not have it! For one mad moment, the thought crashed through her mind – why not hijack it, and damn the consequences! But the consequences were plain to see – four sentry pistols, loaded for bear, at close range. They couldn't miss.

Gemma had to have more time! Zara, like a lock in a Rugby maul, propped herself against the thrust of bodies behind. The aspirin lady, next in line, was growing impatient. Zara deliberately ignored her. What did the woman mean to her, anyway?

There seemed to be a jostle and the sound of voices raised in protest from further back in the queue. Zara ignored that also, except when her own arm was jerked by someone who had obviously incurred the displeasure of the sightseers by jumping the queue. Now the newcomer was trying to force her out of her key position!

Zara swung round angrily.

It was Menty.

Like a lap-dog currying favour, half guilty and half pleased at her rashness, Menty attempted to blend an apology into her half-smile.

'Here I am,' she fluttered. 'I thought –'

The eye-contact specialist started coming towards them. Zara tapped Gemma's shoulder. 'Get on, for God's sake! Don't wait! Look who's here!'

Gemma took in the sentry's interest, the crowd's restiveness, and Zara's fury in a brief sweeping glance. She gave a distasteful shrug at the untidy, grubby, jeans-clad figure, turned away from the display cabinet, and moved into the queue gap which had been opened by previous viewers.

Zara grabbed Menty by the arm and propelled her away from the cabinet before the guard could arrive.

'You bloody, bloody, stupid little ass!' she muttered in a low, savage voice. 'Do you want to spoil everything? Draw attention to us, when the last thing we need is attention! Didn't you see the way the guard – for Chrissake!'

'I came to see if I could help with anything –'

'Keep your voice down! Better, shut up altogether! Can't you understand!'

Menty suddenly tore her arm free of Zara's grip. Something came into the nondescript face which had never been there before and pulled its muscles into a contortion which, if Zara had not been overwhelmed by fear and anxiety, she would have found alarming.

'OK! If that's the way you want it!' For once, Menty's eyes were not evasive and self-effacing. She swung round and stalked off.

Zara and Gemma found themselves alone. They edged their way through the talkative, excited crowd, elated at having witnessed first-hand the reality of such a resplendent symbol as the silver oar, reaching back in history to the reign of Elizabeth the First. The paddle shape of the oar strikes still deeper into British origins, to the time when Viking paddles propelled the long ships into England's creeks and estuaries. The silver oar, once borne in procession to London's Execution Dock for hangings, saw the justice pronounced as well as the justice carried out in all its medieval gruesomeness: the last light a pirate would have seen as the noose went round his neck would have been the bright blade of the oar with its masterly engravings of Royal and Admiralty authority.

Now the two oars lay on their velvet cushions in the Silver Gallery behind the two Rote Zora women, awaiting their key role in a different kind of execution.

Chapter 36

The Villa Montana's telephone gave one ring, next a strangled half-ring, then died.

Rayner had already jumped to his feet and taken a couple of paces from the kitchen, where he was indulging in a kind of force-feed breakfast against his will, towards the instrument when it stopped.

His senses seemed to intuit unerringly that this was no usual call; the frustrated backlash when it choked quiet added to his islanded isolation of mind and body, which had grown with each successive day since Fenella's disappearance.

That was four days ago. It was now Friday. Every morning when he had awoken and started about the grave-like stillness of the villa added yet more desolation to the trauma of the morning he had gone up to take Fenella her tea and found her gone.

Nor had there been a single trace of her since.

Rayner had gone into action right away after Hugh Perrot had phoned the name Zara Hennessy from London. Routine telephone checks, personal legwork, hotels, airport lists – he had come to realize very quickly how tight-shut these sources of information could remain without official accreditation. His net result after a day of it had been – nil.

Hugh, on his arrival back on his one-man mission with the *Alabama* oar, had made an undercover visit to Rayner. They had discussed in depth Fenella's disappearance. Hugh had been gravely concerned. To him, the kidnap had classic hallmarks: first, the snatch; second, the utter disappearance of the victim; third, the silence – of the grave.

The days following had yielded nothing, and he had even risked phoning Hugh the previous day out of sheer desperation. Hugh had been understanding, but reserved. He was completely tied up with the security arrangements for the Simonstown ceremony. There was nothing he could do to help.

Now, after the aborted phone ring, Rayner went back to his breakfast.

The phone downstairs started to ring again. Rayner started for the stairs. He only got halfway down when the instrument gave a similar strangled ring, sputtered, and died.

This time there had been two and a half rings.

Was it a signal? Rayner agonized. Could it be that Fenella was trying to get over a message and was being hamstrung? Were the calls meaningful, or someone merely dialling a wrong number and realizing the mistake before it went too far?

He decided to wait at the phone.

It rang.

Rayner's super-quick snatch of the instrument from

its cradle caught the actor emerging from the wings, so to speak, off-balance. It was a child's voice backed by an adult woman's presentation: the result, as on the stage, was phoney.

'Er – I am your friend –'

The words came out coyly, rustily, as if they had lain in the caller's repertoire for a long time. Especially to a male.

All Rayner's senses went on full alert. What he was hearing was the classic preliminary to a kidnap ransom deal, the attempt to bamboozle a relative driven crazy by anxiety and fear into a false sense of security and trust. Relatives in a human heist will believe anything. Rayner had once played out a kidnap drama as a professional go-between; now he was involved emotionally himself, up to the neck.

Keep 'em talking, play along, there is always a give-away, to the trained listener.

'Yes?' Rayner was non-committal. The caller had said nothing to indicate it, but he knew instinctively that it was to do with Fenella.

'– and I have something of importance to tell you.'

The lead-in had been carefully rehearsed; Rayner could tell it was being delivered by rote. Half hesitant, half determined.

It was that determination which Zara had trodden ruthlessly and uncaringly into the ground when Menty had jerked away from her in the Silver Gallery. Here was the pay-off.

Rayner's caller was Menty.

She had spent hours the previous night with the telephone in her hand speaking into the mouthpiece to get it right, what she would say to Rayner at the other end. Twice that morning her nerve had failed: the result had been those stuttering rings which Rayner had suspected.

'Concerning what?' Rayner remained neutral.

'I think you know.' Menty's laugh sounded silvery and worldly-wise. Only at her end of the telephone.

Keep 'em talking! Rayner hoped with every fibre of his being that Keyter's team were tapping the villa's phone; it would give them time to trace the origin of the call.

'If I knew who was calling, I could perhaps guess.'

The earpiece membrane jarred to another silvery laugh. Menty was beginning to enjoy herself. It felt good to have someone squirm instead of being the squirmer.

'It was very clever, the way they used an ambulance, wasn't it? I bet you never thought of it, although the TV said you were such a top security guy.'

Ambulance? Was she hurt? Rayner went cold. He hadn't got the hang of Menty's *non-sequiturs*.

'They?' he asked, in order to keep the conversation going.

'The other girls. I wish now I'd come. I would know what the place looks like where you're staying.'

The other girls! A gang of girls! A terror gang?

He *had* to get his hands on the woman at the other end of the line! Did this auntie-type conversation, delivered in the young-old voice, conceal a killer underneath?

He said in a nonchalantly deceptive manner, 'You could always come and have a look.'

Her open-ended reply left his pulses racing with a great surge of hope. 'I could always think about it.'

Rayner tried to steady his voice. 'So you didn't take part in kidnapping Fenella?'

The reply was petulant, small-girl. 'I stayed behind. Zara didn't want me any more. I could have fixed it to get her in, like I got her in when she shot him.'

Zara! Zara! Where in heaven's name was this woman talking from? He tried to do mental hand-springs to keep up with what she was trying to say – who had shot whom?

280

Could she possibly be talking about the attempted gunning-down of Pittock-Williams?

'Got her in?' he echoed.

'Yes. It was a good job, I say so myself. I could have beaten the security at Admiralty House too, but Zara wanted Gemma. Gemma! That bitch! Now they're in on it together.'

Rayner's mind reeled. Menty's voice changed from its initial stagey articulation as bitterness and jealousy poisoned it. She was telling him something, back to front. He had to have the key! Admiralty House could mean only one thing. Where did Fenella fit in?

He had to risk a question straight from the shoulder. 'Are you phoning to demand a ransom for Fenella?'

Menty gave a giggle. 'You know, I never thought of it. It would be a way of getting her out, wouldn't it? It must be damn cold down there, after all this time.'

Rayner's emotions overcame his studied caution. 'She's OK, then?'

'Yes.' Menty didn't seem interested. 'But she won't be, once they're finished. She knows too much.'

Rayner felt sick. 'About what?'

'About what I'm telling you.'

It was no good saying to her it was a jumble of half-expressed inferences, each successive one seeming to bear a more awful consequence.

'Before or after the kidnapping?'

'They couldn't have planned it without what she told them.' The note of deep-seated jealousy supervened. 'Gemma, especially. She gave the job to Gemma and left me out in the cold, even after what I'd done before. Then of course Fenella had heard too much.'

Rayner's mouth was dry. He was about to try and probe further among the morass of mixed-up words when he saw a crevasse open up before his feet. A trap! Could this whole thing be a neatly baited trap into which he had already half-fallen? Had he failed to recognize the elementary principle that emotion was being exploited while his reason and judgement were lulled by the rubbish fed to him, which really meant nothing?

He asked tersely, laying everything on the line, 'What are you going to do about your problem?'

A quick right-left to the jaw couldn't have sent Rayner reeling more than her reply.

'I'm going to get even. I want to show you where your girl is.'

Rayner still couldn't believe what he had heard. Where was the snag? Was he about to walk open-eyed into the trap? If he threw his chance away, would he be throwing Fenella's life away with it?

Rayner knew his voice sounded wrong, but he couldn't help it. 'When?'

'Now. Right away. It's quite a way, but we can use my car.'

'*Now?*'

Mistrust blazed through Menty's voice. 'What is wrong with that? Don't you want to – ?'

Rayner tried to cover up, but he knew he'd lost a move and left the woman wary. 'It's just that I didn't expect it.'

The adult took over from Menty's childish other-half. 'Listen. If you don't believe what I'm saying, we'll just leave it and your girl will die down there in the dark. It doesn't matter to me.'

The fish was slipping off the hook, rapidly. He said, 'It does, to me. More than anything else in the world. Does that satisfy you?'

'You looked like a nice guy on TV, and you speak like one,' Menty said. 'But you never can tell with a man. I'll come – but if you let the police or anyone else know or if there's anything I don't like the look of when I get to your place, you won't see me, and your girl will die. And if she does, you'll be responsible.'

It had crossed Rayner's mind, while the call was in progress, that he would chance one quick call to Hugh before she came, but the rapid way things had developed had left him flat-footed. He dared not risk anything now, he decided.

'Come right away – I'll leave the front door open,' he said.

'Ten minutes,' she answered, and hung up.

He hadn't got his gun any longer, but there was time for him to secrete his commando knife under his shirt.

Chapter 37

Five minutes.

Ten minutes.

Rayner double-checked his watch. He had taken up his position by the open front door, so that he could see the front and side entrances of the Villa Montana.

Fifteen minutes.

Rayner had not expected this; his anxiety was growing insupportable. Had she weaselled on him? Had the call been a hoax? There are always the types who love to exploit a tragedy for the sake of a vicarious thrill.

Rayner's super-stressed senses detected, before his ears heard, a presence at his back, from the interior of the house. He went into a low, swinging, dodging movement, his hand reaching for the knife inside his shirt. As his vision first picked up the scuffed sandals, then the grubby jeans, and finally the mousy, unbrushed hair above the indeterminate, evasive eyes, he knew he was reaching for heavy artillery when a popgun would suffice.

'My, you're as tight as a fiddler's bitch!' Menty said.

Rayner recognized the ingenuous, little-girl voice at once as his phone caller. How, though, had she insinuated herself into the house and come so stealthily up behind him (the plank floor was a sounding-board for any kind of shoe) so that he had not even heard her? There must be more behind that child's face and flat-chested teenage figure under a nondescript washed-out shirt than met the eye.

He straightened up; she measured only up to his shoulder.

'I expected you from the other direction,' he said.

She eyed him with devastating candour. 'You're handsomer than you looked on TV.'

What kind of attributes – perverted talents might be a better description – qualified the figure in front of him for membership of an international terrorist gang?

Rayner was so unsure that he asked, 'You are the person who is going to take me to Fenella? The one who rang?'

She laughed, a squeaking, unpleasant little effort. 'It'll slay Zara. But she had her chance. I could have fixed it, for Admiralty House.'

Rayner did not want to get involved in another *non-sequitur* conversational cross-fire.

'Let's get going, then,' he said.

Menty said – was it magnificent acting, or unstaged naivety? – 'It's a long way – don't you want to have a wee before we start?'

Rayner didn't know whether to laugh or make a smart come-back. Her eyes couldn't hold his for long; they slid away, not out of embarrassment but habit.

'I'm OK,' he began to say, when the phone rang from down the hall.

If Rayner had not turned to go and answer, he would have noticed the jerk which pulled Menty's muscles tight, followed by a controlled stillness. Mice learn to freeze to survive when the cat claws at their hole.

Rayner picked up the instrument, his back to Menty. 'Why, Hugh–'

He turned. Menty was gone.

'See you!' He slammed down the phone, sprinted to the front door. Which way had she gone? He could not see any car in the street near the front entrance: it must be the side. He whipped open the door as a buff-coloured car started to pick up speed down the hill. Menty was its driver.

Rayner threw himself after it, dragged open the passenger's front door, projected himself in.

Menty's gaze was fixed ahead. He might not have been there.

He said tightly, 'That was a bloody silly thing to do.'

She said, stalling at the corner stop street, 'You thought you'd trap me, didn't you, Mister Smart-arse? How dumb do you think I am? Give her a quarter of an hour, you told your security pals after I'd phoned, and I'll keep her talking, then give a buzz and come and pick her up. Fenella's off, I tell you. If you try anything on, I'll stop the car and start screaming that you're trying to rape me.'

It felt to Rayner like the occasion in the SAS when he had had to talk down a would-be suicide poised on a ledge fifteen floors above the street.

He said quietly, 'Listen! I don't know your name, but listen to me for a moment, will you? Go on driving, or pull in to the side, just as you wish.'

'Now you're trying to get my name by your soft talk,' she replied. There was a dead, dangerous note to her voice. She was to be taken very seriously, Rayner warned himself. Dangerous. Very dangerous.

'I don't know the rest of the story you tried to tell me

285

on the phone, but it is not important to me, even as a security man,' he said.

'You expect me to believe that?' she jeered.

'Fenella is Number One. Perhaps you as a woman can realize that. The rest means nothing.'

Menty slowed, pulled aside from her hectic flight into the mainstream of traffic.

'You're in love with her?'

'Yes.'

Menty drew off to the kerb and stopped. 'I never was. No man ever wanted me. I guess it's the way I am and I haven't got any tits.'

She sat staring through the windscreen. Rayner said nothing.

She asked abruptly, 'Have you got a gun?'

'No. The police confiscated mine when I backed down on an assignment I should have undertaken back to London. But I couldn't leave Fenella.'

'Zara made us all take one, when she cleaned out the bunker for your girl. There was too much stuff – all the mines and grenades and detonators and things – for the old family tomb there in the churchyard. A Makarov pistol, I think she said. But I don't like it, it's too big. So I didn't bring it today.'

An arms cache! What else would this defector let slip in her back-to-front way of talking?

'Is that what Zara intends using for the job?'

'No, no. It's much cleverer than that. Semtex. They'll fill the shaft with it and Gemma will fix a trembler.'

Rayner went cold. Semtex! The answer to a terrorist's prayer! A trembler fuse! The most diabolical of all booby-traps! What shaft? What was she talking about? He knew by now that to question Menty would make her back-track, and Fenella would be lost.

Rayner gestured at the traffic. 'If we stay here, you'll get a ticket. That won't help you stay anonymous.'

'Menty's the name,' she said unexpectedly. 'OK, we're on our way. Watch out for Zara when we get there, though. She'll kill you. Me too. She's got a special gun that foxes the airport checks, the one she used to try and kill him.'

'Him? Pittock-Williams?'

Menty set the car in motion. 'Who else? Because of him she hasn't got any guts left – woman's guts, I mean. She couldn't stuff with a man if she wanted to, and she wants, by God!'

'A Glock 17?' he asked tentatively.

'That's the name,' she replied. 'It's not a grease-gun, but it's very quick-firing. She used a silencer, too.'

Where in hell, Rayner asked himself, had this girl (he couldn't think of her as a woman) picked up a slang term like grease-gun for an automatic pistol? Maybe it made her walk tall, to use it in the company of a security man.

She added, sententiously, 'Those who live by the sword shall perish by the sword.'

Not necessarily, Menty, as you will find to your cost later today.

Rayner noted that Menty had taken a big freeway which became the main highway to the north out of Cape Town.

Menty's voice rasped. 'I got her in and they never suspected the invitation was a fake. I say it myself, it really was good.'

She would like to have known that Scotland Yard endorsed that opinion. Rayner knew the answer before he asked the next question.

'Was it made out to Zara Hennessy?'

Menty fell into the trap. 'Noways,' she answered. 'I inscribed it to Ms Z. White – White was her great-great-something who built the place we're going to where Fenella is.'

They headed northward, with the gigantic landmark

of Table Mountain, the sea, and the famous island prison of Robben Island on Rayner's left.

'Do you know the way we're going?' asked Menty.

Rayner shook his head, truthfully. 'I've been in the Cape far too short a time.'

'Well, it doesn't really matter. It's the end which counts, as the bishop said to the actress.'

Had he not been so concerned, Rayner might have marvelled at Menty's particular style of conversation. It was the sort of spurious bonhomie which would make a male run a hundred miles.

Menty said, apropos nothing, 'It must be damn cold down there, despite the fact that winter hasn't come yet.'

It was no good, Rayner had quickly learned, trying to unravel Menty's mental knots and snarls by questions; they only made her dig her toes in.

He said in a neutral tone, 'So?'

'It was bad enough for us when we carted the mines and grenades and ammo out and we were having the exercise to keep warm, but to be cooped up there for nearly a week now in the dark would be really tough. Zara gave her the radio, but that doesn't keep you warm, does it?'

'It certainly doesn't,' he agreed with the self-evident Menty-type hypothesis.

'It was this old guy – the great-great-something of Zara's whom she hero-worships so – that built it. He must have planned it at the same time as the church, otherwise he couldn't have dug under it when the building was already there, could he? The altar, too. You couldn't have the secret door and steps and things without planning the funk-hole first and then building the church, could you?'

Now he knew! The convoluted story told him mostly everything, except the location of the place they were heading for. Once he knew that, Menty became irrelevant. He would find Fenella for himself: a church, a secret hide-out under it, with an entrance via the altar!

Rayner decided to risk a question. 'Why did this great-great of Zara's build it in the first place?'

Menty tried a man-luring pout. 'Everything there is the great-great's. You'd think he was still alive, the way she keeps his memory fresh. Even that bloody fish in the tank. It gives me the heebie-jeebies. Deadly, if you touch one of its spines. Great-great kept one, so Zara keeps one. That's the way it is with everything there, even the family tomb. We filled it up with guns and ammo and stuff from the funk-hole. Of course, we couldn't leave it for Fenella.'

'Naturally,' Rayner agreed, digesting this new mass of data.

They went on and on, then turned westward, in the direction of the sea.

At the summit of a low hill Menty waved at the far glint of water.

She said in a voice which was perhaps twelve years old, 'What a super day for a picnic! We could go swimming in the nudie-nude, you and me, and then lie on the beach and drink wine, and you could make love to me over and over in the sand until it gave my bum a rash.'

Rayner replied as seriously as he could, 'Salt water would be bad for that.'

'Oh, it's not sea water, that's why the flamingos are there. Millions of them. You can see them from the windows, and the beach is down below. They look like pink water-lilies on the lagoon. Maybe the lagoon is salty, but it's not sea water. All those marshes and things couldn't stand sea water.'

A house on a lagoon: he was getting warmer.

They came to a four-way junction where they halted. The main sign read 'Saldanha'.

Menty did not follow it but carried on straight ahead, still heading towards the sea.

'The tar ends in a minute,' she said. 'The road from there on is hell. It takes a long time to get there.'

Menty did not exaggerate. She had to slow right down to avoid the non-stop potholes, corrugations, and washed-out sections of the white, sandy track.

'What do you intend to do when we get to Zara's?' he asked.

Menty shrugged. 'We'll play it by ear. If she isn't at home, then it's a piece of cake. I'll show you where the secret door is in the altar, and you'll have to break it open and get Fenella out. If Zara's in –' she shrugged. '– we'll have to make a plan.'

'Why not phone ahead, and if Zara answers, we'll know she's at home?'

Menty burst out laughing. 'There's no phone at Zara's place! In fact, there's no phone anywhere. I guess the nearest place would be at the village on the other side of the lagoon, and you'd have to drive about thirty kilometres round to get there. The road is like this all the way.'

Rayner was uneasy. Never had he gone into an operation less prepared, and with a maverick like Menty around anything could happen.

The dust rose up in the interior of the car as it cavorted and bumped over the appalling surface.

'I dunno how the other girls go on putting up with this,' said Menty. 'It's easier when Renate brings them in the Combi. They'll all be there later today to spend the weekend. They're going to try and work out how they'll get their hands on the oar long enough to arm it.'

It could have been the dust or shock at what she was saying that brought the crepitation into his query. 'Get their hands on it?'

'Didn't you see the TV feature about the oars on display?' she asked. 'Zara said she'd kill you if Fenella didn't tell her how they fitted together. That's stage two. They've got the loading part all worked out. Stage one is how to get hold of Pittock-Williams's oar and fix the Semtex and a trembler.'

She crashed the car through a big runnel and threw them up in their seats. 'That's why we broke up. Zara treated me like shit when I only went to look when they were at the gallery. She only wants Gemma. OK, she can have her. I'll get even with her.'

That's why he was here, Rayner told himself, hitching his star – probably his life and Fenella's – to an unstable girl's revenge-lust. The rescue operation seemed foredoomed, through lack of planning, lack of any knowledge on his part of the set-up or the lay-out.

'The whole gang's coming, this afternoon?' he asked. 'How many of you are there?'

'Five – and Zara makes six,' she replied. 'We'll have to get clear well before they arrive.' Rayner didn't like the sound of her laugh. 'I'll show her – I'll show 'em all! They'll say when they find out, that worm, that mouse, we never suspected she had the guts of a rabbit! They'll laugh on the other sides of their faces!'

Rayner decided to try and lead her back to the logistics of this wildly unlogistical operation.

'How then can we tell whether Zara is or isn't at home? What about her car? Where does she park it?'

'That's it!' Menty responded, too readily, too thoughtlessly. 'We can check whether it's in the garage or not. She usually leaves the doors open.'

The car jerked and pitched like a rowboat in a rough sea. They were now cutting through low scrub; the hummocky, sandy terrain spelt dune country, not far from the sea.

Menty said, 'It doesn't look much now in the autumn,

but in the spring it is nature's wonderland of flowers, a townsman's dream made reality.'

She managed the tourist quote well.

Chapter 38

They crested a hummocky hillock, and there it was.

Langebaan. The lagoon, with a fringe of bright green marshland and saltings like a monk's tonsure, a kilometre and a half wide, and, beyond, a tranquil lake at least a dozen kilometres long, astonished Rayner. He had prepared a mental picture of the setting in which he hoped to find Fenella; even a dream would have found it hard to emulate the reality in front of his eyes.

'– imagine waking up here to the sound of whirring wings as tides rise and fall –' Menty was still on the quote.

'Where is Zara's house?' His demand was brusquer than he intended; it bordered on abrasive because of his inner knowledge of how unprepared he was.

'You can't see it from here,' she answered. 'There's a place a couple of kilometres further on where we can stop. It's a kind of small peninsula. Lots of bushes and trees. We can hide the car there and then go on foot. You can see the house from there. You can't mistake it. On the cliffside above is the church tower, the one old great-great also built. It's white. It looks like a lighthouse.'

'Let's get on.' Rayner was taut and impatient. Menty seemed to regard the whole affair as a kind of relaxed picnic.

She said, gesturing at the placid scene, 'You can see why Zara is doubly the hell in with Pittock-Williams. He wants her place as part of the public national park –'

'OK, OK,' Rayner broke in. 'Get going, Menty!'

She moved the car slowly forward and said, in anticipation of Rayner's impatience, 'If I go faster, it'll kick up dust and Zara could spot us, if she's there.'

Finally, Menty turned rightwards off the road itself, towards the lagoon's side, into a track which led into a thicket of small trees. She halted in a clearing.

They got out; Menty led via an overgrown path. 'You can see Zara's place from the top,' she said.

Suddenly they broke clear of the trees.

On the water close by the point was a big naval crash-boat. The point had hidden it from view as they had approached along the road; perhaps the concealment was deliberate.

It was. Menty explained. 'It's a crash-boat from the naval station over on the other side of the lagoon near Langebaan village. They also help out the lake rangers against poachers. Look, they're waving! They've spotted us!'

The lagoon ranger and naval crew on deck were not the only ones who had sighted the two figures which now emerged and stood waving in reply from the summit of the point.

Further along the lagoon shore, a powerful pair of binoculars in the hands of a solitary figure halfway down the cliff had been eyeing the crash-boat's activities with suspicion. Now they transferred to the two waving figures, who sharpened into identifiable focus. The watcher gave a gasp, knew who they were. The image blurred as the hands shook with realization.

It was Zara.

She was midway down the cliff path which led from the church tower to the little rocky cove which harboured the yacht dinghy. Earlier she had seen, from the lounge, the crash-boat pass, travelling slowly and keeping as close inshore as the shallow water would permit for its relatively deep draft. Curiosity turned to suspicion: had it any wind of Fenella? Then the craft pulled in behind the point and stopped.

Now – the waving figures!

Rayner Watton! She recognized the lean, tall figure immediately from his TV pictures. With him was – Menty!

If Watton was on her doorstep with Menty, it meant only one thing, she had been sold down the river. Menty! Why had Menty, of all the gang – then she recalled the wrench away from her in the Silver Gallery. What hidden, dangerous fires smouldered under that mousy self-obliterating exterior? Hell, what a fool she had been not to recognize the symptoms of a worm turning! And now here they were, the two of them in collusion, signalling a naval patrol vessel: what tie-up was there?

She turned and went up the steep path at a stumbling run. Her strategy formulated itself as she ran. They must be given to think the house was deserted. That meant getting her car out of the garage and hiding it, quick. Down the lagoon-side road, in the opposite direction from Watton and Menty. She knew a place, not far.

She dodged into the house. There were a couple of things she needed. The Glock, keys. She snatched the keys she needed, as well as those of her car, from a hook on the kitchen door, raced through her bedroom and whipped the Glock out of her suitcase. She snapped a fresh magazine into place.

Now!

She backed the car out of the garage and eased it cautiously up the incline to the main road. She resisted the overwhelming desire to hurry – and kick up dust.

Beyond the graveyard hill the road dipped and she passed over a cattle grid. A hundred metres beyond, a track ran lagoonwards and Zara pulled in amongst the thick tree cover. She jumped out, started back at the double towards the church and the graveyard, gun in hand. At the graveyard, she sprinted between the headstones to George White's family tomb, unlocked the small door, and threw herself in among the boxes of grenades, pistols, mines, detonators and ammunition.

When she had regained her breath, she reopened the door a crack, eyeing the only approach Rayner and Menty could make.

She was not to know that Rayner, with his commando training, had made skilful use of the roadside cover. Menty had been inept at hiding herself; none the less, they had arrived unspotted (he believed) at the turn-off from the main road to Zara's house.

The garage doors were open.

'There!' exclaimed Menty. 'She's not here.' She started to stand up.

'Quiet!' whispered Rayner from his cover. 'Down!'

He edged forward warily, checked the house, the empty garage, and the church. 'Looks OK,' he said quietly.

He was so well hidden that it was not until he stood up that Zara spotted him. She watched Menty also emerge from a clump of small trees. The two headed towards the garage and house.

Zara flexed her gun wrist. A difficult shot, a moving target.

She decided to revert to her original strategy. They would try the church, of that she was sure. Equally sure, the altar door leading to Fenella.

She watched the pair head cautiously towards the house door, which she had left open. Watton seemed to be carrying something in his hand, she couldn't make out what.

Now was her moment!

It would mean losing sight of her victims for a minute because the church would block her view, but it was the safer, surer shot in the end. And she meant to get them both.

Zara opened the tomb door, darted across the open spaces between the graves, jerked open a small outside vestry door, and slipped in. She shut the minister's private door into the church, sited just below the high carved pulpit, until only a crack remained.

It was less than five minutes before Rayner and Menty entered.

'I told you it would be a piece of cake.' Menty was chattering. She indicated the altar. 'All we've got to do now is to break open the secret door and we'll get your girl out.'

She was relaxed; Rayner was not. He walked up the aisle stepping carefully, as if his knee muscles were ready at the slightest suggestion of danger to project himself sideways. Zara saw, too, what he carried in his right hand. It was a razor-sharp commando knife. Here was a very dangerous man.

The dim light inside the church seemed to worry him also. Shadows are the friends of enemies.

Rayner and Menty reached the altar.

'Here – this is it,' said Menty. 'It's very smart. You can't see it at all, unless you know.'

Rayner bent down. He was tall, Zara noted, she'd have to give his shot more elevation than Menty's. The Glock's safety was off.

Rayner half-bent down; Menty peered over his shoulder.

Zara used the Glock barrel to ease open her door, just wide enough for her to slip through. She moved in swiftly, down behind one of the big, old-fashioned, full-backed mahogany pews. All that was visible of her was her head. The pistol rested on the pew in a no-miss position.

Which of the two first?

Menty said, 'You'll have to use that knife of yours to force it –' and half-turned.

The heavy nine-millimetre parabellum slug took her in the right eye.

She went down on her knees with her thighs splayed, and then on down the altar steps in a ludicrous half-copulatory series of bumps. Her head jerked back in an ecstasy of agony, until she smashed to a standstill against one of the communion railings, spilling the contents of her eye and brain onto the floor.

A second shot thundered round the peeling old walls like the ultimate declamation of doom.

But it was milliseconds too late. Rayner went down, sideways, and rolled as the second slug tore into the beautiful wood of the altar, chipping and splintering.

Rayner's reflexes took him clear of the line of fire into cover behind the altar. In a flash, he was up on his knees, braced, with the knife ready.

The silence was stunning – and more menacing – than the loud-voiced Glock had been.

Where was the gunman? – gun-woman, he corrected himself grimly. There was no doubt who it was. Zara.

She couldn't get at him where he was, unless she exposed herself round the sides of the altar, of which he had a clear sight.

He waited.

Silence. He *must* hear her if she moved!

How long could each keep up this lethal game of Russian roulette?

There was a minuscule whisper of sound – of some sort – from nearby. The front of the altar! A wooden box just over a metre across between him and his would-be killer!

Rayner could not identify what he had heard – perhaps some residual sound squeezed from the unfortunate Menty's lungs by an already dead muscle contracting –

There it was again!

He knew now what it was. A creak from the secret door.

His take-off at a low crouch, knife ahead, equalled a Grand Prix grid.

As he projected himself round the corner of the altar, the door slammed shut.

Rayner hesitated for one split second. It was long enough to lose him the game.

If he had gone straight after Zara, he could have cornered her on the flight of wooden steps between the inner and outer doors of the funk-hole. He could have crowded Zara at close quarters in the ready-made trap before she could have used her gun on him, and all would have been finished with one lethal, upward thrust of the razor-sharp blade of the commando knife as he held her, chest to breast, against the inner door –

As it was, he was just in time, as he yanked wide the altar door and plunged in, to see the inner door slam a few paces ahead.

He hurled himself at it.

It gave. Beyond was half-dark.

'Stop!'

Zara had Fenella by the throat with her left hand, and her right jammed the pistol against her right ear.

There are hells and hells.

Rayner's would always be that dim little icy underground room lit by an inadequate oil lamp, and Fenella, dishevelled and shivering, her feet wrapped in strips of torn blanket, her eyes wide and luminous from the darkness and trauma.

'Stay where you are, or I'll shoot!'

The gun wasn't aimed at him but at the dark head of tousled, unbrushed hair. Could he get there first, before the trigger – ? His body was anticipating. Zara saw the predator-like poise on the steps, one leg behind the other to give him take-off purchase, the other to guide him at her. The knife-blade, held like that, meant only one thing, death.

Fenella gave a strangled gasp. 'Rayner!'

'She doesn't matter to me!' Zara rapped out warningly. Perhaps nothing mattered. She was on a high, the same way as she had been psyched up the day she had homed the Glock in on Pittock-Williams.

She changed the position of the gun-mouth slightly so that if the heavy bullet went clean through Fenella's head, it wouldn't catch her on the other side. Rayner saw.

'Throw down the knife!' Zara ordered. 'On the step. In front of you. Don't bend –' she knew the danger of a powerful leap from that position '– *throw it down!*'

Fenella's eyes agonized into Rayner's. His arm sank. He dropped the weapon.

'Now kick it away – towards me. Don't move!'

She feared what was already racing through Rayner's mind. He would combine the apparent surrender with a lethal come-back.

Once the knife was gone, he was no match for the Glock, even if he could get to close quarters with Zara.

'*Kick it! Away!*'

He watched her all the way, then kicked it, so that it fell close to Fenella's swathed feet.

With a sudden, deft movement, Zara hurled Fenella from her, grabbed the knife, and made a quick circling movement so that she covered Rayner from the side instead of the front.

'Across there! To her!' Fenella was picking herself up from the sandy floor. Rayner came on, step by step, the ugly mouth of the pistol mocking him all the way.

'Round there!'

Zara had manoeuvred her back to the stairway now for a quick getaway. Rayner helped Fenella to her feet. Her hands were like the kiss of death itself from cold and shock. She led him, as Zara had indicated, into the L-shape of the bunker. He strained backwards in Zara's direction, seeking the slightest loophole in her defences.

But she was safe now. She waved the gun threateningly at him, then leaped up the stairway and away before he could go after her. The door banged in his face, the heavy key turned from outside in the lock.

Zara did the same for the altar door. She slipped both keys into her pocket, and the Glock into her waistband. She ran her finger regretfully over the splintered hole the slug had made in the carving.

Then she went to Menty, hefted the inert, bloody form over her shoulder, passed through the outer vestry door into the daylight beyond, and pitched the body untidily into the tomb among the mines and detonators.

Chapter 39

'Dearest, wonderful darling!'

Fenella's lips sought Rayner's, claimed and reclaimed his, pressing, panting, sobbing, as if to draw some of his warmth into their own iciness. The only warm thing about her body was her tears; the lovely eyes were drawn, even in the dim light, with relief mixed with desperate fear.

She was hard against him, the accumulated cold of days triggering tremors which he could feel running the length of her where she touched his body.

'Why did you have to come and throw yourself away!' Her eyes in their dark sockets tried to focus on his, but they teared to an extent she could scarcely see.

'I came because –' There was no need for him to say

it. He tried to kiss some warmth into her lips and quell the shaking of her shocked muscles.

'The shots – two shots – oh God, then the silence! I knew deep inside me that it was you! The silence! It was for ever!' She held him as if she never meant to let him go.

He said gently, 'She would have killed you, if I hadn't –' He couldn't bring himself to articulate his surrender.

She said, burying her head against his throat, 'You smell of sun and dust.' She kissed him. 'I don't think I'll ever see the sun again, or smell the dust.' Then, like a nightmare returning, she got out, 'Those shots – what *happened*, Rayner?'

'I'll tell you –'

'Come and sit on the bed,' she said. 'The warmest place is among the blankets. You'll soon be cold, like me.'

Rayner's eyes went round the L-shaped hide-out. The unstable soil of the cliff-face had been built over with brick and the roof was wood. The only furniture was a low truckle-bed, a straight-backed chair and a washbasin. There were also two wooden sea-chests with mildewed brass clamps.

'What is in those boxes?'

'Old newspapers, very old. One of them is the *Cape Argus* of August 1863. There's a report on the arrival of the *Alabama* in Table Bay. In fact, all the newspapers seem to have been kept because they mention the *Alabama*. There's even one from Richmond, in Virginia, reporting the arrival there of Captain Semmes, the raider's commander, about six months after the ship had been sunk off France, together with one of his officers, Lieutenant George White. I think this must refer to Zara's ancestor. Great play was made of his bravery and service to the South. The paper says that both Semmes and White were honoured by President Davis and Congress, and White was presented with an engraved ceremonial bronze handspike as a mark of appreciation of his war effort. Reading the papers helped to pass the time. At one stage I thought of burning them to keep warm, but I was frightened the smoke would suffocate me.'

Fenella indicated a small radio on top of one of the chests. 'But that probably saved my sanity – when I could hear. There are some places in this cell which, oddly enough, are better than others for reception. I heard about the *Alabama* oar arriving – did you have a good trip to London?'

'I didn't go.'

'What!'

'Do you think I could have gone, not knowing whether you were dead or alive?'

She said in a small, choking voice, 'Why, why, didn't you tell me you felt that way, on that Sunday? I don't think I felt so miserable in all my life as when I went to bed that night. And then – the hands on my throat in the night and the way they bundled me away –' She explained how she had been blindfolded and strapped down and lowered to the ground.

'A stretcher!' exclaimed Rayner. 'So that is what the strange straight smear was on your bed! Hugh and I couldn't make it out. Nor could Keyter's team.'

'They didn't take me far in the ambulance, a few blocks maybe. Then they transferred me to a car, and came on here.'

'Where is here?' asked Rayner.

'You don't know where you are?' she exclaimed in astonishment.

'Menty –' Rayner told her what had happened. Finally, he checked his watch. It was shortly after one o'clock. 'It doesn't seem possible. A couple of hours ago

302

Menty fetched me from the Villa Montana, and now she's dead.'

Fenella took his face in her hands and kissed him as if she had never seen him until that moment. He saw, now that his eyes had grown more accustomed to the poor light, her deadly pallor, relieved here and there by flecks of smut from the lamp, like mascara carelessly slopped about.

She said, 'Rayner, you're a marked man in her eyes. She could come down and shoot you in cold blood, now that you're a prisoner.'

'Not for long, I hope. I mean to take a good look round.'

Fenella replied quietly, 'Rayner, my dearest, I searched and searched for any possible way out except the door. There isn't, I assure you. This is a dead-end funk-hole. You can't see or hear anything. Except,' she added a little shakily, 'the ghost's footsteps.'

Rayner eyed her penetratingly. 'Ghost's footsteps?'

'I know what you are thinking: she's hallucinating, being locked up in the dark all this time alone. Just the way people go round the bend in solitary confinement and see and hear things which aren't there. Zara warned me about the ghost. The footsteps come in the middle of the night. Up and down, up and down, for a couple of hours. I thought I was going crazy. I even tried to track down the source of the sound. It was there.' She indicated the L-shaped corner the cell made. 'Somewhere half above my head.'

'Half above?'

'I thought the steps might be on the floor of the church, but they weren't. I think the roof of the bunker and the floor are separate. It was a steady, monotonous sound. It seemed to die down about daylight. If you can tell it's daylight. Night and day are the same. She brings me food, early and late.'

'You haven't yet told me the name of this place,' said Rayner.

'It's called Churchhaven. It's now part of a national park near Saldanha Bay. Zara's great-grandfather founded it and built the church a century and a half ago.'

'Plus this bunker under it,' added Rayner thoughtfully. 'I wonder what he was running away from? It's certainly in the blood, if Zara Hennessy is any criterion.'

'What do you mean, Rayner?'

'It's a long story, and it can wait, but Hugh phoned me from London – he deputized for me over the *Alabama* oar – to say Scotland Yard had got a tip-off from an informer in Germany. Zara Hennessy is an international terrorist. She is a member of a notorious women's terror gang called Rote Zora. I know now from what Menty told me that there's a Rote Zora cell at the Cape led by Zara which is operating to try and assassinate the British Prime Minister, the South African President and other VIPs at the Simonstown ceremony next week.'

'Go on.'

'Their method is diabolically simple. The shaft of a silver oar is to be loaded with a charge of Semtex plastic explosive. When the Marshal's baton is unscrewed it will detonate by activating a trembler fuse – what is the matter, Fenella?'

'Oh God, I told them how the oar fits together!'

'*You!*'

'That is why they kidnapped me,' she replied brokenly. 'I had no choice. Either I explained the set-up of both the silver oars, or else Zara said she would go to the Villa Montana and shoot you.' She raised her anguished eyes to his. 'She would have, too.'

He took her close. 'She meant it, just as she meant what she said when she held the gun at your head a little while back in here. I understand what it means to have no choice. But I mean to get out of here before she can carry out her hellish plan. We have four days. Knowing the structure of the oar is only half the solution to Zara's plot. Before she can prime it and turn it into a bomb, she has to get her hands on it to do the arming. How does she intend to do that?'

'How do you intend to do that?'

Kerry-Ann's clear enunciation scraped along Zara's taut nerves like a kid's pencil on a slate.

'Oh, shut up being negative!' Zara snapped. 'Haven't any of you any positive ideas?'

It was dusk, that same evening. The Rote Zora gang was sitting in Zara's lounge watching a re-run of the video Zara had made of the TV feature on Admiralty House showing Pittock-Williams unscrewing the Marshal's baton from the shaft of the silver oar.

Renate stood at the back of the group (she was a head taller than any of the other girls), restless and impatient; Rikki sat cross-legged on the floor, her rather untidy blonde hair half-masking what was going on in the wide grey eyes; Gemma's frustration at the fuse project made her nose appear ugly and more prominent under the coarse cap of hair as she shifted about on the settee next to Kerry-Ann, who looked as groomed and suave as she always did. No one had bothered to ask where Menty was, if indeed anyone noticed her absence.

Gemma fiddled with a length of black plastic pipe a couple of feet long.

Zara snapped at her, 'For Pete's sake, stop playing with that damn piece of pipe! Why'd you bring it along, anyway?'

'To get an idea of how much Semtex we can get into the shaft. It'll be a bit of a guess, but we don't want to have to carry a lot of surplus explosive around, wherever we go.'

'Don't be so bloody reasonable!' Zara's voice jarred

with nerves. 'You know as well as any of us that we don't know where we'll have to go to arm the oar.'

Renate said, 'I'm pie-eyed watching this same old re-run. Screw in, screw out, over and over.'

'Let's keep sex out of this,' remarked Kerry-Ann in her penetrating voice.

The girls started to laugh, but Zara said, 'Stop it, damn it! This isn't a hen party! Has no one any constructive suggestion to make?'

Rikki said, 'Now that we have Watton, couldn't we make a ransom plan for them both? Either, or, you know –' She trailed off under Zara's withering stare.

'How does a ransom demand get us any closer, eh? Either you lend us the oar to enable us to prime it, or else we shoot 'em both, eh? Tell me!'

Kerry-Ann asked, 'Is this guy really as tough as he looks?'

Zara snapped off the video. It was a sign of retreat, if not of defeat. 'You can come with me soon and have a look when I feed the animals behind bars,' she replied. 'I need two of you anyway to be with me, plus guns. I'll have my own. Renate?'

'I didn't bring my pistol along,' she replied. 'I had no idea then you had another captive.'

'Anyone else of you with a gun?' she asked. The girls shook their heads.

'OK, it doesn't matter. We've got plenty of them on tap. Rikki, take the key to the tomb and get a couple of Makarovs with magazines. Renate, what about a grenade also?'

Renate shook her head. 'If we have to use a grenade on him in that confined space, we would kill ourselves as well. No, there's enough firepower without it.'

'The key's in its usual place?' asked Rikki.

Zara nodded. 'Behind the kitchen door. Take a torch.'

They heard her go; the girls milled round indecisively.

Zara stood by the fish tank looking beyond the windows into the gathering dusk, the burning of her eyes in their strained settings seeming to act as a brake on any light conversation.

It took less than five minutes for the clatter of feet to come stumbling down the uneven path to the house, a little cloud of white dust managing to hang on to the terrified, racing heels.

Rikki precipitated herself into the startled group. Her usually well-groomed face looked as if it had been made up with chalk, so that her make-up stood out stark and brash, like a tart's.

Renate grabbed her as she doubled over, gagging as if she meant to throw up all over the floor.

'*What* –!'

All that was left of Rikki's voice was a shock-struck thread.

'It's there – among the guns and stuff – it's only got one eye – the other, oh God!' She doubled over from the waist. Renate yanked her upright.

'Pull yourself together! What are you talking about?'

Rikki's eyes jerked round the electrified group. Zara stood back coolly.

'There's only a great big bloody patch for the other!' she mouthed. 'It's horrible, it's hideous, I tell you! She never was much to look at, but now!' She half-fell in Renate's strong grip and hung on to her arm. 'Her legs and arms – they're all over the place –'

Zara came forward now; Renate shook the half-fainting figure back to reality.

'*Who?* Who is it? Where?'

'Menty,' she whispered. 'She's back there, in the tomb, there's blood –'

Zara's voice pulled her to her senses as she toppled. 'Corpses don't bleed after death, and she was dead when I put her there this morning.'

307

'You – knew!' exclaimed Rikki in an unreal voice.

'Yes, I knew,' retorted Zara in a harsh tone. 'I shot her.'

'*You shot her?*' Rikki faced round the group, wildly questioning.

'I shot her because she brought Rayner Watton here. They were on their way down to the bunker to free the woman. It would have meant the end of all of us. Yes, I bushwhacked them. He managed to dodge.'

'In the church?' asked Kerry-Ann.

'Where else?' retorted Zara roughly. 'Do you expect me to have taken them outside first because of some fancy idea about a church? He had a knife, he's damn dangerous. That is why I want two of you with guns to come with me when I go down to the bunker. OK?'

Renate released Rikki from her arm. Rikki could not keep her hands still over her face.

'It is – too awful,' she managed to get out.

Renate said, 'I'll go and get the pistols.'

Zara looked round the dumb-struck group. 'Well, would you like me to have let her go?'

Renate observed, 'We've now got a murder as well as a kidnap on our plates.'

Zara eyed her. 'Nothing, but nothing, is going to stop me.' She became suddenly incisive and authoritative, like a nurse slapping a hysterical patient's face. 'One of you – no, it had better be two, because there'll have to be a spare driver – take the Combi and go and collect Menty's car. It's hidden among the trees near the point. Bring it back here. We don't want any nosy-parker weekend visitors finding it. Gemma! Kerry-Ann!'

Kerry-Ann asked in a small voice, 'Where are Menty's keys?'

'Ask Renate to look in her pockets,' Zara retorted. 'If they aren't there, she probably left them in the car. You know what Menty was.'

'We know what Menty was.' Gemma wrote the obituary, rather gently.

'Don't waste sentiment on her,' snapped Zara. 'She was a traitor, and she got what a traitor deserved. It was her or us.'

She held the leadership on a tight rein. 'You all know what you have to do – go and do it!' They went.

Renate was back first. Her face was as grim and as uncompromising as the mouths of the two Makarovs she carried, one in either hand. Menty was not for the squeamish.

Rikki sat in the lounge, snivelling and whimpering into a stiff drink. She wouldn't sleep tonight.

Zara was in the kitchen, busy at the stove preparing food for the captives.

Renate asked her, 'Did you clean up the church? I mean, it could be incriminating to leave a lot of blood around.'

'And you too, Renate?'

'I'm not criticizing, only pointing out facts.'

'Well I did clean it up.'

Renate went on, 'Zara, this whole business seems to be developing in a way I don't think I like. Menty –'

Zara's look silenced her. She went back into the lounge.

Rikki was no company. Renate hoped the other two would not be long. They should not be more than another ten minutes.

She laid the two pistols on the low table, and was about to switch on the TV.

Then she heard the sound of humming, a woman's voice humming, from the kitchen. Even Rikki snapped out of her trauma for a moment and looked up from her fixated contemplation of the amber contents of her glass.

Renate went through to the kitchen. Zara was stirring a pot and humming softly to herself. She smiled at

Renate, the sort of smile Renate hadn't seen on the leader's face since the early days before the acid of Pittock-Williams had eaten away her face's residual attractiveness.

'Everything OK, Zara?' Renate asked.

'Very much so. Any sign of the others with the cars yet?'

'No, but they should be here any minute.'

Renate was turning to go when they heard the sound of the Combi and Menty's car coming down the dusty driveway slope.

Renate went first, and Zara followed, after she had turned off the stove.

'The car was there, among the bushes at the point, as you said –' began Kerry-Ann, but Zara waved her silent. Instead, she drew them all into a rough half-circle facing her.

'Listen!' she told them. 'I've got it! Even if there are a dozen tough guys with guns guarding the silver oars, this is how we'll set about it –'

Chapter 40

'I think she means to starve us until you're too weak to be a threat.'

Fenella and Rayner were sitting together on the bed in the bunker. It was after nine o'clock.

The Rote Zora gang and Zara were as oblivious of food and hot coffee in the lounge as Rayner and Fenella in the bunker were conscious of their need for it.

They sat in a tight circle, carried away by the logistics of the masterplan which Zara was expounding.

Gemma was the first to warm to it; as Zara went on, she

glowed; after half an hour she was aflame. 'Wonderful, wonderful!' she enthused. 'Zara, you're a genius!'

Renate said, 'I can't see how it won't work. It's got the big plus going for it that none of us has to be anywhere near the scene of operations.'

'Thanks to trembler and baton,' added Kerry-Ann.

Rikki's sense of shock seemed calmed as Zara went into detail, assisted by Zara's exposition and her liberal slug of Scotch.

Zara added, 'Gemma knows better than the rest of you what I'm talking about. She was there at the Silver Gallery with me.'

'And I'm going to be there again,' Gemma added with a grin. 'Do we make another recce?'

'Tomorrow,' replied Zara. 'It'll work, you'll see. Now, we've got unfinished business in the kitchen for those two in the bunker.'

In the bunker, Rayner checked his watch before replying to Fenella. 'I've only been here something over nine hours, but it seems like nine days.'

Like Fenella, he had drawn a blanket round himself. He was wearing only stone-washed jeans with a faded work-shirt, and the cotton-lined jacket faced with soft nappa leather was never meant for anything more than soft days in the sun.

'It all goes to show, Fenella, we're got to make our exit out of here as quick as – '

'Listen,' Fenella interrupted him. 'There's something coming on the radio about next week's ceremony.'

'You're better than I am at hearing what is being said through impossible interference,' he remarked.

'It's better round there.'

Like Red Indians making their way through the smoky interior of a wigwam, they went round the corner of the cell to where Fenella indicated was the best reception spot.

The announcer's voice became more audible.

There is a feeling of mutual public excitement and anticipation both in Britain and Cape Town this weekend with the impending departure of the British Prime Minister by air for South Africa for the signing ceremony on Wednesday of the reinstated Simonstown naval agreement. Apart from the colourful ceremony itself, there will be an eye-catching array of ships dressed and at anchor in the famous dockyard.

Leading the Royal Navy contingent will be the famous aircraft carrier *Invincible*, which, with a cruiser and destroyer escort, has signalled that the squadron is at present off the Cape and will dock in Simonstown tomorrow –

'*What is that?*' Fenella's voice cut across that of the announcer. 'Listen! On the stairs! They're coming, Rayner, take care! Don't attempt anything! She means business!'

Zara did. Rayner recognized immediately the Glock barrel which appeared at hip level and, less readily, the two Makarovs behind, at shoulder level, as Gemma and Renate stood poised on the stairway behind the leader.

'Keep clear of the steps, or else you'll both get blasted!' snapped Zara. On went her flashlight. Its beam searched the dark hole, as if making sure there was no one else there except the two forlorn blanket-clad figures.

She gestured to Gemma, who also carried a tray of food, a hot-water vacuum flask, plates and cups. She put it down on one of the sea-chests, leaving her pistol with Renate. She also brought a sleeping-bag for Rayner.

There was a kind of false jollity about Zara in the way she addressed them.

'I debated whether I should shoot you tonight, or leave

312

it till later. The trouble is, I'm rather short of room for a couple more corpses. So it'll have to wait.'

'Be my guest!' mocked Rayner.

Zara remained equable. 'Until next Wednesday, at least. Until the signing ceremony, you're much too dangerous having the knowledge you do to go free. Afterwards, you'll be more dangerous still when security follows up on the blast.'

'If this is softening-up talk, I'd much rather get on with my supper,' said Rayner.

She eyed him over the Glock barrel. 'They said on TV you were a cool customer. But it won't help you.'

Rayner said, 'You'll never get away with your bomb plot – Zara Hennessy.'

'Did Menty tell you my name?'

'No. Scotland Yard.'

'You're bluffing, Watton. They couldn't possibly know. Scotland Yard is still chasing its tail over Nelson's head.' She eyed him with a kind of off-beat admiration. 'You must have been pretty smart not to have been taken for a ride – over the rainbow.'

Fenella said, 'I was with him when he took the head out of the box. It was the most hellish device any sane person could concoct.'

Zara remained relaxed and half-turned to Gemma. 'Not as ingenious as next Wednesday's, eh?'

Rayner interjected for an answer. 'You'll never get past the security screen to get your hands on Pittock-Williams's oar long enough to prime it and fit a fuse.'

Zara was amused. 'That's what my girls said, too – at first. Eh, Renate? Eh, Gemma?'

Zara terminated the interview with a gesture of her hand and started to back up the stairs. Gemma and Renate did likewise in unison, so that the three guns covered Rayner and Fenella all the time.

She held on to the door for a moment before she disappeared, and said mockingly, 'Gemma and I will be taking a final look-see at our target tomorrow, if it interests you at this late stage.'

If the mountain won't come to Mahomet, Mahomet must go to the mountain.

That is the way Hugh Perrot felt next day when he picked up the phone to Brigadier Keyter.

It was mid-morning, Saturday. It was about the same time as Zara and Gemma were arriving in Cape Town from Churchhaven on their way to inspect, for the second time, the two silver oars on display.

It was only Hugh's status in Scotland Yard which even got his call put through to the Security chief.

'Yes?' The terse response was enough to have killed any would-be conversation.

'Brigadier – Hugh Perrot here. Do you know Rayner Watton is missing?'

'Yes. He failed to report to the police yesterday morning. There's a warrant out for his arrest.'

'Do you know where he is?'

'If I did, we would have pulled him in already.'

'Aren't you jumping to conclusions, if I may say so, brigadier?'

'He's a maverick, a lightweight. I thought so right from the beginning,' retorted Keyter. 'Brilliant, maybe, but no ability to carry anything through.'

'I worked with Rayner overseas. You've given a dog a bad name.'

'So?' Keyter's voice had been sandpaper previously, now it was abrasive. 'Would it interest you to know that Watton was seen going off with a woman in a car yesterday morning? In a hurry, according to my information. Couldn't wait for his long weekend. Hah-hah. That's where he is, but we'll get him, when I can spare anyone for trifles. I've enough on my fork as far as next Wednesday is concerned without worrying about that sort of thing.'

Hugh hadn't expected this. He swallowed hard. 'Who was your informant, if I may ask?'

'You may ask. We had a tail on Watton. He was just coming on duty when he spotted Watton's hurried take-off. So hurried that he left the front door of the Villa Montana open.'

'Have you thought that he might have got some clue about Fenella Gault and went to follow it up?' asked Hugh.

'Then why in hell didn't he act through the correct channels and let me know? There's no room for the loner in this game. You know that well enough, Perrot.'

'Have you any further lead on Fenella?' persisted Hugh. 'It could have an important bearing on next Wednesday's ceremony –'

'Don't try and teach me my job!' snapped the Security chief. 'Fenella Gault's disappearance is a non-issue, something personal. Nothing to do with the broad security picture. She – and Watton – are involved in something I can't put my finger on. That's the way I read it, and that's the way it stays for the present.'

'I still think –'

'I'm a very busy man. I can't waste my time speculating. Your friend has gone off on a lost weekend, it's plain enough. He'll surface in due course. I have a thousand things to organize. You also have an important place at the Admiralty House ceremony. If you want to know anything about that, you may telephone me. Otherwise, forget about Watton and his woman.'

He hung up.

About the same time as Hugh Perrot's conversation foundered, Zara and Gemma arrived at the museum and joined the queue waiting to see the silver oars. Despite

· the early hour, the crowd stretched into the street outside. It took them nearly half an hour to reach their
objective.

When they reached there at last, they did not follow
the crowd.

They turned aside at the entrance to the Silver Gallery
and went into the life-size reconstruction of the old
pharmacy.

At Churchhaven, Rayner had fretted for the arrival of
breakfast in order to carry out a full inch-by-inch search
of the walls and ceiling of the bunker. Time, as measured
by light and dark, was meaningless.

The meal came earlier than Fenella had expected; the
double supply of hot water in vacuum flasks meant to
her the same as when Zara had been missing for the
whole day previously in Cape Town: they would not see
their captors again that day.

When he and Fenella had finished, Rayner asked,
'How high did you explore the walls, Fenella?'

'As far as I could reach.'

'That's not very far. I'm going to take one of these old
boxes to stand on and give the place a thorough
going-over.'

He went towards the two old sea-chests which they
used as tables.

Take the other box, Rayner! That one holds only junk!

Chapter 41

'Listen! Rayner! Footsteps!'

Fenella jerked upright in the bed she and Rayner were
sharing. 'It's the ghost, Rayner! That's the way it was
before!'

316

The slow, even-paced thump-thump sounded faintly light and muted through the bunker.

It was well after midnight on Sunday, nearer one o'clock.

Rayner sat up, wrenched wide awake at the urgency in her voice. There was fear, too. He asked in a low voice, 'Is it coming from the same place?'

'Yes, round the corner of the wall. Up above there somewhere. I thought – I thought – it was haunting the church –'

'I'm going to light the lamp and have a look,' Rayner answered.

He slipped out of bed, putting on his shoes and finding matches for the miserable lamp. Like an Eskimo's strip of blubber in his igloo, even the faint glow seemed to bring some life-giving warmth with it.

Thump-thump. Thump-thump.

Rayner stood listening intently, pulling on his outer clothes. He said, after a minute or two, 'It never varies its pace. It must have put in a lot of training to keep that up.'

'You don't believe it's a ghost?'

'I'll tell you when I see it – if I do.'

Rayner set out for the part of the hide-out behind the L-shape. He had spent a lot of time investigating the walls and ceiling the previous day, but they had yielded – nothing. Except –

'Look at this,' he had told Fenella, holding out a spoon they had used for breakfast. Zara had been too cagey and alert to allow a sharp instrument like a knife or fork near Rayner. It was full of sand from the floor. But for hours Rayner had been tapping the walls with the inadequate tool of the spoon to try and find a possible hollow spot.

'Sand,' Rayner had told Fenella. 'But not just the white dune sand which is everywhere. Here's brown sand, and gritty black sand as well.'

'What are you trying to tell me?'

'I don't know, except that it's different, that's all. It probably hasn't any real significance as far as we are concerned. Hell! for some decent light! And something with which to chip properly at the walls. This spoon –' he made a helpless gesture '– we can't dig our way out with a porridge spoon.'

'Rayner,' Fenella had said quietly, 'I think we just have to accept the fact that there's no way out of here except the door, and that is that.'

They had finally gone to bed in a mood of total frustration.

Thump-thump.

Rayner cocked his head towards the sound, and then exclaimed excitedly, 'Fenella, you've been in here for nearly a week now and I for a couple of days. Yet the air never seems to get stale or worked out – why?'

'You tell me.'

'The man who built this place intended it as a hidey-hole. He was frightened that someone would come looking for him, not so? In those days, there were no towns nearer than Cape Town, and if a police or an army patrol came all that way, they wouldn't just take a quick look-see at the church and house and be on their way, would they?'

'I don't know what you're driving at.'

'They'd camp out, stay a week, maybe longer, searching. Our fugitive knew it would be no good holing up in a bunker in which he'd die in a few days from lack of air, would it?'

'And so?'

Thump-thump, thump-thump.

Rayner grinned and jerked a thumb vaguely in the direction of the sound. 'And so, he put in a ventilation system. Fenella, those aren't a ghost's footsteps. That's moving air! It's a ventilation system!'

She laughed, a little shakily still. 'That's very smart, but where does the air come in?'

Rayner went on quickly, 'Our fugitive would have been at great pains to conceal the inlet and outlet.'

'Why doesn't the sound happen all the time, if it's only moving air?' asked Fenella.

'My guess is that it's something to do with wind direction. This place is on top of a cliff, the sea's on one side and the lagoon's on the other. It may be wind from an unusual quarter. I think it's something swinging loose in the wind in some kind of a shaft leading out into the open. The first thing is to try and pinpoint whereabouts it sounds loudest. The ghost footsteps will provide a kind of sonic guide to home in on an opening.'

'With that spoon?'

'And one of these old chests.'

Thump-thump. Thump-thump.

Rayner reached for the handle of one of the big old boxes to drag it round to where the footsteps seemed to come from. The other chest, which he had used previously, now held their food tray.

Rayner tugged, the box stuck fast. He gave a sharp jerk. The sides broke away from the rotten old wood of the bottom. A pile of disintegrating old newspapers and other clutter was left behind.

Fenella, who was holding the lamp, suddenly pointed and exclaimed. 'Rayner – look!'

Time and damp had reduced the newspapers at the bottom to a kind of congealed mess, mingled with some military-looking badges, buttons, a clay pipe, an ink bottle and some thick old pottery mug fragments.

It was not at them that Fenella was pointing. 'What is this?'

A rounded metal handle, its bronze green with verdigris, projected from the rest of the junk.

Rayner dropped on his knees, reached for it. 'Bring the light closer!'

He started to reveal what seemed a solid length of metal. He wiped the clinging debris clean on his sleeve.

The object was bronze, green with age. It was about half a metre long, round, solid, tapering from handle to point –

Rayner weighed it in his hand, grinning at Fenella. 'A weapon, Fenella, and, my oath, what a weapon!'

'There's an inscription on it!' exclaimed Fenella, sharing his excitement. 'Let's clean it off more –'

Rayner wiped the verdigris off the old-fashioned cursive handwriting, which was engraved into the metal.

It read:

This replica of a naval handspike is presented to Lieutenant George White, third officer of the Confederate raider *Alabama*, in recognition of his distinguished service and outstanding heroism, by President Davis and a grateful Congress. Richmond, Virginia, January 1865.

'A naval handspike!' repeated Rayner.

'What is a handspike?' asked Fenella.

'It was a sort of lever they used to shift guns into position or work at the anchor capstan,' replied Rayner. 'I was always under the impression that a handspike was bigger than this.'

'The inscription says it's a replica,' Fenella pointed out.

'What a weapon!' Rayner enthused again. 'Now we've got ourselves something we can really use to get out.'

Fenella put her hand on his arm. 'My darling, don't try anything rash. It's only one piece of metal against three guns.'

'We've got the strongest weapon of all on our side –

surprise,' replied Rayner. 'I can't understand why Zara left the handspike down here in the first place.'

'She couldn't have known about it,' said Fenella thoughtfully. 'I remember hearing one of the girls ask her about the two chests when they were clearing out the explosives and pistols and she replied that they were only full of old papers and junk. Being a heavy object, it must have migrated through the rotten paper to the bottom in the course of the years.'

Rayner fingered the rounded, blunt tip of the handspike. 'It'll be an ideal probe for the walls and to try and locate the ventilation shaft inlet. What is the time?'

'One-thirty,' she answered. 'Why?'

'It means we have got six or seven hours to probe the walls before we can expect anyone here with breakfast,' he said.

'If you start chipping at the walls and making a mess, you'll put Zara wise right away,' said Fenella.

'We'll use the other chest for the debris.'

He dragged the sound box into the shelter of the L-shape.

Thump-thump. Thump-thump.

Both Rayner and Fenella tried to pinpoint where the sound was coming from. Finally, it seemed strongest high up in one corner against the ceiling, which was a likely spot for a ventilation aperture.

He struck at the wall with the point of the handspike. 'This stuff's as tough as iron,' he remarked.

After five hours, when the first light had begun to tinge the lagoon beautiful (if they could have seen it) Rayner and Fenella, working in shifts, had barely cleared a patch of wall as wide as the stretch of his extended arms.

There was no sign of an opening.

With the light outside, the ghost stopped walking.

It was Fenella who first noticed the absence of the sound. They had grown so accustomed to its metronome-like regularity that they hardly noticed it any longer.

'It's gone,' said Fenella.

'And it's seven o'clock,' added Rayner. 'Monday morning. Blue Monday, for my part. I was sure we'd strike something in the direction the ghost's footsteps came from.'

He climbed down stiffly off the old chest. The bronze tip of the handspike had become burnished in its attack against the hard old plaster. His hands were feeling the strain and had several small blisters. Fenella's were red and sore.

They washed their hands in disappointed silence at the tin basin which stood on top of the chemical toilet seat. There was no other place for it in the cell. Water was supplied from an old ten-litre petrol can. No hermit could have wished for better mortification for the flesh.

'In case they come early and surprise us, let's switch on the radio and make-believe we've just woken up,' said Fenella.

'It's just on news time,' observed Rayner.

The announcer said:

Today is the start of a red-letter week for South Africa with the signing on Wednesday at Admiralty House in Simonstown of the reinstated naval agreement between the two countries. This morning the residents of Simonstown awoke to the magnificent sight of a squadron of Royal Navy ships tied up in the famous old Dockyard, fully dressed with flags and bunting. The squadron consists of the aircraft carrier *Invincible*, one of the most modern warships of its kind in the world, escorted by four of the latest Type 23 frigates, *Norfolk*, *Iron Duke*, *Monmouth* and *Montrose*. The colossal size of HMS *Invincible* drew gasps of admiration from early-morning bystanders as it towered above all ships and buildings in the vicinity.

Another striking sight was a squadron of eight South African offshore missile strike craft, all similarly dressed, and the big naval supply tender, SAS *Tafelberg*.

In Britain, an aircraft of the Queen's Flight is standing by ready to take off this afternoon carrying the British Prime Minister to South Africa. On its arrival in Cape Town tomorrow morning, the aircraft will be escorted on the last part of its journey by supersonic fighters of the South African Air Force.

At Admiralty House, the most extensive security screen ever mounted in South Africa will be in force for Wednesday's ceremony. Tomorrow, the two silver oars which are to be exchanged will be conveyed from where they have been on public display for the past few days in the Cultural History Museum under a special armed naval guard to Admiralty House for safekeeping until Wednesday.

We are fortunate in having with us in the studio this morning the man who is responsible for the immediate security arrangements inside Admiralty House on Wednesday, Commander Jan Enslin, of the South African Navy, who will liaise with Inspector Hugh Perrot, head of a special Scotland Yard team which has been flown from Britain to work with the South African Security forces, under command of Brigadier Neels Keyter.

'Commander Enslin, what is your role during the Admiralty House ceremony?'

'I will be in immediate command of the men inside the building, from the time the VIP party makes its way from the old waterfront jetty through the garden into the house. Their path will be lined

323

by naval personnel. Once the party enters the building, they will be my responsibility. Brigadier Keyter's men, of course, will also be there in force.'

'Plain-clothes?'

'Yes. Like the Scotland Yard squad under Inspector Perrot.'

'Where will you be stationed?'

'Both myself and Inspector Perrot will circulate inside the dining-room, which, as you know, has been converted into a replica of the old Vice-Admiralty Court which once sat in Cape Town, but during the ceremony itself we will be in close vicinity to the judge's bench where the actual signing and exchange will take place.'

'All of you will be armed?'

'That goes without saying.'

'Are you quite happy with the security arrangements, Commander?'

'Even a mouse couldn't get past our screen.'

Rayner broke in on the broadcast. 'Zara's mad to think she can lay her hands on a silver oar and prime it as well as all the rest of it.'

'Yet she's so sure of herself that she's killed one person and kidnapped two others already,' said Fenella.

'The question goes round and round in my head – how? How? How?' exclaimed Rayner. 'Like a way out of here – how?'

'Go and hide the handspike, Rayner. We don't want them coming in unexpectedly on us. It's our only chance of salvation. Try burying it near where we were working.'

'We've less than forty-eight hours in which to do something!' Rayner replied grimly. 'We've got to stop her!'

When Rayner returned from hiding the handspike, they heard sounds at the door and Zara opened it.

'Stand back!' ordered Zara. 'Well back!'

Gemma and Renate, both with Makarovs, took up formation on the steps behind the leader.

She put down the tray.

'There are two vacuum flasks of hot water here,' she said. 'They'll have to last you the day.'

'Going some place?' Rayner asked.

She responded with a twisted smile, 'You'd like to know, wouldn't you?'

Rayner persisted. 'You'll never get away with it, Zara! The security net is about as tight as any I've heard of. Moreover, I intend to see you hang for Menty's killing.'

'You'll never get the chance,' she answered derisively. She took the Glock from Renate's care and held it on him, backing up the steps. 'Listen on Wednesday morning,' she jeered, her eyes flaring in their charcoal sockets. 'See how it's done. Wednesday's a deadline for a number of people. That includes you.'

The three Rote Zora women made their strategic withdrawal in perfect formation. The door banged, the key turned from outside.

Rayner and Fenella ate their meal in almost total silence. They were too tired and too dispirited to revive the same suggestions which had got them nowhere during the long hours of the night.

They put out the oil lamp and slept.

When they awoke again in the afternoon, they started again on their treadmill task. They chipped, changed places, chipped, changed places, until their arms ached and their hands started to become raw. They wrapped a piece of cloth round the handspike to stop even the slight chafe of the engraved inscription on their hands.

Finally, they gave up.

They found nothing.

They had thrown away twelve hours of the forty-eight.

Chapter 42

'Cut-off time in ten minutes! Cut-off time in ten minutes!'

The uniformed museum official went up and down the long queue baying the announcement.

The crowd had lined up, four abreast, since long before opening-time that Monday morning outside the Cultural History Museum to catch a final close-up glimpse of the two oars which had caught the public fancy to an extent never seen before at the Cape. They had endured the slow drag; the initial pace was determined by spectators in the Silver Gallery who were lucky enough to reach the display case where the two oars lay on their black velvet cushions. Four guards were there, as before, and one each at the entrance and exit. Their pistols lay snug in their holsters, flaps loose for instant use.

As the hours passed and the crowd showed no sign of lessening, museum officials started sheepdogging the onlookers, rationing everyone to approximately two minutes at the showcase.

Now it was afternoon, shortly before four o'clock.

Gemma and Zara were on the home straight towards their objective. They formed part of the queue which was inching its way along the passageway before it took a final right-angled bend to head for the Silver Gallery entrance. Before that, however, on their left, stood the full-size replica of a Victorian pharmacy, complete with dummy customers.

'Hear that – ten minutes! We'll never make it, Zara!' Gemma's voice was thick with tension and disappointment.

'He's talking about the Silver Gallery closing, not the rest of the museum. That's at four-thirty.'

Gemma's coarse hair seemed to become untidier when she became agitated, her lips thicker, and her nose more prominent.

Soon the town-crier was back. 'Five minutes to cut-off time!' He marched up and down the queue. 'Five minutes!'

Gemma fiddled nervously with her handbag. 'Keep still!' muttered Zara. 'Don't let that handbag of yours snap open and show the world what we're carrying!'

Gemma wasn't worried about the bag's contents exploding. Semtex is a rough lover and doesn't object to a beating. But, when in passion at the kiss of a detonator, its frenzy will tear down the roof. It takes only a couple of kilograms of Semtex to blow a hole in the side of an airliner.

The Semtex in Gemma's handbag, plus a similar supply in Zara's, was enough to do just that.

Zara and Gemma rounded the final corner. The Silver Gallery lay ahead. Before that, on the left, was the doorway to the old pharmacy mock-up.

Gemma said, without consulting Zara, to the woman next to her who trailed a teenage daughter, 'Would you mind asking the museum official whether the whole museum closes at four?'

'Cut-off time –' She stopped the man with Gemma's question.

'Only the Silver Gallery, the rest as usual,' he replied brusquely.

The queue was pushing and jostling from the rear. Gemma was smiling at the reassurance.

'You fool!' snapped Zara under her breath. 'I told you not to!'

The crowd's momentum propelled them opposite the pharmacy door.

'Here!' said Zara.

The woman behind started to exclaim to Gemma, who began to follow Zara into the exhibit. 'You're not giving up, at this stage –'

'My friend's not feeling well,' Gemma answered hastily. 'She thinks she's going to faint.'

The press swept on uncaringly.

There was an old-time rocker chair, in which Zara sat down, face away from the crowd, to keep up the charade.

Zara said tightly, 'Why don't you obey orders? There are at least half a dozen people now who'll remember us. And memory means description.'

There was a commotion from the direction of the Silver Gallery. Two burly guards were pulling the glass entrance door closed. There was a groan of disappointment from those left outside. Beyond the pharmacy door, the crowd milled about in frustration.

Several people started towards the pharmacy entrance, but then shrugged and walked off. Old-time coloured bottles, herbal remedies and half-baked cures of yesteryear were no compensation for the splendour of the silver oars.

Zara stopped her rocking. 'Let them get clear first. Pretend we're interested in something here. And then –'

Gemma checked her watch nervously.

Zara added, 'Get as near to the counter as we can.' Then she asked, 'Where's the guy who called the time?'

'I don't see him. But all the guards are there – look!'

The pharmacy had a glass frontage in imitation of an old-fashioned shop window which was painted at shoulder-height a discreet brown-green. 'Green's Pharmacy' was emblazoned on it in gold-leaf letters. It effectively shut out the passageway passing alongside from view. The Silver Gallery – which had plate-glass and aluminium partitions to demarcate it from other sections of museum exhibits – was also almost hidden from inside the pharmacy by a section of counter backed by a cupboard topped by a row of big old coloured medicine bottles. There was, however, a small open section through which Zara and Gemma could observe the guards. They were relaxed and at ease now, standing chatting round the silver oar display case.

Their job was done. So they thought.

The L-shaped counter ran the whole way round the interior of the pharmacy and there was a hinged section at one corner which gave access to the cupboards behind.

It was, however, the lifelike dummies which truly gave the impression of stepping back in time. There were four of them: the pharmacist himself, leaning over the counter near a quaint old-fashioned till whose wildest dreams could not have conceived a modern computer, complete with regulation sideburns and moustache and high, buttoned-up Victorian waistcoat. He was listening (so it seemed) to a smartly dressed young woman, who inclined her head towards him in an attitude of confidentiality from under her bonnet. The other dummy woman, back to the door, seemed interested in some patent medicine on the shelf behind the counter. A man, bowler-hatted and sporting a cane, looked bored enough to be her husband.

'I think that pharmacist is a smoothie,' said Gemma.

'You'll have all night to get used to him,' responded Zara.

'Where do we go from here?' asked Gemma.

'It depends on two factors, time and opportunity,' replied Zara. 'What time the guards knock off, and when the opportunity presents itself.'

Gemma again checked her watch anxiously, and then glanced across at the Silver Gallery. The four display-case guards were still chatting; desultory groups of hopefuls, in ones and twos, came to and went away from the gallery door.

Four-fifteen.

'We must not be seen going into action, and we still can be spotted by the passers-by,' said Zara. 'We'll hold it, until the coast is clear.'

'Can't we get rid of our handbags beforehand? That'll leave our hands free for when we're ready,' asked Gemma.

'Good idea. Drop 'em behind the counter.'

She smoothed her hands involuntarily down the side of her pants. They were a shade of dark green-brown; she also wore light, flat-heeled sneaker-shoes. Her outfit might have been chosen to match the colouring of the floor-length dress of the dummy holding converse with the pharmacist.

Gemma also wore pants and sneakers. Her putty-brown rig could have colour-toned with the Semtex in her handbag.

The two women edged over towards the counter near the quaint till.

Zara glanced round. There was no one in the passage-way outside. The guards were laughing at something.

'Quick – here!'

They thrust their bags on the floor and under the hinged section of counter, then pushed them out of sight as far as their feet could reach.

As they straightened up, Gemma exclaimed, 'He's coming back!'

The museum guard passed the pharmacy door, paused, and called out, 'Closing time's four-thirty, ladies. Everyone out, please.'

'OK, we're on our way,' replied Zara.

'What do we do if he sticks around?' began Gemma.

'Where's he now?' Zara's voice rasped with tension.

'Gone into the Silver Gallery. Towards the guards –'

'This is it!' snapped Zara. 'Down! His back's towards us! Down! Quick!'

Zara dropped on all fours, crept under the hinged section of counter and into the enclosed section it made behind, collecting the handbags on her way. Gemma followed. She edged in beside the leader.

'Tuck your feet right in!' ordered Zara. 'Knees up to your chin, foetal position. That guy may do a spot check of the place before he shuts up shop for the night.'

'A couple of hours of this and I'll be so cramped I won't be able to stand,' whispered Gemma.

'We're blind now,' replied Zara softly. 'We don't know how many guards will be inside the Silver Gallery tonight. Or what the museum's own checks will be. We'll just have to stick it out until things settle down a bit.'

Things didn't – for a while.

The two women became acutely sensitized to sound, and tried to interpret it, focusing all their attention on the Silver Gallery. They continued to hear the guards' noisiness; then there was a cluster of heavy footsteps (at least six men, they reckoned) thumping past the pharmacy entrance. Gemma looked questioningly at Zara in the dim light under the counter, but Zara shook her head in puzzlement.

The unmistakable voice of the 'town crier' gave the answer from near the Silver Gallery entrance.

'You guys like jam on it,' he called to the guards. 'The best two armchairs we could raise.'

'Not for us, fellah,' replied a voice. 'For the night staff. Lucky so-and-so's. My feet are dropping off.'

'Two enough?' asked the 'town crier'. 'They're big and comfortable enough to sleep in.'

'Don't you believe it,' replied a guard's voice. 'Our boss is a real bastard. Do you know, the two night guys have to report *personally* by phone every two hours throughout the night to this Brigadier Keyter? He's shitting himself that anything can go wrong. I wonder what his missus has to say?'

'Looking at that sourpuss, I guess she won't miss much in the way of sex for one night from him.'

'That's the way he always is – sex, sex, and more sex,' came a guffaw from a second guard. 'Spent the ruddy day trying to chat up the girls with his eyes while he stood on duty here.'

'Well, there won't be any women around here tonight,' said the museum man. 'When do the night shift come on duty?'

'Six o'clock,' came the reply. 'They're on until midnight. Then a completely new set of guys takes over, from then until tomorrow morning. And another lot when it gets light, and a further whole squad to be ready for the naval guard when it comes to take the oars to Simonstown. The brigadier's taking no chances.'

'OK, boys,' they heard the museum man say. 'I'm on my way. But Jannie will be standing shift later for the whole night ahead. If you want anything, you'll find him downstairs. He's got his own spot next to the office.'

'Can we use a phone there?' asked a voice.

'Sure. Help yourselves.'

The floor acted as a sounding-board for the rush-hour traffic noises in the street outside. It got dimmer in the pharmacy as the light faded. The traffic sounds became progressively muted.

'I think my hand's getting cramped up,' whispered Gemma. 'I'll never be able to prime the oar with it like this.'

'Here – give it to me.'

Zara massaged the hand briskly between hers for a couple of minutes.

'Better?'

'Thanks, yes – but what's that?'

Light suddenly flooded the pharmacy. The counter remained in shadow. There was a clump of boots outside.

They were joined by others from inside the gallery. They met, halted, close to the pharmacy door.

A voice they recognized as one of the day guard's said, 'Well, it's all yours. Sweet dreams, you guys.'

'Anything to report?'

'Dead as the grave.'

'That's the way I want it to stay.'

'Does the Brig know you're here?'

'I phoned as we came in. Next call, eight o'clock.'

'Why doesn't he come and check himself, if he's so screwed up about the security?'

'They never do, those buggers at the top. Just so they can't take the rap, or so that they can shit on us unfortunates below from a height if anything goes wrong.'

'Can you imagine anyone being so crazy as to try on anything with those oars, even if they are worth such a fortune?'

'They'd have to get past Kalie and me first. Plenty of firepower in these Smith and Wessons.' They heard the sound of a holster being slapped.

'OK Piet, OK Kalie. *Totsiens*. Sleep well.'

'That will be the bloody day.'

Four pairs of boots retreated down the passageway.

'Two hours to wait!' exclaimed Zara. 'We'll make our first move then.'

'I could wet myself, the way my arm's cramping,' whispered back Gemma.

'Use one of those big bottles if you can't hold out,' retorted Zara unsympathetically.

'It was just a figure of speech,' muttered Gemma. 'Jeez, my hand!'

She again passed her right hand to Zara, who worked at it.

The next two hours were the longest in Zara's life. After a while, Gemma said, 'I've got to straighten out, Zara! I can't take it any more!'

Zara herself had begun to feel cramps in her legs. 'Keep well behind the counter – don't stand up, for Pete's sake!'

Gemma edged herself clear, wincing and grimacing. She crawled on all fours to the hinged gap in the counter, stretching and doubling herself over at the waist to relieve her stiff muscles.

Then it was Zara's turn. Outside, nothing stirred. From the direction of the Silver Gallery came the faint sound of a radio. What were the guards doing? She risked a half-rise to her feet.

The two guards sat in armchairs near the display cabinet, legs and feet outstretched. She could barely make out their heads in the deep cushions. No pathway there!

Her plan required time, and opportunity. She had neither yet. But the night lay ahead.

She was about to chance standing up straight when her ears caught a sound from the passageway. She shrank back below counter level.

There was a clump of boots along the passageway and a strongly accented voice called, 'OK in here?'

There was an affirmative murmur from the guards, and Zara heard them come out of the gallery.

'Just checking,' said the accented voice, which Zara took to be that of Jannie, the night-watchman.

One of the guards said, 'I'm half asleep – how do you manage to keep going all night, night after night, Jannie?'

'Easy,' replied Jannie. 'I was an alkie once. Never slept any more as a result. So I cashed in on my sin and got myself an all-night job. Good pay. Nobody wants this sort of job. Plenty of free coffee. It helps. Drink it all night. Come down to my den and have some.'

'Later,' replied one of the guards. 'We sure will. Got to report to the boss in about half an hour. He's pissing all over the place about the security round the two oars.'

'No one around, I suppose?' asked Jannie.

'Nix.'

'We don't want all this light in the pharmacy, do we? Mind if I switch it off?'

Zara froze. 'He's coming in here, Gemma!'

They did not know where the light switches were situated. They compacted their legs, arms and torsos into as tiny a space as possible.

The man came in. He seemed to be coming straight for them. They could hear his breathing as he leaned across the counter near the till.

Then – darkness.

It was not complete darkness. The overhead lights from the passageway still gave a measure of illumination in the pharmacy.

Jannie clumped away.

Chapter 43

Eight o'clock.

'He said they were going to phone – we've got to risk it then!' whispered Zara. 'Give me the scissors and safety-pins! We'll go first for the dummy with her back turned!'

'Here they come!' answered Gemma.

'There's only one, not two,' Zara corrected her. 'They're not leaving the showcase unguarded!'

'We'll never make it, that way!'

The footsteps passed the pharmacy. Both women crawled out. Through the window slit behind the cupboard, they could observe the remaining guard, back to them, in his armchair.

'Here!' Zara took the scissors, slit the dummy's dress from waist to high neck, and dragged off the cumbersome garment. Then they laid the dummy out of sight under the hinged counter, also dragging off bonnet and shoes.

Gemma stepped into the dress. 'It's too tight!' she whispered. 'It'll never get past my waist!'

'It must, it will!' Zara snipped at the material. Gemma squirmed, wriggled, eventually shoehorned herself in. Zara fixed the back with safety-pins. She jammed the bonnet on Gemma's head, thrusting the coarse hair out of sight.

'Shoes – they're too small –'

'OK, leave them. Pitch 'em there after the dummy. Keep your own. Now – me!'

It was Gemma who now took the scissors and ripped off the other dummy's dress. Zara was pinned into it. They shoved the dummy itself under the counter to join the first. Zara took up the bonnet and what she hoped was the dummy's pose by the till.

Gemma was grinning. 'I like it! I like it, Zara!'

'Keep your voice down – get into position yourself!'

Gemma tried to remember her own dummy's pose. Her attempt was less successful than her leader's. She looked stiff and unnatural.

The guard who had gone downstairs to phone Brigadier Keyter was back surprisingly quickly. His thundery air preceded him. He strode past the pharmacy to the gallery.

'That bloody nit-picking sonofabitch!' His anger could be heard all over the quiet gallery. 'Chewed me up – when I say report, I mean report! Can you believe it! Why didn't you report also! That's what he said. *Both* men report! You could be covering up for your pal, who's doing something else I don't know about! You'd better get down there right away to Jannie's phone.'

'That's a hell of a thing, not trusting us,' responded the other.

'OK, if that's the way he wants it, next time at ten we'll both go down and report together.'

Zara's heart leapt. Keyter's overreaction would give them the opportunity they wanted! She darted a sideways glance at Gemma. Gemma was also looking her way. She winked in reply.

The man on his way downstairs halted at the gallery entrance. 'The alarm's still off – OK?'

'Dammit, yes!' answered the other. 'The Brig doesn't need us to sit on these bloody oars like hatching eggs. There's no one here, no one for miles.'

The guard didn't spare a sideways glance as he passed the pharmacy. Nor did he when he returned shortly afterwards.

Eight-twenty.

Zara dared not turn her head from its position held by the dummy, but Gemma was able to observe the guards. They settled back in their deep armchairs, the radio between them.

Zara said softly, 'Gemma, relax! We can't hold this pose until ten o'clock. But don't shift around much. We don't want to be surprised with our pants down, so to speak.'

Both women were riding on a high; they hardly noticed how quickly the time passed. It was Gemma who first caught the sound of footsteps down the passageway.

'He's coming – Jannie, from downstairs!' Gemma's voice was hoarse with excitement.

'Does my pose look OK?' Zara asked tautly.

'Come round a bit more. You're supposed to be listening to the pharmacist guy behind the counter.'

Jannie's bonhomie prefaced his arrival in the Silver Gallery.

'Come and get it!' he called. 'Jannie's special – keeps sleep away. Rusks, too! The old woman's special!'

Both the guards (Gemma could see them) rose and stretched. She noted that one of them had taken off his revolver belt and hung it over the arm of his chair. Now he restored it to place round his rotund belly.

'The Brig will get his bloody call, on the dot, Greenwich Mean Time and all!' he exclaimed. 'Let's go!'

'The alarm?' asked the second man.

'Leave it off – we won't be that long,' replied the first. 'We don't want it suddenly activating itself for some false reason and creating a scare. There's not a damn soul in this place. Clean, sanitized. Eh, Jannie?'

'There never is. You get used to it.'

The three men came opposite the pharmacy door. One of them pointed.

'No women either, eh?'

'Sometimes I think they're alive – that's what the silence does to a man. See that one there?' Zara felt his pointing finger boring into her back. 'Sometimes I could knock a strip off her, and then I tell myself, it's all a fake. But I would still like to stroke her bum.'

'I'll bet he does, just to overcome his frustration,' the younger guard jollied him.

The two guards laughed at Jannie's discomfiture. One of them checked his watch. 'Let's get on down. I don't want the Brig beefing again.'

They went.

Zara felt the sweat running down inside her clothes.

She waited until the sound of the three men's footsteps had vanished. Then she said, 'Ready?' Her mouth was dry.

'In this rig?' Gemma asked.

'Yes. Let's go!'

Gemma pulled off the face-enveloping bonnet. Despite the impediment of the long dresses, they moved swiftly out of the pharmacy door. The Silver Gallery entrance stood wide open.

Gemma had a jeweller's fine-pointed screwdriver and

a stainless steel tool which looked rather like a blunt dentist's probe, for the display-case lock.

She thrust it into the lock with a deft twist. It gave a click.

Zara lifted the glass lid of the case. She reached for Pittock-Williams's oar, with the ivory baton and its silver head screwed into the end of the shaft.

She lifted it out. It was lighter than she had expected.

They high-tailed back to the pharmacy. Zara laid it on the counter, near the old till.

Gemma said, 'I'll have to have light. I can't work like this.'

'The torch –'

'It'll be twice as quick with the electricity.'

'Here goes, then.' Zara threw the switch. 'I'll stand guard at the door. Quick!'

Gemma ripped open the first plastic bag of the brown, putty-like Semtex, taken from her handbag.

'Stick!' she told Zara.

They had rehearsed it all, practising with Gemma's plastic pipe, back at Churchhaven, after their previous in-depth reconnaissance. The cane carried by the male dummy was to be a ramrod to tamp home the Semtex into the shaft of the oar.

Gemma unscrewed the ivory baton. She stuffed the first charge of explosive into the shaft with her fingers, making sure that the sticky stuff did not clog the screw-threads. Then, with the cane, she rammed it home as far as it would go.

Zara stood watch at the door, listening for the slightest sound.

Gemma worked swiftly, expertly.

When the shaft was full of Semtex, Gemma thrust home the detonator, pre-prepared at Churchhaven, snipped off a couple of wires, and then inserted the batteries. The trembler came last.

'Now!' she told Zara. 'I'm going to fix it, once and for all. Once I screw in the baton again and anyone tries to screw it out, she'll blow. OK?'

'OK. Shoot!'

Gemma fiddled for what seemed to Zara to be an eternity. She snipped a little with her tiny pliers, inserted the screwdriver, then reached out, grasped the baton, and screwed it swiftly and decisively into place.

'If it had been wrong, it would have blown us all to hell then,' she said.

'Back! It's OK to carry, Gemma?'

'You can soon find out.'

Zara didn't hesitate. She slung the beautiful object over her shoulder as if imitating Pittock-Williams's Marshal's pose when she had shot him. Together they raced back to the showcase.

Zara started to lay it on its velvet cushion. It looked so beautiful, so innocuous. She pressed the silver blade against her lips. 'Go well, my sweetheart,' she said.

They closed the lid gently.

'Now – the pharmacy!'

They were just in time. They heard the men coming up the stairway as they swept the tools and remnants of Semtex into their handbags. They resumed their dummy poses and switched out the lights.

It was the longest two hours of the night. After a while, Zara and Gemma could not tolerate the muscle-straining poses any longer. They decided to get rid of the heavy dresses, reclothe the dummies out of sight on the floor one at a time, and put them back in position. It was easier than they thought: they could monitor the guards' movements through the slit behind the counter. The two moved in very limited orbits from the depths of their chairs to sitting on an arm, and then back again.

They never looked at the lock of the display case.

Shortly before midnight, the Rote Zora women heard a noise from downstairs. The guards heard it too, and sat up.

'Under the counter again, quick!' Zara ordered.

Now would come the riskiest – or the easiest – part of the escape plan. It all depended –

There were heavy footsteps outside. Jannie was chattering to the two new guards. He rejoiced in the all-night company.

'Report – *personally*!' The aggrieved guard's jeer coincided with his greeting to the two newcomers. Zara and Gemma could hear everything.

'You must be joking!' This was a new voice.

'Each one of us – *personally*! No second-hand messages. *Personally!* Must be your own voice.'

Jannie's voice cut in. 'It's five minutes to midnight. Be my coffee guests, all of you!'

'Fine. That'll enable me to get the taste of his bloody high-and-mightiness out of my mouth before I go to bed. I guess he's checking his stopwatch at this very moment. Let's go.'

Zara pressed Gemma's arm. 'Ready?'

She nodded.

The five men booted their way past the pharmacy door. Immediately Zara rolled out sideways from under the counter. Gemma followed. The men were walking in step down the passageway.

The Rote Zora women came after at a safe distance, crouching back against the walls and behind exhibits on the way downstairs. They kept the men in sight. They followed the stairway to the office. Zara and Gemma, once they were clear, took the other branch into the narrow passageway with the sign 'Staff toilets'.

They went on, and found the judges' private exit door.

There was no need for their duplicate key. Its own key was in the lock.

Zara opened it, and they made their way out into the silent, deserted side street beyond.

Chapter 44

Black sand, building sand.

The incongruous, half-rhythmic stab of the words prodded Fenella out of sleep.

The peculiar quality of the dungeon's blackness brainwashed the captives out of any sense of time. It might have been midnight, or it might have been high noon outside.

It was, in fact, late on Tuesday afternoon, the day after Zara and Gemma had successfully raided the Silver Gallery and primed Pittock-Williams's oar with its killer-charge of Semtex.

Rayner and Fenella had been aware, that morning when Zara came with their breakfast (plus the two-gun escort of Renate and Gemma), that her masterplan had reached a critical phase. She had been so tight with tension that as she swapped her Glock with Renate to take up the tray, she had dropped the pistol on the steps and then grabbed at it, half-upsetting the tray's contents. As she went into a crouch to retrieve the weapon, Rayner regretted bitterly his lost opportunity to put into effect the option which was rapidly becoming the only one left, namely, to attack the trio with the handspike and risk their guns.

It was a last, desperate throw, and he had been talked out of it again by Fenella, who saw it as straight suicide.

Now a golden opportunity had slipped by. Zara quickly recovered; Renate, at the rear, remained unruffled and kept her Makarov steadily on Rayner.

Zara's half-fluffed stairway attempt had a plus factor for Rayner and Fenella: it had prevented her, in her haste to get back to the cover of the circle of pistols, from looking round the bunker and probably spotting the growing pile of debris which they had chipped off the walls. It was only good luck which had saved them so far. The two old chests had been filled and they had taken to strewing the floor with chips from the walls and trying to flatten it to a semblance of the previous sandy surface. But it was, in fact, futile. Zara would spot what had been taking place the moment she rounded the L-shaped corner.

As she had started to withdraw up the steps, Zara had said with sarcastic mock-apology:

'I'm sorry I can't let you out to see the TV's special showing this morning. The Navy is moving the two silver oars from the Cultural History Museum to Admiralty House.'

Rayner was ragged from lack of sleep and hopeless frustration.

'Thanks for nothing.'

Perhaps it helped Zara to needle someone who could not retaliate.

'You should listen on your radio. It's to be quite a function.'

'The way you talk makes it seem you have a vested interest in the move.'

Zara laughed. It wasn't a pleasant sound. 'Ask Gemma.'

Rayner recoiled inwardly at the inference. He could hardly credit that a silver oar had been primed.

Zara gave a parting jeer. 'Don't forget – nine o'clock for the commentary. The Prime Minister's arrival is scheduled for immediately afterwards. The media have been boasting that they're the two most spectacular events that Cape Town has seen since the last Royal visit.'

They were.

Zara paced up and down the lounge drinking cups of coffee waiting for the transmission to begin. Her tension and anxiety communicated itself to other members of the gang, except Gemma, who seemed dull and listless.

The programme began; the commentary was parallel to that which Rayner and Fenella heard as they threw themselves once again into a task as unrewarding as convicts sewing mailbags. Except that mailbags have a function.

The street outside the Cultural History Museum had been barricaded off; thousands crowded the nearest vantage points, including balconies and roofs of buildings opposite. Armed naval guards formed a human barrier along the sidewalks; there were even sharpshooters on the flat roof of the museum itself.

'Here they come!' exclaimed the commentator.

Zara said, under her breath, 'For Chrissake, hurry! Don't let it happen here!'

'It can't,' said Gemma. 'Unless some clot gets it in his thick head to fiddle with the Marshal's baton.'

A naval band appeared first, followed by a squad of hand-picked sailors; in their midst was an armoured security van. An armed man sat next to the driver. There was enough fire-power in the street to restage the Battle of the River Plate.

The squad and the van drew up outside the museum's front door: two officers emerged.

The *Alabama* oar on its black velvet cushion came first on the outstretched hands of one man, and then the Pittock-Williams replica held by the next. The bright sunlight made the two masterpieces even more sensational than the spotlights of the exhibit case inside.

'Look! It's OK, it's there! The baton's screwed in, just as we left it!'

'If it hadn't been, they would be commentating on a

different note altogether this morning,' observed Renate dryly.

Zara turned to Gemma. 'We've won! We've made it! Nothing can stop us now!'

The Oar Squad (the commentator coined the name) moved majestically as a battleship into the open doors of the security van. They swung closed. There were bugles, bands, marching feet. The procession headed up the street.

'We've won!' repeated Zara.

Down in the bunker, the walls were blanker than ever; Rayner and Fenella's hands rawer than ever; their chances of escape slimmer than ever.

Their sense of futility grew to such an extent that when the radio commentary came on describing the arrival of the British Prime Minister's motorcade in the same street which the navy had so shortly before vacated – it was on its way to the presidential residence Tuynhuis nearby – they stopped in their frenetic efforts and listened instead. There are many ways of showing you have thrown in the towel.

The pomp and pageantry of the Prime Minister's arrival in an open limousine preceded by a police escort on horseback made the event splendid TV material; in the Churchhaven lounge, the Rote Zora women watched. Zara was completely relaxed.

As the Prime Minister's limousine edged its way along and the famous face came into shot, acknowledging the cheering, flag-waving crowds, Renate said to Zara:

'There's your target for tomorrow.'

Zara shrugged indifferently. 'It's an occupational hazard. Too bad.'

In the bunker, Rayner and Fenella heard out the commentary in silence. Then, by tacit consent, they lay down and slept.

Black sand, building sand.

Fenella's rising consciousness clawed at the signal which her unconscious had given in sleep, and she jerked upright into a sitting position.

She had it! It was Rayner who had used the words, but they had allowed themselves to be swept along in the wrong direction when the answer lay right there at their feet.

Literally, at their feet. Black sand, building sand!

Fenella threw herself across his shoulder, her breasts hard against him. Only this wasn't passion, it was salvation.

'Rayner! I've got it! What fools we've been! The one place we didn't look, and it was staring us in the face all the time!'

Rayner came awake. 'Fenella, what – ?'

The words avalanched from Fenella. 'I'm lighting the light, just to show you it's not a dream! We can beat them yet, Rayner! You had it in your hand, and you let it go!'

Rayner was still shaking the sleep out of his eyes when Fenella found the matches and lighted the lamp with shaking hands. She came to him holding the poor little illumination high, and smiling.

'What's the time?' he asked.

'Nearly four o'clock – afternoon. It's cutting it very fine, but we can still get out tonight and warn them –'

'Tell me!' he said urgently. 'Start at the beginning.'

'It *was* right at the beginning,' burst out Fenella excitedly. 'You remember, before we began chipping the walls, you picked up some sand in a spoon which you said was alien to the type of sand the floor is made of –'

Rayner caught some of her excitement. 'Go on! I remember it very well. It's what gave me the idea that there might be an escape tunnel there.'

'Black sand, building sand!' echoed Fenella. 'There *is* a tunnel there, with black sand used perhaps for ballast

346

or something, and building sand for the mortar for the tunnel's bricks –'

'But there is nothing there!' Rayner exclaimed. 'You know that for yourself. We fine-combed every inch of the walls.'

'Old George White fooled us, just as he aimed to fool everyone else who came to his bunker,' Fenella raced on. 'The natural conclusion anyone draws is that, because the bunker is deep under the ground, an exit tunnel must start from a point which would lead by the most obvious route to the surface. In other words, from the roof or the walls. Upwards, to get out.'

'Of course.'

'What if that cunning old fugitive sited the tunnel right under the light, so to speak, where no one would expect to find it?'

'What are you saying, Fenella?'

'That the mouth of the tunnel is under the floor. That we've been walking over it all the time. It's the only place we haven't looked! We were in the right quarter all right, but searching upwards instead of under!'

Rayner stared at her for a long moment. Then he swung his legs out of the bed and checked his watch.

'Every minute is precious! We've got a couple of hours clear before they bring our supper. We have simply got to find that tunnel mouth!'

Fenella said, 'We'll have to probe the floor to locate it. I know, the handspike! It's perfect for the job.'

'We can't start any serious operations before they've finally been for the night,' said Rayner. 'It would be madness to throw away our only remaining chance with a tell-tale heap of sand.' Then he added as the thought struck him, 'We'll spread out one of these old sheets of newspaper and use it as a grid, so that we won't work over the same patch of floor twice.'

'Where do we start?'

'Where I found the different sort of sand. That's where the fresh air is coming in from above. That is what really fooled us, thinking that the tunnel and the ventilation system were the same. I'm sure now that there's a separate air duct or conduit higher up, perhaps between the church floor and our ceiling. Fenella, you're a genius!'

'We haven't found it yet.'

Chapter 45

They laid out the old newspaper on the floor as if they were about to begin an archaeological dig. Then Rayner thrust the handspike into the sandy surface.

They had expected that it would go deep, but it didn't. The floor seemed to have been deliberately compacted. Rayner had to throw all his weight on the handspike, coupled with a twisting movement, for it to penetrate its entire length.

Fenella helped him, probing, feeling, searching.

There was nothing.

Nor had they found anything by the time they judged it wise to give up before Zara and the two Rote Zoras arrived with supper. Zara was withdrawn, untalkative. She merely thrust the tray at them and withdrew.

Rayner and Fenella resumed work immediately the women were gone, eating as they searched. At first, they spaced the holes in the newspaper at six inches apart, but later altered it to a foot, in order to speed up the operation.

They worked over a floor area of two full newspaper sheets.

Nothing.

Their next option was to try further into the room itself, away from the wall, or close against the wall itself.

'Let's try inwards,' suggested Fenella.

'Your guess is as good as mine.'

The spike went in, for the hundredth time. Fenella gripped the rounded haft first, in order to save Rayner's hands.

As it went in, Fenella exclaimed, 'Rayner! There's something hard underneath! It's rasping against the point! Like something catching on to a tooth!'

They left the handspike in as a guide, scooped a cup-like pocket round it, tried thrusting it deeper.

'Fenella, it's hard! It won't go! Feel! The way it scrapes means only one thing to me – metal!'

About six inches of sand kept from view whatever lay beneath, but by shifting the handspike on its own axis, they could feel – and hear faintly – the scrape of metal against metal.

They first cleared the lip of the hole they had burrowed, and then scooped the sand clear with their washbasin.

Then they lay on their faces, scuffling the dirt back like feverish desert rats.

They saw.

It was a small half-moon of black, rusty metal.

'What is it, Rayner?' Fenella whispered.

'Don't let us throw our hats over the moon at this stage,' he replied. 'I don't know. But it looks good.'

It was good when, after shovelling out endless basin-fuls of sand, a circle of metal stood exposed.

'A ring-bolt, Fenella! It's a ring-bolt! It's a man-hole!'

They set to work again, redoubling their efforts, burrowing, scratching, clearing with their hands, even using the supper cups and plates, anything which would free the overburden of sand.

First, the metal cover of the man-hole became visible, and then the concrete socket into which it fitted.

At nine o'clock Rayner grasped the ring-bolt and heaved.

It came clear in his powerful grip.

Fenella threw herself full-length on her face and thrust the oil lamp into the space.

It was a small brick chamber, about six feet square and the same deep. The man-hole had been accommodated by a vaulted brick roof, supported by a brick arch.

But it was not upon this that their eyes rested.

Set into the wall at floor level on the far side was what appeared to be, in the dim light, a small fireplace with an arch. It was about as high as a man's chest and about half that distance wide.

Fenella leaned further into the man-hole to try and see.

'Watch it,' cautioned Rayner. 'The air in there is probably dangerous. If it's what we think it is, the place has been sealed for a long, long time.'

He drew her back into the bunker.

'Rayner! We can't leave it just because of the chance of stale air!'

'The air could be plain poison,' he replied. 'We can easily test it, though. We'll lower the lamp into the place, and if it goes out, we know it's not for us.'

'That fireplace thing – it could be the start of our tunnel.'

Rayner quickly undid his belt and hooked it round the handle of the lamp. He lay on the edge of the man-hole and lowered it until it touched the floor. It flickered once or twice, but kept burning.

'We can't spare more than five minutes,' he said. 'Then we'll venture down ourselves. There must be a source of air somewhere. Do you spot anything?'

'There seems to be some kind of vent near the shoulder of the arch – there, on the right, at the top.'

'Maybe an airbrick,' ventured Rayner. 'Perhaps it's

linked to the airstream which comes in under the roof.'

'Let's go down and investigate.'

Fenella swung down by holding on to Rayner's wrists. Rayner followed.

Fenella stood and eyed the arched structure in disbelief.

There was no hole, no tunnel, no aperture. They seemed to have exchanged one dead-end for another.

Rayner thrust the light close to the brick structure. What seemed to be a vaulted roof rested on two brick shoulders which were built on blue stone columns on either side, resting on a broader stone footing. Under the main arch was an additional arch of red brick. Stretching transversely across the lower side of the solid brick wall below the arch was a very distinctive double line of small yellow bricks, laid in a completely different pattern from the ones above.

'Fenella!' His voice vibrated with excitement. 'The bricks in this centre section aren't the same sort at all as the ones above and below it. Look – they're blue for a start and professionally finished, as if they had been made by a machine. The others – look here – are irregular in size, and some of them are really quite crude. Also, the mortar is whiter on the upper and lower sections, whereas here in the middle it's darker –'

'What are you trying to tell me, Rayner?'

'At a guess, I'd say that the two lots of bricks were manufactured at two widely separated periods of time, one by hand, and the other by machine. This centre section has all the hallmarks of a tunnel mouth, beautifully constructed of vaulted brick and old stone. Later – much later, when bricks were made by machine and not by hand, this middle section was bricked up. My interpretation is that old George White built the tunnel at the same time as the bunker and that one of his descendants, many years later, bricked up the mouth – here!'

'You may be right, but where do we go from here, Rayner?' Fenella's query was desperate.

Rayner held up the handspike. 'We dig out the new bricks – with this. Find the tunnel on the other side.'

Ten o'clock.

Thirteen hours to Simonstown.

Rayner attacked the wall with the handspike, targeting on a brick in the centre. He explained to Fenella that it might be the quickest and easiest way to enlarge a gap through which they could see what lay on the other side.

The work, for hands already blistered and painful from days of chipping at the bunker walls, was cruel. Within minutes of his first powerful overhand cracks at the brick, the force of his blows slackened.

'Wait!' said Fenella. 'Take one of my socks and use it for a mitt.'

Rayner did, but the blunt, rounded point of the handspike seemed to make no impression on the brickwork. Fenella joined in, but after an hour all they had to show for their efforts was a small chipped-off section of mortar round the perimeter of the brick.

Fenella also tried scraping at the mortar holding it with the shaft of one of their eating spoons, but this was hopeless. It buckled and bent. They even tried the spout of their stainless steel teapot, until it broke off short.

After a blow with the handspike from Rayner's hands, a fragment of the spike's point broke off, leaving it jagged. It was a blessing in disguise. Work went quicker.

At eleven-thirty Fenella exclaimed, 'It's coming loose, Rayner!'

They redoubled their efforts, but it took them another half an hour before they got the brick free.

Rayner thrust his right arm and hand in as far as he could to explore.

'There's space beyond,' he told her with satisfaction. 'I can also feel a kind of paved floor.'

In turn, Fenella shoved her arm in as far as it would go. She could only detect with her fingertips the paving Rayner had mentioned.

'It's a bit eerie,' she remarked. 'It's worth going on now, isn't it?'

'It's worth going on with,' he echoed grimly.

At 4.00 a.m. they inched aside the last brick which would provide an aperture large enough to reconnoitre the dark, damp-smelling space which lay beyond.

'I'll go, I'm slimmer,' said Fenella. 'Hold my legs. If I yell, pull me back – but quick!'

She went in, light ahead.

She squirmed until her hips caught. She could go no deeper.

He heard her muffled call. 'OK – help me back, Rayner!'

'Yes?' he asked anxiously when she re-emerged.

'Yes, and yes, and yes again.' Fenella was smiling, jubilant. 'It's a tunnel, all right, Rayner. It goes on and on. It's got a proper paved floor and a vaulted roof. You were right! It was meant to be a tunnel, and it is!'

At 5.00 a.m. the brickwork looked like gaps in the Berlin Wall.

Finally, Rayner said excitedly, 'Now, here we go! I'll lead, you keep a grip on my ankles. I'll take the light to see the way.'

Rayner first squeezed through the gap, Fenella followed. The roof of the tunnel was too low for them to crawl on all fours; they propelled themselves forward by flexing elbows and knees.

After a while, the tunnel widened, trumpet-shaped, and they were able to crawl. Fenella still held on lightly to one of Rayner's ankles. It was too dark for her to see past him.

Suddenly, she felt Rayner's leg muscles go steely. He stopped dead. She could feel the tension coursing down his leg.

'Rayner! What is it? Is there someone –'

'You could call it that, I suppose,' he answered quietly. 'Fenella, in a moment the tunnel widens further. I think we could go on at a crouch.'

'Then what stopped you?'

He replied, 'It wasn't only an escape tunnel which old George White built. There are coffins ahead.'

'We must be under the graveyard,' answered Fenella. 'Go on, Rayner, I can take it.'

The tunnel had been widened to accommodate the dead, and there were small vaulted side-chambers on either hand. In these were half a dozen coffins. One or two had crumbled; the dim light showed skulls.

They went on. The vault heightened. Now they could stand, side by side. They hurried on. Their way ahead was barred by a small swinging door like a pub's.

Rayner gripped the handspike, went into a precautionary crouch. He flung open the door, recoiled.

'*Rayner! What is it?*'

He said levelly, 'There are grenades and pistols and what look like boxes of explosive. There's also something which I don't think you should see. It's not very – ah, photogenic.'

Menty had never been pretty in life; in death, less so.

Rayner added, 'I'm going to get myself a gun. I may need it. Wait here. Face the other way. I won't be a moment.'

He came back with a Makarov, two magazines and a grenade.

'There's another outer door, but it doesn't look much,' he said.

They hurried to it; the wood splintered under the handspike.

Rayner flung it open.

Five-thirty in the morning.

George White had chosen the cliff-top site for its great view across the lagoon towards the far hills. It was still too dark to see them but there was a faint line of light which would conjure up the splendid vista when day came.

On their right, flanking the church, Zara's cottage was wrapped in darkness.

Fenella burst through the doorway to his side.

'Rayner! We're out! We're free!'

Chapter 46

They stood on the cliff-top amongst the graves, gulping in the clean fresh air off the water for the sheer joy of being alive. The family tomb was at their backs, the lagoon at their faces. Behind was death, ahead was life. They had no words.

It was Rayner who pulled them back to reality. 'I'll shut that door.'

He eyed Fenella. Her face was grimy from the tunnel, her hands more so, and she had pushed her dishevelled hair back from her forehead. But her deep eyes had the luminous glow he had seen only once or twice before.

Before he could go, she moved close to him. Her lips said all he wanted to know. They stood like that, oblivious that in the dark house so near at hand was a force which could still separate them for ever.

Then Rayner said, 'Shall I give you a gun, too?'

She shook her head. 'I wouldn't know what to do with it.'

He said, 'We've got to act, and act quickly. We've a

355

little over five hours before the Simonstown ceremony. It has got to be stopped, at all costs.'

Fenella gestured towards the house. 'You're not going in there – to shoot it out, are you, Rayner?'

'The situation is beyond the stage where Zara can be of any use,' he replied. 'She couldn't recall the loaded oar even if she wanted. No, Fenella. The moment Pittock-Williams unscrews his Marshal's baton, the Semtex will detonate. Its teeth have got to be drawn. We still have time to do just that.'

'What have you in mind?'

'There are three cars there at the house. If we could get our hands on one of them, we could make a break for Cape Town and warn Hugh –'

'Hugh? Why Hugh, Rayner?'

'Because he's the only person who will listen to me, Fenella. I'm *persona non grata* with Keyter. Can you imagine his reaction if I were to break in on him and tell him this fantastic story? He wouldn't believe a word of it!'

'Not you alone, Rayner. I'll back you up.'

'Hugh is one of the inner security circle round the VIPs,' he went on rapidly. 'He is the only man at this advanced stage before the ceremony gets under way to stop the schedule – Fenella! Down! Quick!'

A light had come on in the house.

On the ground, Rayner eased back the catch of his Makarov and sighted it on the window, using his elbows as a stand for a steady shot.

'They can't have heard us!' Fenella whispered.

'That's the kitchen light, I'd guess,' Rayner replied in a low voice.

It was coming from the rear of the house, illuminating the Combi and Menty's car parked against the garage, whose door was closed, presumably housing Zara's.

'It washes out the idea of grabbing a car, even if we

had to risk a shot or two,' said Rayner. 'The element of surprise is gone now. Let's get out of here, where we can't be spotted from the house.'

They crawled away on all fours, dodging the mounds and headstones until the cliff fell away at a low stone wall which was the boundary of the cemetery. They swung themselves over, behind its cover.

Rayner said, 'If we can't get to Cape Town in person, there's still the telephone. Hugh would accept what I said, even at a distance.'

'He's going to be a very busy man today,' Fenella said.

'It's very early still,' Rayner reasoned. 'I could speak to him before he leaves his hotel. The problem is, there are no phones at Churchhaven. Menty told me so. Our first task is to get well clear of this place.'

'Which way?' asked Fenella.

'Menty said the nearest phone was at Langebaan resort, which is on the other side of the lagoon.' Rayner gestured towards the line of hills, becoming more defined now against the hidden sunrise. But it's thirty kilometres to it. Wait, I've got it! That is what we'll use!'

He pointed to the tiny rocky cove which lay at the foot of the cliff below Zara's house.

A dinghy was drawn up on the natural rock ramp.

'We can row across the lagoon to the other side in that!' Rayner went on. 'It won't make a noise. We can get clear away without Zara and the gang even suspecting it!'

'Except – the path down to the cove runs down the cliff in full view of the house,' said Fenella.

They sat staring dispiritedly across the lagoon. A faint haze was delaying the advent of the sun.

Fenella said, 'We can't swim across the lagoon.'

Rayner wheeled on her. 'Swim! That's it! We could swim into the cove from the lagoon side, and nobody would be any wiser! Wonderful, Fenella! That is what we'll do!'

'The gang could still spot us approaching –'

Rayner was on his knees now, scanning the water's dim surface. 'That's Zara's yacht out there. We could take to the water here at the foot of the cliff and make the yacht our staging-post to the dinghy! It's not far out – it looks less than half a kilometre to me. You wait for me there while I go and tow the dinghy to the yacht and then we can row ourselves across the lagoon!'

Fenella was smiling now. 'Wonderful!'

'How well can you swim?' Rayner asked, standing up.

'I've swum since childhood,' she replied. 'Let's get going!'

It was six o'clock.

They made their way down the cliff, slipping on the friable sandy surface and catching their clothes in the rough vegetation. There was no beach, but only a dried mudflat.

They stripped. Fenella went into the water first, breast-deep.

'Glorious!' she exclaimed. 'There in the bunker, I thought I'd never know water again.'

She turned round, went to him. It wasn't only the autumn chill which made her breasts and nipples erect. She thrust her body hard against his. 'It's a promise,' she said softly.

They went ashore for their clothes, which they tied on their heads for the swim out to the yacht. Rayner dumped one Makarov magazine in the bushes, but he kept the other, and lashed the grenade on top of his pile like a Sikh's topknot.

They headed out into the lagoon, before circling back to reach the yacht on its blind side from the house. There was a light now in Zara's lounge. They reached the yacht, hung on to the mooring-buoy cable, left their clothes on deck.

Rayner prepared to go.

'Watch yourself, Rayner!'

He grinned back. 'I've too much to lose if I don't.'

In about ten minutes, Fenella heard the sound of stealthy strokes approaching, and Rayner reappeared, towing the dinghy by its painter.

'Let's first get clear – clothes can wait.'

'Hold it,' said Fenella. 'Your hands took an awful beating in the night.'

He held them out to her, blistered, red and raw in places.

'Socks!' exclaimed Fenella. 'Both our pairs on both your hands.'

They headed into the morning mist.

They went on for about a quarter of an hour. They had no landmarks ahead to steer by because of the haze and dimness; it was only when Zara's light at their backs became muted that Rayner stopped rowing and they dressed.

'My turn now,' said Fenella.

Seven o'clock.

The sun rose, the mist dissipated. They seemed no nearer the far shore. Fenella's rowing appeared to be getting them nowhere. Rayner turned anxiously astern, and then checked ahead. The low hills seemed to be in exactly the same position: there was no prominent landmark or feature. To their immediate right, however, a great patch of marsh and reedy saltings intruded into clearer water away in the direction of the lagoon's centre. Thousands of birds were starting to call and move.

'Hold it, Fenella,' Rayner said.

The dinghy's bow, once it lost headway, started to swing slowly towards the marsh patch and the head of the lagoon – the opposite direction from their objective.

'There's a current. It must be a tide or a set flowing into the lagoon from the sea at the mouth,' he exclaimed. 'We're travelling crabwise. We are being pushed in completely the wrong direction. We've wasted a lot of effort covering a great deal of unnecessary distance.'

Fenella added, 'Plus time.'

In unconscious unison, they both checked their watches.

Half past seven.

It was heartbreaking, backbreaking, muscle-cracking work. What they did not realize was that, by making a ninety-degree turn in order to beat their previous crabwise track, they had headed into the main thrust of the inflowing tide. This tide is the lagoon's lifeblood. Once a day, the great mass of water has a transfusion from the sea, bringing with it the organisms which feed not only the bird and fish populations, but the aquatic plants of the saltings.

It was the salinity which worried Rayner and Fenella, too. They tasted the water and realized it would increase rather than slake their thirst. There was no strong heat yet in the sun, but later it would come. Nor had they had any sustaining food since their bunker meal the previous evening.

Fenella spotted a plastic shopping-bag under a thwart. It contained a loaf of stale bread; this had obviously been used for bait. There was also a two-litre plastic milk bottle, three-quarters full of insipid water. They ate the stuff the fishes rejected, with relish.

Eight o'clock.

The sun started to get hot. The village of Langebaan was visible, far away to their right. Rayner guessed that it was between five and seven kilometres away. It could have been more.

They rowed in shorter, more desperate shifts as time slipped under their boat quicker than the incoming tide.

Had they known it, a little to the right towards the shore, the lagoon-edge was fronted by long, wide, underwater sandbanks, round which the tide scoured into the main channel in which they now fought their way at steadily diminishing speed. By going closer inshore, they would have been in still water.

Rayner stopped, gasping for breath. Fenella poured water from overside over him, trying, like a marathon runner, to cool him down.

He lifted his right hand off the oar. The woollen socks in which it was cased stuck. Fenella saw the tinge of blood.

'Rayner, you can't go on – we can't go on – like this! There must be a better way.'

He dipped his damaged hand in the water. 'That feels good.' Then he indicated far ahead. 'That's the better way.'

Kilometres away, in the gap which the lagoon formed as it narrowed towards the seaward entrance, they saw a cream of foam under the bow of a fast craft. It arrowed towards the village which was their objective.

'That's a Search and Rescue crash-boat – I saw one of them with Menty,' he added. 'Ten minutes, and we'd be at the village, in one of them.'

Rayner stripped off his shirt. It was also warm enough now to need a hat. Fenella improvised one by making a crude turban out of her jersey.

She joined him at the oars. Rayner was now throwing his main weight on his left hand, and the stroke on the second oar with Fenella's lesser power was out of synchronization, erratic. Their course was correspondingly erratic, bringing them nearer the shore.

After a spell, Rayner paused and shipped his oar.

Eight-thirty.

'Fenella,' he said. 'This is getting us nowhere – fast. We've missed our chance of catching Hugh at his hotel, that I'm sure of. *We've got to get to a phone – quick!*'

'Brigadier Keyter?' she asked hesitatingly.

'I say again, he certainly won't listen to me. Not today, of all days.'

'Why don't we make our way ashore and play the phone call by ear? We could try hitching to the village.'

'We'd have to get through all that rough scrub up the cliff along the water's edge first,' Rayner pointed out. 'We could wait at the roadside all morning. Let's rather stick with the devil we know.'

They continued their lop-sided progress. Then Fenella suddenly exclaimed, 'Rayner – the pull is different! We're making headway! We're not being held back all the time!'

They did not know it, but they had drifted, by virtue of their crabwise progress, over the great sandbank which projected out into the lagoon.

They bent to the oars. They made progress. The first houses of the village came into view. But even their euphoria couldn't heal Rayner's hands. The stale bread and half-rancid water made him feel nauseous, too. He surrendered the oars to Fenella.

Nine o'clock.

It was the change of places which made him sight the radio masts.

'Fenella!' he burst out excitedly. 'I've got it! I've got our solution! Those masts – radio – we don't need a telephone! The radio's the thing! We'll get to the crash-boat base and get them to radio Simonstown and warn them!'

'This is our biggest break yet!' exclaimed Fenella.

Rayner went on excitedly, 'We'll have them radio Commander Enslin – you remember, the South African Navy man who was liaising with Hugh at Admiralty House! We'll ask him to contact Hugh, who'll vouch for me that it's not a hoax – we can make it still, Fenella! There's two hours to go!'

Rayner seemed to find a hidden strength which he had not suspected before. He needed all the protection of the two pairs of socks over his raw hands.

They rowed past the village on their right, using the high radio masts slightly beyond to the north as their datum point.

They edged round the final low headland. There was a jetty and a slipway. Three fast Search and Rescue craft, one slightly larger than the others, were tied up in line abreast. Ashore were prefabricated buildings, and a central brick complex. A big notice board on the roof read: 'SAS *Flamingo*, Naval Shore Establishment. Search and Rescue. Entry prohibited.'

There were fences and barbed wire. A gaggle of radio transmitting masts towered overhead.

Rayner rowed in.

Chapter 47

Nine-thirty.

Rayner headed for the biggest of the three craft. The dinghy bumped against its side; Rayner threw a line to make fast.

'Hey!'

A sailor, in brown working overalls, emerged from a deck door. He gave a startled glance at the two dirty, dishevelled figures. Rayner had on the incongruous double mitten-socks over his hands. His beard and six-day-old stubble had bits of dirt from the escape tunnel attached to it; the lagoon water and his own sweat made it worse. Fenella's slept-in pants and shirt were crushed so that the swell of her lovely breasts was lost under the shapeless top.

'Hey – what –'

Rayner started to pick up the Makarov and grenade from the dinghy's bottom-boards.

The sailor catapulted himself backwards, dived behind an Oerlikon thirty-millimetre gunshield, swung the ugly muzzle in the direction of the dinghy. But the barrel would not depress enough. He danced out from behind the metal shield with a side-step back through the deck door.

Within seconds, there was a metallic clatter and the barrel of an R2 automatic pre-empted his fighting crouch behind.

He swivelled his aim alternately from Rayner to Fenella, but addressed Rayner.

'Terrorist!' He gave the rough consonants full value. 'What are you up to, eh? Thought you'd catch us with our pants down just because everyone's on holiday, eh? Drop that gun and that – that –' The automatic barrel indicated the grenade.

Rayner tossed the Makarov on to the deck.

'We're not terrorists,' he replied. 'This grenade is dangerous if I throw it down. It's Russian. Watch the pin – here!'

The man recoiled, bumping the back of his head against the depressed mouth of the Oerlikon. 'I'll shoot –'

Rayner then pulled off the bloodied socks from his hands. He put them on the deck and laid the grenade on top of them.

'Get back! Hands high!' the sailor rapped out.

Rayner repeated, 'We're not terrorists,' and added, 'Take me to the officer in charge of this base.'

The sailor's glance travelled from Rayner to Fenella. 'You've got to be kidding. What are you up to? Don't you know civilians aren't allowed in here? Base commander!'

Rayner said tightly, 'Listen, for reasons you don't know, time isn't on our side this morning. Cut the jaw-jaw. Take me to your commanding officer. What's his name?'

'Lieutenant Faure.'

'Tell him – no, I'll tell him myself. Only, for Pete's sake hurry, man! This is a life-or-death situation. We've only an hour and a half left, if important people are to live!'

'You're kidding –' the man repeated.

Rayner jumped impatiently up on deck. 'Listen, man, I've never been so serious about anything in my life.' The sailor shrank away, making a wavering attempt to hold his aim. 'Take me to Lieutenant Faure. You won't ever regret it.'

Fenella added, 'We appreciate that you're only doing your duty.'

The man eyed them, taken aback by their lack of hostility. His glance went over Fenella. 'Say, is this a TV stunt or somethin'?' He added, with disarming candour, 'You wouldn't look bad, if you had a wash and brush-up.'

Rayner said urgently, 'Lieutenant Faure!'

'This wasn't the way I was trained to handle a terrorist situation –'

'Shall I bring the pistol and grenade, or will you?' Rayner pressured him.

'I guess I'd better,' he replied. Rayner picked them up and handed them to him. He thrust them into his voluminous overall pockets. His voice and bearing changed. He rapped out in his best sentry voice, 'March! Prisoners, march!'

He indicated a concrete path from the jetty to the central brick complex. 'They're all in there, watching the telly. We drew for who'd be on duty. I lost. Fanie's luck.'

Rayner strode ahead. As they drew near, they could hear the commentator's voice.

He was saying:

Never in Cape Town's long history have there been such crowds and such excitement as there is at this moment in the Gardens outside the official presidential residence Tuynhuis, where we are waiting for the presidential limousine to emerge carrying the British Prime Minister and the South African President on the first leg of their historic journey to Admiralty House in Simonstown.

Waiting at the gate is a mounted escort of South African police, which will precede the motorcade to the nearby helipad, from where a naval helicopter from HMS *Invincible* will fly the party to Simonstown –

The crash of Fanie's boots on the floor drowned out the commentator's voice for a moment as he came to attention and sounded out:

'Reporting, sir! Two prisoners under arrest. Attempted terrorist attack on ships in base.'

He pushed Rayner and Fenella forward with the barrel of his R2 into full sight of about a dozen men in civilian dress who were sitting watching the TV screen.

A tall, sun-tanned, slightly ginger-haired man with a toothbrush moustache and unmistakable air of authority, who sat alone in a big armchair, jerked upright.

'What the hell –!'

'Male terrorist demands an interview with base commander,' Fanie went on. 'Weapons of war for attack confiscated.'

He whipped out the Makarov and grenade from his pockets.

Lieutenant Faure got to his feet. 'Switch that TV down

for a minute,' he told one of the viewing circle. 'Now, what is going on here?'

Rayner intervened. 'You are Lieutenant Faure, the base commander?'

'Yes.'

'I have to see you urgently. What I have to say is confidential.'

Faure's eyes fixed acutely on Rayner, and then travelled to Fenella, as if he were trying to place them somewhere in his mind.

The TV commentary had been switched down only enough to enable the circle to go on hearing. Faure glanced irritably at it and said abruptly, 'Come to my office.'

Fanie bleated, 'Weapons of war, sir – what'll I do with them?'

Faure asked Rayner, 'These yours?'

'In a sense, yes.'

'Give them to me. Fanie, stay here until I want you.'

'They could be dangerous, sir –'

For the first time, a smile brushed the naval man's disciplined lips. 'I'll take that risk. Come.'

He strode down a corridor and entered the first office next to the mess. A notice read: 'Lieutenant D. Faure, Base Commander'.

Faure sat himself down behind his desk, still with his eyes fixed on Rayner and Fenella. He put the grenade and Makarov on the blotter in front of him.

'Well –' he began and then exclaimed suddenly, 'Wait, I have it! I know you now, I thought I recognized you both. You are the guy who was on TV, the man who found the silver oar from the wreck of the *Alabama*, eh? And you –' he addressed Fenella. 'You were the person who identified it, not so? You also went missing, the police are looking for you. Right?'

Rayner broke in. 'Lieutenant, we are who you think

we are. Fenella Gault, Rayner Watton. But time is running out.' He tapped his watch. 'In about an hour and twenty minutes, if we don't do something quickly, there will be the most spectacular assassination in modern times. We need you, we need your communications set-up, your radio –'

'If I hadn't recognized you, I'd lock you up for a nutcase,' Faure interrupted. 'Go on.'

'One of the silver oars you mentioned has been converted into the most cunning and lethal weapon a diseased mind could have ever conceived –' Rayner's words flowed. He told the story disjointedly, Fenella filling in, supplementing the technical aspect. She outlined how she had been kidnapped by Zara and her gang and been forced to reveal details of the oar's make-up, how she had been held captive in the bunker under the old church. Rayner endorsed what she said, talking rapidly, glossing over their escape through the tunnel, and finally the desperation row across the lagoon.

It took about ten minutes. Faure's face was as impassive as a judge's at a murder trial.

When they had done, he said, 'Why did you come here, to SAS *Flamingo*? I can't do anything about a situation which is to happen a hundred and fifty kilometres away. I can't stop the ceremony.'

'I want you to send a radio signal, top priority, to Commander Enslin, the officer who is in charge of the security screen on the South African side, for him to pass on to Inspector Hugh Perrot of Scotland Yard, who has the same position with the British team. He's part of the Prime Minister's personal bodyguard inside Admiralty House. I know Perrot well, we worked together.'

'Scotland Yard,' echoed Faure. 'Yeah, I know, again from the telly.' He said apologetically, 'You see, there's not a hell of a lot else to do in a place like this except watch TV –' He pulled himself up and said tightly, 'So

368

you want me to send a signal to Commander Enslin?'

'That's it. We can draft it. Radio. Urgent –'

'Do you know what you're asking?' Faure's voice was hard.

'I don't know, if you're talking about correct channels. But I do know, with these VIP lives at stake –'

Faure shook his head. 'You ask me to believe that there's an international women's terror gang called Rote Zora operating across the lagoon, from peaceful old Churchhaven?'

'The gang won't be present. They don't have to be. The trembler and the detonator will do their work the moment the Marshal's baton is unscrewed.'

Faure went on, almost as if he hadn't heard, 'I am a lieutenant, a very minor lieutenant. Enslin is a commander, a big shot in the hierarchy. I haven't the right to signal him.'

Fenella said, 'A cat may look at a king.'

The way he smiled, Rayner realized they were beginning to win. 'Moreover, I am not permitted to signal unilaterally. All my radio signals have to go through the main naval base at Saldanha. Except –'

'Except what?' Rayner demanded.

'If there's a critical time factor involved, such as a rescue out to sea. When the time taken up by signalling could mean the difference between life and death.'

'The difference between life and death,' Fenella echoed.

Faure went on, as if speaking to himself. 'My radio has the range to Simonstown. But I have no guarantee that the message would reach Enslin. Not today, of all days.'

'You'll do it, then?' Rayner asked hoarsely.

Faure spread his hands out on the blotter, palms up, like a shady bookie accepting an impossible bet.

'I'm laying my career on the line,' he told them. 'You

realize that? Just signalling Simonstown, let alone what the contents of the signal may be.' He shrugged and reached into a drawer for paper. He glanced at his watch. 'Time is getting damn short. Now – short and sweet.'

SAS Flamingo Search and Rescue Base, to Commander Dockyard, Simonstown. Top priority. Top secret.

He grinned at them. 'In the navy, it doesn't come hotter than that.'

Rayner suggested:

For urgent personal attention Commander Enslin at Admiralty House. From Rayner Watton. Advise –

'What's your status?' Faure interrupted.

'I haven't any. Just say, Rayner Watton. Hugh Perrot will accept it.'

'OK.'

From Rayner Watton. Advise Inspector Hugh Perrot of Scotland Yard, also on duty at Admiralty House, that Pittock-Williams silver oar contains a charge of Semtex in its shaft. Will be detonated by trembler fuse when Marshal's baton is unscrewed. Rote Zora terrorist plot –

'Spell that – I'm not with these odd names.'

'Rote Zora,' repeated Rayner, and Faure went on writing.

Suggest scheduled procedure for Pittock-Williams be amended to exclude removal of baton. Oar remains safe if baton undisturbed.

Rayner stopped, and Fenella nodded.

'Anything more?' Faure asked.

'Isn't that enough?'

He shook his head. 'I hope they don't order my arrest for going off my head.'

Faure got up and went to the door. The muted sound of the TV commentary came through from the mess. 'Signals,' he shouted. 'Signals officer! Here!'

A thin, academic-looking young man with big glasses appeared.

Faure said, 'Shoot that off – now! Quick as hell!'

The man's eyes went over the slip Faure handed him. The magnification of his strong lenses made his eyes look wider. He looked uncertainly at his commanding officer as if doubting his sanity. 'Any reply, sir?'

Faure snorted. 'None. Unless it's a message for my arrest.'

'Aye, aye, sir.' He vanished.

'Now –' began Faure.

Rayner said quickly, 'Lieutenant, I have another request to make to you.'

The naval man's face closed and his eyes became less friendly. 'What is it?'

Rayner's tension made him frame the request badly. 'I want your help with the Rote Zora gang.'

Both Rayner and Fenella saw the quick flare of anger tighten Faure's mouth.

'I've taken your unsupported word for what anyone else would say was plain crazy,' he said abruptly. 'That's enough. I've risked my career. My duties are very well defined. I am not authorized to use my men to flush out a terrorists' nest.'

Rayner glanced at Fenella and said, 'I'm not asking for your men. I have unfinished business on the other side of the lagoon. All I'm asking for is that you run me across in one of your fast craft and drop me off. That is all.'

Faure eyed him with something approaching admiration in his hard glance. 'By yourself? An armed gang? What about –' He indicated Fenella.

'Where Rayner goes, I go too,' she replied.

Faure stood and held her eyes with his own. He said at last, 'Either you're both crazy or very brave.'

Rayner added, 'I must be at Churchhaven before the eleven o'clock signing ceremony.'

Faure asked, with a shadow of disbelief still in his voice, 'That's all? Just a lift to the other side of the water? No strings?'

'Nothing.'

Faure gestured at the grenade and the Makarov still lying on his blotter. 'You'll need to take your visiting-cards.'

'Thanks, lieutenant,' said Rayner. 'How long will it take to get across?'

'Where exactly do you want to go?'

'Close to Churchhaven, but out of sight.'

'There's a point of land thereabouts which we've found pretty useful to hide the boat behind when we're after poachers,' he said.

'How far is it from Churchhaven?'

'About a kilometre and a half.' Then he hesitated, as if having second thoughts. 'How many are there in this gang?'

'Five,' Fenella answered.

'It's your decision,' he said briefly. 'You need to see it through to the end. Let's go.'

As they left the office, the bespectacled signals officer appeared and handed Faure a signal slip.

'Thanks,' he told the man. 'That will be all.'

'What does it say?' asked Rayner.

'Signal received.'

'Is that all?'

Faure shrugged. 'Bureaucracy. Whoever received our signal is keeping his yardarm clear. His reply could mean something, it could mean nothing. The golden rule is, never commit yourself.'

'Do you mean the warning could never reach Commander Enslin?'

'It's anyone's bet. Depends what the person who has to pass it on thinks. His options are open. Maybe, maybe not.'

'So the bomb could still go off!' Fenella exclaimed.

'Yes. Only time will tell.' Faure consulted his watch. 'There is just about an hour to go. The trip across the lagoon will take about ten to fifteen minutes. We'll use one of the smaller crash-boats with a shallower draft. In any event, you'll have to go overside into the water when we get there. I can't put you right ashore.'

They went to the door of the mess. The TV screen showed a huge crowd jostling as close as the security cordon would permit as the President's limousine emerged from Tuynhuis; the mounted escort formed up in front with the expertise of a well-drilled corps-de-ballet.

The announcer was saying:

In an hour from now, the historic ceremony will take place within the confines of Admiralty House, which harbours so much history and tradition of these two great seafaring nations –

Faure called, 'Engineer officer! Here!'

The man, in shorts and open shirt, cast an agonized look over his shoulder at the TV. That note in the commanding officer's voice spelt only one thing, duty.

'Wayne,' said Faure. 'We'll use M3. Now. Across the lagoon to that point near Churchhaven. How long will it take?'

'Fifteen, maybe twenty minutes at the outside,' he replied. 'The engine's still warm from that run this morning.'

'Good! Fanie!' The brown-overalled sailor who had

arrested them left the TV screen as reluctantly as the engineer officer.

The five of them hurried down the concrete path to the lean, fast crash-boat tied up to one side of the one on which they had landed.

Near the seaward entrance, there was a gaggle of drying sandbanks and saltings. Faure at the wheel dodged through them expertly at speed.

They reached the far shore of the lagoon and started to run parallel with it.

'Not far now,' Faure said tersely.

Then Faure slacked off speed, and cruised inshore. A final cliff, thick with scrub and small trees, masked the onward view to Churchhaven.

'Astern! Hold it, Wayne!' Faure turned to Rayner and Fenella. 'This is where you jump. It's not deep. I'll see you over.'

Rayner went first, up to his thighs in the muddy water. Fenella followed.

Faure leant down from the deck and passed the grenade and Makarov to Rayner. 'Good luck!' He looked as if he wanted to say something to Fenella, but remained silent.

Rayner said, 'Watch that TV!'

'Nothing will stop me.'

They waded ashore. They stamped their feet to get the water out of their sneakers. They plunged into the cliffside bush and scrub. The road itself was at the top. The road to Churchhaven.

Ten-thirty.

Zara poured another cup of coffee, but her hand was unsteady. It slopped on to the table-top where the Glock lay. She didn't bother to try and mop it up.

Zara and the four other Rote Zora women sat riveted to the image on the screen.

Ten-fifty.

The famous old dining-room at Admiralty House had the seriousness of a law court, coupled with the illusion of a theatre. The high oak wooden screen with its mock-carved arches hung with sombre maroon curtains imitated what the interior of a Vice-Admiralty Court once had been. The judge's bench was there, with two ornate high-backed chairs instead of the customary one. A large foul anchor in a frame above proclaimed that this was exclusive Admiralty territory. The only thing that wasn't an illusion was the massive old central chandelier which had seen so many famous admirals beneath its lights was still in position – it could not be shifted.

The court was as packed as any theatre could wish to be. The two central actors in the piece – the British Prime Minister and the South African President – held centre stage. They occupied the two big chairs at the judge's bench. An aide stood beside each, both of them in white naval uniform. Their swords and medals were commonplace in an audience which was dominated by uniforms, diplomatic pinstripes, beautiful dresses, beautiful women.

On special silver brackets, sculpted to resemble miniature sailors, rested the two silver oars.

Pittock-Williams, in light blue old-fashioned Marshal's uniform with medieval knee breeches and velvet coat, stood out uniquely. He was the darling of the cameras – and he knew it. He was in position to the right of the judge's bench, in anticipation of unscrewing the ivory baton from his ancestor's oar and then handing the oar to the President for the formal interchange.

Zara edged forward on her chair and breathed, 'Get on with it – for Chrissake, get on with the proceedings!'

The other four women were silent. They had seen the change come over their leader ever since she, Renate and Gemma had gone to the bunker that morning and found the birds flown. Their escape route was clear. Smashed bricks littered the floor of the brick chamber, and the dark mouth of the tunnel showed their route. None of them would venture into it. Where the captives had gone – they might have even been stuck fast in that narrow drain – was anyone's guess.

As soon as they got back to the house, Zara deployed the Glock on the lounge's low table in front of the TV, and two Makarovs as well, one in the kitchen and the other in Renate's bedroom. 'Dispersing our forces, in case of surprise attack,' she explained.

Her fear and nervousness grew as the time of the Admiralty House ceremony approached. The gang had watched the progress of events since switch-on. They had seen the motorcade's exit from Tuynhuis, the VIP helicopter flight to the deck landing in Simonstown, the ceremonial stepping-ashore from the Admiral's barge at the bottom of the Admiralty House garden, the measured procession up the path past the two old cannon, the entry into the refurbished diningroom.

When Pittock-Williams appeared leading this procession, a silver oar on either shoulder, Zara could no longer sit in her chair, but paced up and down, gulping down more strong coffee.

The other women were withdrawn, unspeaking. Perhaps the reality of what they were seeing, the enormity of what they had engineered to take place in a few minutes' time, had homed in on them. Perhaps Gemma had even calculated mentally how far the Semtex blast area would reach, and how many of those composed VIPs who now sat waiting for the grand finale would soon be ripped and bloodied corpses –

There was a stir at the back of the courtroom. Zara watched an officer in South African naval uniform come through the side-door, say something briefly to another officer on the inside, and then make his way on tip-toe to a civilian who stood close to where the Prime Minister was seated.

The naval officer whispered something, drew a sheet of paper – it could have been a signal sheet – from his pocket and passed it to the civilian.

The man read it, gave the officer a startled glance, nodded and indicated Pittock-Williams, at the same time moving to speak to a uniformed British aide at the Prime Minister's back.

Commander Enslin eased his way through the audience and reached Pittock-Williams. The professor's gaze was fixed on nothing but his public showing, now so near at hand, when he went forward to the two oars and unscrewed the crowned ivory Marshal's baton for himself, leaving the two silver oars for Prime Minister and President. He would, in any event, bear them out of the courtroom on his shoulders at the conclusion of the ceremony, as he had done on his entry to the court.

Commander Enslin put a hand on Pittock-Williams's shoulder, spoke urgently, emphatically, indicating the replica silver oar. Pittock-Williams gave him an incredulous look, even more so than Hugh Perrot's had been to Enslin.

Zara half-rose in her chair.

'What's going on? What's happening in there – what's he saying to him about the oar –?'

The two heads of government rose to their feet. They would accept the silver oars, one country to another.

Pittock-Williams moved forward as the procedure dictated, but he made no attempt to remove the baton from the shaft of the oar.

'Unscrew it! Unscrew it, you bastard! Go ahead – unscrew it!'

Zara hung in her seat, eyes transfixed on the TV screen.

'*Nobody move! Stay where you are!*'

Rayner's voice was stark, scarifying.

He stood in the doorway, Makarov in his left hand, the grenade in his right. Fenella was with him.

Zara did not have to turn to know who it was. The anger which had festered and suppurated over the years pulled her face into a contorted mask. She was already half on her feet, it required little to project and launch herself forward.

She didn't dive for the Glock.

Perhaps she knew from Rayner's voice that she would never reach it alive.

Instead, she flung herself at the tank with its big fish. It gave her a shield against Rayner's fire.

She lifted herself to her full height, and plunged her right arm shoulder-deep into the tank. Her fingers groped for the spines along the fish's back.

She stood like that for a moment, grinning contemptuously at Rayner and the gang.

Then her face blanched a dirty clay-white colour and deep pits formed where her eye-sockets were; the same livid blueness seemed to reach down and give instant coloration to her lips. Her arm jerked as if a 10,000-volt current had hit it.

She fell on the floor, her body writhing under some awful uncontrolled strychnic impulse, jack-knifing as the poison ripped into her nervous system.

The gang was on its feet, appalled. Fenella moved in hard against Rayner. He still held the Makarov aimed at Zara.

He missed Renate's move to the Glock. She was at the table in one swift action, snatched up the pistol, held it to the head of the kicking figure with unfocused eyes on the floor, and fired.

In the same movement, it seemed, she thrust the hot muzzle of the gun into the tank so that it sizzled. The great fish came up for another apparent victim. The shot crashed out. The heavy bullet went through its head, ripping a small hole also in the tank's side. Water and blood spurted out and joined the flow from the shattered head on the floor.

Rayner's gun tracked her, but she threw the Glock on the floor before he could fire.

She faced him defiantly. 'She needed mercy,' she said. 'And she got it.'

They all watched in awe for a short while until the last few convulsive kicks ended; the fish came to a head-down halt at the same time.

It has been a long revenge, George White, ever since the day you smashed your way out of the Vice-Admiralty Court with the silver oar. Now there is no heir left to keep alive the hate. Even Churchhaven won't be yours much longer.

On the TV screen, the safe exit of the silver oars passed unnoticed.

They carried Zara's body in a blanket, Rayner and Renate, and put it under the altar inside the secret door. Menty was a job for a mortician. Renate was passive, co-operative. Gemma seemed to have lapsed into a strange, withdrawn guilt state. Rikki and Kerry-Ann whimpered like frightened puppies.

Rayner borrowed Renate's Combi to report to the police. Fenella took the wheel to spare his hands. It would be a long drive to Saldanha, where the nearest police station was. Their road would lie round the salt-ings and marshlands through whose innumerable channels the life-giving tide was now starting to ebb.

The lagoon never looked lovelier.

Acts of Betrayal
John Trenhaile

THE PENALTY FOR TREASON IS DEATH

When an IRA plot to assassinate the Queen is foiled, an outraged public demands vengeance. Before long Frank Thornton, barrister, businessman, finds himself standing trial for treason. If found guilty, he will hang.

Driven by a long-standing emotional debt, Roz Forbes, deputy editor of *The Times*, launches an impassioned campaign to prevent a miscarriage of justice. As she struggles to clear his name, she unearths shocking links with a shady underworld of drugs and terrorism.

But before she can act on her discovery, Roz herself becomes a pawn in the terrifying world of international politics. While she remains a helpless hostage, time is running out for the condemned man . . .

'This is a novel full of lies and moments of truth: none of the truths is palatable and all of the lies are deadly'
Evening Standard

'Shocking . . . the suspense, woven by a British writer hailed as the heir apparent to le Carré, is killing'   *Today*

Fontana

Hold My Hand
I'm Dying
John Gordon Davis

'This is the best novel coming out of Africa that I have read for a number of years. *It is Africa today*. It has the inevitability of a Greek tragedy . . . both moving emotionally and full of adventure' Stuart Cloete

The great heart of old Africa is dying. Joseph Mahoney, the last colonial commissioner in the spectacular Kariba Gorge, is there to witness the death throes. Somehow, he must also ease the birth pangs of the new Africa that will take its place. His companions are Samson, his Matabele servant, and Suzie, the girl he loves.

But Mahoney and Suzie are drifting apart, and now Samson has been accused of murder. And all too quickly, it seems, the country is heading towards a bloodbath of revenge.

Hold My Hand I'm Dying – a compelling story of freedom, friendship and love in the face of hatred, violence and death.

'A great, compassionate and deeply moving book. I did not know how to put it down' Marguerite Steen

Fontana

Hold Down a Shadow
Geoffrey Jenkins

A daring plot to destroy a mighty dam and release a killer flood . . .

Masterminding the terror is the sinister Maluti Rider from the 'mountains of death' who is determined to avenge the loss of his family, the loss of his land. At his side are four of the world's most wanted men – the Chunnel Gang.

Caught in the web of terrorism are the beautiful Grania Yeats who crafts in gold and the brilliant barrister Sholto Banks. Theirs, the impossible task of finding Grania's masterpiece, the Eagle of Time, before the golden bird spreads its wings to reveal its secret – deadly – treasures.

Fontana

Fontana Fiction

Fontana is a leading paperback publisher of fiction. Below are some recent titles.

- ☐ THE SUM OF ALL FEARS Tom Clancy £5.99
- ☐ THE HOUSE OF MIRRORS Michael Mullen £4.99
- ☐ THE DOOMSDAY CONSPIRACY Sidney Sheldon £4.99
- ☐ RAVEN ON THE WATER Andrew Taylor £4.99
- ☐ ACTS OF BETRAYAL John Trenhaile £4.99
- ☐ PALINDROME Stuart Woods £3.99
- ☐ NOW AND THEN, AMEN Jon Cleary £3.50
- ☐ THE NUTMEG OF CONSOLATION Patrick O'Brian £4.99
- ☐ A CAUSE FOR DYING Brian Morrison £4.99
- ☐ UNDER SIEGE Stephen Coonts £4.99
- ☐ HUNGRY GHOST Stephen Leather £4.50

You can buy Fontana Paperbacks at your local bookshops or newsagents. Or you can order them from Fontana, Cash Sales Department, Box 29, Douglas, Isle of Man. Please send a cheque, postal or money order (not currency) worth the price plus 24p per book for postage (maximum postage required is £3.00 for orders within the UK).

NAME (Block letters)_____

ADDRESS_____

_____